I0824115

The Moonlight Runner

Also by Karen Robards

The Ultimatum
The Moscow Deception
The Fifth Doctrine
The Black Swan of Paris
The Girl from Guernica
Some Murders in Berlin

The Moonlight Runner

KAREN ROBARDS

Recycling programs for this product may not exist in your area.

ISBN-13: 978-0-7783-0584-2

The Moonlight Runner

Park Row Books
22 Adelaide St. West, 41st Floor
Toronto, Ontario M5H 4E3, Canada
ParkRowBooks.com

HarperCollins Publishers
Macken House, 39/40
Mayor Street Upper,
Dublin 1, D01 C9W8, Ireland
www.HarperCollins.com

Printed in U.S.A.
26 27 28 29 30 LBC 6 5 4 3 2

This book is dedicated with so much love to
my beautiful new daughter-in-law, Amy, and my son
Christopher, who were married on October 13, 2024.

And, as always, with love to Jack, and Peter and Del.

All changed, changed utterly/
A terrible beauty is born.

—W. B. Yeats

The Moonlight Runner

Chapter One

Please God, don't let me be too late.

With no breath left for speech, Rynn sent the plea silently winging away into the night. The racing of her heart far outpaced her frantic footfalls on the slippery grass. She had to get there before the trap was sprung, had to warn them. The prospect of violent death was no stranger, not after the Easter Rising, not after years of war. But minutes before, out of nowhere, it had sprung up terrifyingly close at hand.

It wasn't that she, the Honourable Mary Rynn Carmichael, had the Sight, as Granny did and, for most of Rynn's twenty-two years, had claimed Rynn did as well. It had nothing to do with the color of her eyes, so dark a brown as to be almost black, which Granny said appeared once in every second generation and were a sign and a throwback to Granny's own Romany grandmother. It was, merely, that she had ears like any normal person and could hear. And what she had heard, or overheard, on this Christmas night in 1918 a few steps outside the crowded ballroom at Ballyshannon Court had upended her world, which had just started to seem safe and settled again. It had sent her flying out into the cold and windy darkness toward the treacherous cliff edge that overlooked the stormy waters of Donegal Bay.

"It's tonight. They're bringing in the guns," Lieutenant Colonel Maurice Pelly of the British Army's Fifth Infantry Division had said in a confidential tone. Resplendent in his uniform, he was there, in the officers' convalescent hospital that the formerly private seaside mansion that was Ballyshannon Court had been turned into in the last years of the Great War, to put an official stamp on its decommissioning now that the Armistice had been signed. "The bloody buggers think we're blind and deaf. But we know what they're up to and we're ready and waiting."

"Your men are in place?" Chief Inspector George Fallon of the Royal Irish Constabulary leaned toward Pelly as he spoke. Like Pelly's, his voice was low. The music and laughter filling the house almost drowned out the conversation. But it was the *almost* that made the difference. Coming upon the two men standing apart from the party in a hallway window embrasure as they blew smoke from their cigars out a cracked-open window, Rynn caught the exchange and stopped dead.

"On the beach as we speak," Pelly replied. The satisfaction in his voice sent gooseflesh racing over her skin. Their backs were to her. They didn't know she was there, clutching the tray of medicines that she, a trained nurse, was on her way to administer to the patients who were too ill to join the party, including one very important one, Lord Thomas Dunne, the second son of the Duke of Hartford, who owned the property. Listening for all she was worth, Rynn didn't dare so much as breathe. "As soon as the boat lands, we'll have them. Given the mood the Castle's in, the traitors will be facing a firing squad within a month."

The Castle being a reference to Dublin Castle, the seat of British power in Ireland. Rynn's mouth went dry as she grappled with the realization of what must be afoot.

"You ask me, shooting's too good for them. Turn them over to us, and we'll take care of them, and in the process make sure to send a message to any who might be contemplating the same." The anticipatory cruelty in Fallon's tone made Rynn's blood run cold.

The conversation wasn't over, but she'd heard enough. Taking care that the bottles on the tray didn't rattle and alert the men to her presence, Rynn backed away until she no longer feared being discovered. Then she shoved the tray onto a convenient table, picked up the skirt of the hand-me-down ball gown she'd pulled from an old trunk of her late mother for this festive occasion, turned and ran.

The tuneless voices of a houseful of tipsy men bellowing "It's a Long Way to Tipperary" followed her through the kitchen garden and across the fields until the sound of the ocean drowned them out. The wind whipped her skirt, tried to snatch away the shawl she'd flung around her shoulders, tore her long black hair from its pins. It was cold out—and so dark. The pale quarter moon hid behind a blanket of heavy clouds. She was fortunate that she knew the way along the cliffs as well as she did. A fall from such a height onto the rocks below would almost certainly prove fatal, as everyone who'd grown up thereabouts knew. She had to mind her feet and yet she couldn't keep her eyes off the vast expanse of undulating blackness that was the bay and, beyond it, the white-tipped turbulence of the wild Atlantic.

Out there somewhere, if what she'd overheard was right, two boats were headed for a secret rendezvous. One was on a mission to deliver its illicit cargo. The other was there to claim that cargo and bring it to shore.

When it did—Rynn shuddered at the thought of the soldiers lying in wait. In the immediate aftermath of the Rising, sixteen of the ringleaders had been summarily executed while hundreds more had been killed in the fighting. Since then, the British had been merciless in their zeal to put down any hint of rebellion.

And now, with the war over and the December election having lit a fire under the nationalists by handing a major victory to Sinn Fein, rebellion was what the brainless lunatics bringing in the guns would be about.

Tiocfaidh ar la. Our day will come. The Irish had been promising themselves that for generations. Overthrowing the British oppressors had become akin to a second religion for many, and like true fanatics they were willing to lay down their lives in its cause.

At the thought Rynn's stomach cramped. With her pulse pounding so loudly in her ears now that she could barely even hear the unsettled ocean's roar, she ran like all the demons from hell were giving chase.

She had to reach the Point, the farthest end of the promontory that jutted like a thumb out into the bay, in time to signal them not to come in. Her grip on the electric torch she'd snatched along with the shawl from the hook by the kitchen door tightened until the metal edges of the square box felt like they were cutting into her palm.

Whipped by the wind, her increasingly unmoored hair was in her face, her mouth, all but blinding her as she slid to a stop just short of the outermost cliff's edge. Shaking the wayward strands back, sucking in great gulps of briny-smelling air as she fought to recover her breath, she narrowed her eyes against the blow. Her hands were unsteady as she took the few steps out onto the very edge of the Point, then lifted the light high and turned it on, and as quickly turned it off again.

A thousand one, a thousand two—

In an almost perfect echo to her count, the incoming tide slammed thunderously against the ancient arched stones of the Fairy Bridges that edged the bay to the north, sending geysers of seawater shooting up through their blowholes to rain back down on the bay.

Quelling her fear, her anger, her disbelief—any emotion that might hamper her ability to do what she needed to do—she carefully kept the count, flashing the light at four-second intervals in the age-old signal that screamed "Mariners beware! Turn back!"

They—all of them who'd grown up in this string of fishing villages by the sea—knew what that signal meant.

If only the men out there in the turbulent waters somewhere below would look up in time to see!

Donal O'Reilly—the boy she'd grown up with, her love—was among them. She knew it with a fierce certainty that, again, had nothing to do with the Sight, but everything to do with knowing her man. He'd be out there in the thick of it, with his cousin Seamus and their cronies.

Even though he'd given her his solemn promise he would not.

We'll be bringing in guns to match their own, see if we don't, and then you just watch how fast the cowards turn tail and run home to England. I've been talking with some boyos from Liverpool. They can get us anything we need. Seamus, the idiot, had bragged about it openly in the pub.

You'll have no part in that, I trust. Seamus's words having been passed on to her as a warning by Molly Kincaid, the pub's barmaid who was Seamus's sweetheart and her good friend, Rynn had confronted Donal with it. Her tone, and the look she gave him, were fierce with warning. He knew how she felt about the horrors she'd seen during the disaster that was the Rising, when the British Army had turned their overwhelming numbers and weapons on the ragtag band of rebels whose efforts to wrest control of Ireland from Crown rule had ended so tragically. At the time, she was still in Dublin, having just completing her nurse's training there, and the deaths of the innocents she'd witnessed were forever branded on her soul.

Don't fash yourself, acushla. If it's true—and I'm not saying it is, you know what a big talker Seamus can be—it's nothing to do with me.

Promise me. She'd caught his arm, looked up at him searchingly. He'd only been back from the war for a little more than a month. The fear that had haunted her every day of the two years he'd been gone raised its monstrous head once more. If she lost him—she could feel the familiar cold dread start up again until she reminded herself that, well, she wouldn't lose him, because he was safe home.

I promise. He'd smiled at her, that same beguiling smile that he'd been using to get around her since they were children. And she'd believed him.

Until she'd overheard the soldiers in the hall. Then she'd known.

Now, icy with fear, she aimed the light out to sea, carefully counting off the seconds between flashes as she desperately searched the all-enveloping darkness for sign of a boat. The sting of the wind, the unaccustomed cold, the danger to herself if she were caught—none of that mattered compared to the enormity of what was about to happen to people she loved if she couldn't stop it. When, finally, the moon ventured out from behind a cloud, spilling its light down over flat-topped Ben Bulbin Mountain to paint the fields and then the water silver clear to the horizon, she caught her breath.

There it was, the *Merrow*, Seamus's currach, unmistakable because of the bright red hair of the mermaid painted on its prow. She'd been looking in the wrong place, it seemed. It wasn't out in the ocean, or even in the middle of the bay. It was, rather, battling through the waves less than a furlong from shore. And it was coming in. Watching, she knew they hadn't seen her, hadn't seen the flashing light or her warning.

Turn back! She opened her mouth to scream it at them, then caught herself before so much as a squeak left her throat. They would never hear—the distance was too great, the wind would snatch away her voice, the sea would drown it out—but even if they did not, the soldiers might.

Desperately she flashed the light again. *A thousand one—*

Where *were* the soldiers? Were they even there at all? They would have come from nearby Finner Camp, and a rowdier bunch she had yet to meet. Impossible to imagine them staying silent for so long. A frantic glance up and down the Strand revealed no sign of them. Neither rocks nor shadows were proof against the sparkling moonlight. Cut off by the cliffs that walled it in, the long, pale crescent of sand appeared deserted.

Had she somehow got it wrong?

Hope died stillborn as the answer hit her with the force of a blow. The soldiers were in the cave, Lion's Paw Cave, as it was known. They must be; there was nowhere else they could hide. It was part of an enormous cave system that burrowed under the cliffs. It filled with water on the high tide but would be safe enough now. The fissure in the rock that opened onto the beach was narrow, allowing no more than a single person to pass through at a time. As children their name for it was Dead Man's Hole, and they'd spent many an hour exploring inside it as far as they dared. The cavern just beyond the opening was large enough to conceal a hundred men and a labyrinth of passages connected it to many more as large.

Shutting off the light, Rynn snatched up her skirt and ran. Her every sense was on high alert as she went down the twisty path to the Strand like one of the mountain sheep that had carved it out of the rock. Giant boulders, long shadows, waves flinging themselves at the shore—the moonlight revealed everything, and nothing.

An ambush was in the offing. Rynn could feel the building danger like a storm charge in the air.

Chapter Two

Out in the bay, the *Merrow* plowed through the waves, drawing closer with every stroke of her oars to what Rynn felt in her very bone marrow was disaster. Even as she watched, the oars were shipped and a dark figure jumped out of the boat into the water. Whoever it was—Seamus or Fergus Boyd or Paddy Colgan or even Donal himself, really any of what was most likely the usual band of four that had been finding trouble together all their lives—started dragging the boat the last of the way in against the teeth of the outgoing tide.

Heart pounding, she leaped down onto the sand just as the moon ducked behind the clouds again. In an instant the night turned so dark that she could barely see the giant driftwood tree that had been the focus of many a childhood game lying in her path. Skirting it, sprinting toward the sliver of denser darkness in the rolling gray breakers that the *Merrow* had become, she was thankful for the obliteration of the light. If she should be seen by the soldiers who she was as certain as it was possible to be were waiting . . .

At the prospect she thought she might burst from fear. She couldn't shout a warning—even the crunch of sand beneath her feet sounded terrifyingly loud—couldn't flash the light, couldn't do anything that might draw the attention of the soldiers. The entrance to the cave was behind her, tucked into a wrinkle in the cliff face, but it was near and there was sure to be a lookout. The thought that hidden eyes might spot her, or the boat, and armed British soldiers would then erupt from the cave sent blood-curdling darts of panic through her.

Reaching the shoreline, she ran into the surf. Within moments she was knee-deep, then thigh-deep, battling through surging water that was cold enough to take her breath.

"Jesus, Mary and Joseph!" Seamus—for it was Seamus in the water—yelped, stopping short with the boat in tow and whitecaps breaking around him as she, waving her arms in silent warning and thanking the Lord that the crash of the waves prevented his voice from carrying much beyond her ears, drew near, plunging toward him through the swells. His attention caught at last, he peered at her through the darkness. "Wait, hold, is it a kelpie you are, then?"

The humor in that last as he recognized her won him an infuriated hiss which she knew he couldn't hear.

"Hush, you blithering idiot! It's an ambush! Go back!" Losing her footing as the ebb current pulled at her and her soaked skirts wrapped around her legs, she forced the words out through chattering teeth just as a wave, bigger than the rest, caught her up. She barely managed to save herself from being bowled over by throwing herself at Seamus at the last second. He grabbed her to steady her as another swell rushed past and almost lost his anchoring grip on the *Merrow*.

"Rynn!" Donal's horrified exclamation as he, too, recognized her sliced through Seamus's muttered curses as he struggled to hold on to both her and the boat.

"Here, now. What're you on about?" Seamus shook her arm to recall her attention. Though the boys were a year older than her, they'd been childhood playmates and schoolmates all, and thus stood on no ceremony with each other. As Seamus leaned close she could smell the whiskey on his breath. Of course she could. Seamus had ever had a fondness for strong drink and would have fortified himself for the night's doings by, as he would put it, having a wee dram.

"Go back! Soldiers! They're on the beach!" Her voice cracked with urgency.

Another wave broke around them, slapping her in the face with a shower of freezing spray. The sandy floor was sucked out from under her feet as the current beneath the surface receded. Tottering sideways, she was torn away from Seamus by the undertow and would have tumbled headlong into the surf if she hadn't been grabbed in the nick of time by a pair of strong hands.

Donal. He'd jumped into the water to catch her.

"What the devil? Are you daft?" Wrath warred with astonishment in Donal's voice as he hauled her against him. Catching a hint of whiskey on his breath, too, she felt a fresh surge of anger. He'd clearly joined Seamus in his wee dram.

"It's an ambush!" Shaking what was now the entirely fallen, inky-black mass of her hair back from her face, she looked up at him with fire in her eyes. "They *know*! About the guns! Get back to the boat! Turn back!"

"The hell you say!" His face was pale in the darkness. His black hair, soaked like the rest of him, clung to his skull. His eyes, a warm brown, were hidden in shadow and impossible to read. He'd left his coat behind in the boat. His skin still felt warm beneath his sodden shirt.

"They're on the beach. *Soldiers.* We have to *go.*"

The tightening of his grip on her was his answer: he understood.

"You promised me!" This wasn't the time for accusations, she knew. She couldn't help it.

"Seamus needed a man he could trust."

"Hurry!" Seamus called. Having recognized the danger at last, he was doing his best to hold the *Merrow* in place for them.

"You there! In the boat! Bring her to shore! In the name of

His Majesty the King!" The bawled command was surprisingly clear. Rynn's heart leaped into her throat. Her head snapped around toward the shout. She could just make out the dark figures of the soldiers, spilling from the fissure in the cliff as she had feared, then pelting across the pale sand toward the bay. One stood still as the others spread out around him. From his movements and the sound of his voice, she realized that he possessed a megaphone that he was using to amplify his shouts.

Dear God, they were out of time.

"Donal–" The arm she had wrapped around him tightened with fear. Her fingers dug into his waist.

"Hell and the devil!" Dragging her the rest of the way to where Seamus now practically danced with alarm, Donal snatched her up out of the water and tossed her into the boat with as little ceremony as if she'd been a sack of potatoes. As she landed hard between the seats another furious shout of "You there! I said bring that boat in!" from the shore was accompanied by a desperate flurry of movement on the part of the men around her.

"Take her out! Let's go!" Seamus's words were barely audible over the crashing surf.

Freezing cold, tangled in drenched skirts that, like the ends of her hair, poured water everywhere, Rynn managed to roll onto her hands and knees in the cramped space as the boat heaved and rocked beneath her. Her shoes were gone, she discovered, lost to the sea. So was the shawl, and the torch. The currach, normally so light, rode heavy in the water. Because of its load of guns, she realized with horror as she spotted the oilcloth stretched tellingly across unseen cargo in the stern. If they were taken with guns on board . . .

The thought of the firing squad that would await them made her light-headed and nauseous and *furious*. The *fools*—

Without warning the moon slid out into the open again,

capturing them all in its eerie glow. Rynn caught her breath as she realized the soldiers massing on the beach were now easily visible, which meant that they must be visible, too.

"Damn it, put your backs into it!" Donal cried to Fergus and Paddy as they worked the oars. He and Seamus were on opposite sides of the boat now, using brute strength to push her out through the incoming waves.

Scrambling across the planks toward Donal, Rynn shivered as she was caught by the wind that fought their progress with every gust. She reached the gunwale and grabbed on, sinking to her knees, holding tight to the worn-smooth wood that edged the hull. The beach, she saw with a quiver of thankfulness, was rapidly receding. Under the combined power of the oarsmen and the two men in the water, the *Merrow* had successfully reversed course and was heading back out to sea.

"You shouldn't have come," Donal yelled at her. He was so close she could see the bunching of the muscles beneath his soaked shirt as he put all his strength into his task.

"If I hadn't come you—all of you—would be under arrest by now!"

"Better us than you!"

"Better no one at all!"

"'Ware the rocks! Pull to port!" Seamus cried, and they did, avoiding the pyramid-shaped sea stack with little room to spare.

"Halt! I *command* you to bring that boat in! Now! In the name of His Majesty the King!"

"Pull, Paddy, pull!" Fergus urged. Faces grim, legs braced, the two strained mightily as they dug the oars deep into the waves.

Caught between wind and tide, the *Merrow* bucked like a wild horse on the frothing sea. Wary of being pitched out, terrified of what might come to them, Rynn huddled close to the gunwale and held on for dear life.

"You! In the boat! This is your last warning!"

Heart pounding, she looked back. The soldiers had fanned out into an amorphous black blob along the shoreline. It was difficult to be certain at that distance, but she thought—were they pulling out the carbines they wore strapped to their backs? Her chest tightened until it was hard to breathe.

"*Sit flat on your arse.*" Donal threw the order at her as the *Merrow* pitched up over the crest then plunged down the back of an especially large wave.

"Get in."

Rynn grabbed Donal's wrist, held on. The brunt of propelling the *Merrow* out to sea had to be on the oarsmen now. He and Seamus could do no more in the water. It was too rough, and too deep.

"I'm aboard," Donal yelled to his cousin, and heaved himself up and over the *Merrow*'s side.

The crack of a gunshot split the air, sudden as a thunderclap. Rynn froze at the shock of it as she identified the sound.

A pained outcry as Donal tumbled down on top of her, knocking her flat in the bottom of the boat, almost stopped her heart.

"He's hit!" Fergus cried.

Her worst fear. She sucked in air, grabbed at his deadweight as he sprawled on top of her. "Donal?"

He was breathing. He was moving.

"Stay down!" Reinforcing that with a shove to the back of her head, Donal catapulted off her, scrambling along the deck like a crab. Seamus rolled in over the side, landing with a curse and a burst of icy droplets that distracted her not at all as she kept her attention on Donal. *Was* he hit? She didn't think so. He didn't move like it. She glanced toward Seamus.

Partway there, her gaze stuck on Paddy's seat. Paddy's *empty* seat. Abandoned, his oars clanked against the thole pins that held them in place.

"Paddy! Paddy!" Fergus cried.

"Keep rowing! Or we're all dead!" Seamus swarmed onto his knees.

"Oh, Jesus, he's took one to the chest!" Donal crouched over the dark shape that Rynn only then realized was Paddy, fallen in a heap onto the planks below his seat.

More gunshots rang out in quick succession, cracking overhead, smacking into the hull, sending up tiny geysers as they hit the water. Panic quickened Rynn's breathing, churned through her stomach. Impossible to believe that Paddy was shot, or that they were in a position where another bullet could find any one of them at any second. Every instinct she possessed urged her to stay huddled right where she was, tucked out of sight against the dubious protection of the hull. But she had to go to Paddy, to do what she could for him.

Careful to keep low, Rynn crawled toward Donal, who glanced around at her as she reached him.

"I told you to stay down!"

"I can help him."

Donal grimaced, a sign of reluctant acknowledgment, then yelled, "Throw me my coat, Fergus."

Rynn put a testing hand on Paddy's bent leg, the only part of him she could reach with Donal in her way. The limb beneath the wool trousers was motionless. Except for an involuntary slip and slide caused by their plunging flight through the waves, Paddy was motionless. As Donal caught the tossed coat and draped it around her shoulders—ah, blessed protection from the wind!—she elbowed him out of the way and began to frantically unbutton Paddy's coat.

"Rynn?" Fear thinned Donal's voice. "How bad?"

"I can't tell yet. I need to—"

"Bring that boat *in*! In the name of His Majesty the King!" The shout from the beach was punctuated by an explosion of gunfire. Rynn flinched as bullets flew past. Donal, flinching too, threw a protective arm across her shoulders.

"Take Paddy's oars!" Seamus roared at Donal, who obediently flung himself into Paddy's vacant seat. As Donal began to row, Rynn saw that Seamus, now wedged into a secure spot in the bow, had snatched up a rifle.

No. But whether she said it aloud or not didn't matter. It was already too late to share her conviction that shooting at the soldiers could only worsen their situation. Taking aim as best he could given the instability of his perch, Seamus fired back.

Darkness fell over the boat like a blanket as the moon went into hiding again. A flicker of hope that the soldiers' inability to see what they were shooting at might stop the onslaught was almost immediately doused by the barrage of answering bullets.

Ears ringing from the rifle's explosions so close at hand as Seamus returned fire in a fierce volley, Rynn clenched her jaw against the terror that threatened to immobilize her and determinedly focused on Paddy.

He lay curled on his side. Although she bent close, it was difficult to be sure of much given the lack of light. But a distinctive smell that she was sickened to recognize as fresh blood was stronger even than the salt smell of the sea.

"*Paddy.* Paddy, can you hear me?" His coat, his chest, were already a flood of wet, sticky warmth. Yanking his coat open, she pressed both hands hard against the gushing wound that was its source. The barely-there glint of his eyes through the darkness told her they were open. His lips were parted. She could detect no hint of air passing through them, could feel no respiratory movement of his chest although her hands were flattened against it. A thin black line that could only be blood trickled from the far corner of his mouth to mix with the shallow film of water in the bottom of the boat.

Dread squeezed her heart as she reluctantly acknowledged

what the sheer volume of blood oozing though her fingers meant. No one could lose that much blood and live.

"Is it bad? Is he bad?" Fergus sounded frantic. Like Donal and Seamus, Fergus and Paddy were kin and close as brothers.

"Keep rowing!" Seamus yelled at him before she could answer and snapped off more shots. Curses and prayers intermingled as, bent almost double in their seats, Donal and Fergus rowed feverishly while the furious exchange of gunfire split the night.

Refusing to give up even though she knew it was useless, Rynn tried everything she could to save Paddy. But, finally, she had to face the truth: he had no pulse. No heartbeat. No breath. One of the soldiers had found his mark. There was no mistake.

The *Merrow* hit rougher water, which Rynn knew from long experience meant they were nearing Mullaghmore Head. The gunfire from the Strand had fallen off until it was no more than a few distant pops. As her hands dropped away from Paddy's chest at last and she sank back on her heels in defeat, Seamus lowered his rifle.

They must be out of range.

"Paddy?" Fergus's anguished question pierced her heart. "In the name of all the saints, Rynn, how bad is he?"

A hard knot formed beneath her breastbone. She wet her lips. The salt on them, was it from the sea or her tears?

"Rynn?" Donal pressed.

She didn't want to answer. She didn't want to tell them. To give voice to it made it real.

She bowed her head. Of its own accord, the familiar litany left her lips: "'Hail Mary, full of grace . . .'"

"Dead?"

Ah, Donal knew her. She replied with a jerky nod even as more tears slid down her cheeks.

"'Intercede for us now and at the hour of our deaths . . .'"

"No." Fergus's oars stilled. "He can't be dead, not just like that, not so fast. Are you *sure*, Rynn?"

She wiped her eyes, looked at him. "I am."

Fergus gave a choked wail and rose from his seat. "Ah, Paddy, he skipped confession today. We were going to stop after mass but we went to the pub instead."

Rynn's heart broke at the anguish in his voice.

"*Fergus. Donal.* See to your oars. There's a bloody great trawler off the starboard keel. From the look of her, she's been laying back waiting for us." Sharp as a knife, Seamus's warning cut through the rising fog of grief. Crouched in the bow, he shouldered the rifle again. "Here she comes. Damn the Brits to hell, they'll not take us without a fight."

Chapter Three

"*Don't shoot.* They'll blow us out of the damned sea." Donal's voice was tight with tension. His strokes slowed, maintaining just enough momentum to keep the boat steady in the water. Any attempt to go to Paddy put on hold by the immediate danger bearing down on them, Fergus dropped back in his seat and picked up his oars.

"And what do you think they'll do to us if we're taken?" Seamus demanded fiercely.

But he held his fire as the force of the current pulled them inexorably out past the rocks that marked the end of dry land, into the rippling waves of the open sea and the trawler's path. There was no turning back, no changing course, nowhere to go. Running without lights, the bigger boat took on shape and mass as it swooped toward them. Cloaked in darkness, under sail, sporting canvas as inky black as the night sky itself, it reminded Rynn of nothing so much as a giant bird of prey.

Black sails meant near invisibility at night on the open sea. Adopted during the Great War to foil the Huns, they were a chilling sight.

Watching the other boat's approach, Rynn quaked inside. If, as she feared, their luck had run out, soon they would be prisoners, with worse to come.

"Pitch the guns overboard. It's the only way." The solution came to her in a flash fueled by desperation, sparked no doubt by Paddy's fate. His lifeless body, heavy and limp as it curled against her bent knees, served as a terrifying warning of what awaited them.

"That's it! There's the answer!" Donal shipped his oars. Bent almost double for balance as the *Merrow* rocked over the waves, he flung himself toward the stern, where the cargo—the thrice-damned guns, Rynn presumed—was stored beneath the oilcloth that stretched tightly across the width of the boat.

"We can't! We'll be owing the Sullivans a fortune! They paid us five thousand pounds for those guns, and believe me, they'll be wanting either their guns or their money back!" Seamus pivoted in his direction.

Five thousand pounds? It was a staggering sum! At the idea of having to repay it, Rynn felt sick.

"Don't you see? Rynn's in the right of it. Without the guns onboard they can't be proving a crime." Dropping to his knees, Donal started tearing at the fastenings that secured the oilcloth in place. "For all they know, we've been out fishing and they've attacked innocent men!"

"No!" Careful of his balance as the waves picked up, Seamus clambered toward Donal.

"D'you want to die, then?" Donal flung over his shoulder.

"If we don't deliver these guns to the Sullivans after they fronted us the money—" His rifle tucked under his arm, Seamus stopped abruptly just short of his goal to peer through the darkness at the looming boat. "Wait, is that the *Reaper*? The Maguire's boat?"

The Maguire, Rynn knew, referred to Owen Maguire, current head of clan Maguire. He and his kin had lived in and around Killybegs for generations. Since the famine, when blight had decimated the potato fields and thousands had died of starvation, the Maguires, formerly farmers like most thereabouts, had become, by and large, fishermen, surviving off what they could pull from the sea. Like most everyone else, they barely eked out a living, except, lately, for this particular one. A trawler, a fleet of smaller fishing boats, a stake in a fishery, a house in Killybegs and the rented farm where his widowed sister lived, had been, if gossip were to be believed, all purchased by him in the year and a half since he'd been wounded and come home from the war. A fortune, everyone agreed, for one such as he.

Donal stopped what he was doing to look closely at the boat that was now almost upon them. "It is."

"The Hero of the Somme's no traitor." Relief laced Seamus's voice.

All four—Donal, Seamus, Fergus and Paddy—had signed up in the wake of the Somme, one of the longest and bloodiest battles of the war. They'd joined together, along with six more of their friends from the area, spurred on by the widely circulated tales of battlefield valor on the part of their countrymen, seeking such glory for themselves along with a steady wage as a way out of the unemployment and poverty that was rife in Ireland. Rynn had begged Donal not to go, to, as it turned out, no avail. Six of the ten had been lost to the war. She considered it a miracle of the highest order that not only Donal, but Seamus and the other two as well, had survived to come home.

Which made it all the more terrible that, scant weeks later, Paddy lay dead at the hands of the British soldiers he'd so recently fought alongside.

And County Donegal's vaunted war hero Owen Maguire, who according to all the newspapers was an expert marksman who'd single-handedly stormed a German machine gun nest at the Somme, capturing the gun and killing the gunners and afterward performing countless other feats of derring-do that had him winning all manner of medals for his gallantry under fire, should be considered a possible enemy by men who had heretofore idolized him.

"Merely because he fought bravely with the Thirty-Sixth doesn't mean he's not working with the Brits now," Donal said. "He's been home awhile. Allegiances change. Many things could have changed."

"The Maguire wouldn't be betraying his own countrymen."

"What's he doing out, then? Fishing for herring on Christmas night? Not bloody likely."

"We don't know, do we? We don't even know that he knows about the guns."

"Oh, he knows, all right. Why else would he be doing *that*?" Donal's savage nod toward the *Reaper* came as she cut across the *Merrow*'s bow while at the same time signaling them to stop.

It was too late to speculate more, because the trawler was at that moment dropping anchor and sail. Rynn's mouth went dry. Given the currach's limitations as to speed and maneuverability, there was no chance of escape. And with the soldiers behind them, and possibly more positioned at any point along the shore by this time, there was nowhere safe to go to land.

They were trapped. The chill that went through her at the thought had nothing to do with her sodden dress, or the wind, or how to-the-bone cold she was. Soon enough the four of them remaining might be following Paddy in death.

Even across the expanse of water that separated them, the *Reaper* loomed threateningly large. Looking up at the shadowy outline of her twin sails and the smokestack that was not presently in use, Rynn's eyes widened. Two men stood amidships at the rail facing the *Merrow*. Like the trawler itself, they were no more than black outlines against a slightly less black sky. She couldn't see but could *feel* the weight of their gazes.

Neither of the men she was looking at moved, but a rope ladder reaching almost to the water unfurled down the trawler's side. Given her size, the *Reaper* probably sported at least a nine-man crew. An order had obviously been given to drop a ladder.

One of the men at the rail lifted an arm, waving them in closer.

"He's wanting to talk," Seamus said.

"He's being quiet about it. No engine, no shouting." Still kneeling beside the cargo, Donal frowned at the bigger boat.

"No *shooting.*" A tiny flicker of hope reared its head as Rynn emphasized what, to her, was the most important part. Her already pounding heart felt like it would beat its way out of her chest. The *Reaper* was aptly named, and only lacked a *Grim* in front of it to spell out exactly how she feared this encounter might end. "If he was wishing to do us harm, I'm thinking he'd be doing it already."

"He might be under orders to bring us in alive," Donal said. "For questioning. They'd like to know who sold us the guns."

"We don't know that he knows about the guns," Seamus objected. "And it's the *Maguire.*"

"So you're thinking this is just a social call, is that it?"

"My sister knows him." Fergus's voice was a thin approximation of his usual hearty tone. "She says he's a good man."

"Oh, well, your sister, then," Donal said.

Seamus looked at Donal. "You know we can't make a run for it."

"I know." Donal's answer was grim.

"So we talk, see what he wants."

"It's a risk."

"I don't see what else we can do," Rynn said. The sheer practicalities of the matter settled it, as far as she was concerned. They couldn't escape. Therefore, the best thing to do was talk and see where it took them.

"Aye, you're in the right of it, as usual." Grudging acceptance was plain in Donal's voice.

"We're in agreement, then." Seamus answered the *Reaper*'s summons with a sweeping wave of his own.

"If we're to talk, it might be best not to go confronting them with your rifle," Rynn said.

"She's right again," Donal said. "In the event this *is* just a friendly chat."

"Put it away, then," Seamus said to Donal. Passing the rifle off to him in a clandestine move that Rynn was *almost* sure the darkness prevented the men in the trawler from observing, which she was equally sure was the purpose, Seamus took the seat Donal had vacated and picked up the oars.

"Let's take her alongside," he said to Fergus.

Donal, meanwhile, slid the rifle out of sight beneath the edge of the oilcloth while keeping it within easy reach. Then he looked at Rynn. "Sorry as I am to deprive you of it, I'll be needing my coat back. Fergus, pass it over."

Rynn frowned—to ask for such a thing wasn't like Donal—but slid out of the coat and handed it to Fergus. A moment later her unspoken question was answered as Donal, having yanked off his wet shirt and shrugged into the coat, pulled a pistol out of the pocket and checked it before repocketing it. Seamus, who'd shed his own soaked shirt and put on his coat at the same time, did likewise. Rynn couldn't be sure, but she had to assume Fergus was similarly armed.

Her insides twisted as she realized how primed for violence they were. If one little thing went wrong . . .

As Donal and Seamus stamped into the brogues they'd left behind on the boat when they'd gone into the water, she steeled herself and looked down at Paddy again. Dark as it was, she could see that his mouth was slack, his skin the gray white of death. Brushing her hand over Paddy's now-sightless eyes, she caught her breath as she realized she had just closed them forever. When he'd stepped aboard the *Merrow* earlier that evening he'd had no idea that this would be the result, that his life would end, that he would never go home again. Would the rest of them make it home? Would she? Suddenly the small stone cottage on the outskirts of Bundoran where she'd grown up with Granny and Glenna, her younger sister, seemed impossibly dear. Would her family wait in vain for her to come home?

Please God, no.

With a lump in her throat, she said a silent goodbye to her childhood friend.

"Rynn. Here." Voice ragged with grief, Fergus passed her a blanket.

"Instead of my coat," Donal said, and she nodded. The temptation to shed her sodden garments in the blanket's favor was almost overwhelming, but with so many men around and no knowledge about what was to come—no. Anyway, her hands were too cold to work the tiny buttons, and there was no time. Shivering, she wrapped the blanket around herself and was thankful for what protection it provided as the men took them alongside the *Reaper.*

Moments later, ropes had been thrown down and the *Merrow* was secured to the trawler. Positioned between them and the ocean, the bigger boat now took the brunt of the wind and waves. Cocooned in the tattered blanket, blood rinsed from her person as well as she could manage, dripping skirts wrung out and hair twisted into a knot at her nape, Rynn watched uneasily from what had once been Paddy's seat as a man descended the ladder to jump aboard the *Merrow.*

"O'Reilly." Voice deep and curt, the man greeted Seamus, who'd caught his arm to steady him as the boat lurched with the force of his landing. He was a big man, well north of six feet tall and broad in his black fisherman's coat, with a heavy beard and a knit cap pulled low over his forehead. More than that, it was too dark to tell.

There was, however, little doubt in Rynn's mind that this was, indeed, the Maguire. His air of command, the deference shown him by Seamus, and the fact that at least four men now watching from the trawler's rail had rifles trained on the occupants of the currach and appeared ready to fire on them at need told her everything she needed to know.

"Major." With that, Seamus confirmed what Rynn had already guessed. Though promotions through the ranks for Irishmen were rare—Donal, Seamus, Fergus and Paddy had remained privates all—Maguire had been an exception, and each rise had been touted with pride by the local newspaper.

"Who's that?" Maguire's gaze lit on Paddy's still body. The moon sailed out of hiding just then, spilling its light over the currach and everyone in it.

"Paddy Colgan," Seamus answered, while Fergus, having taken Rynn's place at Paddy's side, broke off in the middle of the Act of Contrition he'd been muttering over the body to look up. Tears streaming down his cheeks gleamed in the moonlight. Under Maguire's frowning regard, he dashed a self-conscious hand across his eyes.

"Dead?" Maguire asked.

"He is," Seamus replied.

Maguire grunted and cast an assessing look around that stopped on Rynn.

"You brought a *woman* into this bloody mess you've made?"

"Nobody brought me. I came," Rynn said.

For a pregnant moment, Maguire's eyes met hers.

"Then you've got about as much sense as the rest of these idiots, which put together is less than a bloody sheep's." With that brutal pronouncement, which left her bristling right along with, she was sure, the men he disparaged, he dismissed her by turning back to Seamus. "Where are the guns?"

Seamus hesitated.

Maquire said, "I'm going to tell you straight, you've two choices here. You can give me the guns and come aboard my boat and pray I can get you out of this with your lives, or I can go on my way, and you can take your chances. While you're deciding, you should know that there's a Royal Navy gunboat heading this way that's already captured your supplier. Last I heard of them, they weren't in a mood to be gentle with whoever bought these guns."

"Haney's been taken?" Seamus's obvious alarm sent quivers of panic through Rynn, while Donal stiffened and even Fergus looked around big-eyed, the prayers he'd been mumbling over Paddy dying on his lips.

"He has. A fortunate circumstance, if you think about it, because it might just give you time to get away. But only if you're smart—and quick." His tone conveyed his conviction that they were neither.

"How do you know this? Any of this?" Rynn burst out. The key to what they should do next boiled down to a single question: Could they trust him? If not, going aboard his boat was about as smart as trying to smuggle in the guns to begin with. All right, maybe she agreed with him about that.

"Ah, that would be telling, now, wouldn't it?" His eyes, disconcertingly colorless in the silvery light, met hers again. "Let's just say, a little birdie told me."

Rynn's lips thinned. "Christmas night seems an odd time to be out fishing."

"Consider it your lucky day—or night." Maguire looked around at the men. "I'm going to ask you one more time, where are the guns?"

With the air of one having made up his mind, Donal put his hand on the oilcloth covering them. "Here."

"Donal—" Seamus protested.

"We've no choice," Donal replied.

"The Sullivans—"

"To hell with the Sullivans." Donal stood up, careful to keep a hand on the cargo for balance as a particularly large wave set the *Reaper* to bobbing and sent a substantial ripple beneath the *Merrow.* "I'd rather be dealing with them later than a gunboat full of Brits now."

"You know he's right," Rynn said to Seamus in an undertone when he still hesitated. She'd been settling disputes between the pair of them since they were young. Brave and strong and enterprising as the cousins were, they could be impetuous to a fault. Or, as her granny was wont to put it, they could be a right pair of sap skulls with seemingly half a brain between them.

Seamus slanted a reproachful look at her. He didn't have to say aloud what he often complained of: *You always take his side.* Then he grimaced, and his gaze shifted to Donal.

"Have it your own way," he said.

Maguire's arm went above his head in a twirling gesture aimed at the men watching from the rail of the *Reaper.* Despite the distance, Rynn could almost feel the gunmen's tension ease.

"Go on aboard, then," Maguire said. "We need to be getting under way as quick as we can. That gunboat's not far off."

"Seamus. Donal." Fergus crouched over Paddy, pulling one of the dead man's limp arms around his shoulders and struggling to get to his feet with his burden. "I could use some help here." Unlike Fergus, who was undersized and thin, Paddy was—had been—barrel-chested and stocky. Rynn's heart broke as she remembered the unlikely pair when they were all children together, them a gang of four inseparable boys with her, small but determined, tagging after them whenever and wherever she could. Until one day not long after she turned sixteen, Donal looked at her in a different way and everything changed.

"Leave him where he is," Maguire said as both Donal and Seamus moved to aid Fergus. "My men will see to him, do what needs to be done. Go on aboard, the lot of you. There's no more time to waste."

Chapter Four

"Take care. You drop one of those crates, or even shake it too hard, and it'll go off like a bomb. And we'll be going with it." Maguire's stark warning about the cargo's volatility, barked at his crew as the operation began, had Rynn holding her breath as she climbed the ladder to the *Reaper*'s deck.

Despite her fears, the guns were hauled aboard without mishap. Concealed in long wooden crates stamped Handle with Care: Fireworks in an attempt to disguise the contents, they were hiked up the side by ropes and quickly carried below by Maguire's men. That left the currach—and Paddy.

Clad in dry men's clothes—a collarless shirt and ancient breeches that she had to belt with a rope and a thick white fisherman's sweater, all far too big but that she was thankful for nonetheless—that had been provided along with a private place to wash and change, Rynn watched the tail end of the transfer from the *Reaper*'s rail. She expected to see Paddy, clearly of less importance than the guns to Maquire and his men, brought up next, perhaps slung over the shoulder of a stout sailor, perhaps hoisted up by ropes like the guns. The *Merrow*, which was at that moment being cast free from its present position, would then be tied up behind the *Reaper* for towing until they reached their destination, which so far none of them had thought to question. *Away* was all they knew.

Instead, she found herself watching in shock as the last remaining crewman on the *Merrow* picked up Seamus's rifle, which had been discovered beneath the oilcloth and set aside, and fired it multiple times in quick succession into the currach's hull. Muffled by the rush of the wind and waves, the repeated blasts were still sufficiently loud to make Rynn wince for fear that the gunboat Maguire had warned of might be near enough to be drawn to them by the sound. Then the shooter threw the rifle's strap over his shoulder, turned and leaped onto the ladder after his mates, *leaving Paddy behind.*

"Stop! Go back!" She waved at him frantically. The wind blew her voice away. Given the vagaries of the moonlight, the pitching of the ship and the speed at which the seaman was ascending the ladder, it was clear that he'd neither seen nor heard.

"What the *devil* . . . ?" Standing beside her, Donal stared down at the abandoned boat in disbelief. The *Merrow* was now adrift and taking on water fast through the new holes in her side.

"He scuttled my boat!" On Donal's other side, Seamus sounded stunned.

"Paddy! Oh, Jesus, Paddy!" Fergus gripped the rail with both hands. "They've left Paddy! *Go back!*"

But the crewmen were all aboard now, the ladder was being drawn up, and the four of them could only watch in horror as a wave caught the *Merrow* and swept her away. In the background, a metallic rattling that Rynn belatedly recognized as the *Reaper* weighing anchor made her catch her breath. Even as she identified it, the trawler, freed, surged forward.

"Maguire!" Seamus spun around, looking for the *Reaper*'s captain.

Rynn turned, too. Bathed in moonlight, the deck bustled with activity, making it difficult to identify any one man. The main sail snapped and billowed as it filled with wind. Picking up speed, the trawler plunged through the waves, heading out to sea.

"Over there, by the mizzen!" Donal pointed toward where the triangular sail was going up.

"Maguire!" Seamus strode away.

Fergus, hanging over the rail and focused on what was happening with the currach, looked after them, crying, "Tell them to lower a boat! We have to get him back! I've got to take him home to his family! Oh, Jesus, oh Jesus! Paddy!"

Donal was already only a step behind Seamus, two determined men on their way to right a wrong. Rynn turned her attention to Fergus, who openly wept now, and threw a steadying arm around him. His grief punctured the shock that had protected her. Her chest ached and her eyes stung with tears for Paddy's loss.

"Shh, now, we'll be getting him back and having the biggest wake and he'll be smiling down on it and on us." She fumbled to find words of comfort that she knew were useless even as she said them. "It's all right. It's going to be all right."

But it required only a glance at the small boat that was now at the mercy of the sea to know that it *wasn't* going to be all right, that the currach was lost. Listing badly from the weight of the water pouring into it, at the mercy of endless waves that were no longer blocked by the trawler's bulk, the *Merrow* capsized and was swallowed up even as they watched.

Paddy went down with it. Like the boat, between one minute and the next he was gone.

United in horror, she and Fergus simply stared at the moonlight sparkling on an empty, endless expanse of rolling black water. Not a trace of Paddy or the *Merrow* was to be seen.

A discarded shirt floated up from the depths like a pale ghost to undulate just below the surface before vanishing again.

With that, Fergus let out a howl of grief and rage that was like nothing Rynn had ever heard from him before. Whirling, he shook her off when she would have held him and bolted toward the mizzen where Donal and Seamus, forcefully gesticulating, faced off with a seemingly impassive Maguire. Taking only an instant to recover, Rynn ran after Fergus, her feet in their borrowed stockings slip-sliding on the worn-smooth planks.

"What did you do?" Fergus's shout was aimed at Maguire. "You had no right! He's gone, without a priest, without a prayer! We have to get him back! I have to take him home!"

To Rynn's horror, Fergus punctuated his outburst by pulling the pistol she had suspected was there from his pocket and brandishing it wildly.

"Fergus! No! Stop! Donal! Seamus!" Heart in throat as the three men he was bearing down on turned as one, afraid that at any moment he would pull the trigger and shoot someone or someone would shoot him, she grabbed Fergus's arm. He looked around at her in surprise—and the *Reaper*'s crew leaped on him from seemingly all sides, disarming him and taking him to the deck amid a flurry of shouts and blows.

Moments later, Fergus had been dragged away below while she, Donal and Seamus, the latter two having been searched and disarmed, were escorted to the wheelhouse under guard to await the coming of the Maguire. When he arrived, along with a burst of wind that ruffled the charts on the table around which they'd been ordered to sit and set the flames in the lanterns affixed to the walls to flickering, he dismissed the crewmen who'd been standing watch over them with a jerk of his head. Only the gangly, red-haired helmsman, who didn't look to be a day over seventeen, remained behind. After flicking a quick look at Maguire as the door shut behind the others, the helmsman hunched his shoulders as though to block out whatever might be going to happen next and continued to steer the ship through the night beyond the windows without a word.

"Ungrateful lot, aren't you?" Yanking off his cap, Maguire stalked toward them. The U-shaped room was small, and he seemed to take up most of the available space. His hair, cut short, was a coarse-looking dark brown. His beard was the same dark shade. As Rynn got her first good look at him in the light, her initial impression was that he was a man short on patience and long on temper. He was tight-lipped, with thick brows that nearly met in a frown above his nose. His features were rough-hewn in a face that was squarish, with broad cheekbones and a solid jaw now set hard with displeasure. His skin was baked bronze by wind and sun. The lamplight painted his eyes some indeterminate pale color that she still couldn't quite make out.

"You sank my boat." Seamus sounded aggrieved rather than angry. Rynn guessed he found the situation they were in, coupled with Maguire's size and reputation, intimidating enough to dampen his usual tendency toward belligerence. Despite bearing a strong resemblance to Donal, Seamus lacked his cousin's lean, sculpted good looks. His black hair was curly as a sheep's, his cheeks were round and his brown eyes, red rimmed now with grief, were more mud colored than anything else. Raw-boned and loose-limbed, he made up for any shortcomings in the way of looks by—usually—being charming, loud and brash.

"You're damned lucky I did." Maguire threw his cap down on the table, braced large hands on either side of it and leaned toward them. Rynn had a vague notion that he was no more than twenty-eight or -nine, but his sheer physical presence made him seem older. "Does it not occur to you geniuses that by now, your friend Haney having been taken and all, the Brits know what boat it is that was bringing in the load of illegal guns, and who was in on it?"

As the grim truth of that broke over the three of them, Rynn's stomach turned inside out.

"They'll be coming after us," she said, appalled.

"They will," Maguire agreed, as at the same time Donal shot her a quick look and said under his breath, "*Not you. You had no part in this. You only came out to warn us. And how would they even know you were with us? It's dark as Hades tonight. They will never have seen you. Not well enough to identify you, at any rate.*"

"Miss Carmichael, is it?" Maguire slashed a look at her. His eyes, she was finally able to determine as she gazed directly into them, were the clear pale blue of shallow seawater. How he knew her identity she was at a loss to say. To her knowledge, she'd never set eyes on him before.

"And how would you know that?" Suspicion colored her voice.

A sardonic curl of his lip was his only answer. Seamus said with a snort, "And you the most beautiful girl in five counties? Come on, Rynn, there's not a man around doesn't know your name. No mystery there."

Donal's expression signified agreement. Rynn's lips tightened as she immediately felt self-conscious.

Fortunately Maguire showed no interest in commenting on the matter, and instead continued with, "Whatever the rights and wrongs of how you came to be in this situation, *Miss Carmichael*, as far as the Brits are concerned, the fact that you're here now and you were in that boat with the guns is more than sufficient. It might be unlikely that they'd put you in front of a firing squad, seeing that you're a woman, but they still could. And they will certainly shoot *you*—" he looked at Donal—and Seamus "—if they get their hands on you. As well as your idiot friend who has no more sense—or gratitude—than to pull a gun on a boatload of men who've just done him a huge service."

"Fergus loved Paddy like a brother," Rynn said in Fergus's defense. Raw with grief herself, she still shivered intermittently despite the insulating folds of the wool sweater that enveloped her from her neck to halfway down her thighs. The fact that her hair, despite having been blotted with a cloth as she changed, was still damp and loose now about her shoulders as she tried to let the thick fall of it dry might have had something to do with her inability to get warm, but she suspected that a combination of shock and fear was more to blame. "You left Paddy to the sea without benefit of a priest, or any prayers said over him or any words at all! Without asking or telling us what you meant to do! And you wonder that Fergus is upset? The wonder would be if he was not!"

"Upset, is he?" Maguire gave her a hard look, then expanded that grim glance to include the men beside her. "So, too, am I upset. That a bunch of want-wits should have no better judgment than to be bringing the Crown forces down upon us here in our home territory, where we have heretofore been able to go about our business without notice or interference, is something for any rational man to be upset about, don't you agree?"

"To hell with the Crown forces! To hell with the King, and bloody England!" Seamus burst out. "We're done with them! They'll rule over us forever if we let them! Driving them out by force is the only answer. And for that we need guns! Yes, I'm bringing them in! And I'll be bringing in more, and so will others! If they won't give us our freedom, we'll take it!"

"You were with the Sixteenth, were you not?" Maguire's tone was measured. His glance included Donal.

"All of us were. The ten of us," Seamus said. "Donal and me, Fergus and Paddy, Brian Meagher, Sean O'Leahy, Liam McCarthy, Cormac Byrne, Tyrone Walsh, Joseph Murphy." His tone turned bleak as he said those last names. "We joined up, all of us together, volunteered! Like damned fools! We missed the Somme, maybe, but after that we were in the thick of it. Meagher, O'Leahy, McCarthy, Byrne, Walsh and Murphy fell in battle. Four out of the ten of us made it home. Only four."

"So, like myself and my men, you were at Messines. And Passchendaele. And the rest."

"We were," Seamus said, and Donal nodded.

"Then I'd think you'd have had your bloody fill of bloody war and bloody killing." A barely leashed savagery whipped through Maguire's words.

"We've had our fill of *them*. Six years ago, they promised us Home Rule. Six years! But what happened? Nothing. They blamed it on the war. Just wait till it's over, they said. We'll give you back your country that we took. We trusted their word, trusted that it would happen, fought alongside them and shed our blood and died, by the tens of thousands as you know. But now the war is over, and the time for waiting is at an end, and still they say, wait. Waiting's what we've had our fill of, and we'll wait no more!" Seamus's face flushed crimson as he spoke.

Maguire's lips tightened. But before he could reply, Donal burst out with "Aye, and while we were off fighting, they arrested Eamon de Valera and his men on false charges of traitorously plotting with the Germans and locked them away in British prisons! Where they still rot with the Crown's good will! And now the evil bastards have gone and killed Paddy!"

"The evil bastards!" Seamus repeated with loathing. "Even when we fought alongside them, they looked down their noses at us! They treated us like we were less than them, less than human even, sending us in first to catch the brunt of the machine gun fire and the flame throwers and the rest of it while they hung back. Behind our backs they called us drunks and cowards, when it was us saving their bloody arses! For generations they've starved us, run us off our land, taken our homes. They've outlawed our language, made us into serfs in our own country! We've had all of it we can stand." Passion blazed from Seamus's eyes as they rested on Maguire. "You're known, Maguire. A war hero! You could join us, help us run the bastards out once and for all. A man like you, people will listen."

"So you think to get what you want by fomenting revolution?" Maguire shook his head. "I prefer to wait and give the results of the election a chance."

"Are you a bloody Unionist, then?" Seamus's tone made the word a curse.

"I'm a bloody *Irishman.* I lost two brothers and a brother-in-law in the war. That's three widows left behind, and a passel of fatherless children. And thousands like them throughout the country! Who's to provide for them? See that they have food and a roof over their heads and the like? It's left to me to provide for mine, and that's what I'll be doing, not fighting some damned useless fight that'll leave our people in worse case than they're in already."

"We have to fight. It's the only way we'll ever win free," Seamus said, low and fierce, as Donal nodded agreement.

"Stop! Enough about fighting! I'll hear no more of it! None, do you understand? Isn't it enough that Paddy's dead? Do you want to die, too?" Rynn's chair shot back with a harsh scraping noise as she jumped to her feet. This talk of revolution terrified her. Eamon de Valera, one of the leaders of the Easter Rising, had been imprisoned afterward and had barely escaped with his life when the executions were halted after their swift brutality shocked the world. Now the head of Sinn Fein, de Valera had been in prison in England since May—and she could not think that was an entirely bad thing, as he and his cohorts were bound and set on overthrowing British rule at whatever the cost in Irish blood and anguish. That more violence and death would come to the people she loved and the land she loved, and especially so soon after the end to the worst war the world had ever seen, was unthinkable. Anything, anything was preferable to that. Her glare encompassed the two men beside her before landing on the one in front of her. "And what *about* Paddy? A boat must be launched. If we're to have any chance at all of recovering his body, there's no time to be lost."

Those surprisingly light eyes met hers again.

"His body will be recovered. Did you think he was left on the currach by accident? Whether you know it or not, the currents where he went down are such that he will wash ashore with the morning tide," Maguire said. "And he will be found." His gaze shifted to Seamus. "As will the remains of your boat. And if you are very, very lucky, those hunting you will think that you, too, all of you, went down with the boat and drowned and will, in good time and when nothing more is seen of you, call off the search. Leaving you to carry on with your life in some degree of safety, providing, of course, that you do it somewhere else until these matters settle down."

"Owen," the helmsman interrupted, looking around at them. "We're nearing the harbor. If you're meaning us to go elsewhere, you'd best be telling me where."

Chapter Five

"No, we'll stay to our plan," Maguire said. "Except we'll be putting these fine folks ashore on Inishmurray."

The tiny island of Inishmurray, as everyone knew, was home to a now-deserted monastery known as the Cashel as well as a settlement of perhaps two hundred souls whose families had lived there for generations and who presently survived on fishing and the making of illegal Irish moonshine whiskey and its equally illegal predecessor poteen. Some six kilometers off the coast of Sligo, it was little more than a grassy rock protruding from the bay. The waters around the island were notoriously rough, making access difficult for all but the most experienced seamen, which suited the moonshiners perfectly. As far as she was aware, outsiders rarely visited, and short of hiring or borrowing a boat, which seemed ill advised at present if it could even be done, there would be precious little chance of them finding their way home that night.

She would not be missed until morning, she was almost sure. Would any of the men? There was no way to know. But tomorrow, the families would start to worry. If Maguire were to be believed—and she did believe him, she found—Paddy's body would wash ashore, where it would be found. His death would leave his mother heartbroken. His sisters—Rynn's throat tightened as she pictured them, pictured all the families. The news of their son's and brother's loss would leave them shattered, especially now that they'd counted him safe from the war and let go of the dread that all of them with loved ones at the front had lived under for so long. And she—

"You're thinking to leave us there? On the island?" Donal directed the question to Maguire as the helmsman returned his attention to his job.

Maguire's glance encompassed all three of them. "I am. You'll go ashore with the supplies we'll be delivering and continue your journey on from there."

"What journey?" Seamus asked.

Maguire's grunt of laughter was unamused. "Were you perhaps thinking that you'd just go along home now and bury your friend and then get on with your lives as though nothing had happened? You've well and truly kicked the hornet's nest, and by this time the hornets know exactly who you are and where you live. Your only chance at escaping the King's justice is to disappear until this whole disaster you've created has died down. To that end—and you're welcome, by the by!—I'll be passing you on to an acquaintance of mine who lives on the island. He'll convey you to Liverpool, where if you've a grain of sense you'll be aboard the next boat to the Continent. Or America. Yes, America's probably best."

"What?" Rynn grabbed the edge of the table for balance as the boat bounced over a series of giant swells.

"America?" Seamus's eyes widened.

"You can come back, of course," Maguire said. "In a few years."

"A few *years*?" Rynn nearly choked. The thought of simply picking up and leaving Granny, Glenna, her friends and job and home and *life* took her breath. And to leave without a word, letting everyone think she was dead—

She could feel panic building.

"We can't be doing that." After a quick glance at her, Donal shook his head. "We've people here. Families. Anyway, we've no money to go anywhere."

"We could sign on as ship's crew and earn our passage that way." Seamus's tone was thoughtful. His expression told Rynn that he was turning the idea over in his mind. "The crossing isn't so long—only about seven days."

"Are you truly talking about going to America? And what would we be doing when we get there, pray?" Donal demanded.

"We'll find something. Work the docks. Hire ourselves out to the fishing fleets. Maybe make our fortunes. There's pots of money to be earned in America, I'm hearing."

Maguire shrugged. "What you do after I put you ashore is up to you. But you will get off my boat on Inishmurray, because I won't be bringing any more trouble down on my own and my crew's heads than I've already done. If you're smart, you'll take this chance I'm offering to get well away while you can. But if you fancy ending up facing a firing squad at the Castle instead, you'll not find me standing in your way."

"He's in the right of it, you know," Seamus said to Donal. "We have to go. And America—it'd be an adventure, for sure."

"No!" As alarm coursed through her, Rynn's grip on the table tightened until her knuckles showed white. She held on for dear life because the sea was getting rougher, and because of the sudden spark in Donal's eyes. She knew him. She knew that brightening; he found the prospect exciting. The last time she'd seen it, he'd wound up going off to fight the Huns despite his solemn promise to her that he would not. What she had to say to Donal she would much prefer to say in private, but she was afraid there would be no time. Her gaze locked with his. Her voice went low. "Have you forgotten? We're to be married. You asked me to wait until you got back from the war, and I did. When you got home, you said there's no more reason to wait and I agreed. We're to talk to Father Doherty on Sunday, with the banns to be said right after the New Year."

Donal said, "Would I be forgetting that? No, I would not! You'll be coming with us, of course. Were you thinking I'd leave you behind? We can be married along the way. In Liverpool, or on the ship, or in America or wherever we end up. Wouldn't that be grand, though, to start a new life in America? You and me, and Seamus, and Fergus? And Paddy along with us, in spirit."

Her mind reeled.

Donal's eyes blazed with excitement as he got to his feet beside her. Oh, she knew that look! When she didn't answer immediately, he took her hand—pried it from the table, more like—and held her cold fingers tightly in his warm ones and smiled that impossible-to-resist smile of his at her. "Well, Rynn? Will you come adventuring with me?"

As if from a distance, she took in the handsome face of the man that she'd been in love with for what felt like most of her life, the coaxing tone that he always used to get around her, the warmth of the oh-so-familiar hand gripping hers.

"No." She snatched her hand from his.

"Oh, for the Lord's sake," Seamus said, and stood up. Looming behind Donal, he shook his head at her. "This is no time for one of your crotchets, Rynn Carmichael, and so I warn you."

The look she directed at him in turn should have by rights taken him to his knees.

"Why not?" Donal demanded of her, nettled.

"To begin with, we've nothing," she said. "No papers. Not so much as a full set of clothes among us. Not even a toothbrush. And as you said, no money. How do you propose to survive?"

"We'll make do. We'll find work. We'll find *something*. Ah, you worry too much, *acushla*. The matter will sort itself out, you'll see."

"That's pie-in-the-sky talk, you great looby." The look she gave him was as much despairing as angry. He was ever the dreamer, with scarcely a practical bone in his body. And as she had learned over the course of a penurious lifetime, one couldn't eat dreams. "What about our families? Have you thought of them?" She glanced at Seamus. "And not just your mam, but Molly Kincaid? Will you leave her without a word?"

She cast a significant look at the silver St. Michael pendant Molly had given him for protection before he left for the war, which he wore on a chain around his neck.

Seamus had the grace to look slightly abashed. "I'll be sending for Molly. When I can."

"And what if she doesn't want to come? What about how much she'll grieve in the meantime?"

"She'll grieve, 'tis true. But she'll come."

Giving him a disgusted look, Rynn turned back to Donal. "And while you might be able to hire on as ship's crew to get across the Atlantic or wherever you choose to go, I don't think that's an option for me and that still leaves you with nothing when you get there."

"What would you have us do, then?" Donal threw up his hands in exasperation. "Do you *want* to see me facing a firing squad?"

What answer could she give to that? Her throat tightened with fear and dread and a host of other soul-crushing emotions.

"You know I don't."

"Then what? I know this isn't what you bargained on. I know you don't want to leave home like this, leave Ireland. I—we've—made a right mess of it, I admit that freely. But Maguire's talking sense—after tonight, I don't think we can stay."

A lump formed in her throat.

"I don't think so, either."

"And Molly—our families—would a sight rather think us

dead for a wee while than have us be dead in reality, as we will be if the Brits catch us," Seamus said, in the tone of one delivering a knockout blow to the argument.

"So we'll go." Donal had been watching her face all the while. Now he spoke with the confidence of one who'd never once failed to persuade her to his way of thinking. "And we'll be together. And once we're safely away, all will be just as we planned, you'll see."

A thousand thoughts and images and memories chased each other through her head as she looked at him. It was as if her whole life passed before her eyes in a single second. Her beautiful Irish mother, dying days after Glenna was born. Her feckless British father, abandoning his two young daughters within weeks of that event, leaving them to the care of his dead wife's mother as he slunk back home to the aristocratic family that had disowned him upon his scandalous marriage to an Irish actress. Her tiny, indomitable granny, standing strong, managing the bits and pieces of money he sent to them as best she could, until he died less than four years later and there was no more. The aching poverty that followed, the sting of always being seen among the villagers as an outsider because of who her father was, the fear of Granny dying and leaving them totally alone, were the constants of her childhood. But Donal—and Seamus, and to a lesser extent Fergus and Paddy as well, that whole gang of boys——was a constant, too. From their earliest years, they'd allowed her into their group, sometimes bullying her, sometimes protecting her, sometimes, as they grew older, even openly appreciating what they came to call her "managing ways." But always they'd wrapped her in the shield of their friendship, and she, in turn, had looked up to and looked after them. And then Donal had become her love. And now he held her heart and future in his hands.

It terrified her to realize that she found the thought unnerving.

"The O'Reillys in America." Seamus clapped Donal on the shoulder. "The more I think on it, the more I like it!"

Donal's smile widened into a broad grin as he looked around at his cousin. "It does have a grand sound to it, I admit."

Watching the two of them exchange glances, a shaft of anger so strong her hands involuntarily clenched into fists shook Rynn. It occurred to her then that, just as Seamus claimed with some truth that she always sided with Donal, it was equally true that Donal always chose to follow Seamus into whatever reckless scheme he thought up next without regard to common sense, his own safety or any objections she might raise. To top off countless incidents from their growing-up years, he'd gone to war at Seamus's urging, he'd smuggled guns at Seamus's urging and now—

"We'll need to be getting the guns to Ori Sullivan," Seamus said. "Or—"

"How can we get the guns to him if he and everyone else thinks we've drowned?" Donal asked impatiently. "Forget the guns, will you? Haven't they brought us enough trouble?"

Without warning, the *Reaper*'s bow pitched up. Rynn staggered, then grabbed for the table again as the trawler bucked and shuddered its way to what felt like a complete stop in the water. Even before the helmsman looked around to ask Maguire "Will we be sending them ashore in the skiff, then?" she realized that the trawler had once again dropped anchor, which meant they'd reached their destination. Bracing against the movement as the boat tested the limits of the anchor chain, she faced the truth: with much—everything!—at stake, the time for looking to the future was at hand.

Chapter Six

Maguire shook his head. "They can go in with Tremaine's people. Have him come aboard when the boats get here, and I'll have a word. And Tim, make sure Tremaine and his crew hear no mention of those guns we've acquired."

"Aye." The helmsman, Tim, nodded, secured the wheel and went out.

Maguire looked at Seamus. "Here we are, then. Tremaine will get you lot to Liverpool. After that, you may do as you wish." He strode for the door, saying over his shoulder, "I'll send someone to fetch you when it's time."

"Wait." Rynn's voice was sharper than she intended as she released her death grip on the table. Maguire stopped, eyebrows lifting in surprise as he looked at her. "I need to speak to you."

His eyebrows went higher. "Speak, then. There's nothing that I see stopping you."

"In private." Waving off Donal's surprised look, she swept past them all and out the door.

A cold blast of wind hit her as soon as she stepped outside, whipping her hair out behind her like a banner. She let it go. The wind smelled of the sea, of course, but also carried on it a hint of woodsmoke that told her that they were close to land. The moon was out in the open now, riding high among the racing clouds, bathing the deck in a ghostly light. On the island that stretched out before them, the moonlight illuminated a rough stone wall and a sprinkle of small houses beyond the narrow fingerling of the natural harbor in which they were anchored. Dim lights showed in a few windows, as if someone inside waited for a family member to return home. Metallic scrapes and clangs, the whoosh of a collapsing sail, the slap of waves against the hull, formed the backdrop to the rise and fall of masculine voices, many masculine voices, far more than should have been on the ship.

Glancing around curiously even as she stepped out of the wind to press her back against the wheelhouse wall where it was sheltered and warmer, she was surprised to see what looked like a score or more of men moving purposefully back and forth across the deck. The ones striding toward the rail bore large sacks of something slung over their shoulders, which they lowered to, presumably, the boats Maguire had mentioned waiting below. Those moving away from the rail carried large wooden crates that were obviously far heavier than the sacks.

"What are they doing?" Her question was spontaneous, born of surprise.

"Their jobs." Maguire stopped in front of her, blocking her view. "I've work to do. What is it you want of me?"

Backlit by moonlight, he looked big enough to be intimidating, if she'd been in a mood to be intimidated. But she was too heartsick, and too heartsore, for that.

"The guns," she said. "If they're to remain in your possession, you should be paying us for them."

"What?"

"It's only fair," she said.

"You think I should pay for the privilege of saving your lives?" Maguire sounded as if he couldn't believe his ears.

"No, I think you should pay for the guns."

"The cheek of you!" he marveled.

"If you're not wanting to pay for them, then we'll have them back. I've no doubt they can be sold for a tidy sum. If not on Inishmurray, then certainly in Liverpool. Maybe not for what was paid for them, but for enough to provide a little cushion until something else comes along."

"So now you're proposing to take up gunrunning, are you?"

"No," she said, not having quite thought of the matter in that way. "I'm proposing to get value from that which we already possess."

"It appears to me like I possess them, for the moment. And what if I say I'm keeping them as my price for saving your sorry lives?" Maguire folded his arms across his chest.

"Then I'd say I'd be sorry to learn that the famous war hero Owen Maguire, head of clan Maguire, is a thief." She folded her arms across her chest in turn.

"What?" Maguire's eyes narrowed dangerously at her. "The hell you say."

"Either you intend to sell them or keep them, and whichever you choose it's you reaping the value from that which doesn't belong to you."

"They don't belong to you, either. Or, more properly, to yon idiots who thought to smuggle them in."

"At least they paid for them, which is more than you can claim."

"As I understand it, they paid with someone else's money. I don't think that makes them the owners."

"More so than you."

"Perhaps I intend on turning them over to the Crown, as any good subject of the King should do."

"Ah, but if you did that you'd have to explain to the Crown where you got them, wouldn't you? And I'm thinking that would prove awkward for you, since the *Merrow* will have supposedly sunk with all hands and the guns on board, though you could, I suppose, claim to have fished the crates out of the sea after the boat went down. But then they might well start to ask themselves, as I do, why you're out after herring on Christmas night with no nets out and no sign of fish on board and an island that produces illegal whiskey as your destination."

An almost imperceptible stiffening of Maguire's shoulders was the only outward indication he gave that she'd hit a nerve. Still, she *knew.* It was there in the air between them, in the sudden crackle of antagonism she could feel radiating from him like heat from the sun, and logic backed it up. The only reason she could see that he would be sailing to Inishmurray in the middle of Christmas night, a time when most were with their families and he could have expected the surrounding waters to be deserted, which, except for the unfortunate appearance of the *Merrow* and, not coincidentally, a British gun boat they *were,* was to pick up a load of the illegal whiskey that the islanders made. And the only reason to pick up such a load would be to sell it, which was also illegal. Engaging in such trade would account for the huge success of his fishing fleet, which, come to find out, did not appear to have stemmed from fishing at all.

It might not have occurred to Donal and Seamus that Owen Maguire was every bit as much engaged in a criminal enterprise as they were and was so concerned about their endeavors because they might call attention to his, but it had occurred to her.

And she meant to make what use of it she could.

Maguire met her gaze with a long, cool look. "It might interest you to learn that I'm out on Christmas night delivering much-needed supplies to the islanders, though what I do with my boat and my time is no concern of yours."

"Oh, my, have I offended? I hope you'll forgive me for letting my imagination get the better of me! I quite see my mistake. But I do still want you to pay for the guns." Rynn returned him measuring look for measuring look. "It's my understanding that they're worth upward of five thousand pounds."

"You may believe me when I tell you I have no intention of paying you five thousand pounds for them."

She clucked sympathetically. "It is a great deal to ask, isn't it? I'm not so unreasonable as to expect that! We'll take half for them. You may keep the balance as our thank-you for the rescue."

Maguire laughed. "And if I refuse? Do you propose to take the guns off me by force? Or will you go running with your preposterous story to the authorities?"

The mockery in his tone told her he knew he had her there. There really was nothing she or any of them could do.

Rynn lifted her chin at him. "I will think poorly of you."

"Oh-ho." It was a jeer.

"You'll still be coming out well ahead, you know. You may sell them for the full five thousand pounds or even more, and two thousand five hundred pounds' profit, at a minimum, is quite a return on your night's work. And you will have our undying gratitude, and the satisfaction that comes with knowing that you did the right thing."

"And what of the Sullivans? Who are, quite properly, expecting to receive the guns they paid for?"

"They cannot expect such a thing with the boat sunk and all aboard perished."

His lips compressed. "Quite the opportunist, aren't you?"

"Only a fool doesn't take advantage of opportunities."

Before anything more could be said between them, someone called, "Owen!"

Maguire turned slightly in answer. With him no longer blocking her view Rynn saw Tim striding toward them, with another, bulkier man following a pace or so behind. Spotting Rynn, Tim stopped, clearly hesitant to approach.

"What is it?" Maguire's tone was testy.

"Uh, I have Mr. Tremaine with me," Tim said, gesturing at

the other man, who stopped beside him. "And Mulally wants to know what he should do about the one in the brig."

By "the one in the brig" Rynn understood him to mean Fergus.

"Tremaine! I'll be right with you! Just give me a minute to finish up here." Maguire greeted the second man heartily, then said to Tim, "Have the prisoner brought up, but tell Mulally to keep him under close watch until he's off the *Reaper*."

As Tim nodded and withdrew, Maguire raised an acknowledging hand to a shout of "We need to hurry, Major! A storm's blowing in," that came from someone out of Rynn's sight before he turned back to Rynn.

"Much as it goes against the grain with me to reward what I can only characterize as blackmail, I'll give you five hundred pounds for the lot. And that's only because it's Christmas and I'm feeling generous." His voice was low and growly with annoyance.

"It's a paltry sum compared to what they're worth."

The sound he made in answer to that persuaded Rynn to take what she could get.

"Very well, we have a deal," she said before he could rescind his offer. Then, because he looked so out of temper, she smiled at him.

He blinked, pulled a wry face, nodded curtly in acceptance of their deal and started to turn away.

She caught his sleeve. "You understand that we need payment before we leave the ship, and we need it in cash."

"Do you now?" His eyes glinted at her.

"We do."

"Mercenary as well as ungrateful, aren't you? Rest easy, you'll have it." Pulling his arm free, he walked away. "Fetch your friends," he ordered over his shoulder. "It's time the lot of you got off my ship."

He was talking to Tremaine as Rynn went back inside the

wheelhouse. Donal stood in the middle of the small room frowning at the door as she entered, while Seamus stood beside him with a calming hand on his shoulder.

"And what was that about?" Donal asked with an edge to his voice as she closed the door behind her. After the blowing wind of the deck, the wheelhouse seemed warm, if a little stuffy. The air smelled of whale oil and damp wool and men. Of Donal's tone she took little notice. Jealousy had long been one of his faults, and one moreover that she'd learned to ignore.

"Since it seems Major Maguire will be keeping the guns, I asked him to pay for them. He agreed and will be giving you five hundred pounds for them before you leave the ship."

"What?" Donal's whole demeanor changed. "Never say you bargained with the man for such a thing!"

"Well, I did. And a good job I made of it, too."

"Rynn! You angel! Five hundred pounds!" Surging forward, Seamus snatched her up off her feet and swung her around in a circle. "It's far less than they're worth but 'twill make all the difference!"

"Put her down, you oaf!" Donal pulled Rynn away from Seamus. "That was some good thinking, *acushla*." He smiled at her. "What would we do without you to look out for us?"

As their eyes met, she didn't smile back. Instead, she felt a pain worse than the ache of a sore tooth start up somewhere in the region of her heart.

"Be five hundred pounds the poorer, that's for sure." Seamus was jubilant. Then he frowned. "Still, there's the Sullivans."

"If they think you're drowned, and the *Merrow*'s lost, they'll not be looking for their guns or their money," Rynn said, adding, "Major Maguire told me to fetch you. They're bringing up Fergus from the brig. It's time to get off this boat."

"We'd best not tell Fergus of the plan until we have to." Seamus headed for the door. "He's not going to like it."

"He'll like it well enough once we explain the alternative to him." Wrapping an arm around her to pull her along, Donal started to follow Seamus. Rynn stopped him by the simple expedient of planting her feet and shaking her head at him.

"You go along to Fergus," Donal said to Seamus, who, having reached the door, looked around at them. "Rynn and I need a moment."

Seamus groaned. "Donal, man, can't it wait? You can kiss the girl later."

"Go away," Rynn said to him.

"I'll be right along," Donal promised.

With a heavenward roll of his eyes, Seamus departed.

"So, *acushla*?" Donal said when Seamus had gone. His arm dropped away from her waist. His expression had turned wary. Ah, he knew her! Her heart gave another pang.

"Leaving Ireland is best, I quite see that," Rynn said. "But it's best for you and Seamus and Fergus. Not for me." She took a deep breath. "I won't be going with you."

"What! Now, Rynn . . ." He took her hand, held it prisoner in both of his. "You're overwrought about Paddy and everything that's happened tonight. I know that, I understand, but you and I, we belong together. I know this is not what we planned but it'll still be *us*. You and me."

His tone was that of a patient man, only slightly exasperated by what he saw as the vagaries of womenfolk. He still thought he could talk her around. She could see it in his eyes, hear it in his voice, feel it in his touch as his hands cradled hers. But she'd seen the future, seen her life with him unspooling in her mind's eye in a bright burst of illumination that revealed much in their relationship that she had never questioned before, and it had felt *wrong*. He was handsome and charming and so very dear, but little more than a boy. A feckless, reckless boy.

While the girl that she was when he'd left to go to war had grown up in his absence.

"You know how you said that you came out tonight with Seamus because he needed a man he could trust?" She hated having to say such things to him, but she'd seen the truth now. As much as facing it hurt her and would hurt him, denying it would only lead to deeper, greater pain for them both. "So do I need a man I can trust. The truth is, we are neither of us ready for marriage, me no more than you. I release you from your promise, and our engagement."

"What! You love me! You know you do!"

"I do, but—"

"But what?" His hands tightened on hers. He looked baffled, with hurt and a little outrage beginning to creep in.

"We're very different, Donal, which you know as well as I do if you would but take the time to think about it, and we want different things. I . . ."

"You've met someone else." Cutting her off before she could finish, his voice turned harsh. The hands holding hers tightened until his grip hurt. "While I was away fighting. Haven't you?"

"No, of course not." She jerked her hand free. "Don't be ridiculous. It's as I told you, we're too different. Unsuited. As tonight proves, you want excitement and adventure and to see the world beyond here and I—I am no adventurer. I want a quiet life, safe in my home, surrounded by family and friends. You would hate being tethered in such a way and would hate me for being the one to tether you."

"Hate you! Damn it, woman, I love you!" Grabbing her, he wrapped her in a crushing embrace and kissed her, forcefully. The heat of his mouth on hers, the strength of his arms around her, the feel of him against her were so familiar that for the briefest of moments she was motionless, soaking it in, heart aching even as she did so because she knew that, her pain notwithstanding, this was goodbye.

The door was thrust open and a harsh voice barked "O'Reilly!" before the incoming footsteps stopped abruptly.

Rynn pushed out of Donal's arms to find Maguire standing in the doorway frowning at them.

"Tremaine and his men are leaving. The pair of you need to come now," he said.

"I'm not going," Rynn said. Her face was turned away from Donal but she could feel the tension emanating from him. "I am returning home."

"What?" Maguire looked surprised.

"You can't." Donal grabbed her arm. "If the Brits find out you helped us—"

"They won't." She pulled her arm free. "How could they? As you said yourself, it was too dark for those on shore to see me, and the only ones who know are on this boat and in no position to tell."

If Donal thought that was a reference to Seamus, Fergus and him, he was right, but not entirely. It was also a reminder to Maguire of her—correct, she was certain—suspicions about his activities.

"Rynn." Donal reached for her again. She eluded him by shaking her head and taking a step back, then looked at Maguire.

"Will you allow me to stay aboard, then put me ashore at Mullaghmore? I can find my own way from there."

His face revealed nothing, but there was something in his eyes; he knew what she was holding over his head and didn't like it.

"If that's your choice." Maguire's response was curt. "Although I'm not sure it's a wise one."

"I think I'm the best judge of that."

His lips compressed.

"Owen." It was Tim's voice, which she recognized although he was out of her sight. "Tremaine's holding a boat. And if they miss the tide, they'll have the devil of a time getting back in."

By that time, he was standing behind Maguire, peering at her and Donal over Maguire's shoulder.

"O'Reilly." Maguire's attitude brooked no argument. "Time to go."

"Rynn." There was desperation in Donal's voice and in his eyes as he looked at her. "Don't do this. I know you're angry because I came out with Seamus tonight, but . . ."

"It's not that." She shook her head, although she could feel her heart cracking. It was impossible to put into words everything that had gone into her decision, especially with Maguire and his henchman watching and listening. "It's what I told you. Other than that, there's no more to be said."

"O'Reilly. The boat won't wait," Maguire warned.

"Go. I'll not be changing my mind." Hard as she found it to do, Rynn met Donal's gaze without flinching.

"I'll not be sending for you." Donal was breathing hard, focused on her.

"I'm not asking you to," Rynn answered. "Take care of yourself, Donal. You'll be thanking me for this one day, whether you believe it now or not."

Donal stared at her. She put up her chin at him.

"Go to the devil, then, Rynn Carmichael," he said.

Then, his face like stone, he all but flung himself past Maguire and out the door.

Chapter Seven

By dawn, a steady rain fell, pattering on the slate roof, turning the world outside the tiny window through which Rynn observed it a depressing gray. An earthy dampness pervaded the huge old mansion that was Ballyshannon Court, adding its own touch of misery to the grief that throbbed like an open wound inside her. Though fires were lit below—she could smell them—it was cold in the attic where she hurriedly fastened the last button of her blue nurse's uniform even as she headed for the stairs. She had to remind herself that it was St. Stephens Day, a holiday celebrated as enthusiastically as Christmas itself, which didn't mean that she and the other nurses were off duty. But it did mean that she would have to pretend to be in a festive mood—at least until Paddy's body was found.

Shuddering at the thought, she pushed it from her mind. She must just get through this awful day as best she could, and not dwell on what was to come until it did. Not much more than two hours before, she'd crept up all three flights of the servants' staircase to her small room under the eaves, wincing at every creak lest someone should appear with questions about where she'd been. But no one did, and she'd made it to her room unobserved. She'd spent the ensuing time hiding her borrowed clothes and bathing and brushing her hair until all visible traces of the night's ordeal were gone. If her head hurt from exhaustion and her legs ached from her recent frantic journey, which had seen her walking from the beach where she'd been put ashore to Mullaghmore, where she'd "borrowed" a bicycle and then ridden on through the night until she reached Ballyshannon Court, those were minor discomforts. Now, with her hair pinned up securely and, she hoped, her lack of sleep camouflaged by having splashed her face repeatedly with the icy water left in her pitcher, she would take up the familiar routine of caring for the convalescents, while doing her best not to be shattered by the knowledge that her life as she had known it was changed forever.

Paddy was dead. Donal was gone. Her heart broke over both. Shock and its accompanying sense of unreality provided a layer of protective cushioning, but that would wear off, she knew. The practical repercussions of what had happened—she had no idea what they might be. All she knew was that there was no going back. She had chosen her path and must live with the consequences.

"There's sugar for your tea, brought special clear from Dublin," Mrs. Frampton greeted her as Rynn emerged into the warm, heavenly smelling kitchen from the narrow back staircase. Plump and white-haired, Mrs. Frampton was the long-time cook/housekeeper for Ballyshannon Court, recruited with most of the rest of the staff to stay on when the Duke of Hartford had offered up his Irish retreat to the war effort. She hovered protectively over the turkeys she was roasting for the evening's feast while the kitchen maids bustled about preparing breakfast for the dining room, where at nine o'clock sharp the patients would gather to eat. Before then, medicine must be administered, wounds checked, dressings changed and all the other early-morning activities associated with the care and feeding of the twenty-two remaining soldiers accomplished.

"What good fairy visited us overnight?" Rynn kept her response light as she went to add a bit of sugar to the cup of steaming tea Mrs. Frampton poured out for her, then carried it to the large wooden table that was the kitchen's centerpiece. Sugar had been the most precious of commodities in the last months of the war, and it remained scarce. Under better circumstances she would have been excited at the treat, but as things stood it would take more than a little unexpected sugar to brighten her day.

"Colonel Pelly, although I dunno if I'd be calling him a fairy, good or otherwise," Lynnette giggled. Lynnette and Anna were the kitchen maids. Under Mrs. Frampton's rule they worked, cheerfully enough, from before dawn until long after the rest of the household was abed. Feeding so many hungry soldiers was labor-intensive work.

Rynn smiled as she was meant to—Colonel Pelly was the approximate size of a lorry—and sat down at the long table. The other nurses—two professionals like herself, who needed to work for a living and thus had gone to school for formal training and now got paid for their services, and six VADs, who were affluent enough to take the more socially acceptable route and volunteer—were either already present or arriving in the kitchen more or less on schedule. There was much general talk along with the clatter of plates and utensils as everyone gathered around the table and began to eat. Rynn drank her tea and took small bites of the toast and jam that was her usual breakfast as she listened with half an ear to the morning's gossip. Although the hot tea was welcome, she had to choke down the bread. She was wound so tightly it was difficult to eat, but she thought it was important to carry on as though this was a morning like any other.

Soon enough she would have to slip into the role of mourner for the man and the friends she loved, and the prospect was making her feel increasingly desperate. She had ever been a poor liar. And to have to playact in the face of Donal's family's grief—and Seamus's family, and Fergus's—and mourn with Paddy's family while being unable to tell them the truth was something she was unable to contemplate without feeling sick.

"There's a rare kerfuffle over in the Ladies' Cove." Alberta Grisham rushed into the kitchen, her eyes wide, her face rosy from her trip in from the village, where she lived with her parents. A VAD, she customarily rode a bicycle, and her route took her past the part of the Strand closest to Ballyshannon Court that the villagers called the Ladies' Cove, because in earlier days modesty had restricted its use to bathers of the female sex. It included the sheltered beach where the *Merrow* had attempted to come in and where Rynn had entered the water last night to warn them off. "Soldiers everywhere, and I heard some of them talking about finding a body washed up. A *dead* body."

Rynn's heart skipped a beat. Paddy! So Maguire had been right about his body turning up on this morning's tide. Her stomach knotted, her pulse leaped and it was all she could do to swallow the tea she'd just sipped. What her face looked like she didn't know, but her eyes were riveted on Alberta. Which, as soon as she realized, she remedied by glancing away, only to discover that the eyes of everyone at the table were riveted on Alberta.

"A body?"

"Who is it?"

"Never say it's someone we know!"

"Did they drown?"

The questions came thick and fast as Alberta, having scooped up a cup of tea and a scone, dropped into the chair across from Rynn.

"I heard gunshots last night as I was getting ready for bed." Alberta spoke in a hushed tone as she leaned in to share her news with the table. "A lot of gunshots, like some sort of battle was going on. And they sounded like they came from that direction. I think it might have something to do with that."

Rynn blanched as she realized that Alberta had to be describing the soldiers firing on the *Merrow*. Had anyone else in the village or at Ballyshannon Court heard? They must have! Why had she not thought of that before?

The more pertinent question was, had anyone gone to investigate? Were there witnesses to what had happened after all?

Her stomach threatened to rebel against the toast.

But wait. A lightning review of the previous night's events proved reassuring. Even if the gunfire had drawn someone out, even if that someone had rushed immediately to the scene, by the time the soldiers had opened fire the *Merrow* would have been too far out and the darkness too concealing for anyone on shore to have seen anything, including *her*. It would, in fact, have been impossible.

She was—almost—sure.

No longer able to swallow, she put down her cup half finished as excited voices peppered Alberta with more questions.

A jingling bell caused a break in the conversation and had them all looking toward its source. Each of the mansion's thirty-plus rooms had a button to push if help was required by its occupant or occupants. The buttons were connected to small brass bells fastened to a call board on the wall that summoned whoever was needed.

"It's Lord Thomas," Mrs. Frampton announced, and numerous pairs of eyes immediately turned toward Rynn. Lord Thomas Dunne was assigned to Rynn.

"I'm going." Glad of the interruption, she stood up. She was almost at the door when Ellen Green, another of the VADs, came rushing in.

"Have you heard?" Pulling off her coat and in the process slinging raindrops everywhere, she included Rynn, who had stopped just short of the doorway, in the wide-eyed glance she sent around the room. "A woman's dead down in Ladies' Cove. The soldiers'll be bringing her along shortly."

"Someone from the village?"

"Why are they bringing her here?"

"What happened to her?" The questions came from multiple throats.

"A *woman*?" Surprise wrung that one from Rynn. There had to be a mistake, Ellen had to be mistaken. The body in Ladies' Cove had to be that of a man, because it had to be Paddy. Who else could it be?

Ellen nodded vigorously as she hung her coat on a hook by the door and went for the cup of tea that Mrs. Frampton held out to her. She, too, lived in the village, and would have followed approximately the same path Alberta had followed. "They want the doctor to look at her, they said. I passed them on the road."

"Who is it?" one of the girls asked.

"I don't know. They had the body all wrapped up. I couldn't see," Ellen replied, and then everybody was talking over each other as speculation flew.

The call bell jingled again. Rynn almost jumped.

"Lord Thomas," Mrs. Frampton prompted with a reproachful look in her direction.

Rynn nodded and headed out the door. It required every bit of self-control she possessed to leave without finding out more.

If Ellen wasn't mistaken, if a woman had really been found dead in Ladies' Cove, it could have nothing to do with the *Merrow* or what had befallen the boat or its occupants, Rynn told herself stoutly as she hurried up the ornate front staircase to her patient's room. But her nerves were on edge, and that, coupled with the ache in her heart, made it hard to summon the smiles required as a chorus of "Happy Stephen's Day" followed her. A footman carried silver chafing dishes along to the dining room.

The housemaids bustled about with brooms and cloths cleaning up after last night's celebration and preparing for the night's festivities, which everyone had long looked forward to. The garlands festooning the staircase and the mistletoe suspended from the huge chandelier that hung over the front hall twisted the knife still more by reminding her of how happy she had been at this time yesterday. She'd hummed carols as she'd gone about her work, giddy with joy at the knowledge that the war was over, that Donal was home, that it was Christmas Day and they, all of them here in Ballyshannon Court and Bundoran and Ireland and all over the world, could freely celebrate for the first time in four years.

And then . . . and then—

The toast weighed like lead in her stomach as reality came crashing down.

So preoccupied was she with pushing the resulting tsunami of grief away that she entered the big back bedroom that their most illustrious patient had claimed—it was the one he was accustomed to using from childhood—with the quickest of perfunctory knocks, only to stop short just inside the door. Although Lord Thomas usually required assistance in such matters, he'd managed to get himself up, dressed and into his wheelchair and was at that moment in the process of rolling himself toward the door. Like her, he stopped short.

"There you are! I was growing concerned. Are you all right?" His eyes, a somber gray blue, moved over her anxiously. Fair-haired and pale skinned, he was about six feet tall—she knew because lately they'd been getting him up on crutches for part of the day—and painfully thin. At present his face was so gaunt that there were hollows in his cheeks and his bones seemed determined to press through his flesh, but she knew from the family photograph he kept beside the bed that before the war had left him in his present state he'd been sturdily built and quite handsome. His exposure to mustard gas at Ypres the year before had weakened his lungs, leaving him with a chronic cough and labored breathing if he exerted himself to any degree at all. But the real injury had been to his legs and spine. An exploding shell on that same battlefield had peppered him with shrapnel. By the time he was transferred to Ballyshannon Court in response to the fear that the Spanish flu then sweeping the military base where he was hospitalized would be too much for his weakened lungs and carry him off, the consensus had been that, aged only twenty-four and after two unsuccessful operations, he would never walk again. Lately, though, thanks to Dr. Lowry's dogged insistence on continuing treatment despite the dispiriting diagnosis and her own diligent efforts as his nurse, it seemed that maybe he would, after all.

"Why would you ask me that?" She was so rattled by then that the question was sharper than it should have been. The room was warm thanks to the embers that glowed in the hearth, but she felt cold to the bone.

"Close the door," he instructed, rolling forward.

Rynn realized she was still standing in the doorway with the door wide open to the hall and anyone who might be passing by. She closed it carefully and, tray in hand, started across the room.

"I was sitting at my window last night, watching the storm clouds roll in over the mountains and waiting for you to bring me my medicine and I saw you running through the garden. And not long after that, I heard gunfire."

His eyes were fastened on her face.

Rynn's stomach sank. Had all the world and its brother heard? Why had she not thought of that, thought of the danger it might pose? And she'd never, not with him, not with any of her patients, neglected to take proper care of them, including bringing their medicine on schedule. And for her to miss the nightly dose for

Lord Thomas, whose sleep was interrupted by the most intense coughing spells because of his damaged lungs, how to explain that?

"One of the nurses also mentioned hearing gunfire last night, but she lives in the village. With all the noise you lot were making, I'm surprised you heard a thing." *Keep it light*, she told herself. *And deflect. Deflect, deflect, deflect.*

"I told you, I was up here. As merry as everyone downstairs was, I doubt the other chaps did."

Instead of attempting to lie—Donal had spent most of a lifetime telling her that she was beyond terrible at it because her face telegraphed her every thought—she kept her back to him as she set the tray down on the table in front of the window. A glance through the rain-streaked panes confirmed it: he would have had a perfect view of her running through the kitchen garden. Fortunately, the west wing of the house would have prevented him from seeing her turn toward the cliffs, or anything after that.

That didn't stop her heart from thumping.

Casting a quick glance at him—he'd swiveled in his chair to face her—she managed a smile and assumed a rallying tone. "Look at you! You got out of bed and got dressed and got into your chair all by yourself. Soon you'll have no more need of me at all."

"I'm not a child, you know. I can do what I must." There was no answering smile from him. "So, what happened? Why were you running? Where were you going?"

Chapter Eight

"Did Your Lordship ever think that perhaps you were mistaken, and it wasn't me you saw at all?" With that borderline teasing response—he hated it when she called him Your Lordship, had urged her to call him Thomas which, given his position and hers, she didn't feel able to do—Rynn moved to pick up his nightclothes from where they lay discarded on the floor. "It could have been anyone. Or no one at all. It could have been a dream."

"It could have been, but it wasn't." He sounded so sure. He watched her broodingly as she folded his nightshirt and placed it under his pillow. In an attempt to hide her too-expressive face, she went back to the bedside table and began to pour out his medicine. "Trust me, Rynn Carmichael, no one, but no one, looks like you. Even in the dark, even when you're running like you're dodging bombs on a battlefield."

His words were no surprise. He had a crush on her and owned up to it freely. Actually, he'd had it for years, or so he claimed, ever since he used to visit Ballyshannon Court as a little boy with his family for a month every summer and watched her running wild with the other local children along the cliff edge and below on the Strand, and paddling in the sea. As a Brit, and shy, he'd never got up the courage to try to join in, although, he assured her, he'd wanted to. For her part, if she'd ever seen him, she couldn't remember it.

"Ugh. What a terrible image." Without looking at him, she mixed powder with liquid and stirred.

"It's what I see when I close my eyes. Only it's me running, not you. Which is why I missed my sleeping draught that you failed to bring up last night."

"I'm sorry." She was genuinely contrite. His screaming nightmares when he'd first arrived at Ballyshannon Court were the stuff of legend. "I won't forget again." She had the first potion ready and turned to hand it to him.

"From what I saw, you seemed to be upset. Last night." He was watching her keenly. "Was it Donal?"

Of course she'd told him about Donal. Of their love, that he was off fighting and most recently of his return home and their engagement. Nothing dangerous, nothing of what Molly Kincaid had told her, but snippets of her life just as he had shared snippets of his. Because over the months she'd been caring for him, they'd become not just nurse and patient, but friends.

"Take your medicine," she said, more sharply than she'd intended.

He made a face at her, swallowed the medicine, then accepted the second dose she handed him and drank that down, too. A handful of pills, and they were done.

Before he could return to the subject of last night, she said, "Since you're already up and dressed, why don't we get our walk in before breakfast? Before the festivities start?" A walk meant trading the chair for crutches. Since it was raining, they would use the long gallery at the rear of the house. Traversing the gallery on crutches even once required a huge effort on his part, but now that he saw walking again as a real possibility, he was determination personified. It was all she could do to dissuade him from trying it for more than the doctor prescribed: half an hour twice a day.

"Yes, all right" was all he said, but she knew him well enough by this time not to think that he was going to let the topic of what he'd seen go forever. She was, however, glad enough to put it aside for the time being. Fetching his crutches, she gave them to him to hold and proceeded to wheel him along the hall to the Red Staircase, so called because of the vibrant color of its walls. It led directly down from the back bedrooms to the hall connected to the gallery. A ramp had been installed to accommodate those patients in wheelchairs, and they reached the ground floor and then the gallery without incident.

"I'll be leaving here in a little less than three weeks," he said abruptly as she set the brakes on his chair then took the crutches from him and leaned them against the wall preparatory to getting him up. "I'm going home. My father's sent for me, and Dr. Lowry cleared me to go. I was going to tell you last night, but you didn't come."

Frowning, Rynn turned back to him. Positioned as he was in his chair, he had to look up at her, and as she stopped in front of him, he tilted his head back to regard her intently. With a heavy lock of his honey-colored hair falling over his forehead and the gray light of a rainy morning filtering in through the windows to turn his skin ashen, he looked very young and alarmingly frail. Too frail to leave hospital? But they all would be leaving soon, because the war was over and this particular hospital would revert to the privately owned home it had been before.

"That's wonderful news," she said, and meant it. She was happy for him but she would miss his friendship, just as she would miss the hospital and its people and the security it represented. One more loss following the seismic ones of the previous night.

"Is it?" he said.

His hands rested on the wheels of his chair, and she watched them tighten. The look in his eyes—what was that look?

"Certainly it is."

"Not for me." He hesitated, then seemed to make up his mind about something before continuing with, "I'm hoping you'll come with me, actually. As my nurse, of course. You've been doing such a splendid job, and I—I feel I'm not quite ready to manage without you."

Rynn looked at him in surprise. Such a possibility had never entered her mind.

"Are you offering me a *job*?"

"Yes."

"I . . ." She hesitated, at a loss.

"Don't say you can't," he said. "As I know you're meaning to do. I know you'll say that there's O'Reilly, and you're to be married, and this is your home and all you want in life is here. But a whole world exists beyond this place, you know, and you've seen nothing of it! Don't you want to at least have a look? I can show you London, and Paris, too, and all the great cities of Europe when I'm better and we go traveling as I would like to do. The war is over, and all the world is open again, and you can see it all if you come with me—" Something in her face must have given him pause, because he faltered slightly then added, "As my nurse."

Before she could even begin to make sense of her thoughts, much less frame a reply, a series of hasty footsteps behind her caused her to glance around.

"There you are! I've been looking everywhere! Miss Carmichael, you're wanted in the music room right away." Cyril, the gray-haired, slightly stooped first footman who'd grown old in the service of the family regarded her with what looked very much like distress. A glance past him told her why: two British soldiers in their khaki uniforms had followed him into the gallery. There was nothing to read in their faces, but they were there, standing shoulder to shoulder a pace or so behind him, armed to the teeth, looking at her. *Waiting* for her.

Rynn's stomach dropped clear to her toes.

"Who wants her?" Lord Thomas asked.

"Colonel Pelly, sir," Cyril answered.

Then one of the soldiers spoke directly to her. "We've been sent to escort you. If you'll come along, miss."

The walls seemed to tilt and the floor seemed to shift beneath Rynn's feet.

Someone must have seen me. The thought struck up a panicked drumbeat in her mind.

"You don't have to—" Lord Thomas began, frowning up at her.

"No, it's fine." Remembering her telltale face, she forced a smile even as she shook her head at him. She had to behave as if she had no idea that anything could possibly be amiss.

"You'll stay here with Lord Thomas, won't you?" she asked Cyril. At the footman's nod, she said to Lord Thomas, "I'll just go see what Colonel Pelly wants, and be right back."

Before anything more could be said, she swept past Cyril and the soldiers. The soldiers followed her like a unit from the Praetorian Guard through the maze of connecting hallways until they reached the music room.

The door was open, allowing her to see the fire that blazed in the marble fireplace opposite, as well as the Christmas decorations adorning the mantel, as she approached. With the soldiers behind her she didn't so much as hesitate on the threshold even though inwardly she quaked with fear. She walked into the wood-paneled room as if she owned the place. Head high, shoulders back, taking care to reveal nothing of her inner turmoil in her face or demeanor.

Would it be enough?

The warm glow of the fire was augmented by pale morning light pouring through the tall windows. The familiar combined aromas of woodsmoke, pine and the sea masked another, elusively familiar, far less pleasant smell.

Even as one of the soldiers escorting her said, "Miss Carmichael, sir," she saw Colonel Pelly with Chief Inspector Fallon and another man she didn't immediately recognize. They stood together with their backs turned to her near one of the long sofas on which guests were wont to sit as they enjoyed musical performances. Having the trio turn as one to look at her would have sent her pulse galloping if her gaze, at that moment, hadn't fallen on the dead woman lying on the sofa.

Rynn stopped in her tracks. Yes, there was no doubt about it: the woman was *dead*.

"Ah, Miss Carmichael. Come join us, please."

Colonel Pelly's greeting seemed to reach her from a thousand miles away. Gathering her composure, Rynn resumed her approach while trying not to focus on the woman, whose long, matted dark hair trailed toward the floor. The sickly-sweet scent of death, with which she'd become familiar over the last few years, was the odd smell she'd noticed mixing with the more Christmassy ones. Someone had placed an oilcloth and layers of canvas beneath the corpse because she was wet, soaked through in fact, so that her white blouse and gray skirt clung to her slender form and her shoes left muddy markings on the canvas. It was not a fresh death; her slim, pale arms curved stiffly away from her body, while her exposed flesh was already turning gray. Severe bruising marred her face.

"Molly." The shattering realization that the poor lifeless creature was someone she knew, her friend, hit her like a brick, stopping her in her tracks once again. It made the room swim, made her go weak at the knees. She tottered sideways, braced herself with a hand on the lamp table at the end of the sofa, and registered blood staining the canvas beneath the body before tearing her eyes away from the terrible sight.

Striving to catch her breath, she looked at the trio of men who, she discovered, watched her intently. "Dear God, what happened to her?"

"Excellent. I was told you would know her, and it appears you do." Colonel Pelly's voice was ripe with satisfaction. Then, glancing past her, he snapped, "A chair for Miss Carmichael."

One was brought by a soldier, and, thankful to do so, Rynn sat.

"Can you confirm the deceased's identity for us, please?" Colonel Pelly stood over her. Rynn hadn't even been aware that he'd moved. Instead of looking up at him, or across at Molly, she looked down at her hands that were clenched in her lap. Her ears rang . . .

"Molly Kincaid," she said.

"And you know her how?"

"She's a friend." It was all she could do to talk. Her throat felt tight.

"When did you last see her?"

"On Christmas Eve." When Molly had told her about the guns. Dear Lord, she needed air . . .

"And where was that?"

"At Brennan's. In Bundoran. She works—worked—there." Her voice cracked as she realized she needed to refer to Molly in the past tense now.

"What did you talk about?"

Molly had taken her aside, whispering her warning about Seamus and the guns. The accompanying thrill of fear as she remembered that went a long way toward clearing Rynn's head. Horribly conscious of Colonel Pelly's eyes on her, she did a lightning-fast review of the scene. The pub had been dark, crowded, noisy—anyone might have seen them with their heads together, but had anyone overheard what was said?

"Just woman talk. Christmas."

"Do you know of any reason why she would be out on the Strand last night?"

"No." Had Molly gone down to the beach to warn the men, too? Or to meet them?

What other reason could there be? Rynn's heart thumped. Hands clenching in her lap, she looked up at Pelly, then, fleetingly, at the other two men. *"What happened to her?"*

"That's what we're trying to determine, Miss Carmichael." As Colonel Pelly spoke, the third man turned into the light, and she recognized him as one of the local constables, Titus O'Shea. He knew her, too, of course. Just as everybody thereabouts knew each other.

"Do you know Seamus O'Reilly?" Colonel Pelly asked.

Rynn's stomach clenched. This *was* about the guns. He already knew that she knew Seamus. Even if she hadn't been sure that Constable O'Shea would have told him, she would have known it from his tone.

"I do," she said.

"And Donal O'Reilly?"

"I do," she said again, even as her heart sank. "Why are you asking?"

Instead of answering her question, he said, "You are, in fact, Donal O'Reilly's sweetheart. Are you not?"

"I am." Because as far as anyone in that room knew, that was still true.

"When did you last see them? The O'Reillys?"

"I saw Donal yesterday. And Seamus, that would be three or four days ago, I can't be quite sure." A truthful answer, if she ignored last night. She was still quietly panicking. It was clear that Pelly knew what Donal and Seamus had done. Of course he did; hadn't Maguire said their supplier, Haney, had been captured? It was less clear what else he knew. Did he know about Fergus and Paddy? Did he know about Maguire and the *Reaper* or, God forbid, about her? She felt her palms grow damp and tried not to think about what he might be able to read in her face. Tried not to think that her life might depend on exactly what he knew—and how well she lied.

"Where are they, Miss Carmichael?" Another change in tone. A hint of steel had crept in.

"Right now? Probably getting ready for the Wren Day celebration." Wren Day celebrations, in which everyone took to the streets to parade about in straw costumes and fancy dress, were part of the St. Stephen's Day tradition, and that was what they *would* be doing if—

Calculating wildly, she tried to work out how things would be if last night hadn't happened. If Paddy's body hadn't yet been found, Colonel Pelly would have no reason to think that Donal and Seamus were anything other than alive and well. Thus she herself would have no reason to think anything was amiss with them, either. If, in fact, Haney had been taken, and talked, which the Brits had very effective methods of making someone do, efforts were probably underway at this very moment to find them, and *that* was why Colonel Pelly was questioning her. It was, therefore, quite possible that he did not suspect her of anything except knowing the men involved. Even as the knot in her stomach eased a bit, she saw a way to escape the interview.

"Oh, my. Oh, no. Seamus—he doesn't know about Molly. Oh, he'll be devastated! He—has someone gone to tell him? And Molly's family?" Martialing all her resources, she stood up. "I must go—"

"Sit down, Miss Carmichael." Colonel Pelly's voice was sharp. She was instantly reminded of how much authority he wielded, how much power he and his kind had over her and all her countrymen. Here, as always, it was the oppressors and the oppressed. "We haven't finished yet. Where were you last night?"

She sat. Not so much because he ordered her to, but first because her knees felt wobbly, and second because it gave her an excuse to duck her head while she frantically tried to work out the safest possible answer. It was all she could do to not wet her lips. *Did* he know? *What* did he know? Just imagining the possibilities left her petrified. *Please God, don't let it show.*

"She was with me." Wheels silent on the carpet, Lord Thomas's chair rolled up beside her as he answered the question for her. She was so glad to see him, so thankful to have Colonel Pelly's attention distracted, that the hands she'd unconsciously fisted in her lap relaxed, and she threw him the smallest of grateful smiles. Thin, pale and not at all physically imposing in his chair, he wasn't looking at her, but was rather regarding Colonel Pelly with the kind of cool superiority that she was accustomed to seeing directed at herself and her countrymen from the despised Ascendancy, as the locals called the British aristocrats who owned the big houses that they only occasionally visited. His manner was at odds with his youth, but as Colonel Pelly's expression changed, she was reminded that Lord Thomas was the son of a rich and powerful man. A man, moreover, who was known to be a close friend of the British prime minister, David Lloyd George.

"With you, Lord Thomas?" Colonel Pelly asked.

"Miss Carmichael is my nurse, and last night I was quite ill. She was with me through the night. And this morning finds me still ill, and still in urgent need of her services, so if this interview is at an end I will take her away with me so that she can provide them."

Colonel Pelly frowned. "I have more questions—"

"I'm sure you can find another time to ask them. Or even

someone else to give you the answers. But as my father has sent for me to rejoin him shortly and I must be well enough to travel, I know you won't wish to deprive me of my nurse when I so sorely need her."

"No," Colonel Pelly said after the briefest of pauses. "I don't wish to do that." He looked at Rynn. "Thank you for your help, Miss Carmichael."

Getting to her feet, Rynn inclined her head in acknowledgment. Then she took a firm grip on the handles of Lord Thomas's chair and pushed him out of the room.

Chapter Nine

After that, they abandoned any idea of walking and went back up to Lord Thomas's room. Rynn was so shaken she didn't say a word until they got there. *Molly*—Molly was dead. The coincidence was too great; her death had to be connected to the guns. The horror she was feeling must have shown in her face because Lord Thomas had her sit in the big armchair in front of the fire and pulled a quilt from the bed for her to wrap around herself. Then he rolled his own chair up so that he was facing her.

"Are you all right?" His eyes were dark with concern.

She nodded. It wasn't true, but she was trying.

"I gather you knew the poor girl on the sofa?"

Rynn nodded again. Then, taking a deep, steadying breath, she said, "It's Molly. Molly Kincaid. My friend. From the pub."

He'd heard her talk about Molly, and the pub. Her promise to take him to visit both when he was up and on his feet again had been one of the first incentives she'd dangled in front of him if he would just *try*.

"God, I'm sorry." He reached for her hand, held it comfortingly. She realized how cold hers was only when he began lightly chafing it. "You're freezing. Can I get you some tea or something?"

By that he meant he'd ring the bell and send whoever appeared for some, she knew. Shrinking from the thought of anyone else seeing her before she'd recovered her composure, she shook her head.

"Why did you do that?" she asked.

"Do what?" His head was bent over her hand that, thanks to his ministrations, did indeed feel several degrees less icy. Returning that one to her lap, he reached for her other one and began chafing it.

"Tell Colonel Pelly that I was with you last night."

"Because when he asked where you were I thought you seemed afraid."

The idea that Colonel Pelly might have thought that, too, appalled her. "You were behind me. You couldn't possibly have seen my expression."

"It wasn't your expression that gave you away. It was how you clenched your fists."

He'd turned her hand over so that her palm was uppermost. Now he held her hand up so that she, too, was looking at her palm. To her surprise, four red crescents from where her nails had dug into her skin were clearly visible. She remembered with dismay how tightly her hands had fisted under Colonel Pelly's questioning. A glance confirmed identical marks on her other hand.

"I was upset," she said with what dignity she could summon. "Not afraid."

"My mistake." He ran a gentle finger over the marks. Instinctively she closed her fist to hide them. His head came up at that and he gave her a considering look.

"I think you need help," he said. "I can help you, if you'll let me. Tell me what happened last night."

For a moment, tempted, she hesitated. She *did* need help. But he was, after all, a Brit, and a soldier to boot, and his loyalty to his country might outweigh their friendship. And there were so many others involved: Donal, Seamus and Fergus, and Owen

Maguire and his crew, too, and now Molly, poor Molly who was, so unbelievably, dead. Telling him her secret would reveal their secrets, too. How many times had she heard Granny say, "Three may keep a secret if two of them are dead"?

For all their sakes, it was imperative that she keep what she knew to herself.

But she didn't want to lie to him, either.

"I can't," she said.

His eyes searched hers. Then he made a face that told her that, however reluctantly, he accepted her answer.

"Whatever it is, however you're involved, I'm on your side. Remember that."

"I'll remember," she said.

Before any more could be said, a brisk rap on the door made her jump and him release her hand. Her heart knocked as he turned his chair around and bade whoever it was to come in. To her relief, it was only Dr. Lowry come to check on his patient.

Dr. Lowry had finished his exam and was leaving when she felt she'd regained enough composure to ask if he'd seen Molly. He said that he had, and, shaking his head, opined that it was a terrible thing.

"What happened to her?" Rynn asked one more time and steeled herself against the answer.

"She was beaten. Badly."

"Beaten to death?" It was incomprehensible.

Dr. Lowry shook his head. "Not to death. What killed her was a gunshot wound."

"She was *shot*?" Hit by mistake by the soldiers firing at the *Merrow*? Or, God forbid, by Seamus himself as he returned fire? But why, *why*, was she on the Strand?

"That she was. Took a bullet to the back. From a pistol from the look of the wound, although that's up to the coroner to determine for certain."

Not a rifle, then. So not hit in the exchange of gunfire.

"Who would do such a thing?"

"If I were to give my opinion, I'd say she was running away from whoever beat her and he shot her."

The horror of it clutched at Rynn's heart.

"Colonel Pelly seems eager to ascertain the whereabouts of Seamus O'Reilly," Dr. Lowry said. "I'm guessing that he's the one they'll be blaming."

"No—" Rynn began, then broke off abruptly. She couldn't give Seamus the alibi he deserved without revealing how she knew that whoever had killed Molly, it wasn't he.

"That's what I think, too, but the good colonel is not likely to take my word for it, or yours." He cast a grim look at Lord Thomas. "You're leaving us at a good time, my lord. What with one thing and another, we're sitting on a powder keg here, I'm afraid. If you're lucky, you'll be gone before it explodes."

Rynn was still trying to come to terms with what that meant for her and all of them who would be left behind when word came that Paddy's body had washed up with the tide.

Chapter Ten

"You're bearing up like a true O'Brien, my dotey pet," Granny whispered to Rynn as they joined the procession following Molly's coffin to her fresh-dug grave. Overhead, seabirds circled and dived, their cries as doleful as the assembled company. Underfoot, the thick grass, worn down by several days of rain, was slick and treacherous. Black robe flapping in the wind, Father Doherty led the way to what would be Molly's final resting place high on the hillside behind the Church of Our Lady Star of the Sea, where her funeral mass had just concluded. It was Wednesday, January 8, 1919, but there was no heart in anyone for celebrating the turn of a new, war-less year. The atmosphere in Bundoran had never been so tense. Passions ran high. Tempers quivered on a hair trigger. The death of Molly Kincaid and the uncertainty over the fate of the missing men of the *Merrow* had brought the forces of the Crown and the residents of the area into all-but-open conflict. "O'Briens have never lacked for courage, and never will, come what may."

Granny's thin hand gripped Rynn's arm for support. Even through the wool of her loose black coat, Rynn could feel the strength in her gnarled fingers. Nearing her seventy-fifth year, Granny was finding the climb arduous, although she'd never admit it. A small woman even in her youth, she was tiny now—scrawny as a plucked chicken, was how she described herself—with her once-black hair turned stark white and her thick eyebrows gone gray and wild and fine wrinkles etched into her fair skin. But her eyes that were so like Rynn's own were as sharp as ever, as were her mind and especially her tongue.

The three of them—her sister, Glenna, was on Rynn's other side—were somewhere in the middle of the throng of mourners, the service having been attended by what seemed like the entire population of Bundoran along with many from the surrounding farms and villages. The murder of a local young woman out on the Strand, with rumors running wild about who might be responsible, brought forth the curious along with the sorrowful. Organ music from the church followed them up the hill, adding its own lament to the shrieks of the birds and the weeping of the bereaved.

"I know, Granny." Rynn spoke with only the merest trace of resignation. Being called a true O'Brien was the highest compliment Granny could bestow, given that O'Brien was her matriarchal clan and the bloodline she honored. Never mind that Granny's own father's name of Dolan or her married name of Shaughnessy—Cliona Shaughnessy she was—or the name of Carmichael bestowed by their father on her two granddaughters, were the names of record. Having been lectured for as long as she could remember on the superiority of the O'Brien bloodline, whose number included both the legendary Brian Boru and the great-great-grandmother whose dark eyes and gift of the Sight Rynn was held by her to possess, Rynn accepted the compliment in the spirit it was meant.

"Sure, she's bearing up. There's no need for her to despair. We don't *know* that Donal was on Seamus O'Reilly's boat. Not for certain." Her own whisper fierce, Glenna spoke across Rynn to their grandmother. Unlike Granny, whose head barely topped Rynn's shoulder, nineteen-year-old Glenna was only a little shorter than her sister. She was blessed, moreover, with a curvier figure of which she was pardonably proud. Her hair, currently twisted up in a high knot as was Rynn's, was a soft auburn, her eyes were a bright hazel and her complexion warmly cream in comparison with the pale porcelain skin that, coupled with her raven hair, dark eyes, fine-boned features and tall, slender figure, had seen a much younger Rynn taunted by some of the village girls as the Banshee's get. In her first year as a teacher at the local school, Glenna was held to be quite the beauty in her own right. She'd had several suitors although no one for whom she had expressed a particular preference. Now that the war had taken the lives of half the men in her generation and left much of the other half, as she put it, "damaged," she openly despaired that she would ever find "the one" as Rynn had found with Donal. Both Granny and Glenna, in their own way, were doing their best to support her through what they thought were the soul-crushing emotions she was experiencing as she waited to learn Donal's fate.

The *Merrow* had begun washing up, in pieces, not long after Paddy's body had been pulled from the surf. As Seamus's boat would hardly go out without him, and him nowhere to be found, Seamus was counted most likely dead along with Paddy, who was presumed to have been aboard. With Donal known to be close with Seamus, and Fergus known to be inseparable from Paddy, and all four missing over the same time frame, they, too, were presumed to have been on the *Merrow* when it went down. The discovery that Paddy had been shot to death and the *Merrow* riddled with bullet holes was held by many, including the Brits, to be proof positive that Seamus and Paddy, at least, had been aboard the boat the soldiers had exchanged gunfire with on Christmas night and thus guilty of gunrunning just as suspected. The longer Donal and Fergus were missing the more likely it was thought to be that they had been a part of it, too. Although no one could say precisely how, Molly's brutal death was felt to tie into that as well.

And each side blamed the other for it all.

"Hush, now. We're here to say our goodbyes to Molly." Rynn quashed the conversation as they reached the growing semicircle of friends, relatives, neighbors and acquaintances gathering around the grave.

Except for the expected weeping of the close relatives, the crowd went respectfully silent as the coffin arrived graveside and Father Doherty began the usual prayers. Rynn lowered her head along with everyone else, but besides uttering the rote responses she'd known from childhood she mentally removed herself from the proceedings.

Fear, grief, dread—they were only the most identifiable of the feelings that threatened to overwhelm her. The autopsies that had seen the bodies held long after the proper time for burial, the ongoing investigations, the descent upon their town of a small army of Crown forces, were a nightmare in and of themselves. The twin wakes, first for Paddy and then for Molly, with their songs and weeping reminisces of the deceased, their covered mirrors and long tables laden with food and drink and small rooms packed with black-shrouded mourners, had been an almost unbearable ordeal. She was barely eating, barely sleeping—but she was functioning. Bearing up, as Granny said.

The sounds and sights around her no longer touched her as they should, and that would be, she knew, because she had deliberately closed herself off from them. And she did that by focusing on small things, like how much the fluttering veils that covered nearly all the women's heads including her own looked like blackbirds taking wing. Or how worn many of the women looked—was she, too, so pale and thin, with haunted eyes and a tight mouth?—and how shabby were their clothes. The war had left its mark on the men as well. Gaunt, with hardened faces and twitchy hands, those who'd newly returned from the fighting were easy to separate from the rest. As for the others . . .

Her wandering gaze hit on Owen Maguire and stopped short. Somber in a black overcoat over a tweed suit, his height making him impossible to overlook, he stood among the mourners a short distance away. His hat was in his hand, his dark head was bowed and, unlike most of those around him, he looked well-fed and prosperous. At his side was a woman who appeared to be about a decade older, whose red hair was just visible beneath her black veil. She looked vaguely familiar, but Rynn couldn't quite place her. Tim, the helmsman, stood on his other side, his uncovered hair a bright beacon in the sea of black. A boy of about sixteen, two other boys who were younger and two little girls were with them, all with hair in varying shades of red.

Surprise kept her focus on Maguire. She'd had no thought of seeing him here or, indeed, ever again. Whether he felt her looking at him or not she couldn't have said, but he glanced up just then and their eyes met. After the briefest of pregnant moments, he inclined his head in acknowledgment. She looked away.

Her pulse quickened and her chest felt tight. Seeing Maguire brought memories of her last moments with Donal rushing back. Sometimes, like now, when thoughts of Donal caught her unaware, she felt as if some vital part of herself had been ripped away.

What have I done?

Should she have gone with him? The conviction that had driven her to say no seemed to have dissipated. Conscious of Granny's hand on her arm, of Glenna pressing close, of the uncertain future Donal had represented and the trouble he always seemed to find, she told herself she'd made the right choice. Then she took a deep breath and pushed the unsettling doubts from her mind.

What was too late to fix should not be fretted over. Wisdom, again, from Granny.

The wind was cold and the sky was heavy with clouds. The

smell of rain was in the air although so far today not a drop had fallen. In the distance, Killybegs Peninsula and the towering sea cliffs of Slieve League dominated the horizon. The Great Northern Hotel, all but empty now as the tourists that filled it in summer were gone, crouched close to the bay. Closer at hand, she sought out Brennan's, where Molly had worked. It was located on the one main street that was divided into two halves by the narrow slice of muddy water that was the Dobhran River as it joined the sea. Its roof was just visible among the neat rows of shops and houses that made up the town. The pub was closed and the village all but deserted as nearly everyone had come out today to bid farewell to one of their own, unjustly taken from them as the feeling was. The mood in the crowd was ugly and growing uglier by the minute. Even the bay, which from that elevated vantage point seemed as endless as the sky, frothed with anger, throwing out waves like weapons that crashed against the rocks with distant booms. Everywhere Rynn looked was as gray as the low stone walls that crisscrossed the countryside for as far as the eye could see.

Her *life* felt gray.

And then her heart lurched as she realized that the boats she could distantly see belonged to the Royal Navy fleet. They trawled the bay, back and forth, leaving ruffles of pale foam in their wake. It was obvious from the deliberation with which they charted a grid through the rough water that their purpose was other than the netting of fish. That they were, in fact, searching for something—probably the bodies of the missing men, or the smuggled guns. Or both.

Father Doherty's voice rang out: "'Blessed are the dead who die in the Lord,'"

Knowing the words, knowing what they portended, Rynn clutched the ends of her mantilla-like veil together so that the prickly lace would lie close against her face and thus, perhaps, hide her expression in case it revealed too much. Head bowed, she forced herself to focus on the funeral service, which was ending.

Ropes lowered Molly's coffin into the grave. Molly's mother's weeping turned into sharp cries of grief that rose above the ritual prayers as the casket disappeared from view. Her remaining daughters surrounded her, sobbing loudly, too, as they did their best to comfort her in her grief. In the crowd nearby, among the Kellys and McCarthys and Ryans and Walshes and other neighbors who made up the fabric of the village and her life, she spotted Fergus's family, and, next to them, Donal's. Pale and slumped with grief, Donal's mother leaned against her daughter, her only other child.

Rynn set her teeth, looked away. Impossible to comprehend that Molly, her laughing, lively friend, was dead. That Paddy was dead. That Donal and Seamus and Fergus were gone away, perhaps forever.

The church spire pointed up toward the clouds like a finger showing Molly the way to Heaven. The mound of dark, fresh earth that was Paddy's grave was farther up the hill to the right.

They'd buried him yesterday.

Reality crashed down on her like one of those thundering waves. The force of it tore at everything that made up the foundation of her existence. She felt unmoored, rudderless, a boat adrift in a raging sea. Dropping her head, she closed her eyes and faced the truth. This was real. All that had happened could not be undone. Choices had been made, lives had been lost, families and futures had been forever changed.

Now was the time to face the consequences.

As soon as the last word was spoken, as soon as the family finished dropping handfuls of dirt down on the coffin and the grave diggers set to work with their spades, Rynn turned and started back down the hill, threading her way through the dispersing crowd, leaving Granny and Glenna to commiserate with the friends who were nearby. She couldn't wait, couldn't bear a repeat of Paddy's funeral, where she'd had to pretend to the families of Donal and Seamus and Fergus that she, too, was in agony over their fate, had to say nothing of what truly had befallen him to Paddy's family, had to present a false front to the entire community and, terrifyingly, to the soldiers sent by Colonel Pelly to spy on the gathering. Khaki-uniformed soldiers with their weapons and military lorries who even now, knowing that they were unwelcome at the service and that the mood of the crowd could turn against them at any time, lined the road at the bottom of the hill.

Watching and waiting. For what? Were they expecting the missing men to turn up?

"Rynn! Rynn, wait!" Donal's sister, Sarah, called from behind her. Recognizing the voice with a sinking sensation, Rynn turned to see Sarah, who resembled Seamus more than Donal with her curly black hair and tall, angular frame, hurrying toward her with both hands outstretched.

She'd known Sarah forever, although since she was a year younger than Glenna they hadn't been in the same group of friends. But Sarah was Donal's little sister, and they were fond for that reason. They embraced, and then Sarah stepped back and caught her hands. What Sarah had in common with her brother were his eyes. Rynn met those achingly familiar thickly lashed brown eyes, damp now with fresh tears, and her own eyes stung.

She was so, so sorry it had come to this. So sorry for their pain.

"Will you come talk to mam? She thinks if anyone knows where Donal is, it will be you."

"I do not," Rynn protested, resisting the pull of Sarah's hands.

It even had the benefit of being partially true. What she did know was that he wasn't dead, and that was the secret that tormented her.

"Please," Sarah begged. Glancing beyond her, Rynn saw Donal's mother, Brigid, beckoning and gave in. No matter how distressing such an encounter would be, it was not in her to simply turn and walk away.

"Ah, Rynn." Mrs. O'Reilly practically collapsed against her, wrapping her in her arms, hugging her as if she never meant to let go. Not yet fifty, she was small and plump, with neat salt-and-pepper hair and a smooth, round face. She stood back at last and looked at Rynn beseechingly. "Have you heard from him?"

There was only one *him* as far as Mrs. O'Reilly was concerned. Donal was the center of her world, her only son.

How could he put his mother through this? was the thought that instantly popped into Rynn's head. But then she remembered the fate Donal most likely would have faced if he'd stayed and knew that if Mrs. O'Reilly had been asked to choose, she would have chosen this way.

That didn't make it any easier.

It seemed to Rynn that dozens of pairs of eyes fixed on her, dozens of breaths were caught and held, as the entire O'Reilly clan and Fergus's family too, along with Granny and Glenna, who'd caught up, and what seemed like at least half the mourners present, gathered round to hear what she had to say.

Under the weight of all those eyes, she felt as if she might suffocate.

I could end this. I could free Mrs. O'Reilly and Seamus's and Fergus's people from such suffering.

All she had to do was tell the truth. In confidence, say, by pulling Mrs. O'Reilly aside and whispering in her ear. Or she could do it later, visit her in her home, before making her way back to Ballyshannon Court.

Three may keep a secret if two of them are dead.

"No, I haven't. I'm sorry to have to say it," she said to Mrs. O'Reilly, to everyone who had stopped to listen.

"It's been a fortnight." Mrs. O'Reilly's voice shook. "He's been gone a *fortnight*. I can't—he can't be—" Her face crumpled as she broke off, and then she laid a hand over her heart and whispered, "I would *know*. In here, I would know."

"Ah, mam." Sarah gathered her mother in her arms as the older woman broke down in tears. She was still weeping as Sarah led her away.

Rynn fought the urge to close her own eyes.

"This waiting, it's a terrible thing." Fergus's sister Trena Doyle, some fifteen years his senior and as much a mother to him as a sister, came up on Rynn's other side and looked at her with sad eyes. "Although why I'm telling you, I don't know. It must be as hard on you as it is on us."

Rynn managed a nod and glanced away. With Trena was the red-haired woman who'd stood beside Maguire earlier and that's where her gaze landed. Seeing Rynn's eyes on her, Trena said, "Are you acquainted with Moira Clary, from out near Magheracar? She's sister to Owen Maguire, who's very kindly sent his boats out to search the coastline for any sign of our men."

Magheracar was about a twenty-minute walk from the western edge of Bundoran and was about the same distance from Ballyshannon Court. Although they'd never met to Rynn's knowledge, she had seen Moira Clary around the village, she realized. Even as Rynn nodded acknowledgment of the introduction, Moira snorted and said, "'Twas nothing 'very kindly' about it. The army came to him, as a former officer, to do it. He didn't feel he could say no."

"Mam, Owen says you should come away now." Tim the helmsman came up behind Mrs. Clary. It was her he was calling mam, Rynn realized, and that's when she made the connection:

Tim the helmsman must be Tim Clary, Moira Clary's son, and thus Owen Maguire's nephew, which explained the familiar Owen he'd called Maguire on the boat. The younger boys and the two little girls were with him, his siblings without a doubt. This, then, must be the widowed sister with her fatherless children that was part of the brood Maguire had taken responsibility for. Tim studiously avoided meeting Rynn's gaze, but everything from the pinkening of his cheeks to the uneasy shifting of his feet told her how uncomfortable he felt in her presence. A quick, almost involuntary glance around found Maguire himself standing a short distance away. He was talking to a group of local men, but as his sister called to him, he excused himself and came to join them. Mrs. Clary took her brother's arm as he reached them and drew him into the circle.

Chapter Eleven

"Major Maguire, I don't know if you've had a chance to meet Mrs. Shaughnessy and her granddaughters, Miss Rynn Carmichael and Miss Glenna Carmichael," Trena said to him.

Maguire's face could have been carved from stone for all the expression it showed as he tipped his hat to the three of them. "Ladies." His gaze was no more particular as it touched on Rynn than it was as he looked at Glenna and Granny. Rynn, who feared her face would betray her at every turn, had to give him points for that.

"And these are my children," Mrs. Clary said. "Tim, who's learning the shipping trade under Owen, Alfie, James, Joseph, Maeve and Grace."

Each of the younger children bobbed their heads politely as they were introduced. Tim's face grew redder than ever.

Maguire looked at his sister. "I'm sorry to pull you away, but we need to be going if you're to make the four-forty, especially if you still want to stop and say hello to Mrs. Walsh."

The four-forty, as everyone knew, referred to the train that left Bundoran daily at that time for Dublin. And Mrs. Walsh was the elderly widow who'd once been head of the local branch of the Irish Women's Suffrage Society, for which, among the females at least, there was a great deal of enthusiastic support, especially since, in a tremendous victory in the last election for which the Suffrage Society took much credit, the vote had at last been granted to women over thirty.

"Oh, I must. She'll be so excited about Countess Markievicz's election to Parliament," Mrs. Clary said. "The first woman, fancy that! And her one of our own, too!"

"She can't take her seat. She's in prison," the second-oldest Clary boy, Alfie, said, sotto voce. His mother waved that reminder away.

"I didn't know you had plans to go to Dublin." Trena looked at her in surprise.

"It was just decided yesterday. You know my late husband's people live there. They've been after me to come visit. And to bring the children, of course. So now that the holidays are over that's what we're going to do. Although I hate to leave you at such a time. You know you'll be in my prayers. As will Fergus. And everyone."

"Moira—" Maguire tilted his head toward his sister. But before he could say anything else, another woman hurried up to them: Mrs. Cheadle, a sturdy forty-year-old whose husband owned the greengrocer. From the look of her, she was big with news.

She cast a quick glance around as though to gauge who was close enough to overhear, then leaned in. Voice lowered, she said, "Did you hear? Cara O'Reilly has been taken to the Garda station for questioning. They think she knows more about what Seamus was up to than she's telling."

Cara O'Reilly was Seamus's mother. Rynn went cold all over.

"What?"

"No!"

"A grieving mother! The bloody buggers!"

"Are there no depths to which they won't sink?"

Outrage shimmered in the air.

"We must go," Maguire said quietly to his sister under cover of the furious chatter. As Mrs. Clary nodded and turned away, with Tim and the younger ones following and Maguire bringing up the rear, Rynn stepped back to let them get through the now tightly packed crowd.

"You'd be wise to go visiting out of town for a few weeks yourself," Maguire said in her ear as he passed.

It took a moment for his words to sink in. Looking after his tall form as he made his way toward the road, she felt a thrill of horror when finally they did. He was warning her that all those close to the suspects might be taken in for questioning. *She* might be taken in for questioning.

The possibility made her insides twist.

Of them all, she had the most to hide.

Something of what she was feeling must have been apparent in her face, because Granny frowned at her.

"Are you unwell, then?" Granny's quiet question acted on Rynn like a dash of cold water, reminding her of where she was and who might be watching and, most importantly, of the secrets she was bound to keep.

Taking advantage of the excuse Granny had inadvertently offered, Rynn nodded.

"I've a bit of a headache." She spoke loudly enough so that anyone paying her any particular attention could overhear.

"I do, too," Glenna chimed in unexpectedly. "I could do with some tea, and to get out of this wind."

"Couldn't we all," Granny agreed.

With that, and murmured goodbyes to those around them, the three of them left. Glenna drove them home in the pony trap that had brought her and Granny to the service—Rynn had ridden her own bicycle in from Ballyshannon Court, the "borrowed" one from that ill-fated night still lying hidden in the stable as she was afraid to even go near it—and went on around to the shed where both the shaggy Connemara pony and bright blue trap were kept to put them up.

Walking with Granny into the small stone cottage that had been home to the three of them for almost as long she could remember, Rynn felt some of her tension ease. It stood alone at the end of the lane, with farmland reaching to the Dartry Mountains on the one side and on the other the bay acting out all its moods in sight. She took in the thatched roof, the faded blue door, the huge old beech tree, leafless now with winter upon them, that stood sentinel in the yard, and felt comforted by the knowledge that some things, at least, hadn't changed. Inside, the small sitting room with its pungent peat fire burning low in the hearth, the well-scrubbed kitchen where they automatically headed to make tea on the old black range, the narrow staircase that led upstairs to the two tiny bedrooms that had sheltered boarders in the lean days and, now that Rynn and Glenna were both earning and able to contribute to the family coffers, provided Granny and Glenna with the luxury of having rooms of their own, brought more comfort. The East End, formerly the separate village of Single Street, might be the poor side of Bundoran, the seat of the "hardscrabble Irish" as opposed to the more affluent West Enders, but it had given her her roots and her strength and she was proud to claim it.

As Granny put the kettle on, Rynn took off her outer garments and hung them and the ones Granny had shed with the others on the hooks by the back door.

"It's something bad, I take it," Granny said out of nowhere as she busied herself about the stove.

"What do you mean?" In the process of getting out the bread to slice and toast and serve with the tea, Rynn almost dropped the loaf. Neat as a pin in her well-worn black dress, Granny never even turned around. Rynn found herself blinking at the back of her head with its low white bun.

"Do you think I can't tell when you're keeping something in?" Granny's tone was scornful. "It'll ease you to tell me, I've no doubt. Just as I've no doubt that it's concerning that jackeen, Donal O'Reilly. Some people are born to find trouble, and that young fellah is one."

"How can you talk about him like that, when he's . . ." Rynn let her voice trail off, unable to complete the lie. Granny was no fan of Donal's, at least not as a husband for her granddaughter. She'd made that clear long ago. With the faraway look she got when the Sight was supposedly upon her, she'd told Rynn that she could see no happy future for her with him.

Rynn's lips compressed as she realized that once again, Granny had been right.

Rynn was no real believer in the Sight, but at times, Granny could be eerily accurate.

"Drowned?" Granny finished for her, looking around with a cocked eyebrow. Then Granny shook her head. Picking up the tea canister, she carried it to the table. "Not he. As they say, those born to hang will never drown. Now why don't you tell me what's the truth of it while we've a minute to ourselves?"

Rynn only realized that she was staring at her grandmother with the knife suspended in midair over the bread when she heard the thud of the front door slamming shut followed by Glenna calling out "Granny! Rynn!" in a panic. Rynn's eyes widened. Setting the knife on the table, she pivoted toward the kitchen door just as Glenna sent it bouncing back on its hinges by shoving through it.

"There's a motorbike just pulled up. With Constable O'Shea." That's all Glenna managed to get out before a sharp knock on the front door was immediately followed by the sound of it being opened without so much as a by-your-leave. Heavy footsteps crossed the sitting room.

"Are you here looking for your lost manners, then, Titus O'Shea?" Eyes snapping, Granny greeted the middle-aged man who walked boldly into her kitchen. Just as she knew everyone in the village, Granny had known him practically since his birth.

"I've come on official business." Despite his blustering tone, O'Shea snatched his cap from his head. Looking uncomfortable, he shifted his gaze to Rynn. "I've been ordered to bring Miss Carmichael to the Garda station."

Rynn froze. Her pulse, having begun to race as soon as Glenna burst into the kitchen, thundered in her ears.

"You're here for *Rynn*?" Glenna gasped.

"For what purpose?" Rynn desperately, desperately fought for calm.

"They want to ask you some questions."

Bristling like a banty rooster, Granny stepped between her and the constable.

"You, Titus O'Shea, will take yourself out of my house this minute. And you can be sure I'll be speaking to your mam about this."

"It's no use." O'Shea sounded, and looked, miserable. "I have orders. If Miss Carmichael doesn't come with me, they'll send soldiers to fetch her. And they're Brits." They all knew what that meant: rough and crude, no respecters of women, prone to violence at the least excuse. He looked at Rynn. "It's best that you come with me, Miss Carmichael. Really, it is."

"Questions about what?" Rynn asked, although she knew the answer. Her voice was commendably untroubled, she thought. She only hoped that her expression was as well. No matter how icily afraid she felt, to let it show could be fatal. Her fingers had curled around the back of the nearest chair for support, she discovered. Unobtrusively, she hoped, she took her hand away.

"I'm not supposed to tell you anything. Just bring you in. *Please*, Miss Carmichael."

Granny picked up the knife Rynn had put down. With the intention of chasing O'Shea from her kitchen and her house, Rynn had not a doubt.

The situation could only go from bad to worse.

"It's all right," she said to Granny and Glenna. Then, to O'Shea: "I'll come."

"I'm coming with you." Glenna followed Rynn as she went for her coat.

"I've only room for the one." O'Shea sounded almost apologetic. To Rynn he added, "Bundle up. It's a sidecar, you know."

"You best be bringing her back here safe and sound if you know what's good for you, Titus O'Shea," Granny warned. She still held the knife, which O'Shea eyed askance.

"It's only for questioning. I doubt that they'll keep her," O'Shea replied.

"They best not." Granny's voice was full of meaning. Looking alarmed, O'Shea took a sidling step toward the door and, where Granny couldn't see, made the sign for warding off the Evil Eye.

"If I'm not back by nightfall, tell Lord Thomas what's happened," Rynn whispered to Glenna under cover of this exchange as she put on her coat and wrapped a wool scarf tight around her head. He was, she thought, the only one who might be able to help her if help was needed. Glenna, who'd met Lord Thomas more than once and heard all about him from Rynn, nodded. Rynn said to her grandmother, "It will be all right, you'll see," and walked out of the kitchen and out of the house with O'Shea behind her.

It was no great distance to the Garda station, which was very near to the Church of Our Lady Star of the Sea, but by the time the motorbike jolted to a stop in front of the two-story brick structure Rynn was sick with fear.

She did her best not to let it show, keeping her shoulders back and her head high as O'Shea, taking her arm, walked her through the busy main room with its glass-fronted reception area where Gillie Johnson, a sharp-featured spinster who—like nearly everyone in the village—Rynn had known from childhood, reigned supreme. There was no sign of Cara O'Reilly, but there were several closed doors that led off the main room and Rynn supposed she must be behind one of them. Or perhaps she'd already been released. Perhaps this would be a few simple questions and over quickly and no need at all for her to be quaking like a jelly inside.

"They're waiting for you in the back," Gillie called to O'Shea as they passed, lowering her spectacles to look Rynn over with interest. He lifted a hand in acknowledgment. Then they were at a heavy paneled door in the far corner of the room and he knocked. Upon being bade to enter, he opened the door.

Preceding him into the room, which was small, unadorned and, with its shades drawn, nerve-rackingly dim, Rynn immediately found herself under inspection. Behind her, the door closed again. She realized that O'Shea had not followed her inside but had rather left her to deal with the three men awaiting her on her own.

"Thank you for coming, Miss Carmichael. Please join us." Colonel Pelly's greeting was polite enough. He and Chief Inspector Fallon stood together beside the sturdy-looking table that took up most of the far end of the room. In response to a gesture from Pelly, she walked over to stand in front of the table. The man sitting behind it did not, as good manners dictated, get to his feet upon her approach. Instead, he steepled his hands in front of him and regarded her unblinkingly over them. The single tall lamp was positioned behind him, casting his face in shadow. It gave him a sinister aspect that made her stomach knot.

"This is Detective Major Charles Kenney, from Crime Special Branch. He's been sent down from London to lead this investigation," Pelly said.

Crime Special Branch? It was a division of MI5. Rynn's stomach sank. A thin-faced man of about forty with slicked-back dark hair and hooded eyes, Kenney continued to simply look at her, unsmiling.

"The investigation into Molly Kincaid's death? Good. I'm glad to hear it," Rynn said, rallying. She knew it wasn't likely even as she said it but mustered the courage to take the first thrust in what she could only think of as the coming duel as a way, hopefully, to keep them from realizing how guilty she felt and how frightened she was.

"No. Miss Kincaid's unfortunate death is of interest to local law enforcement only, not His Majesty's government. This is about another matter. Chief Inspector Fallon, if you'll take Miss Carmichael's coat and scarf." Kenney's accent was not the plummy one of a public school boy like Lord Thomas. It had the shorter vowels and rougher intonation of working-class London.

Looking none too pleased with the assignment, which he no doubt felt was beneath him, Fallon did as he was told. He was hanging the garments on the coatrack by the door when Kenney said, "No doubt you have other matters to attend to, Chief Inspector. You may leave us. You, too, Colonel Pelly. Miss Carmichael and I will deal better on our own."

A tiny pause was followed by Pelly turning on his heel and walking away. Swept by a thrill of unease, Rynn kept her eyes on the man in front of her rather than watch him go, but a moment later the door opened and she heard two pairs of footsteps walking out before the door closed again.

Rynn went cold with dread as she realized she and Kenney were now alone.

Chapter Twelve

"Sit down, Miss Carmichael," Kenney said. It was an order rather than an invitation.

Rynn sat with what grace she could muster in the upright wooden chair he indicated, which was right across the table from him. The light from the lamp behind the table fell directly on her face. No doubt the lamp had been positioned there for just that purpose. She tried not to let any emotion, anything of what she was thinking or feeling, show.

"I want to know where Seamus and Donal O'Reilly are. If you tell me that, I'll have no further business with you and you may go." Kenney's eyes bored into hers.

"I don't know where they are." If she sounded tense, why, what was there to wonder about in that? Worry over the men's fate would be a natural cause of tension. "Everyone is saying that they've drowned."

"I'm sure that's what everyone is saying." He smiled at her, a thin, terrifying smile. With his face in shadow, his eyes gleamed at her. Like a shark's, she thought, if it came swimming at her from the depths. "You haven't heard from them?"

"No."

"Do you expect to?" His tone was almost affable now.

The room was warm. She was not. Her hands, curled in her lap, felt like blocks of ice. Inside, she was cold with fear. *Be careful.*

"I . . . pray to God I will."

"Is that what you're doing? Praying?" He waited, but she didn't answer. "How long have you known they were smuggling in guns?"

"I didn't know."

"Do you know that Seamus O'Reilly is a member of the Irish Republican Brotherhood?"

Of course he was. Somewhere deep inside, she'd suspected it. "No. I no."

"I would ask you the same about Donal O'Reilly."

"He is not. I'm sure he is not."

"You're most emphatic." His mouth tightened. "Oh, that's right. I've been informed that he's very special to you. So special that you would lie for him? If so, I must warn you that lying to me would be a dangerous thing for you to do."

His eyes were intent on her face. She was hideously conscious of how the light must be illuminating every nuance of her expression. The implied threat hung in the air between them, tangible as a dark cloud. And then it hit her: *He's speaking of them in the present tense. As if he doesn't think they're dead.*

She did not wet her lips. She did not blink. What she did was call on every saint she'd ever heard of and every long-deceased ancestor whose name she knew for courage and lifted her chin and returned him look for look.

"I'm not in the habit of lying, I assure you."

He seemed to consider her. Inwardly she quaked. Outwardly she tried her best to remain unmoved. Was she succeeding? Impossible to know.

The silence between them stretched out until she thought she would jump out of her skin with nerves.

"Where were you on Christmas night, Miss Carmichael?" he asked finally, shooting the question at her.

Ah, but she'd been expecting that one. A little of her terror eased.

"At Ballyshannon Court."

"All night?"

"Yes." She had Lord Thomas to thank for the conviction with which she answered. He'd given her the alibi and she would use it, knowing he would say the same if asked.

"Isn't that a trifle . . . unusual?"

"I am a nurse. I was needed by a patient. A very important patient. Lord Thomas Dunne."

"So you stayed at Ballyshannon Court with this important patient for all—the entirety—of Christmas night." He made no effort to hide his skepticism. It was clear the name Lord Thomas Dunne meant nothing to him. Her hope that her patient's identity might give him pause withered and died.

"I did."

"Did you ever, at any time during that night, go to the Strand?"

Why would he ask that? Her pulse quickened. "I did not."

He looked down, reached for something on the floor near his feet, out of her sight. A quiver of foreboding almost gulled her into taking a deep, calming breath. She did not. She did not move, did not shift in her seat, did not change expressions.

All while she thought she might expire of fear.

Straightening, Kenney plunked something down on the table in front of her.

Shoes. The black satin single-strap pumps she'd worn on Christmas night and lost to the sea. The ones with the delicately crafted rosemary blossoms sewn onto the straps. Her mother's shoes, that had been stored in the trunk with the dress they matched. Now splotched with drying seawater and crusted with salt and sand. How had he ended up with them?

It didn't matter. There they were: *her mother's shoes.*

One of a kind. Crafted specially for the acclaimed young actress in her final performance before she left the stage forever to wed. Possibly identifiable by anyone—any woman her mother's age or older who might remember her, at least—in the village.

Rosemary blossoms for Rosemary Shaughnessy.

It was all Rynn could do not to stare at them in horror. She prayed her reaction didn't show. How could she explain how they'd ended up in the bay? To be caught in a lie could prove her undoing.

"I see you recognize them," Kenney said.

Her face, her telltale face!

Dear God, what could she say? Her heart raced.

"They're not mine, if that's what you're asking," she said. Once again, it was the truth. She did much better with the truth.

He stood up abruptly and came around the table to loom over her.

"Look at me." His voice was soft. Terrifyingly so.

Rynn called on every tiny reserve of courage she had left and did as he ordered.

"We've had word that a woman was out gunrunning with the O'Reillys that night. A young woman with long black hair. Tall, slim, very beautiful. Unusually dressed, possibly in men's clothes. Was that woman you?" His hand dropped onto her shoulder. Weighty. Intimidating. Purposely so, she thought, even as she successfully fought to contain a shiver.

"No." There was no other answer she could give and survive. Meanwhile, her mind raced. He'd had word—from whom? If he was asking if the woman in question was her, whoever it was who'd seen her hadn't known her identity. That eliminated Donal, Seamus, Fergus—and Owen Maguire. As well as practically everyone in and around Bundoran. One of the soldiers on the Strand? But it had been so dark, and she'd been so far away. And she'd been described as wearing men's clothes. She'd only changed into them after she was on Maguire's boat. One of the *Reaper*'s crew, then? Or someone who'd boarded her at Inishmurray?

Or was Kenney bluffing? If so, it was a very specific bluff.

His hand slid around to grip the back of her neck. It felt hot and damp and skin-crawlingly repulsive against her exposed nape. She stopped breathing.

Then he trailed a caressing forefinger from her hairline down her spine to the top of her dress.

"Stop that!" Too outraged and horrified to do anything but react, she jerked away and jumped to her feet, facing him with fear and fury combined. "How dare you?"

He smiled at her.

"You'll find that—" he began.

A knock at the door: Rynn had never been so glad of an interruption in her life.

"Detective Kenney!" Gillie's voice, muffled by the door.

"Not now!" Kenny barked, making Rynn jump.

The door opened, and Gillie stuck her head into the room. "It's sorry I am to interrupt, Detective Kenny, but there's a telephone call for you from Special Branch. A Mr. James McBrien says he must speak to you most urgently."

Her words had a profound effect on Kenney. His mouth contorted. Blood rushed into his face, turning it bright red. Glaring in Gillie's direction, he seemed about to dismiss her out of hand before appearing to think the better of it.

"We'll continue in a moment," he said curtly to Rynn, and strode past Gillie and out of the room. With a wide-eyed glance at Rynn, Gillie followed, closing the door behind her.

Rynn's knees sagged. Her hip found the edge of the table, and she rested against it, thankful for the support. She wanted to sit but did not. Kenney would be back, and to give him the opportunity to loom over her again—she wouldn't do it.

What am I going to do?

His actions had already driven home to her how truly defenseless she was. It was within his authority to interrogate her as he saw fit, to have her arrested, sent to Dublin Castle—and worse.

He was gone for just long enough for Rynn to conclude that her only option was to deny all knowledge of everything. If he didn't believe her, well, he couldn't prove otherwise. Could he? Would he even need proof?

As an officer of the Crown, he held all the power.

If he touched her again, she would scream the place down. Although she wasn't sure if it would do any good.

When the door opened, she straightened away from the table. He was scowling as he came toward her. Whatever the call had been about, it had clearly put him in a filthy mood. She kept her face as expressionless as she could while her heart knocked and her insides curdled with fear.

Steady.

He stopped when he reached the far edge of the table. His gaze was darkly malevolent as their eyes met, and she was once again reminded, horribly, of a shark.

"You. May. Go," he said. Each word as it emerged sounded as if it was being wrenched from his throat.

What?

"We will finish this at another time." Despite the unbelievably welcome message, there was no mistaking his underlying rage.

Rynn didn't reply. Instead, she embraced the miracle of it, inclined her head in stiff acknowledgment and walked past him and out of the room, retrieving her coat on the way. Without saying a word to anyone, not to Gillie, who gave her a commiserating look, not to Colonel Pelly, who stood talking with a pair of soldiers just inside the door and stopped to watch her pass, not to any of the onlookers, most of whom she knew, she continued out of the building and down the walk, pulling on her coat as she went.

Head high. Pace measured. When it was all she could do not to run.

The car waiting for her outside was the green DeLion belonging to Ballyshannon Court.

Surprised as she was to see it, Rynn didn't hesitate when the chauffeur, whom she knew, jumped out to open the door for her. Climbing into the back seat, she held herself rigidly erect in case anyone inside the Garda station still watched. Then when the chauffeur—Higdon was his name; he also served as the hospital's groundskeeper in these trying times—got in, released the choke and pulled away down the street, she went boneless, slumping like a rag doll against the seat as she fought to catch her breath.

"What are you doing here?" she asked once she had her breathing under control again, although she was sure she knew the answer.

"Lord Thomas sent me to fetch you, miss."

As she'd thought. Of course Lord Thomas had been involved in her release. How he'd managed it she couldn't fathom, but it was the only possible explanation. Someone—Glenna?—must have alerted him to her situation.

"Can you take me to my grandmother's house? It's . . ."

"I know where it is." He hesitated. "Lord Thomas instructed me to bring you directly back to the Court. In case of trouble, you understand."

Trouble? The mere thought that something else might happen made her chest tighten.

"I'll only be a few minutes. And I'm sure Lord Thomas won't object."

"Very well, miss. If you say so."

The village had come alive again, with cars and horses and bicycles in the streets and people in and out of the shops and pubs. Difficult as it was to accept that after Molly's death and Paddy's death and all that had happened the world still continued on its merry way, it did, she reflected. And not only did it go on, but right at that moment it was achingly beautiful. Above the glinting silver of the bay, the sun sank toward the horizon, limning in bright orange the purpling clouds that hung there. Long shadows from the buildings striped the cobblestones, and starlings wheeled and cried in swarms overhead as they headed for their roosts for the night.

How near the day was to its end was further borne in on her as they drove past the train station and she saw Owen Maguire among those exiting through the tall gates of the iron fence surrounding it. Head down, face partly hidden by the brim of his hat, tails of his long coat flapping in the wind, he strode away from the low brick building, having apparently just seen off his sister and her children on the train that blew its whistle in mournful farewell as it chugged away down the track. From the look of him, he was both deep in thought and in a hurry.

We've had word that a woman was out gunrunning with the O'Reillys that night. Who could have seen her and told? The possibilities were both limited and terrifying.

"Pull over, please," she ordered Higdon.

So urgent was her voice that Higdon complied without argument. The car jolted to a halt by the curb, and with a quick "I'll be right back," she hopped out.

Maguire was still a few long strides away when she stepped onto the sidewalk. As she moved toward him against the tide of those exiting the train station, the wind caught the loose strands of her hair and sent them swirling around her face—ah, she'd forgotten her scarf. Well, it was just going to have to stay at the Garda station forever because she was never, of her own volition, going back. She tucked the wayward tendrils behind her ears and was pulling up her coat collar against the chill when Maguire's head came up. He clearly recognized her, but as she reached him, he touched his hat and said "Miss Carmichael" without slowing as if he intended to walk on by.

Pivoting, she fell into step beside him. "I need to talk to you."

His eyes slid sideways at her and he frowned a little, but he nodded.

"Walk with me." His voice was as quiet as her own.

She understood; there were too many people within earshot for anything resembling a private conversation. They walked in silence until they reached his car, which she only realized was his when he stepped in front of her to open the passenger side door.

"Get in," he said.

She did, but when he closed the door and came around to slide in behind the wheel, she said, "I have a car and driver waiting for me in front of the train station. I can't go anywhere with you."

"This is for privacy." He shifted in his seat so that he could see her better. As big as he was, he blocked most of her view of the street behind him. "We're not going anywhere. You wanted to talk, so talk."

"It's possible that someone on your boat, or from Inishmurray, is reporting on your activities to the Brits," she said.

He went very still. "Why would you think that?"

She told him in a few quick sentences about being brought in for questioning, about Detective Major Kenney from Crime Special Branch being sent down from London to oversee the investigation, about Kenney's seeming knowledge of her presence on the *Reaper.*

"The description Kenney was given of me was accurate enough that whoever provided it must have seen me at fairly close quarters. The most likely way I can see that happening is if one of your crew, or perhaps one of the men who boarded the *Reaper* at Inishmurray, is responsible."

"No one—*no one*—knew you went rushing out into the darkness to warn O'Reilly?"

Before the *Reaper* had set her down at Mullaghmore she'd explained to him, at his request, the circumstances that had led to her being aboard the *Merrow.*

An instant memory of Lord Thomas telling her that he'd seen her racing across the kitchen garden took Rynn aback, but she dismissed it as quickly as it occurred and shook her head. "I was described as wearing men's clothes, which only happened after I was aboard the *Reaper.* Also, whoever it was that saw me doesn't seem to know my name. That lets out you and your nephew as well as both O'Reillys and Fergus Boyd and, indeed, most everybody in and around Ballyshannon Court and Bundoran."

"Could it have been a bluff? A stab in the dark to see how you'd react?"

"It didn't feel that way. It felt genuine."

"If you were truly seen, and described, how is it that this Detective Kenney let you go?"

"He got a telephone call from a James McBrien at Special Branch. When he came back into the room, he seemed angry but told me I could go."

"Ah," he said. When Rynn looked a question at him he added, "James McBrien is Special Branch's commanding officer. Head of the whole shebang. Kenney's boss. The question is, why would McBrien order your release?"

"I suspect one of my patients was behind it. Lord Thomas Dunne. His father is the Duke of Hartford, and a close friend of Lloyd George. A telephone call from Lord Thomas to his father might have done it."

"It might." He seemed thoughtful, as if he were turning something weighty over in his mind.

Rynn said, "You realize that if I was seen on board the *Reaper*, Donal, Seamus and Fergus probably were, too. Which means the Brits know you were involved."

"I do." He grimaced. "Your idiot friends had no idea of the trouble they were stirring up." His eyes sharpened on her face. "Why come to me with this?"

Surprise had her frowning at him. "Why am I telling you that you may be being watched? To warn you, I suppose."

"And why would you do that?"

"You helped me—us—when we so desperately needed it, and then today you advised me to leave town. I thought it only right that I return the favor. Why, what other reason do you imagine I might have?"

"In times like these, one never can tell. And that thing I said about leaving town, I still think it would be the smartest thing you could do."

"Yes, so do I." She reached for the door handle. "I must go. Higdon—my driver—will be wondering what's become of me." As she stepped out into the street, it occurred to her that this was her chance, that he could set her mind at ease on the question that had been haunting her since that night when she'd stayed behind on the *Reaper.* With her hand still on the open car door, she turned back to look in at him.

"Did they get away all right?" she asked quietly.

There was no question who she meant. He knew.

"Rest easy, your man's safe." His voice held the tiniest trace of mockery. "The others, too."

"He's not my man. Not anymore," she said. "But thank you."

She smiled at him. Then she closed the door and left him to his thoughts.

The DeLion was within sight when a burly man in a plaid coat with a knit cap pulled low over his forehead stepped directly into her path, blocking her.

Chapter Thirteen

Startled, Rynn tried to dodge around him, but he reached out and caught her by the arm.

"What . . . ?" she said. He had squinty eyes and a mouth like a frog, she saw as she tried to pull away.

"I'm Ori Sullivan. Your man owes me five thousand pounds," he said.

Rynn's heart leaped. "I don't know what you're talking about."

"You do," he said with conviction, and Rynn realized he'd probably read the truth in her thrice-damned face. "You tell the O'Reillys that I want my money, or the cargo I was promised, and if I don't get one or the other there'll be consequences."

"I don't know where they are," she said, and jerked her arm free.

He laughed, an ugly sound, and as she walked away called after her, "You tell them."

Higdon, clearly having seen the encounter, was stepping out of the car by that time. As he came toward her, Ori Sullivan strode away.

Granny and Glenna both pounced on her the moment she walked into the cottage.

"Did they harm you?" Granny's question was fierce as she

looked Rynn up and down. Her eyes were black as coal, which Rynn knew was a sign that she'd been laboring under extreme emotion.

"They did not." Rynn spoke to Granny over Glenna's head as her sister wrapped her in a hug. She was still shaken from both encounters, but she tried not to let it show.

"I *knew* they'd let you go. Lord Thomas said he'd see to it." Glenna was exultant as she released Rynn and stepped back. "Even if he is a Brit, I *like* him."

"You telephoned him." It was the only way word could have reached him so quickly.

"I know you told me to wait, but Granny had a bad feeling. So directly after you left, I went to the doctor's house and asked to use their telephone. Lord Thomas was really worried about you."

"He's become a friend. And he's very kind," Rynn said.

Behind Glenna's back, Granny's eyes met Rynn's. In them Rynn saw a question: Had her bad feeling been justified? Rynn answered with an almost imperceptible nod.

"I can't stay, but I wanted to let you know that I'm all right. And to tell you they've brought in a man from London, from Crime Special Branch. A Detective Major Kenney. He's terrifying. He asked me questions—there was nothing I could tell him—and they showed me a pair of women's shoes they've fished out of the bay. He asked me if they were mine. Apparently, they feel the shoes are somehow connected to what's happened. I didn't have a chance to answer, but if I had I would have said they're not mine. For all I know, they might come around asking every woman in Bundoran if the shoes belong to her. If they were to ask either of you any such question, you must say that they are not yours and you have no idea whose they are. That, in fact, you have no knowledge of them at all."

That last was directed as a warning to Glenna more than

Granny—Granny's feet were as small as the rest of her—but while Glenna nodded solemnly Granny looked at Rynn with dawning comprehension. She'd watched Rynn take her mother's dress and shoes from the trunk where they were kept and knew she'd planned to wear them to the hospital's Christmas party.

"Do you think they will come?" Glenna breathed.

"They can come if they like, and we'll say we've no knowledge of their wretched shoes," Granny said. She looked at Rynn. "You'd best stay put at Ballyshannon Court for the next little while. The young lord there appears to wield considerable influence. Keep near him."

"I will." Not wanting to worry them further, Rynn didn't say that Lord Thomas was leaving soon and so his protection would only be available for a brief time. Instead she looked at Glenna. "Stay away from the Garda station, and the soldiers. And stay home at night."

Glenna nodded, looking frightened. Rynn hugged them both and left.

By the time the car reached Ballyshannon Court, she was so tired she was beyond feeling any emotion at all. Darkness had fallen, which made her thankful for one thing: this horrific day was finally ending.

But then she saw the military lorry pulling away from the front entrance, its headlamps flashing past in a burst of blinding light before it gained the road and roared off toward Bundoran. The fear that had coiled itself into an unpleasant but largely quiescent knot in her stomach sprang back into shrieking, clawing life.

"That lot's been up to no good, I'll be bound," Higdon prophesied darkly. Pulling up to the front entrance, he added, "You'd best be watching out for yourself, miss."

Rynn's nerves were on edge as she walked through the front door, which she as a member of staff was discouraged from using, into the imposing entryway. Knowing that, between patients and staff, there were at least thirty other people in the building should have been reassuring, but it wasn't. Rational or not, her feeling that the soldiers' visit had concerned her was strong.

Cyril, the footman, was the first to confirm it. As she headed toward the kitchen, where she knew Mrs. Frampton and Anna and Lynnette would be bursting to talk about whatever had just occurred, he appeared from the bowels of the house to greet her with open alarm and an urgent whisper.

"Soldiers were here, Miss Carmichael. They searched your room."

They searched her room? Fear shot through her. With a wordless nod of thanks, she hurried to the back stairs and raced up to her room. What she found as she entered made her go cold with dread. It was obvious from the way things had been left that they'd gone through everything: the wardrobe, the small chest, even the box of cosmetics and personal items that she kept on the shelf beneath the table that held her water pitcher and basin. The bedcovers had been pulled back, the pillows tossed and the trunk at the foot of the bed disturbed. She saw all that with scarcely more than a glance around before she rushed to the window embrasure where she'd stored the clothes she'd been given that night on the *Reaper.* Concealed by heavy curtains, drawn now to keep out the cold, a bench seat was built in beneath the dormer-style window. It opened for storage. Rynn pushed aside the curtains and threw open the lid. Then, slowly, she sank to her knees in front of it. She'd rolled the clothes up, thrust them into a spare pillowcase and hidden them away among the extra linens that were kept in the bench seat.

The pillowcase was there in a crumpled heap on top of the linens.

The clothes were gone.

On their own, the clothes mean nothing, she told herself.

But if whoever had seen her that night identified them as the clothes the woman he'd described had been wearing . . .

Would that be enough to get her dragged back in for more questioning? Or even arrested?

If they add in the shoes . . .

Panic made her chest feel tight.

Such was her anxiety that a timid-sounding knock on her door was all it took to send her leaping to her feet to face it.

"Miss Carmichael?" Anna. The voice on the other side of the door belonged to Anna. If Rynn had been in a normal frame of mind, she would have realized at once that the knock was too soft and tentative to be the soldiers returning, which had been her instant fear. Drawing the tattered remains of her composure around herself as best she could, she crossed to the door and opened it.

"Lord Thomas has been asking for you. He told us to send you to him in his room the minute you got back," Anna said. Her eyes were wide with sympathy.

Rynn nodded. Then she went down to Lord Thomas's room.

"You must marry me," Lord Thomas said. "It's the only way you'll be safe."

She'd told him *almost* everything. About Christmas night. About the guns. About how Paddy had died, and Donal and Seamus and Fergus had not. About refusing to go with them to America, and about breaking her engagement. About what had happened today, with Detective Kenney. About Kenney's threats. About Ori Sullivan and his threat. The only thing she'd left out was Owen Maguire and the *Reaper*, claiming instead that as the *Merrow* had started to sink, they'd been rescued by a passing boat that had delivered her to shore, and carried the men on. That omission was because Maguire and the *Reaper* were still within reach of the Crown forces if her trust in Lord Thomas should be misplaced. He'd listened intently and hadn't questioned her account. Instead this marriage proposal, uttered as he frowned at her in concern as they sat before the crackling fire in his room, was his most unexpected response.

"*Marry* you? I thought to accept your offer to go to England with you, as your nurse."

"If they find solid evidence that you were involved in gunrunning, they'll come for you even in England. And my father strongly condemns any who would support an Irish rebellion. The only reason I've been able to secure his help so far is because I've told him that you're an innocent wrongly suspected. If he's presented with anything that seems to him like proof of your guilt, he'll do nothing to save you." Lord Thomas's eyes bored into hers. "Unless you're his daughter-in-law. My father's a proud man. He would never stand by and see a member of his family arrested."

"I can't *marry* you."

"You can." He reached out and took her hands. Their eyes were on a level and his were a deep, earnest blue as they held hers. "It wouldn't be a love match, not like the one you were planning with O'Reilly, I know. But it could be a good thing for you, and for me as well. This Kenney, and his investigation, could never touch you. Nothing that's happening here, or is going to happen here, could touch you. Whichever way Ireland goes, you'd be safe. And you would have a good life with me. Once I've recovered a little more—yes, I'm now determined that will happen—we could travel. I could show you the world, and you'd have your own home, and—" He faltered, and his grip tightened on her hands. "Forgive me, I know you too well to think that money matters to you, but I'm a rich man. You could have anything you wanted. You'd be secure for the rest of your life."

"Money always matters," Rynn said. "But I wouldn't marry for it."

"Do it for me, then. You've given me so much. The will to fight to get better. A reason to hope I can have a future that's more than just being an invalid in a chair. I want you to be a part of it. You know my medical condition. You know I can't be a real husband to you, at least not right now, not in a physical sense. And I give you my solemn promise that if that were to change, I would not hold you against your will. You could have an annulment anytime you wished. And even if that were to be what you ultimately choose, you would still have my undying regard. And I would see to it that you were taken care of."

"Stop." Rynn shook her head at him. "You can't be serious. You haven't thought this through. You've told me all the ways this marriage would benefit me. But what do you get out of it?"

"You. I get you." For the briefest of moments, naked adoration blazed at her out of his eyes. Rynn recognized it for what it was, before he, too, seemed to realize and glanced elsewhere. The room around them seemed to recede, to grow shadowy and indistinct. The fire's warmth no longer touched her. Lord Thomas himself seemed to fade away. As if looking on from a distance, she could so clearly see the future he described, see a new path opening before her, see the life they could have together, see the happiness she could give him and maybe even find for herself. Possibility twinkled like a bright star in a dark sky, drawing her almost irresistibly in a direction she never could have imagined.

"Please say yes, Rynn." It was the first time he'd ever called her that.

She was back, instantly, totally in the present, with the fire blazing away and his hands warm and firm on hers and everything, the hearth and his chair and hers, and the table and the bed, as solid and real as it could possibly be. And yet the future she'd seen was still there in all its infinite possibility for her to seize if she wished.

"There's Glenna. And my grandmother. I can't just leave them." It was the first, and largest, objection that came to mind.

"I would never ask you to leave them. They can join us whenever you want. But for your safety, I would want you to come away with me on Friday, as my wife."

"That could never be arranged so soon."

He smiled. And she caught another glimpse of the man he would have been had the war never happened, had mustard gas and an exploding shell not decimated his body, had pain and despair not eaten away at his soul.

"You'd be surprised what I can arrange when it's important to me." He leaned toward her, his eyes intent now, purposeful, the adoration she'd glimpsed in them gone or masked. But she had seen it and wouldn't forget. "Will you do me the honor, Rynn? Will you marry me?"

Another crossroads. Another time to choose, to decide. The way forward was murky, the future unknowable, either way. But she could feel a tug in a certain direction, like a magnet being drawn toward the north.

Unlikely as it seemed, she knew where it was urging her to go.

"Yes," she said. "Yes, Thomas, I'll marry you."

Chapter Fourteen

The rain that had held off on the day they'd buried Molly Kincaid was not so accommodating on the day Thomas brought Rynn home to Ashtonbury Park as his wife. Cascades of water pounded the roof of the car, sluiced the windows, soaked the earth. The downpour had doubled the time it usually took to drive from London, where they'd holed up at Claridge's, the impossibly luxurious hotel in Mayfair, to Surrey, where Ashtonbury Park was located. Thomas assured her that on their journey they were passing through some of the most delightful pastoral scenes that existed on God's earth, but Rynn could only take his word for it. It was nearly dusk by the time they arrived. Quite apart from the falling darkness it was impossible to see much of anything through the deluge.

"Nervous?" Thomas reached for her hand as they rattled through a pair of enormous stone pillars and along an avenue that, in summer, would be shaded by the tall trees that were now skeletal and black with rain. They sat side by side in the rear while Meadows, the family chauffeur who'd been sent to fetch them, drove. He was obviously pleased to see Thomas and was properly deferential to his new wife, but Rynn, as much as she fought against it, could not help but feel that she was being silently judged and found wanting by this, the first of the longtime family retainers to meet the new Lady Thomas Dunne.

"Who wouldn't be?" she replied as the house, a large pale blur seen through the windscreen as they left the dubious shelter of the trees, loomed before them. She was familiar with the grand houses of the British aristocracy, of course, at least to some extent. Bundoran was home to several, including Ballyshannon Court. But those were their summer homes, their second or third or fourth residences. This enormous Palladian mansion—Ashton, Thomas called it, with the easy affection of one who considered it home—was the Duke of Hartford's principal seat. It stood three stories tall, with a huge central section flanked by two equally large, forward-protruding wings in the shape of half an H. With its slate roof, innumerable chimneys and dozens upon dozens of windows looking down on the paved courtyard where the car was now pulling in, Ashton put those paltry dwellings to shame.

"Don't be. They're going to love you."

"I hope so." Rynn wasn't so sure. Loathe as she was to admit it, she felt a little queasy at the prospect of meeting Thomas's family. London, huge and crowded to bursting point with returning soldiers, its streets packed with a mix of cars and bicycles and horse-drawn vehicles and electric trams, with its constant noise and never-ending activity, had already proved nearly overwhelming to one whose only previous experience of a large city had been Dublin. Being introduced as a new daughter-in-law to the famously testy (by his own son's account) Duke of Hartford and his blue-blooded wife was something she did not look forward to with pleasure, although her growing trepidation was something she never intended to reveal, to Thomas or anyone else.

Thomas smiled. "I know so. How could they not? My mother, for one, was over the moon when I told her I'd married and was bringing my new bride home with me. She'll have assembled the whole gang, believe me. They were expecting us earlier, but the rain put paid to that, I'm afraid. Hopefully they've saved us some tea."

"Yes, hopefully." She spoke with a calm she wasn't feeling. To make the coming meeting even more anxiety producing, the first Dail Eireann, Ireland's own rebel parliament newly formed in an act of defiance against British rule, had met yesterday—January 21—in Dublin's Mansion House and immediately issued the Irish Declaration of Independence in which they proclaimed themselves to be a sovereign nation. Clearly determined to rub salt in the wound, they also issued a Message to the Free Nations of the World stating that Ireland and Britain were in an "existing state of war." As the newly elected members, most of whom were pledged to the hardline Irish nationalist party Sinn Fein, had refused to take up their seats in Westminster and indeed had vowed to boycott Westminster forever, the assembly itself was provocative even without its revolutionary agenda. To make the situation more fraught, only twenty-seven of the sixty-nine new members were present. That would be because most of the others were either on the run from or imprisoned by the British, the latter group having been rounded up in May after being falsely accused of treasonously plotting with the Germans. Among the imprisoned were Countess Markievicz and Sinn Fein's president, Eamon de Valera, over which circumstance the British gloated and the Irish fumed. This morning she'd awakened to discover that the Dail with its fiery proclamation was the lead story in *The Times* and all the newspapers were apparently full of it. So far, the British reaction seemed to be mainly one of toff-nosed affront at the nerve of the upstart Irish, but still it made for an uncomfortable atmosphere in which to meet her new in-laws.

"Chin up. They can't eat you, you know. And I wouldn't let them if they could."

"Oh, very comforting." She made a face at him, and he smiled again. The one heartening thing in all this was that

Thomas was smiling more, had in fact smiled more since their wedding than he had in all the previous time she'd known him, which had to count for something. Perhaps she hadn't married for all the right reasons, but he at least seemed to have no regrets.

Squeezing his hand, she freed her own to smooth her hair, brushed and twisted and pinned into ebony perfection by the hotel maid Thomas had summoned to attend to her during the course of their sojourn there, and settled her lovely green hat with its turned-up brim more firmly on her head.

As guilty as it made her feel, one of the most enjoyable aspects of her new life was that she was no longer obliged to scrimp and save and count every shilling. Instead, she found herself in a world that offered her the best of everything: beautiful clothes, luxurious surroundings, the finest food—things Thomas took for granted, but she didn't think she ever would.

Best of all was the absence of fear.

They'd been married for twelve days. The strangeness of it had not abated. Being Lady Thomas Dunne still felt uncomfortable, like an ill-fitting dress. But with Thomas himself she was now totally at ease. Beyond their nurse/patient role, which hadn't changed appreciably, they had developed an affectionate camaraderie which, she felt, boded well for their life together.

"We're here." Thomas looked past her out the window as the car stopped. Looking out through that same window herself, Rynn blinked at what appeared to be an entire household's worth of servants, each wielding a large black umbrella, rushing out to greet them.

Her expression must have been typically revealing, because he grinned. "Don't look so scared."

Her door opened before she could do more than throw him a quelling look. Compelled by his encouraging "Go along in, don't wait for me," she had perforce to step out and immediately found a puddle, which soaked her foot and splashed up past her shoe to splatter her ankle in its silk stocking with cold water. The umbrella that instantly appeared over her head protected her from any further assault by the downpour. The bowing footman holding it while murmuring "Welcome to Ashtonbury Park, my lady," ushered her around more puddles that lay like landmines across the pavers. A glance back as she went up the steps to the open front door told her that two more servants plus Meadows were engaged in getting Thomas's chair from the boot and then helping Thomas himself into it, all under the protection of umbrellas being held over the operation by a gaggle of maids. The following car, which held their luggage—the acquisition of what Thomas called a basic wardrobe for them both had occupied a fair portion of their time in London—was directed by someone to drive on, presumably to another entrance.

Then she was inside, in a vast entryway with oak-paneled walls and a high, vaulted ceiling. Her lightning first impression was of welcome warmth to counteract the cold day, a faint scent of lemon polish with an underlying trace of cigarettes and generations of acquired magnificence everywhere she looked. The dripping umbrella was whisked away as yet another footman asked if he could take her coat. She was just handing it and her hat over when a stately gentleman in a black tailcoat appeared out of seemingly nowhere to say, "Welcome to Ashtonbury Park, Lady Thomas. I am—"

"Jansing!" Thomas broke into a broad smile as he was rolled into the entry hall on a huff of rain-scented wind, his chair wheels squeaking as they left wet tracks on the marble floor before the waiting carpet silenced them. "Still here, I see."

"As I hope to always be, my lord! May I say from all of us what a pleasure it is to welcome you home?"

"It's a pleasure to be home, believe me, and an even greater pleasure to bring my wife home with me. Rynn, this is Jansing, who's been at Ashton longer than I have and is the real master of the house." As Rynn smiled and nodded in greeting, Thomas added more quietly, "Where are they, Jansing?"

"In the Blue Salon, sir, and I was to bring you directly in the moment you appeared. The Duchess has had tea held back for your arrival."

"And my father hates waiting. Yes, I know. Rynn, would you like a moment to freshen up before we beard the lions in their den?"

Rynn dearly wanted a moment—several moments—to herself but for no other purpose than to delay the inevitable. She was growing more nervous by the second. But since turning tail and running was not an option, best to do and have done, as Granny would say.

"No, I'm fine. And your family are hardly lions."

"Ah, but you don't yet know them," he said with a wicked smile. In response to the look she gave him reproaching him for his teasing, he laughed out loud. Then he said to Jansing, "Very well, we'll go right in."

Jansing nodded and glanced at her. "If you'll follow me, my lady."

Rynn found herself walking after Jansing with Thomas, being pushed by one of the footmen, following close behind. As they rounded the corner into yet another magnificent hallway a woman's voice reached her. The words were perfectly clear.

"An Irish nurse? Are we really supposed to accept her as part of the family?"

"Thomas has been crippled, remember. We must be kind no matter how awful she is," a second woman replied.

"Yes, that's all very well, but how do we explain her to our friends?"

"I agree it's awkward, but—"

Jansing's back went ramrod straight, while Rynn's stomach pitted.

"Lord Thomas and Lady Thomas have arrived *home*," Jansing boomed, cutting off the speaker before she could finish. His magisterial tone was a rebuke.

The speakers, caught in the act of descending the last flight of a magnificent staircase, froze in place as the converging parties saw one another. Two women about Rynn's own age, one plumpish with dark blond hair pulled back into a tight chignon, the other shorter and thinner with medium brown hair cut short in a fashionable bob, looked startled at the sight of them. Both in their own way were attractive and dressed in the latest style.

As their gazes fastened on Rynn, she found herself extraordinarily thankful that she was wearing the Nile-green dress with its black lace overlay and fringe of black beads that Thomas had insisted on purchasing for her as part of her new wardrobe. With black onyx earbobs—"A mere trifle," Thomas had told her when she'd protested the expense, "I'll get you better when I've had a proper chance to access my bank."—dangling from her ears, and her new wedding band on her finger, she had nothing to apologize for in her appearance, she knew. The knowledge wasn't much help. She still felt acutely self-conscious under the entirely feminine up-and-down looks she was subjected to.

Then, "Thomas!" The brunette flung herself down the stairs, arms outstretched and heels clattering as she fell upon Thomas to hug him in his chair.

"Maud." Thomas's return hug was affectionate.

"Hello, Thomas. And Lady Thomas." The blonde continued down the stairs at a stately pace. "It seems we've been caught out being quite rude," she said to Rynn as she reached the bottom and approached them. "I apologize."

"Think nothing of it. How wretched for you to have been overheard." Rynn managed a smile and received a rather thin one in return.

"Such a charming accent," the lady said. "I predict it will become all the rage."

Rynn blinked. She might be unfamiliar with how things were done in such rarified social circles, but she was perfectly capable of recognizing a barely disguised sneer when she was on the receiving end of one.

"This is my sister-in-law, Alice, Marchioness of Wycomb," Thomas said to Rynn, indicating the blonde as he emerged from Maud's embrace. Rynn knew that his older brother, Geoffrey, their father's heir, was styled as the Marquess of Wycomb. "And this madcap—" he wagged a finger at Maud "—is my cousin Maud. Lady Maud Dunne. Ladies, this is my wife, Rynn."

"Thomas, is that you?" A door was flung open further along the hallway and a beautifully coiffed and dressed older woman appeared, glanced in their direction and, face lighting up, hurried toward them. "Oh, it is! How wonderful to have you home at last!"

"Mother!" Thomas wheeled himself toward her, embracing his mother warmly as she swooped down on him and kissed him on both cheeks.

"Oh, my poor boy, to see you like this!" Straightening, she pressed both hands to her cheeks and shook her head. "It breaks my heart."

"The fortunes of war." Shrugging, he looked around at Rynn and held out a hand to her. As Rynn stepped forward to take it, he drew her closer to his side and said, "This is Rynn, Mother. My wife."

"How do you do?" Rynn dredged up the formal British manners that had been drummed into her by the nuns at St. Louis Convent School who'd overseen the middle years of her education, after Granny had determined that she was too old to attend the local hedge school and run with the lads, and briefly shook the hand the older woman held out to her. Her own, she feared, was cold as ice, from nerves even more than the weather, but there was nothing she could do about it and the Duchess seemed not to notice.

"It is a pleasure to meet you, my dear. Thomas has been singing your praises for, oh, these many months now. Since you first became his nurse."

"Rynn has saved my life," Thomas said. In Rynn's view, the steeliness of his tone made the words a warning. Had the Duchess at some point expressed dismay at her son's choice of a bride? If so, Thomas had said nothing to her about it.

"Yes, indeed, we are all most grateful to you," she said to Rynn. "If you can bring happiness to my poor boy, you will forever secure your place in this family."

"Hang it, Blanche, are you going to stand about in the hall all evening?" A gray-haired man, tall, slender and slightly stooped with age, appeared in the doorway through which the Duchess had exited. He scowled at the lot of them. "Is that you, boy? Well, don't lurk about. Come in. I want my tea."

"Good evening, Papa," Thomas said.

"You're late," the Duke replied. Giving Rynn a comprehensive look, he added, "You're right, she's quite the beauty. At least you didn't make a mistake about that," and headed back into the salon.

Rynn tried not to react. Thomas's hand tightened on hers.

"Still on about me joining up, is he?" His tone was rueful as he looked at his mother.

"Oh, dear, you know how he is when he gets in one of his moods. And he does like things to be on time." The Duchess made shooing motions that had them all heading toward what Rynn presumed was the Blue Salon. Having had attention called to her appearance in such a way made her even more uncomfortable than she was already. Still, there was nothing for it but to go into tea.

Chapter Fifteen

The group that awaited them was larger than Rynn had anticipated. Besides the Duke, whose disposition seemed to improve once he was provided with a cup of tea and a selection of tiny cakes and sandwiches, and the Duchess and the two young women they had encountered in the hall, she was introduced to the heir, Thomas's six-years-older brother, Geoffrey, who was tall, thin and fair-haired with patrician features, an impressive mustache and a strong resemblance to Thomas and their father. Also present were Lady Maud's mother, Lady Jane Moore, who was the Duke's sister and thus Thomas's aunt, her husband, Lord Moore, and younger daughter, Lady Emma, and Lady Maud's much older fiancé, Sir Reggie North. So many introductions meant that some facts escaped Rynn almost as soon as she was told them, but she sipped her tea and made polite conversation while trying not to be overly aware that she was, to a greater or lesser extent, the cynosure of all eyes.

"I don't believe I've ever met anyone named Rynn before," Lady Wycomb said under cover of the general conversation. Her new sister-in-law's smile was in place, Rynn saw, but there was something in her tone that made her not quite trust it. "Is that a popular name among your people?"

"I was named after Lough Rynn," Rynn said, absorbing the

"your people" but determinedly overlooking it. "My father apparently spent a lot of time at the castle there before I was born and fell in love with the area."

"Your father?" The condescension in Lady Wycomb's tone was unmistakable. It made Rynn's lips tighten, but before she could once again choose to overlook it Thomas spoke up.

"Her father was the late Baron George Carmichael. She was the Honorable Mary Rynn Carmichael before she did me the honor of marrying me." The steel was back in Thomas's tone as he turned away from the discussion he'd been having with his brother and Sir Reggie to respond. Rynn realized he'd been keeping track of her conversation with her new relatives for the purpose of coming to her aid if need be, and smiled at him.

Lady Wycomb said, "Perhaps we could call you Mary, then? It would be more . . . usual."

"I'm sure it is, but I prefer Rynn." Rynn held on to her smile with effort.

"Are you saying you're Penelope Carmichael's *sister*?" Lady Maud looked at her wide-eyed.

"Half-sister, yes." Rynn took a sip of her tea as she worked to keep a grip on her equanimity. After her mother's death and her father's return to his family in England, he'd remarried almost immediately. Within a year, that marriage had produced a third daughter, Penelope, who would be around eighteen years old now. Rynn and Glenna had never met, spoken with or even corresponded with their half-sister, and the only contact they'd ever had with her mother had been her signature on the letter sent by the family's lawyer informing them of their father's death—and the resulting immediate cessation of the allowance he had been paying Granny for their upkeep.

"Oh, my." The Duchess stared at Rynn like she was seeing her for the first time.

"Well, that's a relief." Lady Jane Moore's whisper to her husband, who responded with a silencing frown, was just loud enough for Rynn to overhear.

"I told you the girl was perfectly acceptable on the father's side." The Duke left off eating his third sandwich to cast an irritable look around the group. "D'ye think I would have countenanced a *total* mésalliance?"

Rynn's hand tightened on her cup, and she carefully set it down. The usual British assumption of superiority over the Irish was not a surprise; she couldn't remember a time in her life when that hadn't been the case and she had come into this meeting with Thomas's family prepared to face a degree of prejudice. But the idea that the father who had abandoned her and her sister was "perfectly acceptable" with its obvious implication that her mother and Granny were not made her hackles rise. Her eyes must have kindled with indignation, because Lady Wycomb, who was watching her, sank back in her chair in response.

"I consider myself the most fortunate fellow on earth to have won Rynn for my wife, and that has nothing at all to do with who her parents or sister might or might not be," Thomas said before she could speak, which was probably just as well. "She's remarkable in and of herself."

"Hear, hear." Lord Wycomb made a little show of applauding and earned a poisonous look from his wife. Rynn, meanwhile, gave Thomas a quick, grateful smile.

"Penelope Carmichael is quite the heiress," Lord North observed.

"Are you fabulously rich, too?" Lady Maud regarded Rynn with fascination.

"All right, that's enough." Thomas put down his cup with enough force so that it made a sharp sound as it hit the saucer. "I'm sure the last thing Rynn wants to talk about is her family connections. Tell me, Maud, when is the wedding?"

Lady Maud answered, and the conversation once again became general. Rynn drank her tea and said little. Thomas's championship had taken the edge off her budding anger, but the underlying hurt remained. She felt as out of place as a bird in a fishbowl and found herself wishing she was back in Bundoran with an intensity that surprised her. She suddenly missed them all fiercely: Granny, Glenna, even, if she were to face the truth of it, Donal. Seen in the context of his home and family, Thomas seemed a stranger. Looking around at the elegant room and the elegant people in it, she shivered inwardly at the thought that this was her new home, and her new life. The one she had chosen.

What have I done?

But there was no undoing it now. She wasn't even sure that she would if she could. But oh, how she wished she was taking tea with Granny and Glenna in the little stone cottage at the end of the lane.

Jansing, who'd left them, reappeared, gliding over to the Duke to say in a confidential tone, "Your Grace, you have a visitor. I . . ."

"Hello, all!" A cheery voice had them all looking around to find a robust, mustachioed gentleman of perhaps sixty years striding into the room on Jansing's heels. "Duchess, I apologize for interrupting such a charming family party, but I have urgent need of your husband."

"Andrew Bonar Law! What brings you to Ashton?" The Duke rose to greet the new arrival with a handshake, while the Duchess said, "Not at all! Such a pleasure to see you. Won't you join us and have some tea?"

"No time, and I apologize for that, too. I'm on my way to call on Churchill, who as you know has just been named the Secretary of State for War and Air, which makes him the very man I need, and I'm afraid I hope to steal your husband away with me."

"Is Winston at Lullenden, then?" The Duchess put down her cup. "One never knows. He so seldom is these days. I feel sorry for Clementine, as often as she is left on her own."

"He is," Law said.

"What's happened?" The Duke's tone, and expression, were suddenly grim.

"The damned mad insurrectionist Irish, what else? This murderous bunch call themselves Volunteers. Last evening they went and murdered two RIC officers at Soloheadbeg in Tipperary. We've got to formulate a response, and I want to make sure Churchill has all the facts before he goes to Lloyd George with a recommendation. Will you come?"

"I will." The Duke looked around. "Blanche, it's unlikely I'll be back tonight. Jansing, tell Porter to pack me a bag. Law, come along to my study and fill me in on the details while we wait. The rest of you, good night." He was ushering the newcomer out of the room as he spoke, then paused at the door to glance back. "Thomas, late or not, I'm glad you're home. It's time and past. Rynn—may I call you Rynn?"

Already put on high alert by the visitor's jarring announcement, Rynn nodded warily.

"Welcome to Ashton. From what my son tells me you are no doubt as outdone with the villainous rogues and rabble-rousers among your countrymen as the rest of us. Please do not consider anything that any of us may say in the context of these unfortunate events to be directed at you."

He left the room, leaving Rynn sick with alarm over the news even as her Irish born-and-bred heart swelled with indignation on the part of her maligned countrymen. But she said nothing of what she was feeling, doing her best to present a serene exterior as she drank her tea. Thankfully it wasn't much longer before Thomas, pleading exhaustion to his mother, made their excuses. The Duchess herself showed them to their quarters on the ground floor, which, she said, had been specially prepared to accommodate Thomas's condition once they'd been informed of the likely long-term duration of it. It was a suite of rooms that included a private parlor and two bedrooms, one of which had been hastily refitted to accommodate a wife instead of an attendant, as had been its original purpose. Their baggage had already been unpacked for them, Rynn discovered upon being shown her bedroom, and several of her dresses taken away for pressing.

"Parry will have them back in time for dinner," the Duchess promised as she turned to leave. "She'll be waiting on you until we can get you a proper lady's maid. You'll find her satisfactory, I'm sure, but you have only to say if you want to make a change."

"Thank you," Rynn said, and was surprised when her mother-in-law, with a glance at her son, who'd rolled himself over to look at the selection of books that filled the shelves on either side of the fireplace, beckoned her to follow her to the door.

"You will tell me, won't you, if Thomas needs anything?" the Duchess spoke in a near whisper. Clearly she didn't want her son to overhear. "I know he finds his—altered state—a great burden to bear, and his spirits sometimes are low as a result."

"Yes, I will." Rynn's smile at the Duchess was the first genuine one she'd managed since stepping through Ashton's door. Whatever else might be at fault, the woman's love for her son could not be in doubt.

The Duchess returned her smile, patted her arm and left. As the door closed behind his mother, Thomas pivoted his chair away from the bookshelves to raise his eyebrows at Rynn.

"Well, what do you think? Are they lions?" he asked.

"They are not," she said, and sank down upon the sofa that had been placed perpendicular to the fire. Like the chairs opposite, it was upholstered in a gold brocade to match the drapes that had been drawn over the tall windows. The walls, too, were a rich gold. The rest of the furnishings were in shades of cream and green accented with dark wood, making for a cozy but luxurious atmosphere.

"Although you find them sadly prejudiced against the Irish," Thomas said with lurking humor, and when Rynn chose the prudent route of staying silent he shook his head at her. "Oh, don't deny it. Your face tells the tale."

She folded her arms across her chest. "Very well, if you must know, I feel they may not have considered that to be constantly treated as an inferior, to say nothing of being starved, thrown off our land and denied the right to make the rules that govern our own country, might turn an otherwise reasonable people into—how did your father put it?—ah yes, villainous rogues and rabble-rousers." Her reply was tart. "Although I do draw the line at condoning murder, of course."

He gave a snort of laughter. "I knew you were a rebel at heart. Though I'm glad to know you draw the line at murder."

"*Condoning* murder. Oh, don't laugh. You never know when I might become a damned mad insurrectionist myself."

"If you must, I suppose I can live with it. Although I do hope you'll hold off until after dinner."

That wrung a reluctant smile from her. "I'll do my best. I find I am quite hungry."

Thomas eyed her keenly. "This has been a tiring day, hasn't it? How about we skip dinner with the family and have trays brought to us here instead?"

"Could we? That would be perfect." Dazzled at the sudden prospect of escaping what she could only think of as the next ordeal, Rynn let the rest of her irritation go. Reluctantly she added, "Though I wouldn't want to be rude."

"No one will think us rude. Indeed, they'll love the chance to gossip all about us. No doubt our ears will be burning while we eat."

Rynn laughed. "Very well, you've persuaded me."

"I *am* very persuasive, am I not? One of my more admirable traits. I persuaded you to marry me, didn't I?"

"You did."

The merest shadow of a frown flickered across his face as he looked at her. "Are you sorry?"

A complicated question, to which there was only one answer that she could give him.

"No."

"Good." His frown cleared. "You rest while I order dinner."

After that first night, Rynn fell into an uneasy routine. Dinners on a tray might be acceptable, but the Duke had no time for layabouts, and at Ashton breakfast with the family was a ritual all were expected to participate in. Consuming her usual toast and tea in the breakfast room where guests helped themselves from a staggering array of dishes laid out on the sideboard left plenty of time for her to be faced with the contents of the morning newspapers, also thoughtfully laid out for early-morning consumption along with breakfast. The ambush at Soloheadbeg was the main story in every single newspaper and was endlessly discussed over Ashton's table. That a group of eight Irish Volunteers had shot and killed two RIC officers transporting a shipment of explosives roused the British, including most of her new relatives, to volcanic fury. The *London Times* called the killings premeditated murders and described them as "wicked" and "shameful." The Duke loudly and forcefully agreed as the British government was called upon to exact a bitter vengeance. A reward of one thousand pounds was immediately offered for information leading to the capture of the ambushers, and within two days of the ambush South Tipperary was declared a Special Military Area under the Defense of the Realm Act, which was tantamount to declaring martial law. The British then banned the newly formed Dail as an illegal assembly. As a result, tensions between the two sides turned white-hot.

"We are," the Duke announced angrily after yet another meeting with Law and Churchill had him heading up to London to confer with Prime Minster Lloyd George, "within a cat's whisker of finding ourselves in an all-out war. Which is what the ingrates want, damn them. Well, they're about to get it, and have only themselves to blame if they rue the day."

Rynn, too, deplored the violence, but from the point of view of the Irish the terrible wrongs endured under centuries of British oppression had left them with little recourse but to fight back, as she explained to Thomas with a militant glint in her eyes. Recalling one of Granny's favorite edicts—"Bite your tongue before it digs your grave"—she reluctantly did just that with the others, keeping her silence as her father-in-law and his guests raged, not wishing to find herself in what could be nothing less than an ugly (and useless) quarrel with her new relatives. But when the Duchess and Lord and Lady Wycomb joined the Duke in London a short time later, and the visitors stopped, and the houseguests dispersed to their own homes, both she and Thomas heaved a sigh of relief.

Finding themselves alone at Ashton suited them perfectly. All talk of what the papers were calling the Irish problem ceased. Instead, they concentrated on settling into their new life and getting comfortable in their new marriage. Letting go of the vision of her future that she'd clung to over the long years of the war—marriage to Donal, a home of their own and eventually children—was sometimes difficult, but whenever a pang of regret was especially sharp, she was able to push it away by reminding herself that the life she'd once imagined was just that: imaginary. It had never been any more real than a pleasant daydream.

Rynn had a set of parallel bars installed in an obscure back hallway, and Thomas used them to practice walking with the fervor of a religious convert. With his increasing strength he was able to get about on crutches over longer distances and for greater periods of time, and his spirits improved as his mobility did. He still coughed, but not so often or so deeply. He thought, and Rynn agreed, that his lungs were improving, too.

The rain stopped, and although it remained cold, they were able to get outside every day. Mostly she would push him bundled up in his chair around the labyrinth of stone terraces, but sometimes he would attempt to navigate the paths through the closest of the gardens on his crutches. Other times, if it was too cold or he was feeling particularly tired, they would take the car and, with one of the footmen driving, explore the scenic byways of Surrey while Thomas pointed out places of interest for her edification. Then Thomas got the brilliant notion that he would teach her to drive, which was something he could no longer do, so that they could tootle about in privacy, without the need for a chauffeur. Ensconced in the passenger seat, he would patiently instruct her on the use of the three floorboard foot pedals: the left one was the clutch, the middle one sent the car into reverse and the right one was the brake. There was also a handbrake that had to be released before the car would move. The throttle that controlled the gas was a lever on the right side of the steering wheel. Operating all those gadgets at the right moment and in the right order was tricky to say the least. The mishaps that ensued led to much hilarity as she practiced along the country lanes and over Ashton's frozen fields.

By the time Thomas, in between snorts of laughter, pronounced her a splendid driver (after she'd sent them lurching through a row of carefully tended topiaries and barely avoided launching the car over an embankment into an ornamental duck pond by hitting on the right combination of pedals and levers to stop the thing at the last possible second) they'd become the very best of friends, as comfortable in their relationship as if they'd known each other all their lives.

We're going to be all right, Rynn thought with a sense of profound relief as they arrived back at the house, where she managed to stop the car almost where she meant to without hitting anything, including the footman who appeared right on time with Thomas's chair. Glancing over at Thomas, who was ruddy faced and laughing and looking as healthy and carefree as she'd ever seen him, she said the words out loud.

"Now that you've got us home in one piece, certainly we are." He shot her a teasing look.

"I'm talking about me. Us. *This*." Her gesture encompassed the house, the grounds, the car, him. "Our marriage. It's going to be all right."

He stopped laughing. His expression turned utterly serious as he reached for her hand.

"I hope it's going to be more than all right," he said. "I mean to make you happy."

For the briefest of moments, the naked adoration that she had seen in them once before blazed at her from his eyes. Then his lids dropped as if he was afraid his unguarded gaze might reveal too much.

But that one look was enough. Enough to remind her of how he felt. He was in love with her, and while she wasn't in love with him, that was something that would very likely cure itself with time. Anyway, romantic love was a blindness and a folly, as dangerous as a lightning bolt, and as ephemeral, as she had learned the hard way with Donal. Real love, the kind that lasted, was built—yes, built—on a solid base of friendship and respect and trust. And she had those things with Thomas. All she—they—had to do was put in the work.

"I'm happy," she said, and in that moment at least it was true.

"I am, too."

Carrying her hand to his mouth, he pressed his lips to its back.

The warmth of his lips against her skin, the gentleness of his still-way-too-thin fingers wrapped around hers, the growing bond between them and, yes, the laughter they had shared, all came together in that moment to reassure her that she had indeed chosen the right path, the one meant for her. She and Thomas would build a future together using loyalty and affection and kindness and shared experiences and sheer time as bricks, and it would be solid and *good*.

She might miss Ireland, but Ireland would always be a part of her.

She might miss Granny and Glenna, but they'd made plans to come to England in the summer, when Glenna's teaching commitment would be at an end, by which time Thomas had promised they would have their own house where her loved ones could join them as opposed to them all staying with his family, which she did not think Granny especially was constitutionally capable of doing.

She might miss Donal, but the pangs of what-could-have-been were diminishing by the day. What she'd felt for Donal was the blind infatuation of a young girl, while her growing regard for Thomas, and his love for her—that was something she could build a life on.

For the first time since she'd raced out into the night to warn Donal, she felt whole.

She and Thomas had barely made it into the house before her newfound optimism was upended by two unwelcome bits of news.

The first one came in the form of the *Evening Standard*, announcing on its front page that Eamon de Valera and two associates, Sean McGarry and Sean Milroy, had somehow managed to escape the supposedly impregnable stronghold that was His Majesty's Prison Lincoln.

The second was an invitation: they, Lord and Lady Thomas Dunne, were summoned forthwith to London to attend a fundraiser for wounded veterans to be hosted by none other than His Royal Highness the Prince of Wales.

Chapter Sixteen

In light of the recent death of his younger brother, Prince John, a circumstance that was hardly noted by those outside the royal orbit due to the fact that the fourteen-year-old's severe epilepsy had seen him locked away from all save his minders for years, the Prince of Wales had chosen to honor his mother's natural grief by receiving his guests at the Goring Hotel, which was more or less next door to Buckingham Palace, rather than the far more magnificent environs of Buckingham Palace itself, where the King and Queen were in residence.

Those factors, as put forward in the Ladies' Column about the upcoming event that Rynn had read in the gossipy *Daily Mail* the previous morning, had prepared her for a rather subdued and solemn occasion. But on the night of the fundraiser the Goring's splendid ballroom dazzled in its opulence. Floor-to-ceiling gilded mirrors bedecked with flowers and ribbon streamers made it seem as though the six hundred guests were legion. Exploding flashbulbs as photographers took pictures were as ubiquitous as stars in the sky. The guest list, described in that same column as "top of the trees," included military men, government officials, high-ranking aristocrats, the very rich and, everywhere Rynn looked, exquisitely turned-out women, all mingling under the glittering lights of multiple oversize chandeliers. Jaunty jazz music combined with the sound of laughter and chatter and the clink of glasses lent the function a far more festive atmosphere than Rynn had anticipated. It was, in fact, like no gathering she had ever attended or ever thought to attend, and although she would have never admitted it to a living soul, she found it intimidating.

A cat may look upon a king, you know. The Irish proverb, which she'd always understood to mean that no man (or woman) was better than any other, sprang into her mind with perfect timing. Especially since looking upon a king, or so near to a king as didn't matter, was at that moment precisely what she was doing.

"Yes, thank you, it's a tragic loss, especially for my mother," His Royal Highness the Prince of Wales said to a matronly lady who had just expressed sympathy at the passing of his youngest brother. "I am not feeling the loss so keenly myself, as the number of years that separated us precluded my knowing him very well."

When that snippet of conversation reached her ears as she waited in the reception line for her own introduction to the Prince, Rynn was taken aback. But she only realized that her reaction to what could be seen as royal callousness showed on her face when Thomas, who was beside her in his chair with a footman to push him, beckoned her to bend closer, and then when she did whispered, "Don't look so shocked. Empathy for his fellow human beings was never Gretel's strong suit."

"Gretel?" Rynn frowned, not sure she understood the sardonic remark.

"HRH and I were at Magdalen College at the same time. Wales rarely left the side of his tutor, Dr. Henry Hansell, the whole while he was there. Thus we chaps started calling him Gretel."

Hansel and Gretel. As she made the connection Rynn had to smile.

"There! You're looking far less nervous. Though why you should be nervous, I have no earthly idea. You are by far the most beautiful woman in the room. The envious looks I've been getting from every man who sets eyes on you have left me quite puffed up with pride."

"Thank you. You're looking very handsome yourself," she responded, and meant it. In his military uniform, with more weight on his bones, his complexion now healthily ruddy rather than pale, his fair hair brushed to burnished gold and the beginnings of a mustache just starting to darken his upper lip, he was not only handsome but dashing, and she told him that, too.

"Yes, and if only the ladies did not have to crawl about on the floor to see me properly you would no doubt be receiving a barrage of envious looks yourself."

That made her laugh. She was still smiling as she reached His Royal Highness and the introductions were made. She *was* nervous, despite her fashionable hairstyle and the gorgeous bronze silk dress that the designer Lucile had made up for her during the two and a half weeks she and Thomas had been in London. The new pearl earbobs Thomas had given her and the matching double strand of pearls lent to her by the Duchess, who was present along with the Duke and Lord and Lady Wycomb, were gorgeous, and her entire ensemble was as elegant and fashionable as that of any lady present. But she still felt woefully out of place. In truth, all that finery meant little in the teeth of her awareness of the seething hostility toward the Irish that was now as ubiquitous in London as the fog. The escape of de Valera and his associates, coupled with the ambush at Soloheadbeg, had sent the British into a teeth-gnashing frenzy. The search for the escapees, who were, according to a confidential briefing the Duke attended and then discussed at length at home with various visiting cabinet members, suspected to be hiding in a safe house somewhere in the vicinity of Manchester with a plan to move on to Liverpool and from there cross the Irish Sea to Dublin, generated daily headlines in the newspapers.

Since she and Thomas were currently staying with the Duke and Duchess at Hartford House, their magnificent London home, along with the details of the search and the grim fate planned for de Valera and the others when they were recaptured, Rynn heard almost more than she could stomach about the treacherous, lecherous, ungovernable nature of the Irish. As many in the aristocratic circles Thomas's family moved in now knew of her and her background, she was conscious of being the subject of a great deal of gossip whenever she went out, and, as she was tonight, the object of a barrage of curious looks. Meeting Edward, the Prince of Wales, the most popular of the royals and an international heartthrob because of his blond-haired, blue-eyed, choirboy good looks, had been presented to her as a high honor, but under the circumstances it was something she would rather have foregone. But for Thomas's sake here she was, feeling a little like Daniel in the lion's den if the truth were known, and if anyone present had an issue with her race, she was prepared to face them down with her head held high.

"Lady Thomas Dunne, Your Royal Highness," the servant standing at the Prince's elbow announced. Stepping forward to find herself in front of the Prince, who was surprisingly small and slight but as goldenly beautiful as advertised, Rynn managed a creditable curtsy, murmured something she hoped was not too trite in response to his pleasantries and suffered having the most eligible bachelor in the world kiss her hand.

"Perhaps you will save me a dance later," the Prince said.

Without waiting for her reply—she got the impression he took her delighted assent for granted—he turned to Thomas.

"Dunne! Horrid to see you in such a condition, my dear fellow, but I must tell you I envy you your time in France! I would so like to have seen combat in the trenches myself!" The Prince's greeting to Thomas, to Rynn's ears, provided one more bit of evidence of His Royal Highness's surprising lack of sensitivity to the feelings of others, but she clapped politely as the Prince pinned on Thomas's jacket the military medal that had been presented to each of the wounded veterans present as they passed through the line. Flashbulbs popped as photographs were taken, the sudden explosion of light making her blink, and then she was being motioned to move on down the line to the dark-haired young woman standing next to HRH.

Slender and sweet faced rather than beautiful, dressed in the height of fashion, this was Mrs. Freda Dudley Ward. The twenty-four-year-old Mrs. Ward, Thomas had informed her beforehand, was widely known to be the Prince's mistress despite her married state. Notwithstanding the irregularity of their association, she was universally received and accorded every respect.

"Oh, yes, you are the Irish bride," Mrs. Ward trilled as Rynn was introduced, giving Rynn a sweeping look that encompassed everything from her upswept hair to her shoes. "Dear Alice—" it took Rynn a second to connect "dear Alice" with Lady Wycomb "—has told me *all.* You must come visit me one afternoon. Without her, of course, because how can we gossip about her if she is present?"

Mrs. Ward gave a mischievous giggle. Rynn smiled and said she certainly would, with no intention of doing so, and moved on again. After that, she was introduced to a few royal cousins, several government officials and one major general. Then she and Thomas were free of the line.

As they made their way through the crowd, Thomas was swamped with well-wishers: soldiers in and out of uniform, former schoolmates, friends from the hunt with which he used to ride. His popularity with his peers was both touching and eye-opening. It gave her one more glimpse into the boy he used to be and the man he would have become if the war had not permanently altered his path.

For her part, she sipped champagne and smiled as she acknowledged introductions and said what was appropriate. Through it all, she stayed close to Thomas's side, nervily conscious all the while of the tidal wave of mostly silent curiosity directed at her from everyone they met.

After his duties on the reception line were completed, the Prince stepped up on a small dais to welcome his guests and say a few words urging them to donate to the cause. Other speakers followed, and then in a heartbreaking moment the young daughter of a soldier who was killed at the capture of Mons, in the last battle of the war, was called up to read a poem about the fallen. "In Flanders Fields" brought many of those present, including Rynn, to tears.

Immediately afterward, the band struck up an almost incongruously lively tune and the Prince led Mrs. Ward onto the floor as they all were invited to join in the dancing.

Although she had danced many times before, of course, at pubs and parties and dancehalls in Dublin when she was undergoing her nurse's training and in Bundoran and the neighboring villages with Donal and others, Rynn was uncomfortable with the idea of taking to the floor under so many curious eyes. Despite Thomas's urging, she refused several invitations to dance, preferring to remain with him on the sidelines while chatting with those similarly disinclined.

Until the Prince of Wales, having joined their small group of former soldiers engaged in verbally refighting old battles to weigh in with his own tales of being overseas among the troops while bemoaning that he had never actually been allowed by his government to fight, solicited her hand for the promised dance.

"Dunne, if I may borrow your wife? Lady Thomas, if you will do me the honor?"

A quick downward glance at Thomas, who gave her a wicked smile, confirmed what she already knew: there was no refusing such an invitation. So she in turn smiled at the Prince, dropped a small curtsy and found herself swept up in the whirling, twirling carousel that was dozens of couples dancing to the tune of "Smiles."

"I understand this is your first visit to London," the Prince said, and she agreed. Despite his diminutive size, which he didn't seem sensitive about, the arm about her waist was firm, and his grip on her hand was strong. He was an excellent dancer, while she was mediocre at best, and sadly out of practice. Holding up her end of the conversation as they dipped and turned required every bit of her concentration.

"I am to visit Canada later this year, you know. I'm very much looking forward to it. The people seem almost embarrassingly enthusiastic. I have no doubt I should be met with a far different reception if I should attempt a visit to your country. The Irish seem to have little use for the Crown at the moment. Quite a belligerent people, actually. Although I suspect it's only a small group causing all the problems. Do you agree?"

She did not, but she didn't want to contradict the heir to the British throne, and particularly not at the moment. Britain's growing anger toward the Irish, which was beginning to strike her as rather like that of an autocratic parent toward a child who simply cannot be made to mind, was dwarfed by the volcano of resentment that had built up in her countrymen over eight hundred years of mistreatment. Not causing any embarrassment to Thomas and his family had become an objective with her, and with that end in mind she sought for the most noncommittal reply she could give.

"I really couldn't say, sir."

"Well, I am sure they will soon come around. It's not as though they have any real choice. Churchill is champing at the bit to get them sorted out, and I have every confidence that he will succeed."

"David! David!"

Distracted, the Prince glanced in the direction of the female voice that was loud enough to cut through the music and the noise, nodded once as if in answer and then looked back at Rynn.

"That's all for me, I'm afraid," he said. "It seems I'm being summoned to another engagement."

Rynn remembered then that he was called David by his family and friends and blessed the interruption. He was being beckoned to an anteroom, she saw as she glanced in the caller's direction to find Freda Dudley Ward waving at them—or rather at him. Mrs. Ward had donned a sumptuous blond fur coat and hat and stood together with a small party also dressed for the outdoors.

"I've enjoyed our dance." The Prince ended it with a flourish as they neared the doorway where Mrs. Ward waited. "I would be interested in getting your perspective on the unfortunate situation in Ireland in a setting where we may more easily talk. But for now, let me find you another dance partner."

Another dance with a stranger was the last thing Rynn wanted to endure.

"That is kind of you, sir, but I think I should return to my husband now. Please go ahead and don't worry about me. I can easily find my way."

"David!" Mrs. Ward's wave was more urgent.

"If you're certain." The Prince was clearly eager to be off.

She assured him she was.

"Then I'll say good night," he said, and with a smile for Rynn and a kiss of his fingertips to Mrs. Ward as she called again he headed toward her.

Left alone, Rynn took the few steps needed to lose herself among the shifting groups mulling about on the side of the dance floor, then paused to get her bearings. The Prince had gone, along with Mrs. Ward and the rest of her party. The dance floor remained crowded, and she spotted Lord and Lady Wycomb, with separate partners, among the dancers. She couldn't see Thomas but guessed that he still would be on the other side of the ballroom near where she had left him. She was just contemplating the best way to rejoin him without cutting through the middle of the dance floor when she spotted a tall, powerfully built and somehow elusively familiar figure moving toward her through the crowd.

Her eyes widened as he got closer and she recognized Owen Maguire. Clean-shaven, his dark hair brushed smoothly back, elegantly dressed in a black tailcoat with a white waistcoat and tie, he was as far removed from the raffish captain of the *Reaper* as it was possible to be. What he was doing there she had no idea, but for just a moment, as her eyes rested on him, she found to her surprise that she was enormously glad to see him. It was, she thought, because he brought Ireland with him. Looking at him was like looking at a small piece of home.

A wave of longing to be back among the soft mists and green hills of her birthplace arose out of nowhere to hit her like a brick.

Despite how promising her new life seemed, England, she feared, was still going to take some getting used to.

She only realized that she was standing stock still watching Maguire's approach when someone knocked into her from behind. Staggering a little, turning to look, she found herself face-to-face with a leering, middle-aged army officer with a very red face. He'd obviously had too much to drink.

"Dance, lovey?" He reached for her hand, which she instinctively put behind her back, out of his reach.

"No." Realizing that was probably too rude a refusal given the august nature of the company, she added a belated "Thank you."

"The lady's with me." Maguire spoke from behind her. Despite the circumstances, the soft lilt in his voice was music to her ears.

The officer looked past her, then grimaced as if not liking what he saw.

"Sorry. My mistake," he said, and moved on.

Chapter Seventeen

Rynn turned back toward Maguire, who was closer than she'd expected. She had to tilt her head back to meet his eyes, which held a gleam that she misliked.

"My, my, if it isn't Lady Thomas Dunne." Maguire shook his head at her. He had dimples, she saw, which were totally incongruous with the hard, tough man she knew him to be. They'd been hidden by his beard and were now fully in play as he gave her a mocking smile. "Wasn't it just a couple of months ago that you were madly in love with and planning to marry someone else? Well, what is it they say? Once an opportunist, always an opportunist?"

"Hush," she hissed at him, knowing now why that look of his had put her on guard and mindful that they were in a crowd. "What are you doing here?"

"Unless I'm mistaken, this is a fundraiser, and I have funds."

"You were invited?"

"I was. I'm a war hero, you know. That gets you through a lot of unlikely doors. Rather like beauty does for a woman."

"Why are you even in London?"

"Business."

"*You* have business in London?"

"I do."

"What business?" Rynn encountered a curious glance from a passing lady—actually a trio of ladies, young matrons she thought, whose eyes slid past her to look Maguire over appreciatively. How handsome he was had not previously registered with her, but it did now, as she saw the looks he was drawing from her fellow females. Not that it mattered, except she couldn't say what she wanted with so many eyes upon them. She put a hand on his arm. The best way to have a private conversation amid such a throng without attracting excessive attention was to do what everyone else was doing. "Dance with me."

His eyebrows went up. "Tch, tch, what will your husband say?"

"Thomas will be pleased to see me enjoying myself. You can dance me over to him. We can talk on the way."

"And what does Thomas know about me?" His eyes narrowed at her even as he let her pull him onto the dance floor

"Nothing. As far as I know, he's never even heard your name. Certainly not from me. You don't need to worry, I'll be keeping your secrets." She placed her hand on the broad shelf of his shoulder as he put a very solid arm around her waist. They clasped hands—his was big and warm and grasped hers just a shade too tightly—and then they were gliding around the floor with all the other couples.

"We'll be keeping each other's secrets," he said.

A tilt of her chin at him was her only acknowledgment of that, but his grip on her hand eased and she realized that the tightness of his hold had been meant to convey a message, which he apparently considered she had received. Neither of them said anything for a moment, letting the music fill the silence as other couples swirled around them in a blur of color and movement. Dancing with him was easier than dancing with the Prince, she found. His steps were basic and because she didn't much care what he thought of her dancing she didn't have to worry about minding hers. Instead, she was able to simply relax and follow his lead.

"How is . . . the situation . . . at home?" she asked, careful not to get too specific in case she should be overheard.

"In Bundoran, do you mean? I left the area not long after you did, so I'm not exactly up to date on all the news."

"Where did you go?"

"Under the circumstances, I thought it best to relocate my operation to Dublin. It's been a good move, one I don't regret."

She frowned a little as she took that in. "Do you know if they've made any progress on finding out who killed Molly Kincaid?"

"From what I've heard, Seamus O'Reilly remains the odds-on favorite."

"It wasn't he."

"I bow to your superior knowledge of events."

"What of—" she wanted to say *the search for Donal and Seamus and the missing guns*, but again the fear of being overheard made her careful "—the other investigation? About . . . the O'Reillys."

"It's ongoing. You should know that Haney's dead. The official word is he was shot while trying to escape. There's still some disagreement over whether the O'Reillys and Boyd are dead as well, but with no formal finding made there's a price on their heads and they're considered wanted men. But I can tell you that after Detective Kenney's unfortunate accident things in Bundoran have calmed down to a degree."

The news about Haney had quickened her heartbeat. Now her eyes went wide on his face. "Detective Kenny had an accident?"

"He did. His brakes failed, and his car went over a cliff. Most unfortunate. He survived, although he was badly injured. He's in a hospital in Liverpool now, I believe—him not trusting Irish hospitals, you understand—where he's expected to make a very slow, very painful recovery."

"That *is* unfortunate." Her eyes stayed glued to his.

"Yes. And by the by, to refer back to our last conversation, it turned out that my crew wasn't the problem. The trail led back to one of Tremaine's men, who like Kenney has since suffered his own unfortunate accident. One he *didn't* survive."

As the meaning beneath his words became clear, a chill went through her. She missed a step, and his arm tightened around her waist. Their last conversation, in Bundoran, was the one where she had warned him that he was being spied on. Her face must have telegraphed her sudden suspicion—*You orchestrated those accidents, didn't you?*—because he gave her another of those mocking smiles.

"Did anyone ever tell you that you have the most revealing face? And the answer to the question you're *not* asking me is no."

She didn't believe him.

"I'm in your debt, it seems," he said. "Just as *you* are in Detective Kenney's debt. Only think, if it weren't for him, you would never have married your husband."

She stiffened. "If you're implying what I think you're implying, let me assure you that I'm very happy in my marriage."

"I was implying nothing, I promise you."

"Thomas is a lovely man. Kind, and generous, and—"

She broke off, aware from his expression that she was sounding defensive.

"I don't regret marrying him *at all*," she said, chin in the air, and was instantly aware that she sounded defensive again.

Maguire's smile widened. The deepening dimples, the glint in his eyes—he was silently laughing at her.

"Do you *really* have business in London?" she asked, nettled.

"Certainly I do. Why else would I be here? Surely, *surely* you don't think I came all this way merely to check on you? You're quite lovely, my dear Lady Thomas, but—"

"Of course I wasn't thinking any such thing!" Rynn could

feel heat rising in her cheeks. "If you must know, I was wondering if perhaps you're on the run from the law!"

As soon as she said it, she could have bitten off her tongue. A hasty glance around reassured her that none of the other couples were near enough to have overheard.

"I'm sorry to disappoint you—I know your taste in men runs to outlaws—but I'm really not that exciting. I assure you my presence in London is perfectly aboveboard."

He *was* laughing at her. Only now he was making no attempt at all to hide it.

"Stop scowling at me, you'll give yourself wrinkles," he said. "If you must know, I'm here as part of a delegation. We're hoping to head off this conflict before it can escalate."

"What?" If he'd meant to distract her, he'd succeeded. She gave him a skeptical look.

"It's the truth. The state of affairs between our two countries is at a tipping point. One more incident, one more wrong move, could find us in an all-out war. If, for example, the Brits should recapture de Valera and his associates and execute them as they did the leaders of the Rising, there will be no stopping it. Ireland will explode. Hundreds, perhaps thousands of men will die needlessly on both sides. And, more to the point, it will be bad for business."

"More to the point?"

"Politicians don't care about the poor sods shooting at each other. What they care about is business. Profit. Money. Never make the mistake of thinking wars are about anything else."

"That's terrible."

"It is. It's also true. And de Valera's escape could be the flash point that sets off the whole thing. We know the search for him is intensifying. My most pressing fear is that they'll find him and shoot him in the course of trying to bring him in. The consequences of that would be catastrophic. It would put paid to any hope of peace."

"Unless de Valera's somehow managed to get out of England, he almost certainly will be found," she said. "With the size of the reward for information leading to his whereabouts, tips are pouring in. Someone somewhere is going to get it right."

A subtle change in his posture, a tightening of his arm around her, an increased intensity in his gaze told her how much she'd just interested him.

"What kind of tips?" he asked.

And just like that, she knew. Whether she'd suddenly acquired the ability to read faces as easily as everybody seemed to read hers, or whether it was something in his voice or even the Sight making itself felt at last, she was as certain as it was possible to be that Maguire knew exactly where de Valera was and was working to get him to safety before the worst could happen. He was probing to see if she had information that would be of use to him. And once again, she had to choose a path: keep silent out of loyalty to the family she had married into, or reveal what she knew to protect her country and countrymen.

She chose.

"The most promising one seems to be that he's hiding in a safe house in Manchester. As early as tomorrow, soldiers are to begin conducting house-to-house searches there," she said. "If they don't find him, they'll move on to Liverpool, on the theory that he's to be smuggled from there to Dublin. If that's true, I don't see how he can escape."

Maguire's eyes flickered. It was the only sign he gave that the information mattered to him, but she saw it.

"Let us hope for Ireland's sake that he does escape." Maguire's tone was carefully neutral. Then his expression changed; his mocking smile returned. Was he hoping to distract her again?

Too late: she knew what she knew. "Tell me something: How did your new husband's illustrious parents react to the news that he'd so unexpectedly taken a bride? Since I see that they're here with him and you, I take it they didn't quite cast him out?"

This time his baiting didn't bother her.

"They've been very kind."

"Have they? In that case, I wonder if you could introduce me? I've been trying to finagle a meeting with Lloyd George with no success so far. It occurs to me that going through your father-in-law, who has his ear, might be a quicker path."

"I can introduce you to Thomas," she said. "I'm sure he'd be glad to arrange a meeting with his father."

"Thank you." He smiled at her. A genuine smile without the least hint of mockery. It was an acknowledgment that, as far as any threat to the country they both loved was concerned, they were on the same side.

When the dance ended, she took him to find Thomas. He was, as he had been when she left him, surrounded by his mates, including former soldiers, several of whom wore their uniforms for the occasion.

"There you are," Thomas said as she reached his side with Maguire following a pace or so behind. "I was beginning to think you'd run away with Wales. What *have* you done with him, by the way?"

Smiling at him, Rynn said, "His Royal Highness had another engagement," and stepped aside to draw Maguire forward.

Even as she did, Thomas was introducing her to the men around him, adding as he finished, "Gentlemen, this is my wife."

While she acknowledged the introductions, and before she could introduce Maguire, Thomas said to him, "I'm Thomas Dunne," with an appraising look, and held out his hand.

"Owen Maguire." As the two shook hands, one of the men

near Thomas looked hard at Maguire and said, "Owen Maguire? The same Major Owen Maguire of the Thirty-Sixth Ulster who won the Victoria Cross in the Big Push at the Somme?"

Instantly the eyes of all the men in the group fastened on Maguire.

"I am," he said. "We lost a lot of good men in that battle."

"We did," one of the others agreed. "Damned Huns and their dug-in bunkers."

"Bloody machine guns," another said.

"Fucking mud," a third chimed in, then immediately looked self-conscious. "Begging your pardon, Lady Thomas."

She waved the apology away, not that anyone noticed particularly because the men were already off and running with their war reminisces. Rynn was left with nothing to do but listen. As it turned out, several of them, including Maguire, had been at the Third Battle of Ypres, or Passchendaele as it was commonly known, where Thomas had been so badly wounded. By the time Maguire got around to telling Thomas why he was in London and that he hoped to have a chance to talk to the Duke and, through him, the Prime Minister, the two, somewhat to Rynn's bemusement, were well on their way to becoming fast friends.

"I can get you a meeting with my father easily enough," Thomas said. "I could introduce you tonight, but I think it would go better if I warmed him up a bit first. He's quite upset with the rebels at the moment. If you'll give me your direction in London, I'll send word as to a time and place."

That was done, and then Maguire excused himself and was gone. She and Thomas left not long afterward. They rode home with the Duke and Duchess—the Wycombs had traveled separately—and by the time they reached Hartford House the Duke had agreed to meet with Maguire and his delegation.

"I'll send a note around to Maguire's hotel in the morning," Thomas said once they were alone together in their suite of rooms.

"Although at this point, I'm not sure that there's much anyone can do. My father is quite adamant that the rebellion must be put down at once, and he's not the only one who feels that way."

Clad in his dressing gown, his valet dismissed for the night, he rolled up behind her in his chair. Having been helped out of her dress and into her night attire by Parry, the maid Thomas and his mother insisted she needed, Rynn too wore only a thin robe over her nightgown as she sat in front of the vanity brushing her hair.

"Major Maguire is well respected in County Donegal. He and his delegation might be able to act as a bridge between the two sides." Putting her brush down preparatory to braiding her hair for sleep, Rynn smiled at Thomas through the mirror.

"Let us hope." Thomas reached out to run a gentle hand down the length of her hair, which had grown almost to her waist, stroking it as one might a horse or a dog. "You have the most beautiful hair. Black and shiny as a raven's wing."

"Thank you. How very poetic of you." She made a face at him through the mirror as his hand fell away from her hair.

"I've never heard you mention Maguire before. How well do you know him?"

There was something in his voice—she'd never heard that exact note in it. He was watching her through the mirror as she began to braid her hair. She frowned a little. She didn't like lying to Thomas, but to tell him exactly how she knew Maguire would be to put Maguire in danger.

"Not well. He's from Killybegs, which makes him a neighbor, but I doubt I've spoken to him more than a handful of times. His sister is the friend of a friend."

"He seems like a decent enough fellow."

"I've never heard anything against him."

"High praise, indeed." He watched her through the mirror as she finished her braid by tying it off with a white ribbon.

"That's the best I can do. As I said, I don't know him well."

She turned around on the bench to look at him. With him in his chair they were almost of a height, but beneath the maroon dressing gown his shoulders were wider and his arms far stronger looking than they'd been when he'd first arrived at Ballyshannon Court and been assigned to her as a patient. With the lamplight shining on his fair hair and plenty of color in his face, any outside observer would have thought him perfectly healthy if they hadn't been able to see his chair. "You were certainly popular tonight. What a lot of friends you have! I was impressed."

"Were you?" He smiled at her, and the slight constraint she'd sensed in him vanished. "It's always an object with me to impress you, you know."

"You certainly succeeded." She returned his smile. His eyes darkened a little as he looked at her.

"Do you think about him much? O'Reilly, I mean?" His question was abrupt, and so unexpected that Rynn was taken aback.

"No, hardly at all," she answered and realized even as she said it that it was true. And she realized, too, that she wouldn't go back to Donal, to the way they had been, to the life she'd once dreamed of with him, if she could. That dream belonged to a younger girl, a different girl.

"Good," he said, and then he leaned forward to kiss her cheek. It was not much more than a butterfly brush of his lips against her skin, warm and a little bristly because of his blossoming mustache. Surprised, Rynn simply looked at him as he sat back in his chair.

"Well, I'm for bed," he said, and turned and rolled away to his own bedroom before she could corral her thoughts enough to think of anything to say.

Rynn was left to frown after him—and place her fingers over the spot on her cheek where he had kissed her.

Chapter Eighteen

Over the next few weeks, Maguire and his associates conferred several times with the Duke at Hartford House before a meeting was arranged with Lloyd George, who was preoccupied with a hundred other matters including the race riots currently roiling London and the other seaports and hammering out the finer points of the Paris Peace Conference, which effort was ongoing. According to Thomas, who'd been invited to attend the meeting, the Prime Minister seemed to consider the unrest in Ireland as little more than a bothersome distraction that could be crushed underfoot in short order, leaving him free to deal with more important matters. But Maguire, employing what his chief associate, Ernie O'Malley, called his innate gift of the blarney, talked the Prime Minister into agreeing not to send in more soldiers or otherwise escalate the situation as long as the rebels eschewed further violence themselves.

The house-to-house searches in Manchester and Liverpool had so far come up empty. Maguire, who Rynn saw on those occasions when he stopped by the house, did not appear concerned that that would change. What she took from that was that de Valera and his associates, wherever they were, were no longer to be found in either Manchester or Liverpool, although the searches continued.

During that same period, Rynn was shocked to pick up a copy of *The Times* to discover a photograph of herself dancing with the Prince of Wales dominating the front page. The caption read, "HRH the Prince of Wales dances with Lady Thomas's Dunne, the beautiful Irish bride of the Duke of Hartford's younger son, at the fundraiser for wounded war veterans at the Goring Hotel."

The picture was picked up by other newspapers and even ran in the gossipy *Sketch* magazine, which added a horrifying-to-Rynn final line to the caption: "Has Mrs. Ward acquired a rival at last?" When Rynn called on the Prince's mistress at Thomas's insistence—"If you want to convince everyone that the *Sketch* reporter has got it right, all you have to do is avoid Mrs. Ward at all costs" was what he said to persuade her—Mrs. Ward laughed it off. But more pictures of her in the *Daily Mail* and other publications followed. In them she was inevitably described as "the beautiful Irish bride" of the Duke of Hartford's son, with the clear inference that for one of her race to be raised to so elevated a position in the social pecking order was such an oddity that it was worthy of being touted far and wide. The unwelcome exposure made Rynn self-conscious. It also brought what seemed to her like an avalanche of visitors eager to get a look at her to Hartford House, although Alice (as she now called Lady Wycomb) assured her with a shrug that the deluge of callers was nothing out of the ordinary now that Parliament was in session and people were starting to return to town. In other words, it had nothing to do with her at all.

"Pay no mind to her. She's always been a jealous cat. She hates that you're getting more attention than her," Thomas's cousin Lady Maud, who'd come to town to stay with them for a few weeks, whispered after Alice exited the car delivering them to a ladies' tea at the Criterion in Piccadilly on Thursday of the fourth week following the fundraiser. Having looked critically at Rynn's pale peach afternoon dress with its matching belted jacket and cunning veiled hat, Alice had just remarked on how fortunate Rynn was to possess neither a true womanly bosom or hips, as the new dropped-waist dresses such as the one Rynn was wearing were designed to most flatter females with boyish figures like hers.

"I prefer to think she meant it as a compliment," Rynn replied as she stepped out of the car next and was followed onto the sidewalk by Maud, who she was starting to consider a friend. She knew better, of course, but having been the recipient of a number of Alice's barbed compliments she'd learned that seeming to entirely miss the point was the best course and had the added bonus of annoying her sister-in-law.

"If you say so," Maud replied doubtfully. Then they were swept into the restaurant along with a tide of women who were all coming together to hear Helen Gordon Liddle of the Women's Social and Political Union, who'd endured forcible feeding to combat her hunger strike while imprisoned for her "antigovernment" suffragette activities, talk about her experience and the vitally important cause of women's suffrage. Mrs. Liddle was a compelling speaker and was rightfully lauded for her role in winning the vote for women over thirty in the last election, but the most interesting part for Rynn came at the end.

"Is that not your sister?" Maud whispered, nodding at someone in the exiting crowd. While Alice had gone ahead, Rynn had stayed back with Maud, who'd wanted to get Mrs. Liddle's autograph on the pamphlet on women's rights they all had been given, so they were among the last to leave. It took Rynn a moment to realize that Maud didn't mean Glenna had somehow found her way to London but was instead talking about her unknown half-sister, Penelope.

"I have no idea. I've never so much as seen her," Rynn confessed.

"Oh, my," Maud said, and nudged her again before pointing discreetly. "Well, it is her. Up there, in blue. With the feather in her hat. That's Penelope Carmichael. Oh, and she's with her mother, Lady Somerset. Behind her, in pink."

Rynn looked. The woman, Lady Somerset, was plain faced, full-figured, beautifully dressed, with light brown hair twisted up in an elaborate chignon. The girl was young—just turned eighteen, if she had her dates right—of medium height, slim and dressed in the latest fashion. Her strawberry-blonde hair was cut into a fashionable short, wavy bob. Her complexion was fair. Rynn was too far away to discern the color of her eyes, but she was as certain as she could be without actually seeing them that they were blue. Her face was long and slim, with a decided chin. Her nose was a trifle on the long and thin side, too, and her mouth was wide and full lipped. She was attractive and elegant rather than beautiful, and the overall impression she gave was of aristocratic wealth. She looked, in fact, almost exactly like her father—*their* father—and seeing her brought the image of him, of the last time Rynn had seen him when he'd bade her and Glenna goodbye from the doorway of Granny's house, forcibly to mind. She'd been seven years old, and he'd been a stranger. She hadn't even realized she remembered until this, the sight of her half-sister who so unexpectedly resembled him, brought it back.

Rynn was surprised at the shaft of pain she felt. She'd thought she was immune to what had happened by now, but apparently she was not. When her father had abandoned them after her mother's death, *this* was the family he'd created instead. This was the daughter he'd chosen, the woman he'd chosen, the life he'd chosen, instead of her and her sister and his life with them. He hadn't bothered to send for them. Except for that one visit, in which her vague recollection had him signing papers relating to them that Granny had needed, they'd had no other contact. He'd left them behind like they were nothing, like they were trash.

Irish trash, which she supposed was the way he and his new family thought of them.

"Shall we try to catch up?" Maud's tone was eager as she looked after the pair, who were exiting through the main door.

"No." Rynn's reply was sharp, instinctive. She caught herself, not wanting to give Maud, or anyone, a glimpse of the wound that had not yet, to her dismay, healed. "Not today. I'd really rather not have the whole world as witness to what should be a private family moment."

"Oh. Oh, you're right, of course." If Maud was disappointed, she hid it well. They went outside and climbed back into the car with Alice, where Rynn listened to the two of them discuss everything from the horror of Mrs. Liddle's story to the quality of the refreshments to the latest gossip attaching to several of the ladies present. When the car pulled up in front of the gray stone mansion that was Hartford House in St. James Place, though, Rynn decided not to go inside right away. Instead, she told them that she was going to take a walk in the park to clear the headache she could feel coming on. Alice would never have volunteered to accompany her, Rynn knew, so she was safe in that regard. Maud, who would have, gave Rynn a sympathetic look that Rynn suspected stemmed from her conviction that seeing Penelope Carmichael and her mother had upset her and as a result she needed some time alone. Rynn once again cursed her telltale face, but at least it gave her the privacy she needed to come to terms with the distress she most unexpectedly felt.

It was a beautiful sunny afternoon, warm for spring. The sweet smell of a fresh new season was in the air. Green Park was living up to its name: the trees had just unfurled their shiny new leaves, the grassy meadows were coming alive and drifts of early daffodils provided bright bursts of color everywhere she looked. Thomas was out with his father, who was introducing him to influential friends with an eye toward moving him into a career in investing. This evening, he was promised to an all-gentlemen engagement, which meant there was no need for her to hurry back.

She could regain her equilibrium at her leisure.

A fair number of people were about, including a rowdy group of newly demobbed American soldiers, hundreds of whom roamed the city as they waited to be shipped home, but they paid no attention to her and she barely noticed them. She was breathing in the fresh air and listening to the birdsongs and in general enjoying the solitude until she turned down a path bordered on both sides by tall hedgerows. There, most unexpectedly, someone grabbed her arm from behind.

"Rynn."

At the first unwelcome touch, she'd already whipped around so fast that she'd dislodged her hat. Recognizing the voice at the same time as she recognized *him*, she gaped at Donal in astonishment before collecting herself.

"Are you daft? You can't be here." The words burst out in a fierce whisper. Fear that someone would recognize him tightened her chest. She cast a quick, anxious glance around. Fortunately, the dense green foliage of the hedgerows blocked any chance of him being seen by most of those in the park. On the path up ahead, a boy on a bicycle pedaled away. A young woman, a maid from the look of her, pushed a baby in a pram. Two more women, fashionably dressed, walked a dog on a leash. Those were the only ones near enough to get a good look at him and they were paying him no mind whatsoever.

"Do you think I want to be?" He sounded impatient. He looked rough, unshaven, his black hair overlong, with a peaked cap pulled low over his forehead and a worn brown jacket buttoned up over a collarless shirt, and loose black trousers. His hand tightened on her arm. "I need you to come with me."

"What? Where? I can't do that."

"You must. It's Seamus. He's been shot. He's in a bad way."

"What?"

"Come on."

She was, she discovered, already keeping pace with him, from sheer force of habit she supposed, as with his hand on her arm he propelled her along the brick path.

"He's been *shot*?"

"It's his leg. It's turned putrid and he's off his head with fever. I wouldn't have bothered you, *Lady Thomas*, but I daren't bring a doctor to him. Your nursing skills are all we have."

So he'd learned of her marriage. Well, time enough to address that later.

"How did he get shot?"

"We were by an unhappy chance in a warehouse in Liverpool a week ago when soldiers raided it. They were looking for de Valera, who'd been there, but Mick Collins and his crew got him spirited safe away a while ago. What they found instead was us, a whole group of us actually, and when they tried to arrest us, we fought our way out and ran. They started shooting, and a bullet caught Seamus in the leg. I got him out of there, and I thought he'd recover well enough, but he's not, he's getting worse."

"Why did they try to arrest you? Because of de Valera? Because of Mick Collins? Never say they recognized you." There was, she remembered, a price on his head, and on Fergus's, and a far bigger one on Seamus's. If the Brits knew, rather than merely suspected, the three men still lived, they would be relentless in their pursuit of them. As for Mick—Michael—Collins she had little doubt that he had a price on his head, too.

"I'm as sure as sure can be that they had no notion who we are. It wasn't either of those things."

She was walking with him quickly, willingly now, straightening her hat with one hand so that it was no longer ridiculously askew. Belatedly realizing that anyone watching might conclude that he was forcibly marching her away, she pulled her arm free of his grip and settled her hand in his elbow instead. So that they looked, she hoped, like any ordinary couple out for an afternoon stroll in the park. Except he looked like he'd gone on a drunken bender after raiding some church's poor bin, and she was wearing a modiste's elegant best.

"Then what was it?" she asked.

"With the mood the Brits are in these days, I'm thinking it was more than enough that we're Irish."

The look she gave him was sharp. She *knew* him. "What were you doing? And I want the truth, mind."

"Whisht, now." He growled it at her, and she took from that that he was afraid of being overheard, which meant he wasn't as sanguine about being out in public as he pretended.

"Donal." Her tone made it a warning.

"If you must know, we were working, packing up some crates to be sent out that night to Dublin. Seeing as how there's no fancy toff wanting to marry us and we have to earn our living and all."

She ignored his jibe about her marriage to concentrate on the important part.

"What was in the crates?" One look at his face gave her the answer. "*Guns?* Are you still involved in the gunrunning, then, you fool? After all it's cost you, and all of us?"

"Would you hush your mouth, woman?" He glared at her, and that was enough to tell her the truth of it and remind her of the danger and make her remember her surroundings, all at the same time.

"You were supposed to go to America!" It was another fierce whisper.

"Seamus wouldn't. Not after hearing about Molly. He says the soldiers that were on the Strand that night murdered her in cold blood, and he's vowed not to stop until he's killed every last one who was there."

"That's idiocy! He'll get himself—and you, you ninny!—killed. For something that can't be done! There were dozens of soldiers out there that night, and he doesn't even know that it was them for sure. Anyway, even if he's run mad, you could have gone to America yourself."

"And leave him? What do you take me for?"

They'd reached the far side of the park by that time. As they stepped out onto the sidewalk, which was crowded, she could do no more than give him a single, fulminating look that promised him an answer he wasn't going to like for later.

"Your poor mother's heartbroken," she hissed as he hustled her along.

"I sent her a message as soon as it was safe. She knows I'm not dead."

"She got taken in for questioning. So did Seamus's mother. And I did, too."

"I'm sorry for that. They'll pay, I promise."

"Ori Sullivan came up to me on Station Road. He said he wants his money, or the guns."

"I'm sorry for that, too."

"What are you going to do about it? He'll find you and Seamus eventually, you know."

"He already did, and you'll be pleased to know we've settled things between the three of us."

"You paid him back?"

"We cut him in on the job we were doing. He would have made a nice profit, too, if we hadn't gotten raided."

"So he didn't get his money?"

"I've no idea. We had to run for it, remember? But whether he did or not, we gave him the connection. He'll profit from it eventually."

"Granny always said you were born to be hanged."

"Your granny scares me, always did. Have you any money on you? I'm skint." He was looking up and down the street, which was busy with cars and motorbikes and bicycles and a horse-drawn cart or two. More soldiers, British ones, rattled past in an open-backed lorry. He watched it narrow eyed.

"I do. Fifteen pounds." Bank notes from the generous amount of pin money Thomas gave her were tucked away in her pocketbook in case she'd wanted to purchase anything at the event at the Criterion.

"Good. I'll be needing some of that for rent, and it'll pay the taxi, too." He succeeded in flagging down a car, taking it as a matter of course that her money was available for his use. Well, he knew her, too.

Chapter Nineteen

"Where are we going?" Rynn asked as a taxi pulled over and stopped.

"Chapel Street." Bundling her inside, he spoke to her and the driver at the same time.

"Have you medicine?" she asked him in a low voice as the taxi got underway, because she had nothing of the sort with her. If Seamus was in the state Donal claimed, he was going to need more than just her nursing skills to help him.

"We had some iodine. It's gone now. It didn't do much good anyway."

Rynn leaned forward to speak to the driver. "Take us to the nearest apothecary, please. And then I'll need you to pull over and wait."

"Yes, missus."

A moment later, the taxi pulled to the curb beside an apothecary shop.

"You stay here. I'll be as quick as I can," she said to Donal, and went inside. It wasn't very many minutes later that she emerged with several rolls of bandages and a specially compounded jar of BIPP, the miraculous new treatment for infected wounds that had been created by a woman doctor right there in London at the start of the war. Having grown familiar with it in the course of her work, Rynn was able to rattle off the ingredients and the proportions from memory so that the apothecary could easily make up what she needed.

"Still the managing sort, I see," Donal said, after she'd gotten back in the taxi and directed the driver to proceed. Which he did, pulling out into heavy traffic with a blare of his horn at an oncoming tram.

"Depending on the company. Some need more managing than others." With that pointed rejoinder, she handed over what was left of her money. He glanced at what she gave him and thrust it into his pocket.

"So, you've married," he said next, and from the way he looked at her she knew he had a great deal he wanted to say about that.

"I have."

"To the son of a duke, forsooth."

"Yes."

"That was some quick work. The speed of it's put a question in my mind about exactly what was going on at home while I was off at war."

"If your mind was capable of coming up with anything beyond rank stupidity, you'd know better." Her tone, and the blistering look she gave him, was daunting enough to stop that line of conversation, for the time being at least. His mouth tightened, but he said nothing more and looked out the window instead.

"Pardon me, sir and missus, but we'll have to take the long way around, because the worthless Socialists are marching down Lisson Street," the driver said.

So intent were they on what they *weren't* saying, the interruption startled them both.

"That's fine," Donal answered, unsurprised. A protest march by one disgruntled group or another had become a regular occurrence as the euphoria of the war being over was replaced by the harsh reality of a worsening economy, an overcrowded city and tens of thousands of demobbed soldiers returning home to the reality of no jobs.

After that, mindful of the driver's listening ears, neither of them said anything more until they reached their destination, which was in a part of London Rynn had never visited before. It was poor, and dirty, rife with peddlers hawking their wares and children in ragged clothing running unsupervised through the streets and beggars on seemingly every corner.

Chapel Street itself was a narrow, cobbled avenue lined with Georgian and Victorian houses on what looked, from the wash hung out to dry from various windows and the slimy nature of the cobblestones underfoot and the sheer number of persons, animals and vehicles crowded into it, like something out of one of the popular novels by Charles Dickens. There was no space between the houses. They rose up in a solid wall on both sides, blocking out the sun. It was dim and grim and noisy, and, as Rynn noted as she slid out of the taxi, smelled of unpleasant things.

"Couldn't you find somewhere less busy?" Rynn asked under her breath as Donal herded her toward the nearest doorway. What she meant was, wouldn't it have been better to find a more deserted area to hide out in, but with so many people around she was careful of being overheard.

Donal shook his head. "It's all immigrants here. There's Irish, Scottish, Welsh, Italian—all coming and going all the time. The whole street is lodging houses, both sides. We don't attract any notice."

He pushed open the door, and Rynn walked inside. She was just taking in grimy yellow walls and a peeling ceiling when a commotion to her left drew her gaze.

"*Seven come eleven*," a male voice yelled, making her jump. Her gaze flew to a group of men crouched on the floor of a small open room just inside the door. Something rattled across the hardwood, a wordless shout went up as several of them jumped to their feet with their fists raised in jubilation and Rynn realized they were playing a game of dice.

"If you're planning on staying on, Mr. Brady, I'll remind you that the rent on 314 is past due," the woman behind a desk on the other side of the entry hall sang out as Donal hustled Rynn past.

"And you'll be having it shortly, Mrs. Clark," Donal replied. By then they'd reached the staircase at the far end of the hall. At his urging Rynn started up, and he followed her. The banister was rickety, while the steps themselves were dirty and littered with debris. The strong smell of cooking cabbage and the wail of a crying child intensified as she climbed.

"Mr. Brady?" she questioned over her shoulder as another shout went up from below.

He shrugged. "As good a name as any."

The room he took her to was on the third floor, number 314 as the woman had said. It was cluttered and dark despite the feeble sunbeam trying to force its way through the one grimy window. The first thing that struck Rynn as she stepped inside was a wall of heat from the gas fire—and the nauseating smell of rotting meat. She instantly recognized that for what it was: putrefying flesh.

It meant nothing good for Seamus.

"I'm going to need hot water," she said to Donal as he closed the door behind them. A glance around the room had shown her a range with a kettle on it in one corner along with a pair of cupboards. Combined, they made up what passed for a tiny kitchen.

"I'll see to it." He headed toward the range.

"Where's Fergus?" she asked, having ascertained that he was not present. Removing her hat and jacket, she dropped them and her pocketbook on the small dining table in the middle of the room as she walked toward the iron bedstead in the far corner. Seamus lay there on a thin mattress under a pile of blankets. He was stretched out on his back with only his head and right leg uncovered. His leg was wrapped from knee to crotch in makeshift bandages, and a grubby sock adorned his exposed foot. He was pale, shivering, and his eyes were closed.

"He was with us in the warehouse, but we lost him after. We were next door to a freight yard, and that's where we ran. I managed to get Seamus hidden away in a railway car behind some sacks of grain. We stayed put while the soldiers searched and then the next day the train brought us to London. Where Fergus has got to, I don't know."

"If he has any sense, he's left you two to it." Her voice was tart. Depositing the bag with her nursing supplies on the bedside table, she bent over Seamus, laying her hand on his forehead. "Seamus."

"Who's that?" His eyes flew open. They were bleary, bloodshot. His skin was hot with fever even as he shivered as if he were freezing cold.

"It's me," Rynn said, but Seamus stared at her like he'd never seen her before.

"I've brought Rynn," Donal said at the same time. Having lit the fire under the kettle, he was walking toward them. He, too, had shed his coat and hat. In his shirtsleeves, with his shock of black hair as unruly as if it hadn't seen a comb in days, he looked more like his old familiar self. "She'll get you fixed up, don't worry."

"Rynn? But she's in England. Remember, we saw her picture in the newspaper." Seamus shook his head fretfully.

"We're in England, too." Donal stopped beside the bed and frowned down at his cousin. "He's been shivering like this since last night. How he can be cold in this oven I've no idea."

"It's the fever," Rynn said, then shifted her focus to her

patient. "I'm here, Seamus," Rynn assured him, and gently gripped his ankle. There it was, what she'd been hoping for: a pulse. At least there was some blood flow to the leg.

"Rynn?" Seamus peered at her.

"That's right," she said, and started working to untie the knot above his knee that would allow her to unwind the bandage that consisted of what looked like someone's—probably Donal's—torn-up undershirt.

"I'm shot." Seamus closed his eyes. "Hurts like bedamned."

"Yes, I know. I'm just going to have a look at the wound." Once the water was hot, she would clean and drain it, which she could already tell was going to be necessary. But first she had to remove the bandage, and the knot was proving impossible to undo.

She looked at Donal. "Do you have scissors? Or a knife?"

"Scissors, no. A knife . . ." He fetched her one from kitchen, held it out to her. "That I can do."

It was big and cumbersome, but the blade seemed sharp enough. She slid it under the knot and started to saw at the cloth.

Seamus groaned and arched like she was taking the knife to his leg. The blankets shifted enough so that she could see that he was, fortunately, wearing drawers. Not that she hadn't nursed men who weren't, but . . .

"Here, sit." Donal brought over one of the straight wooden chairs from the dining table and set it beside the bed. "If you can manage without me for a minute or two, I'll take the rent down to Mrs. Clark in the lobby before she thinks to come up here for it." He smiled at her, that same charming smile that she'd had a weakness for for most of her life. Its effect had faded considerably, she was glad to realize. In fact, it didn't charm her at all. "Born to find trouble" was what Granny had said of him, much to Rynn's irritation at the time. But Rynn was beginning to see that once again Granny, uncanny prescience or not, was right. "And I thank you very kindly for the loan, by the by."

Dropping into the chair, Rynn waved him off and started to unwind the bandage. More knots held the whole together, and on those, too, she had to use the knife. She heard, rather than saw, Donal leave. Her attention was all on Seamus, who was panting and moaning and pouring sweat. Getting uncomfortably hot herself as she worked, Rynn cast more than one longing glance at the window. The heat was bad, the stench was worse and what she wanted most right at that moment was a blast of fresh air.

The leg was every bit as bad as she'd feared. Looking down at the red, swollen flesh that she'd exposed, Rynn grimaced. The thigh was twice its normal size. The bullet itself seemed to have passed right through it, missing anything vital while leaving a small, puckered black hole that, on its own, would have healed readily enough. But infection had set in, and that was what posed the danger, to his leg—and his life.

As she gently prodded the wound, Seamus yelped and shuddered. His eyes rolled back in his head. He went limp. Had he fainted? If so, it was probably for the best, because she was just getting started. That wound had to be opened and drained.

"I'll be as gentle as—" *I can* was what she was in the middle of saying when the door opened again.

She glanced around to see Donal, as she'd expected, enter the room. What she didn't expect was that he would have both hands raised high in the air—and a man with a gun jammed against his spine following close behind.

Her pulse leaped. She froze, her hands suspended over Seamus's swollen leg.

The man shook his head in disgust as he entered. Dressed in a long black overcoat and bowler hat, he was about Donal's height, fortyish, with a squint-eyed, pockmarked face that twisted into a sneer as he kicked the door shut behind them. "Blimey, you Irish stink! Got a pig or two under the bed, do you?"

Donal's eyes met hers. From his expression she could see just how dire the situation was.

There was nothing she could do. Her hands dropped to her lap, clenched into fists.

"Well, lookee here, I got me a trifecta," the man crowed, spotting her, perched still as a statue on the hard chair, and Seamus, sprawled out, limp and seemingly unconscious, on the bed beside her. He smirked with satisfaction. "The boss told us you was the key." The words were addressed directly to her. "O'Reilly'll come back for her, he said. You mark my words, he said. You watch her, you'll catch him. And, by God, Kenney was right. We been watching you, missy, since you ran off to London. Today, it paid off."

A jolt of terror made every nerve ending she possessed quiver: Kenney. Major Detective Kenney, MI5. He'd sent people after her, set them to watching her. She'd never really escaped at all.

Suddenly she found it hard to breathe.

"Get over by the bed," the man instructed Donal, his tone brutal now as he prodded him hard in the back with the gun. As Donal obeyed, grim-faced, his hands still in the air, the man looked past him at Rynn. "Stand up, sweetheart. You're going to be tying this one to that chair for me. As for this one . . ." He was close enough to the bed now that he could see the state Seamus was in. Eyes closed, limp and pale, his grotesquely swollen leg on full display, Seamus was clearly in a bad way. "Eh, it don't look like he's going to make it to the firing squad. But it's all one to me. I get paid either way."

He shoved Donal into the chair and stepped behind him, out of Donal's sight. "Keep your hands up in the air where I can see 'em. Try anything, and I'll blow your head off," he warned, adding to Rynn, "Don't you move." Keeping the gun on them both—she could see it, Donal couldn't—he shucked his long overcoat and tossed it and his hat on the bed, muttering, "It's a damned furnace in here." Then he stepped up behind Donal and pressed the gun squarely to the back of his head. "I should probably tell you, I get paid whether you're dead or alive. So for me, it's whichever's easiest."

Rynn broke out in a cold sweat. It was clear that he wouldn't hesitate to pull the trigger.

"Them rags will do fine to hold him while I shout down to that lady at the desk to get the police here, so grab 'em." He shoved Rynn to the floor. Donal's jaw tightened, but any other response would have been suicidal, and it was clear he knew it. On her knees, Rynn started gathering up the stained bandages, moving as slowly as she dared.

"If it's pay you want, I can top anything you've been promised." Desperation restored Rynn's wits—and her voice. "My father-in-law is a rich man, and so is my husband. They'll pay twice what you've been offered if you let us go."

The man huffed skeptically. "Jonas Bingle ain't one to fall for empty promises. You might be right, one of them might pay handsome for you, but then I'd have Kenney to deal with. And he's a mean bastard with a long memory and an army of agents to call on. And on top of my pay, there's the rewards. So—"

A piercing whistle from the other side of the room made Rynn—all of them—jump and look around. She was just registering what it was—the water in the teakettle reaching a boil at last—when something large and heavy launched past her in a fast, low dive that made her gasp even as she fell back out of the way.

Seamus—it was Seamus!—tackling Bingle while his attention was on the kettle and sending him crashing to the floor. A startled cry from Bingle, and then Seamus was straddling him with a hand over his mouth and *plunging the knife from the kitchen into his chest again and again* with a savagery that was like nothing Rynn had ever imagined him to be capable of. Seamus's grunts, the driving thuds as the knife landed, Bingle's heels drumming the floor—the sheer horror of it froze her in place. Blood shot up like a fountain as an artery was sliced. Bingle kicked and bucked and gurgled—and went still.

Chapter Twenty

It was all over just as quick as that.

For a moment, an unreal moment that seemed to stretch out for an eternity, the only sound Rynn could hear was Seamus's labored breathing—and the only thing she could see was the terrible scarlet spurt of blood. As a nurse, it was incumbent on her to try to save a life—even the life of a man who might have been the death of them—but the ferocity of the attack left her with no moral question to wrestle. She could only look, appalled, at the bloody pulp that had once been a man's chest. There was no doubt in her mind that Bingle was dead. No one could survive such injuries.

"Jesus, Seamus! And here was me thinking you were half dead!" Donal was on his feet, looming over Seamus and the man he'd just killed. His tone was amazed, congratulatory, relieved. Clearly seeing a man slaughtered right in front of him didn't bother him at all.

"It's not the first time I've had to kill a man when I was half dead." Seamus meant when he was in the war, Rynn knew. Donal had told her about some of the surprise nighttime attacks they'd endured when the Huns had come pouring down on them in the trenches, about the vicious hand-to-hand combat with which they'd fought for their lives and the lives of their comrades, often when they were so sick and weak with dysentery or trench fever they could barely move. This, she supposed, was the result of that.

She was still gaping at the gruesome sight in front of her when Seamus rolled off his victim, dropped the knife and collapsed on his back on the floor nearby. Spatters of blood on his face were eclipsed by his bloody hands and the deep red splotches of blood on his undershirt.

"Cor, my leg hurts! Feels like the skin's gone and burst."

Her nurse's instincts caught by this appeal to them, Rynn's attention shifted to his leg. The wound had, indeed, burst open as a result of his exertions. The resulting purulent drainage was smelly and disgusting but was also a good thing because it was getting the poison out. Shaky with shock but seeing no advantage in wallowing in her own feelings or the horror of it, she got to her feet and went to do the next, practical thing: fetch the kettle and a basin so she could tend the wound. It frightened her to realize that what was motivating her to move so quickly was the thought that she might not get another chance. At any moment, the police might burst in, or a confederate of Bingle's, or someone drawn by the sound of the struggle . . .

"Was the bastard alone?" Seamus asked Donal through clenched teeth.

"He was. I think he was. There wasn't anyone with him when he stuck a gun in my back in the stairwell. He'd been watching Rynn. He must have followed us from the park, then seen me again when I was paying the rent." Donal crouched beside Bingle, pressing a wad of discarded bandages to the man's mutilated chest—the still gushing blood immediately turned the cloth bright red—before grabbing the small rag rug from the floor beside the bed and pressing it down on top of the bandages. "He said he was going to shout down at Mrs. Clark to send for the police. If he'd had somebody with him, there would have been no need. He would have sent them."

"Why are you doing that? He's dead." Nauseated by the gore, by the ripe smell of the eviscerated body, by the violence of the deed itself, Rynn set the basin of hot water on the floor beside Seamus and, with the bag holding the supplies from the apothecary's shop in hand, sank down beside it. If her voice was sharper than usual, well, she considered it a wonder that she could talk at all.

"If he bleeds out all over the floor, some of it might drip through to the room below." Having snatched a blanket off the bed, Donal hauled Bingle's limp corpse up enough to wrap it around his head and torso, binding it tightly over the rug and bandages. It was a relief, Rynn thought as Donal lowered him back to the floor, not to have to look any longer at the gaping wounds—or the dead man's staring eyes. "And we can't leave all this blood. If anybody finds out what happened here . . ."

He broke off, but Rynn had no trouble filling in what he'd left unsaid: they would all, herself included, be implicated in Bingle's *murder.*

Her heart, which she only that second realized was thumping like she'd been running for hours, gave a mighty lurch.

"We can't stay here any longer," Seamus said, then groaned loudly as she pressed a steaming pad of hot-water-soaked bandages down on his wound. "We need to get moving."

"We do," Donal agreed. "As soon as Rynn is done with your leg, we'll go. I don't know where that'll be, precisely, but—"

"We can't be leaving the body behind." Seamus groaned again as Rynn replaced the pad with another steaming one. "Once they find it, they'll be coming after us with everything they have."

"Can you walk a bit, do you think?" Donal asked Seamus as he wrapped another blanket around Bingle. "If you can, I can carry the body out. If I put him over my shoulder, you can lean on my other side. Or you can lean on Rynn."

"I can walk," Seamus said. Donal gave him a doubtful look. Rynn, too, was skeptical. Panting and sweating, Seamus was more gray than white now, and his mouth was contorted with pain. As for his leg, she doubted that it could bear any weight at all.

"That'll make a pretty picture, now won't it?" Gathering her wits about her, Rynn forced herself to focus on the practicalities of the situation even as she applied another steaming pad to the wound, to Seamus's obvious discomfort. The discharge was mostly blood now, which was a good thing. Her hands were shaking, which was not. "You with a dead man wrapped up like a mummy over your shoulder, and another one half dead leaning on your arm? Are you thinking no one will notice? And even if we make it outside, then what do you intend to do? Shall we all pile into a taxi? Or take a tram? I think that just might attract the very attention we most want to avoid. And if we manage all that, where, pray, do you intend to go? I can't take you home with me. The house is busy. There's nowhere I can hide you. My father-in-law is dead set against the rebellion and will summon the police in a trice if any part of this comes to his attention. And Bingle was watching me, remember. Someone else will come to take his place. They'll be watching me, too."

Realizing the truth of it even as she said it, the knowledge struck terror into her soul.

"Eh, you make a good point about Bingle. He'll have had a shift, most likely. The shift will end, if it hasn't already, and he won't be there to hand off the assignment to his replacement." Donal's expression was stark as he looked at Rynn. "They'll start to look for him. They might be looking for him now."

For an appalled moment they stared at one another.

The icy calm that always seemed to claim her when confronted with the worst emergencies took possession of her mind, granting her a clarity of vision that showed her a possible way out.

Rynn said, "I know what to do."

Some twenty minutes later, Seamus's leg was slathered in BIPP and bound up with clean bandages. He was fully dressed—with a seam slit in his pants leg to accommodate the bulk of his bandaged thigh—propped in a sitting position in the bed, and armed with a pistol. Bingle's corpse had been wrapped in multiple blankets and shoved beneath the bed so that it would not be immediately visible should anyone come bursting through the door. The worst of the blood had been cleaned up.

And with a solemn promise to Seamus to return as soon as possible, Rynn and Donal were on their way out of the lodging house.

The Great Eastern Hotel was respectable and well-appointed but lacked the glamor—and cost—of the Goring or Claridge's. With her face and hands washed, her hair tidied, her hat with its veil pulled forward to hide her face and her jacket buttoned carefully over her dress, the bodice of which she had discovered to her horror was liberally splattered with Bingle's blood, Rynn attracted no more than a sideways glance or two from the businessmen who were the hotel's primary clientele as she navigated the reception rooms and rode the lift to the top floor. Maguire and his associates had taken rooms there while they were in London, and she, fortunately, remembered his direction and the fact that he was slated to join Thomas and his party at White's that evening after attending a football match that seemed to be of great interest to every gentleman in London. While making the arrangements with Thomas in her presence, Maguire had stated his intention to retire to his hotel room to change clothes between events. As it was a little more than an hour before they were to meet, Rynn most fervently hoped that she would find him in his room.

She was in luck. Maguire yanked the door open at her first tentative knock. He was tousle haired and in his shirtsleeves, with black trousers and a black waistcoat rendering him almost fully dressed. She appeared to have interrupted him in the process of tying his bow tie, because the black satin ends hung down on either side of his neck.

At the sight of her, his eyes widened with surprise, and no wonder. The gossip that would result if she was caught visiting his hotel room didn't bear thinking of. But she'd had no choice.

"What the *devil* are you doing here?" He glanced up and down the hall, which was empty, then stepped back and pulled her inside. It was an ordinary hotel room, nothing fancy, she saw with a glance. The water he'd used for shaving was still in the basin with his razor beside it. The smell of his shaving soap hung in the air. "The valet went to press my jacket and I'm expecting him to return at any minute. You don't want him to see you."

No, she didn't. She wanted to get the business over with and be gone as quickly as possible. The thought that Bingle might already have been missed, that someone might be looking for him at that very moment, made her want to jump out of her skin.

"I—we—need your help," she said without preamble as he locked the door and turned to face her.

"What's happened?" His voice was sharp.

She told him, as quickly and succinctly as she could. By the time she finished, his arms were folded over his chest and his face was like thunder.

"So, having escaped death by the grace of God—and myself!—when they decided to turn gunrunners, the O'Reillys are having another go at getting themselves killed, are they? Did it not occur to you that it might not be the smartest thing you ever did to get involved in their idiot schemes again?"

He was sounding more Irish than usual, which she'd learned tended to happen when he was in the grip of some strong emotion.

The times she'd noticed it before, he'd been talking to roomfuls of men about the importance of avoiding a wholescale conflict between Britain and Ireland. Right now, what was fueling it was, she thought, anger, both at her and on her behalf.

She squared her shoulders at him. "I'm a trained nurse. And Seamus was in a bad way. Left untreated much longer, he would have died."

"And so O'Reilly came to fetch you. For his cousin. Which was bad enough by itself but might have only earned you a prison term if you were caught. But then they went and involved you in the murder of what is quite possibly, from the sound of it, an agent of the British government."

"Donal had no idea that would happen. He was—we were all—caught by surprise."

"He's always getting caught by surprise, it seems. What surprises *me* is that you keep letting him pull you in to his surprises." His face went hard. "They'll execute you, you know. The Brits. Stand you up against a brick wall and shoot you. Woman or not. With no mercy." His tone had changed. It was harsh, almost cold.

"I'm aware."

"You're aware." Suddenly his eyes blazed hot. "Do you love him so much then, *Lady Thomas*? That you're willing to risk your life for him?"

"No. *No.* If you're meaning Donal, I don't love him at all, or at least, only as a friend, or a brother. Anything more that was once between us is over. But—"

A knock on the door interrupted.

"Get in the dressing room."

She was already darting for the door in the corner of the room even as he pointed at it.

By the time the valet, because it was the valet, left, Rynn was ready to scream with anxiety. Every passing minute seemed to her like an hour. When Maguire, resplendent now in a black tuxedo coat with his hair brushed neatly back and his bow tie tied, opened the dressing room door at last and indicated with a mocking gesture that she could leave the seat she had improvised for herself on his upturned valise, she did, walking past him into the room with her head held high before turning to face him.

"Are you going to help us or not?"

"Am I going to put my life and everything I hold dear at risk to save the lives of a pair of hotheaded fools who are working against the very thing I'm here working for? Is that what you're asking me?"

Their gazes held. When he put it like that . . .

"Please," she said.

"Why not go to your husband for help?"

"I don't want Thomas to know." She made the admission reluctantly. "His father is so adamantly against the rebellion, and—" She broke off.

"There's O'Reilly." The sardonic note in his voice left her in no doubt about what he was inferring.

"Yes. But not in the way you mean. Thomas isn't jealous, he's not that kind of man. It's . . . I don't want to put him in a position where he would be a party to this if anything were to go wrong." And, although she would never admit it to anyone, she didn't think there was anything that Thomas could do. The type of expertise needed to get Donal and Seamus safe away was far outside his experience.

"Just so you know, every man is that kind of man," Maguire said. "What makes you think I'm even capable of doing what you want?"

"I know you are. Just like I know you're in touch with men you can call on to help get Donal and Seamus safe away."

"And how do you know that?"

"I *know*, all right? You may ape the legitimate businessman as much as you want, but we both know it's only an act."

"Much as I hate to disabuse you of the wrongheaded notions you seem to have of me, I *am* a legitimate businessman. It might interest you to hear that I just signed an exclusive deal with Lord Somerset for my company to act as the sole shipping agent transporting the gin and rum manufactured in his distilleries to America. Quite a coup, that. And now that such a bastion of the aristocracy is on board, there'll be more."

"Lord Somerset? You've gone into business with Lord Somerset?" There could only be one—and he would be her half-sister Penelope's mother's *second* husband.

There must have been an odd note to her voice, because he looked closely at her.

"Do you find something strange in that?"

"It's just . . . I've heard he's so very, very respectable." She tucked the information away to be mulled over later and returned to the topic at hand. "If that is indeed the case, it's doubly in your best interest to help us. If Donal and Seamus are arrested, there's no telling what they might be coerced or tortured into revealing. For example, I doubt it would suit your purpose if your role in the events of Christmas night were to be revealed."

"Are you by any chance threatening me?"

"No. No, of course not. We agreed to keep each other's secrets, and I would never betray that. I am simply asking for your help. As a fellow countryman. And a friend."

"Friends, are we?"

"I think so, yes." Casting a hunted look at the deepening twilight she could just glimpse through a crack in the drawn curtains over the single window, she clasped her hands together in distress. "Oh, would you stop wasting time? If someone goes looking for Bingle and finds him there with Seamus—" She broke off as his eyes, which had been regarding her narrowly, dropped to fasten on her chest.

"There's blood on your dress." His words were abrupt.

Having found the dressing room oppressively warm, she'd unbuttoned her jacket, which hung open. Glancing down at herself, she realized that he was looking at the stains that marred the front of her dress.

Seeing them, she barely repressed a shudder.

"Where are they?" He sounded grim. He looked grim, she discovered. He also looked big and tough and like a man who was infinitely capable of dealing with any dire situation that came his way.

As ill-tempered as the question sounded, it was capitulation, she knew. "Seamus is in a lodging house at 200 Chapel Street, Room 314. Bingle's body is there as well. It needs to be carried out somehow without anyone realizing what it is, and Seamus will require help leaving because I don't think he can walk. Donal wore Bingle's coat and hat when we left, so that anyone who might have been watching Bingle enter the lodging house will also have seen him leave, so you won't have to worry about that. If you can get them safely away, and dispose of the body, hopefully we can brush through this without anyone suspecting the truth."

"Sounds like you've thought of everything." Maguire's response was dry. "And where is Donal?"

"In a pub across the street."

To her relief, Maguire was already shrugging into his overcoat. "Afraid to show his face to me, was he?"

"I thought it would be best if I talked to you alone first."

"Did you now?"

She finished buttoning up her jacket as he opened the door. "Yes. At the very least, I knew you wouldn't turn me over to the police."

A grimace was his only answer as he followed her into the hall.

Chapter Twenty-One

Twilight had, indeed, fallen while she'd been inside. The streetlights were lit, adding an eerie yellow glow to sidewalks teeming with pedestrians from all walks of life and a street crowded with traffic. The clanging of an oncoming tram was only the loudest of the city sounds that, paradoxically, lent their conversation a necessary degree of privacy. Although Rynn's intention was to head straight for where Donal had been waiting for far longer than she could have anticipated, Maguire insisted on putting her into a taxi for home as soon as they left the hotel.

"You want to attract exactly the kind of attention we don't need, you go ahead and walk into that pub. Believe me, it's no place for a lady. Every man there will be looking at you." He caught her arm, restraining her from going farther as he nodded at the grimy windows of the Star Tavern, where Donal waited. This was in response to her stated determination not to leave before she put the two men together and judged the outcome. "You either trust me to handle this or you don't."

"I trust you. Truly. But—"

"Then go home and leave me to it. At this point you'll only get in the way. I'll say goodbye to O'Reilly for you, if that's what's worrying you." He was waving down a taxi as he spoke.

"That is *not*—"

"Isn't it?"

"No!"

He smiled mockingly at her as the taxi stopped. There was no time for her to reply with anything more than a hopefully crushing frown before he had the door open and she had, perforce, to slide inside. He gave the driver her direction and was closing the door behind her when she stopped it with an outstretched hand.

"Thank you," she said quietly in response to his inquiring look.

"You're welcome." Leaning closer, lowering his voice so as not to be overheard, he added, "This is the second time that I know of that O'Reilly has put your life at risk. Before I put any woman I supposedly loved in that kind of danger, I'd throw myself in front of a train. Next time he comes for you, you might want to think about that." Stepping back, he closed the door. The last glimpse she had of him was of him striding across the busy street toward the Star Tavern.

She thought about what he'd said all the way home.

Fortunately, none of the family was about when she arrived at Hartford House. Hideously conscious that whoever was slated to take Bingle's place, or even several people searching for Bingle, might be watching the house, she hurried inside without, she hoped, giving the least appearance of hurrying, and gave an inward sigh of relief as the door closed behind her. To Granger, the butler, and the footmen hovering in the entry hall, she merely said good evening as she would on any evening after arriving home and went upstairs. To Parry, who came to help her undress, she trotted out the explanation that she'd come up with on the taxi ride home if a question were to be raised about where she'd been for so long: she'd witnessed a poor dog getting run down in the street and stayed to try to help the animal while its owner was located. That also explained the blood on her clothes, and she was quite proud of herself for coming up with so believable an excuse. Then she'd pleaded a headache, requested dinner on a tray in her room and, after writing letters to Granny and Glenna—both were poor correspondents, but she couldn't complain because she wasn't much better—she tried to read, finally tossing the book aside in frustration after she found herself unable to concentrate.

As it happened, Thomas didn't get home until very late, and in no condition to do anything but go to sleep. Still shaken by what had happened, she was long abed, if not asleep. As much as she was dying to know if Maguire had joined him at any point during the evening she was afraid of revealing too much with her questions, and thus could do nothing but listen as Thomas's valet helped him to bed and, later, to the coughing spells that still plagued him as he slept.

Rynn went downstairs to breakfast the next morning to discover to her surprise that her half-sister, Penelope, had called at Hartford House with her mother, Lady Somerset, the previous afternoon on their way back from the gathering at the Criterion. She, Rynn, had been out on her walk at the time, but Alice and Maud, having just arrived home, had received the visitors. As a result, the agenda for that afternoon was rearranged to include making a return call on Lady Somerset and her daughter.

The streets were as crowded as usual as the three younger ladies plus the Duchess were driven toward Grosvenor Square, where the Somersets' town residence was located. Tucked into the twin seats in the back of the family's big black Daimler with Meadows at the wheel, with each of them wearing fashionable ensembles in the latest spring pastels, they made quite the picture, Rynn was sure. In her old life, she could never have afforded the slim lilac gown that brought out the blue tones in her hair, nor would she ever have had an occasion to wear it or her charming confection of a hat. Now she possessed a wardrobe full of equally costly ensembles, and all she could think about was how much she would rather be wearing one of her old skirts and jumpers and tramping along the Roguey cliff walk with a stiff ocean breeze blowing in.

"This means they've decided to acknowledge you," Alice said in a congratulatory tone as she glanced around at Rynn, who rode with Maud in the seat behind her and the Duchess.

"Perhaps *I* don't wish to acknowledge *them*," Rynn said. The truth was, the thought of coming face-to-face with her half-sister, and her half-sister's mother, had her stomach in a knot. Combine that with the gnawing fear that she was being watched, that someone might come nosing around looking for Bingle at any moment, that the authorities might somehow already know everything and be biding their time, plus her worry over Donal's and Seamus's well-being, and she was, inwardly, a bundle of raw nerves. It was *not* the state in which she'd hoped to first meet her unknown half-sister.

But the best way to keep suspicion at bay was to go out and about as though she had no knowledge that anything was wrong. Thus she was paying an afternoon call that she really didn't want to pay, in the company of her aristocratic in-laws whose presence could only make the ordeal worse, because that was what well-bred *innocent* ladies did.

"It would be so very rude not to return their call," the Duchess said. "And such bad form for it to be publicly seen that there is discord in your family. You cannot wish to figure in the kind of gossip that would occasion. And Lord and Lady Somerset are well-liked, and with her daughter having made her come out only last year they may be encountered everywhere."

"You'll have to meet them sometime," Maud chimed in. "If it were me, I'd prefer to do it in private rather than publicly."

That would have been the deciding factor if Rynn had

needed convincing, but as she'd already made her mind up to it, she did not.

As it happened, they were not the only visitors to the imposing brick mansion that took up half a block in the exclusive Mayfair district that afternoon. Several other ladies were in the lavishly appointed drawing room with Penelope and Lady Somerset when the butler announced them with "Her Grace the Duchess of Hartford, Lady Wycomb, Lady Thomas Dunne and Lady Maud Dunne, Your Ladyship."

All conversation stopped. All faces swiveled toward the newcomers. And then seven pairs of eyes—Penelope, Lady Somerset, and Lady Amanda Davies, Lady Colin Hughes, Mrs. Tarrant-Combs and her two daughters, who as it turned out were the other visitors—fastened exclusively on Rynn.

She knew then that the gossip about her had reached fever pitch.

"Sister!" was how Penelope greeted her. It was said with every evidence of delight as she rose from the sofa where she was seated beside her mother to bestow an air kiss on Rynn's cheek. Rynn realized two things in that moment: Penelope was at least as sensitive to the negative effects of the gossip as she was and, at only eighteen, she was much better at masking her feelings. Looking into her half-sister's eyes, a bright cornflower blue the exact shade of her—*their*—father's, a fact she hadn't even remembered until she'd seen them again in this little sister who was a total stranger to her, sent her mentally reeling. It was all she could do to keep the polite smile on her face.

"Such a contrast as you two make," Lady Somerset marveled as she rose to shake hands. "One might almost be tempted to characterize you as the light and the dark."

It was said with a smile, but Rynn wasn't fooled. The words were a subtle jab. Behind Lady Somerset's placid face lurked a seething jealousy of her husband's previous family.

"I'm held to closely resemble my mother." Rynn turned her polite smile on Lady Somerset.

"While dear Penelope looks like her father" was Lady Somerset's rejoinder. "Fortunately, she inherited my hard head. He was the softhearted one, always easily influenced."

"Which is why we loved him so, as I'm sure you must have, too," Penelope said to Rynn as they all sat down. Rynn's unwavering smile hopefully masked the truth: *My most vivid memory of him is of seeing him walk out the front door of our house in Dublin, where we lived at the time, carrying a suitcase in each hand. I ran after him, a small girl crying because her mother had just died and she was afraid of losing her father, too. He picked me up, gave me a hug and a kiss and promised to come back soon. It was years before I saw him again, and then only for about half an hour one afternoon.*

"There is a third sister, is there not?" Mrs. Tarrant-Combs asked. That she should know such a thing was evidence of just how deep the gossip went. "When will we have the pleasure of meeting her?"

"Glenna will be joining us in London this summer," Rynn said. "Along with our grandmother. Thomas and I are greatly looking forward to seeing them."

"Your grandmother is coming to London?" Lady Somerset's tone was perfectly polite but there was that steel in her eyes—of course, it was Granny who'd had to deal with Lady Somerset in the wake of George Carmichael's death. Now that the matter was recalled to her, Rynn remembered Granny stomping around the cottage in Bundoran, where they'd moved by that time because life in Dublin was too expensive, muttering "Pompous bastard" in reference to Lady Somerset's father. That was after the arrival of the lawyer's letter informing Granny that Baron Carmichael had died without so much as a shilling to his name, that all the money he'd sent for the care of his daughters to that date had come from Lady Somerset and her father, a very rich man, and from that time on there would be no more funds forthcoming. After receiving no reply to her letters of protest, Granny had taken herself to London to confront Lady Somerset and her father in person. The meeting had not gone well, and she had returned home in a fury. In the aftermath, she'd cursed Lady Somerset's father in particular to the skies. "A mean old skinflint," she'd called him, "with a poisonous daughter." Then she'd taken in boarders, sold meat pies out of her kitchen, worked at a draper's in the village and done whatever she could to support them until Rynn was able to start contributing financially to the household. Which she was still doing, sending them money each month out of the generous allowance Thomas made her until such time as they could join her in England.

"She is," Rynn confirmed. Lady Somerset's lips pursed until she looked like she'd tasted something sour.

"I understand you attended Mrs. Liddle's talk yesterday," the Duchess said to Lady Somerset. To Rynn, it was an obvious attempt to redirect the conversation into less sensitive areas. "What did you think of it?"

The gambit worked. Every lady present had an opinion on Mrs. Liddle, and women's suffrage, and from there the conversation branched off in other, impersonal directions.

To Rynn, the remainder of the twenty minutes—the prescribed polite duration for an afternoon call, she'd been informed—felt like a performance conducted for the benefit of the other visitors. They would talk about this meeting with their friends, she knew, and the final takeaway would come down to, were the Carmichael sisters on good terms or not?

It was in everyone's best interest for them to be seen to be friendly.

Lord Somerset entered the house just as the ladies were leaving en masse. Short and stocky, he was in perhaps his mid-fifties, immaculately dressed, with grizzled fair hair and blunt, almost homely features. During the course of the greetings and introductions that followed, Rynn's impression of this man who was Penelope's stepfather and Maguire's new business partner was that beneath his affable manners, he was shrewdly calculating.

"So you're my daughter's sister." Turning to her at last, he gave her an appraising look, then chuckled. "The pictures in the newspapers haven't done you justice. What a surprise you've been to Lady Somerset! Dancing with the Prince of Wales! You've quite taken the town by storm, something she wasn't expecting at all. And married to the Duke of Hartford's son to boot! I certainly hope we'll see more of you, as you and Penelope get better acquainted."

Rynn murmured something polite, and then to her relief the car arrived, and they were out the door.

"I think we brushed through that rather well," Maud said as they rode back to Hartford House. "Although it seemed to me that Lady Somerset had her nose put out of joint because you're having such a success."

"I'm glad to have met Penelope," Rynn said, not wanting to say anything negative about her half-sister's mother in case anyone in the car—Alice's was the loose tongue she was primarily worried about—should repeat it. "Although I do wish we hadn't had such an avidly interested audience."

"Lord Somerset seemed to quite like the idea that his wife wasn't best pleased with you," Alice said. "I've heard that there's trouble in their marriage and that he only married her for her fortune. Just as Lady Somerset's mother, who was the daughter of the Earl of Stanton—he lost everything at the gaming table, you know—married her father for *his* fortune. *He* was a Cit, fabulously wealthy, who owned half the liquor distilleries in England. Now Lord Somerset runs them. Having acquired what he married for, I hear he spends precious little time at home."

"I've heard that, too," the Duchess said. "Now that our

friends have found out that Rynn is Penelope Carmichael's sister, they seem to think I'm interested in every little thing the Somersets do."

There were other calls to be made, at the Duchess's insistence, while they were out, which meant that by the time they returned to Hartford House there was just enough time to change for dinner. Tired from doing the social rounds, which was one part of life as Thomas's wife that she definitely could have done without, and tense with worry at the thought that the search for Bingle must be reaching fever pitch and might wind up on her doorstep at any minute, Rynn had just finished changing for dinner when Thomas appeared in the doorway of their adjoining bedrooms. He, too, had changed for dinner, and was looking dashing with his hair slicked back and his now-full mustache lending him an appealing air of maturity. But what made her eyes widen was that he was walking—walking!—with the aid of his sticks, as he called his new crutches that had cuffs that went around his forearms and handles he gripped in each hand. They'd been practicing with them each morning for several weeks, but as they provided less support than the axillary crutches he'd been accustomed to and were certainly far removed from his chair, she was surprised to see him relying on them for anything other than a practice session.

"You certainly seem to have gotten the knack of those," Rynn said as he crossed the room toward her. "I'm impressed."

"As I think I've mentioned before, impressing you is always an object with me. Since it's just family tonight, I thought I'd give walking into dinner a try."

"Your mother will be so pleased." As Parry had just finished draping a fringed silk shawl over her shoulders, completing her toilette, Rynn said to her in an aside, "Thank you, Parry. I won't need anything else."

Parry left. Thomas came up to Rynn where she still stood

in front of the long cheval mirror in the corner of her bedroom adjusting her shawl. His gait was halting and awkward, but to see him upright and walking, with his legs bearing so much of his weight, filled her with joy. Impulsively, she leaned forward and pressed a kiss to his cheek. His skin was warm and smooth, and the subtle citrusy scent of his aftershave was pleasant.

"You've made such tremendous progress. I'm so proud of you," she said, sinking back on her heels.

"I couldn't have done it without you. I would have given up back there in Ireland. You've given me something to live for, you know." His eyes were intent on hers, as if he was trying to gauge the answer to a question he hadn't asked.

"And you very likely saved my life back there in Ireland, so I'd say that makes us quits." She smiled at him. "Shall we go down?"

"In a minute. I wanted to ask you about something." His tone turned unexpectedly grave. "I was told that you went out walking by yourself yesterday, and then didn't return home for hours because you'd been in an accident of some sort. Is that true?"

Chapter Twenty-Two

She should have seen it coming. Of course someone—one of the servants probably—had mentioned her prolonged absence to Thomas. Why had she not expected it and been preparing herself? Panic set her heart to racing.

I can't lie to him. Her first instinctive reaction was almost instantly replaced by *I must. If someone searching for Bingle should come to the house, he won't have to pretend to know nothing if he actually knows nothing. Donal's and Seamus's lives are at risk if the truth is found out, and so is mine. And Maguire's. Too much is at stake, and telling Thomas would put him at risk, too.*

I'm a party to murder. That was the horrifying reality she had to accept. There was no fixing it, nothing to do. Except pray the truth never came out.

She could almost hear Granny saying it: *Three can keep a secret if two of them are dead.*

Thomas's eyes held hers. She returned his gaze, unblinking, her smile frozen in place as those and a thousand other thoughts ran through her mind between one heartbeat and the next.

"Oh my, yes. I was going to tell you, but you got in so late and so much happened today that I forgot all about it. It was terrible! This poor dog . . ."

And so she lied, and told him the story that she'd told Parry. And, miraculously, he believed her, commiserating with her over her terrible experience, saying what a lucky dog and owner to have had her there to help. Then she launched into an account of her afternoon, most particularly her call on her half-sister, as a distraction, and somewhere in the middle of that the gong rang, summoning them to dinner. Talking animatedly all the way, she went down with him in the hand-cranked lift that had been installed for his convenience. The family had just gone into the dining room, drinks in hand. Everyone glanced in their direction as they entered, and all conversation immediately ceased. The Duchess, as expected, was overcome with emotion on seeing Thomas upright and walking, albeit with his sticks, and fell upon him, hugging him as she burst into tears.

Geoffrey said, "Glad to see you on your feet, old man," and clapped his brother on the shoulder.

The Duke expressed his happiness with a gruff "I knew no boy of mine would let the damned Huns defeat him," swallowed the rest of his drink in a gulp and demanded that dinner be served.

In all the excitement Rynn's lie about the dog was lost, buried and hopefully forgotten. But guilt weighed on her, for the lie and even more heavily for a man's death, and it was all she could do to keep up an untroubled front. The park assumed such a sinister aspect in her mind that even on sunny days it felt dark and threatening, and she doubted that she would ever be able to bring herself to step foot in it again.

The fear of being found out was a constant, gnawing at her over the days and nights that followed. On a happier note, Thomas's health continued to improve, although he still spent more time in his wheelchair than up on his sticks and he still had that troublesome cough. When his mother suggested that perhaps he was pushing himself too hard, he replied that no matter the cost he was determined not to spend the rest of his days as a semi-invalid and meant to reclaim the life he would have had if the war had not intervened. To that end, he applied himself diligently to learning the ins and outs of investing and threw himself into reacquainting himself with the friends and social life he'd left behind.

Rynn found that adjusting to the life of an aristocratic lady was more difficult than she'd imagined. To begin with, the contrast between her working-class existence in Bundoran and the sheer opulence of the lifestyle the Hartfords and all their circle took for granted was staggering. Even in London, the stark differences between the rich aristocrats in their mansions and the poor living in the overcrowded tenements and filling the teeming streets was eye-opening. But those around her, even Thomas, seemed oblivious to the disparity, and she was once again left to contemplate the fundamental truth behind the Irishman's forever lament of oppressors versus the oppressed. To add to her inner unease, it seemed like she was always in company. She increasingly longed to be outdoors, to go for solitary walks and breathe fresh air and leave her worries behind. But fear of who might be lurking made her wary, and London itself was too crowded and dangerous to explore on her own as more and more people flocked to the capital in the face of the widespread unemployment and homelessness that plagued the country.

The warmer weather brought back the terrifying scourge that was the Spanish flu, although it was mainly reported in the western port cities and this wave seemed milder than the ones of the previous year. Other diseases were on the rise as well. Except for her work with Thomas, her nurse's training was expected to be put aside. The Duchess counseled her that if Thomas was to be a success, it was up to her to do her part by cultivating the wives of the influential. This she did to the best of her ability, although the fact that she was Irish and not of their world meant that the barriers never really came down.

Many evenings were given over to socializing. She accompanied Thomas to victory balls, which were grand events celebrating the war's end and were all the rage, and fundraisers for the veterans and families of the fallen as well as more intimate dinner parties and soirees. They attended the theater and the opera and visited the zoo. Glenna wrote to say that she and Granny would be postponing their visit while she went to Dublin with her class to participate in the July victory parades, which meant that searching for their own London house took on less urgency. Still, she and Thomas looked, and between those excursions and his early-morning exercises that she oversaw and their now almost nightly social engagements they spent much of their time together.

Despite the anxiety that was never far away, Rynn enjoyed her husband's company. But she couldn't shake the near certainty that unseen eyes were following her whenever she left the house, and that someone was out there watching and waiting when she was inside.

She was desperate to talk to Maguire but saw and heard nothing of him and finally was forced to ask Thomas, in what she hoped was an offhand manner, where he was. Thomas said that he'd returned to Ireland to try to reason with the rebels, with apparently indifferent success. Along with gloomy reports on the ongoing riots and labor strikes in their own country, the London newspapers carried almost daily stories about the turmoil rocking Ireland. Lloyd George was being urged by Churchill and others who had his ear to send in more soldiers to deal with the rebels once and for all, and those calls grew louder after the rebels killed an RIC officer as they tried to free a prisoner and began launching attacks on RIC barracks for the purpose of acquiring explosives and guns. Listening to cooler heads, Lloyd George kept the British retaliation *proportional*, as the Duke, who felt that there could be no compromising with the rebels, reported bitterly. The rebels responded to this restraint with a series of lightning ambushes against RIC officers and others loyal to the Crown, and the situation grew more volatile by the day.

To the fury of the British establishment, de Valera turned up alive and well in Ireland and was subsequently elected president of the Dail Eireann. He immediately proclaimed that the Crown had no authority there and that the only authority in Ireland was the elected government of the Irish people. The British, in turn, placed an enormous price on his head and launched an all-out hunt for him. He managed to evade capture, which Rynn considered remarkable in a country where he was so well-known, but there were multiple reports of him traveling the country in disguise and in the opinion of most it was only a matter of time until he was arrested. Finally, any fear of that was taken off the table when he caught a ship to America in hopes of persuading the American Congress to back the rebels' cause. The British, meanwhile, declared counties Limerick, Tipperary, Cork, Kerry and Roscommon, where the rebel activity was heaviest, to be in a state of disturbance, putting them under strict military control including a curfew from 5:00 p.m. to 8:00 a.m. Unsurprisingly, this stirred up great resentment among the citizenry of those areas.

In the words of one Irish columnist, it was a right mess.

Glenna wrote again to say that the area around Bundoran was mostly quiet, although the soldiers from Finner Camp were patrolling the streets and in general making a nuisance of themselves, and a failed attempt by some youths to break into the Garda station in the dead of night to steal guns had ended with two of them being carted off to Kilmainham Gaol. Also, she added, her students were learning to play "Molly Malone" on tin whistles, a bit of artistry they meant to perform in upcoming victory parades in Galway, Limerick, Cork and Dublin. Just picturing Glenna at the head of a gaggle of nine- and ten-year-olds tootling loudly away as they marched down the main streets of the various towns made Rynn smile.

During all this time Rynn saw and heard nothing of Donal. She also heard nothing to indicate that he or Seamus had been captured and could only assume Maguire had taken them away with him or otherwise gotten them to safety as he'd promised. Of Bingle she tried not to think at all, but she couldn't help but fret about what had been done with his body and whether it would turn up and had more than one nightmare in which his death featured prominently. The fear that Bingle was still being searched for and that the truth would one day prove the ruination of them all was the bane of her existence.

Her relationship with Penelope advanced by the smallest of degrees as they encountered one another at various social engagements, but they were pictured together in the *Daily Sketch* and other ladies' magazines and were polite when they met, so the gossips largely turned their focus elsewhere. Still, when an invitation arrived from Lord and Lady Somerset requesting the honor of their presence at a fancy dress ball to raise money for the Save the Children fund to help war orphans, Rynn felt it incumbent on her and Thomas to accept even though it meant prevailing on Thomas to cancel plans he'd already made for that same evening.

"I know you said you'd never go to another fancy dress ball, but if we fail to attend, someone's sure to say I'm on the outs with Penelope." Rynn's tone was apologetic. Thomas's grimace as he read the invitation she'd just handed him told her everything she needed to know about his feelings on the subject. They'd arrived home from touring a house in the Knightsbridge district, which Thomas had thought had possibilities but she'd had reservations about, to find the post waiting for them, and she'd opened that one in the lift as they went upstairs. "Besides, it's for a good cause."

"Joe Beckett's fighting Frank Goddard that night," Thomas groaned. Then his face brightened. "It's a costume ball. We can put a mask on Hinkley—" Hinkley was his valet "—wrap him up in some kind of robe, sit him in my chair and send him with you. No one will know the difference."

"No," Rynn said sternly, but she had to smile. "Of course, if you really don't wish to go . . ." Her voice trailed off.

"A ball is no fun for a man who can't dance," Thomas pointed out. He was using his sticks, so when they reached the door to their apartment Rynn opened it and followed him inside. "And any man who doesn't feel ridiculous kitted out like a swami or Napoleon . . . well, there's no hope for him is all I can say."

"So you wish me to decline."

He looked at her over his shoulder as she closed the door behind them.

"I didn't say that. Accept the damned thing if you must." A corner of his mouth quirked up. "Perhaps we can arrive late. My money's on Beckett knocking out Goddard no later than the second round. I can go on to the ball from there dressed as a man who's just been to a fight."

Rynn laughed, and he gave her an exaggerated leer. "If you'll dress in harem pants and a sheer vest like Lady Cadogan did at that last costume party, it'll almost be worth it."

"I'll see what I can do." Rynn made a face at him—Lady Cadogan's scandalous outfit had been the talk of the town for weeks afterward—and then Parry arrived to help her change for dinner and Thomas went on to his room where Hinkley waited.

As it happened, Joe Beckett did indeed knock out Frank Goddard in the second round, just as Thomas predicted. After assuring Rynn that he would leave no later than the end of the second round and get home in time to accompany her to the ball no matter what, Thomas was there at the fight, on which he bet, won and made a handsome profit, and then proved as good as his word.

"A few more investments like that, and we'll be rich as Carnegie," Thomas chortled as he displayed his winnings to her in the car. At this reference to Andrew Carnegie, arguably the richest man alive, Rynn shook her head.

"Or you'll lose every shilling you possess, and we'll end up in the poorhouse," she retorted, and he laughed.

"Spoken like a true wife."

"Spoken like a person of sense," she said, and he laughed again.

It was going on midnight when they arrived. The ball was in full swing. The ballroom at the Somerset mansion was magnificent, with a high frescoed ceiling held up by fluted pillars, arched French doors open to let in the warm night air and masses of flowers everywhere. The guests were no less magnificent, as Lady Somerset's enormous fortune made her lavish entertainments practically de rigueur among those fortunate enough to receive an invitation. It was difficult to tell who was who as couples twirled past to the lively strains of "Pack Up Your Troubles in Your Old Kit Bag," to which a number of partygoers added a full-throated "and smile, smile, smile" where appropriate. The guests were dressed as everyone from Henry VIII—that would be Churchill, according to Thomas, who said the pale round face beneath the half mask was unmistakable—to Mrs. Ward as Cleopatra. The Prince of Wales, easily identifiable by his blond hair and diminutive size, was a Roman slave in a toga and gilt sandals, and Viscountess Astor was a shepherdess complete with gold-topped crook. Rynn's scarlet dress featured sheer chiffon panels designed to float when she danced over a slim silk column. Glittering with spangles that caught the light with her every movement, it was sleeveless and worn with a long jet necklace and her jet earbobs, a black satin half mask and a cunning headpiece topped with three scarlet plumes. She was supposed to be the Firebird, from the popular Russian ballet. Thomas, in a red military jacket buttoned up over the shirt and trousers he'd worn to the fight and a trench cap, was a toy soldier. He was up on his sticks when they arrived, but Rynn had insisted that his chair be brought along in case he should tire. It wasn't long before he settled into it, surrounded by a group of his cronies, all of whom excitedly listened to his blow-by-blow retelling of the fight.

Rynn danced, and talked to her acquaintances among the ladies present, and went into supper with Thomas, and, as he retired to the card room that had been set aside for the non-dancers among the gentlemen, danced some more. The champagne was heady, and she sipped it cautiously as she sat near one of the French doors cooling off in the slight but welcome breeze. The sweet scent of roses wafting in from the garden rivaled the most fragrant of the ladies' perfumes. She'd been talking to Maud, who'd just been whisked away by Lord North, and was enjoying having a minute to herself to admire the dancers and their costumes when Penelope, who'd danced every dance as far as Rynn could tell, detached herself from her partner and pirouetted up to her. As Rynn looked at her in some surprise, Penelope turned back to the young man she was deserting with the laughing admonishment that if he wanted another dance, he must first provide her with a glass of lemonade, because she was parched.

"Your wish is my command, my queen. I shall return forthwith." Seeming to take his dismissal in good part, he gave her a flourishing bow—not so ridiculous once you realized that Penelope's sixteenth-century gown and glittering crown were meant to turn her into Mary, Queen of Scots, while her admirer, at a guess, was meant to be Sir Walter Raleigh—and headed toward the refreshment room.

Chapter Twenty-Three

"He's very sweet, but I don't wish to marry him," Penelope said as she plopped into the chair beside Rynn. Placed for the convenience of the chaperones, or anyone really who chose to sit out, the small gilt chairs lined the walls. From them, mothers could keep an eye on their marriageable daughters, dowagers could put their heads together and engage in a good gossip about the dancers, and wallflowers could hide behind the potted plants.

"Need you do so?" Rynn cast a speculative glance at this young half-sister who seemed to have most of the eligible bachelors in London at her feet. She and Penelope were on perfectly good terms, but this was the first time that Penelope had ever specifically sought her out.

"My mother wants me to. Edward is the Duke of Norfolk's heir. She's very keen for me to marry the son of a duke." A sidelong glance said much that Penelope didn't put into words, and suddenly Rynn understood Lord Somerset's amusement at her own marriage to Thomas. Lord Somerset, it seemed, enjoyed seeing his wife get her feathers ruffled.

"He seems quite nice," Rynn said. Heretofore, she'd seen no resemblance between herself and Penelope, but now, suddenly, she was struck by the realization that their hands were the same: slim and pale, with long, tapering fingers. With Penelope's hand stretched out along her chair's armrest, and her own hand stretched out along her own chair's armrest, they were side by side and there was no mistaking the similarity.

This is my sister, Rynn thought, and for the first time the relationship felt real.

"He is," Penelope agreed. "But there are twenty just like him. They all want to marry, not me, but my money."

"I'm sure that's not true." Rynn reflected for a minute. "Not *all* of them."

Penelope made a wry face. "My mother says there's no reason such a marriage shouldn't work out. She should know, she's made two of them. And that brings me to what I wanted to ask you. How would you rate such a marriage? You seem perfectly happy with Lord Thomas, and he is clearly besotted with you."

Rynn was taken aback. "If you're suggesting that I married my husband for his money, nothing could be further from the truth."

"Oh, really? I beg your pardon, I meant no offense. Only, that's what everyone is saying, you know."

"Well, *everyone* is wrong."

"I was hoping to get your perspective on it." Penelope sounded disappointed. "Mama says that in the most successful marriages, both parties get something they want. Since I have a fortune, but Grandpapa was a Cit, she thinks I should choose a high-ranking nobleman—like Edward—for the sake of my future children. But the truth is, I'd as soon *not* be married for my money."

"You must do as you please, of course, but I'm sure there's a gentleman out there you will prefer to all the others—and he won't want to marry you for your money."

"I hope so. Anyway, if I *must* be married for my money, I'd like somebody more exciting than Edward—" her eyes, which had been restlessly searching the ballroom, suddenly lit up "—like him."

Following her gaze, Rynn was stunned. Was Penelope really looking at . . . *Maguire*? Because there he was on the opposite side of the ballroom, talking to a man she didn't know. Dressed in classic evening attire—did he not realize that the invitation specified fancy dress?—he looked tall and fit and, yes, very handsome. Certainly she could see his appeal to someone as sheltered as Penelope.

"Is he one of your suitors?" She did her best to keep her voice neutral. Her pulse had quickened upon spotting him, and she was afraid her face might reveal it.

Where have you been? was the question that pounded like a drumbeat through her brain.

"No, but I'd quite like him to be. He's gone into partnership with my stepfather, who says he has a good hard head for business. From Papa Somerset, that's high praise indeed."

"Really." Rynn was just debating whether to reveal that she knew Maguire when, possibly because he felt the force of her and Penelope's gazes, he glanced around and saw her. His face brightened, the slightest of smiles touched his mouth and then he excused himself to his companion and cut a straight line through the dancers as he headed across the ballroom toward them.

"Oh, my, he's coming over." Penelope clasped her hands in excitement. "We've been introduced, but I didn't think—" Her head swiveled toward Rynn and her voice went flat. "He's not coming for me, is he?"

"Major Maguire is Irish, you know. We're acquainted. No doubt he's glad to see a face from home," Rynn said with careful composure. She was more thankful than she could say for her half mask, which hopefully kept Penelope—or anyone—from reading what she feared must be the excitement blazing from her eyes at seeing him. She'd been so worried, and now here he was. With answers.

He stopped in front of them. His eyes met hers for the briefest of moments. She always minimized their impact until she was with him again. It wasn't only that in his sun-and-wind-bronzed face they were the unexpected clear pale blue of the sea; it was that they seemed to hold as many secrets.

Some of which she was dying to know.

"Lady Thomas," he said, and then his gaze shifted to Penelope. "And Miss Carmichael. Or should I say Queen Mary of the Scots?"

"Yes," Penelope trilled delightedly. "How clever you are! You got it in one!"

"It's good to see you again, Major Maguire." Rynn did her best to make sure her smile was no more than polite. The last thing she wanted was for some keen-eyed gossip to divine that he was anything more to her than a casual acquaintance. "It seems like a long time since we've seen you in London."

"Yes, I've been busy setting up my offices in Dublin."

An unobjectionable answer. If it was true. It was all Rynn could do not to frown skeptically at him.

"And how did you find Dublin?" she asked, making polite conversation when what she really wanted to do was drag him off somewhere and lambast him with questions.

"Beautiful as always. Lively. Crowded."

Was he giving her a significant look? By "crowded," was he referring to the presence of Donal and Seamus in Dublin?

The look she gave him asked everything she couldn't put into words. He smiled. Tantalizingly? Was he teasing her? He knew what she wanted to know.

"Oh, that's my favorite song," Penelope exclaimed before either of them could say anything more. Rynn realized that the previous dance had ended, and couples were taking to the floor again to the sprightly strains of "I'm Forever Blowing Bubbles."

Even with her mask, the hopeful look Penelope turned on Maguire was impossible to mistake.

"Would you care to dance, Miss Carmichael?" Holding out

his hand, he gave Penelope a charming smile. Rynn practically choked. *She* wanted answers—but she was clearly going to have to wait.

"I'd love to." Jumping to her feet with an eagerness that, to Rynn, underlined just how young she was, she placed her hand in his.

"If you'll excuse us, Lady Thomas?" The flicker in Maguire's eyes told Rynn that he knew how impatient she was. Her lips tightened in response before the realization occurred that if he was still hale and hearty and a free man nothing too terrible could have happened—she hoped.

"Certainly." Rynn waved them away and sat back to wait.

Maguire was far from the most skilled dancer on the floor, but Penelope added grace to his vigor by matching her steps to his with aplomb. Eyes sparkling, previously pale cheeks blooming with color, she laughed and talked and in general made it clear that she was enjoying herself and the man she was with. Maguire, for his part, had a lazy, almost avuncular smile on his face as he listened to her chatter. As a couple, the tall, dark Irishman and the slender, laughing British heiress attracted a good deal of attention. The gossips had their heads together watching them spin around the floor. Lady Somerset, who'd just left the supper room with a group of friends, frowned as she spotted her daughter. Several of Penelope's suitors looked less than pleased as well.

Edward, for his part, when he returned with the requested lemonade, spilled nearly half of it from trying to watch them as he walked.

"Who's that chap?" he burst out as he reached Rynn. Then, realizing they hadn't been introduced, he added, "I'm Arundel, you know."

"And I'm Lady Thomas Dunne," Rynn replied.

"Oh, I know *that*. Everyone does. Dunne's Irish bride." As

that blurted-out-before-he-thought answer clearly appalled him, he stammered and apologized and in general behaved with so much boyish embarrassment that Rynn found herself quite liking him. She couldn't imagine that he was much older than twenty, and thought that when he outgrew his callowness he might actually be a solid prospect for Penelope.

"I, uh, would you care to dance, Lady Thomas?" he asked at the conclusion of his convoluted apology. He started to hold out his hand to her, realized he still held the glass of lemonade and blushed bright red.

Taking pity on him, Rynn took the glass out of his hand and set it down beside her champagne on the small table at her elbow.

"You'll do better waiting for my sister." She nodded toward Penelope as, the song having ended, she and Maguire came toward them. "She's the one you really want to dance with anyway."

"She is," Edward agreed gloomily, before casting Rynn an alarmed, apologetic glance. "Not that I don't wish to dance with *you*, Lady Thomas, but—"

"I'm an old married woman and not a bit exciting," Rynn finished for him with a twinkle in her eye.

"Yes," Edward said, then looked horrified. "No, that's not it at all! I—"

Rynn was laughing at him as Penelope and Maguire reached them.

"Take him away and dance with him," Rynn said to Penelope, thrusting Edward at her. "He brought you your lemonade and now the toll must be paid."

"Yes," Edward said to Penelope. "I did. Brought the lemonade, I mean. Though some spilled, I'm afraid, and, uh—" He gave up, swallowed and concluded with a stiff "Miss Carmichael, will you . . . ?"

Before he could finish asking, Penelope said, "Certainly. I

always pay my debts, you'll find," and Maguire transferred Penelope's hand to his arm and stepped aside.

They walked away, and Rynn was left alone with Maguire at last.

"Where have you been? It's been weeks," she hissed.

"Your friends are safe. Anything else should probably wait for a more private setting." He cast a significant look around, then nodded at Maud and Alice and their respective partners, all of whom were heading their way. "Unless you wish to find yourself in company, I suggest we take to the floor."

"No, I don't wish to find myself in company. Not right now. Very well, let's dance." She put her hand in his and he swung her into his arms. She felt surprisingly at home there, and once again it was easy to match her steps to his. Moments later, they were in the midst of the company gliding around to the plaintive "After You've Gone." The dance floor was crowded, too crowded to afford any semblance of privacy. Any kind of sensitive discussion would have to wait, even though she was practically foaming at the mouth with questions.

"We should probably try to make polite conversation," he said.

She tilted her head back to see his eyes. They twinkled at her.

"You do realize that this is a costume ball, don't you?" If she sounded cross, well, perhaps she was, a little. To be so near to the answers she needed and yet not be able to get them was maddening. "You're supposed to be in disguise."

"I'm in disguise."

"Oh?" Her gaze swept as much of him as she could see. "What are you disguised as, then?"

"An English gentleman."

"Instead of an Irish brigand? That *is* a disguise." Her voice was tart.

"I thought so." He smiled. "And you're a . . . half-plucked red chicken?"

"Oh, ha-ha. I'm the Firebird. From the ballet."

"Ah. Well, I wouldn't know much about that. What was that boy saying to you back there to make you laugh so?"

"That I'm an old married woman and he much prefers my sister."

"He didn't."

"He thought it," Rynn said. "I may have put it into words for him, but he thought it."

"He's an idiot," Maguire said with conviction.

Leaning back against his arm, Rynn succumbed to a reluctant smile. "Possibly. He'll be a nice fellow when he grows up a little, though. Like Penelope, he's very young."

"Says the old married woman. How old are you, anyway? Twenty-one? Twenty-two?"

"Twenty-three. And didn't anyone ever tell you that it's rude to ask a lady her age?"

"I'm sure someone must have."

"How old are you?"

His brows lifted. "Oh, ho, so I can't ask you, but you can ask me?"

"I think you'll find that applies to many topics. But you did ask me, and I told you. So . . ."

"As near to twenty-nine as makes no difference."

"What does that mean?"

"My birthday's in three weeks."

"I see. Happy almost birthday."

"Thank you."

"Ever married?" She couldn't help it. She was dying to know.

"I'm sure that's one of those questions you shouldn't be asking me."

"Well?"

"No."

"Why not?"

"I've been a tad busy, what with the war and all."

She gave him a speculative look. "Now that you're going into business with Lord Somerset, I'm sure it's occurred to you that my sister is a considerable heiress."

He lifted his brows at her. "Are you by any chance matchmaking?"

"No, I'm not. I don't think you'd suit."

"I thought we agreed that only a fool doesn't consider his opportunities."

That brought her back to the conversation they'd had on the *Reaper.* It seemed like a very long time ago now.

"Or a rogue." The tartness was back in her voice.

"Exactly."

They exchanged measuring looks, and then he smiled at her. "You know, when I saw you there on the edge of the ballroom, I could have sworn you looked glad to see me."

"I was. I am. Oh, come outside." They'd reached one of the three sets of open French doors by that time. Casting a quick glance around to make sure no one who mattered was watching, she pulled out of his arms, caught his hand instead and dragged him out onto the terrace.

Chapter Twenty-Four

It was a beautiful night, warm and only slightly cloudy, with the moon riding high among a sprinkling of stars and the scent of roses all around. Light from the ballroom threw long shapes across the stone. They weren't alone, but the terrace ran the length of the house and the couples who were already outside seemed to have no wish to be in company. As Rynn steered Maguire deep into the shadows next to the balustrade before swinging around to face him, the sheer romance of the setting was not lost on her.

But neither she nor Maguire had any inclination toward romance.

"Tell me what happened." Her voice was low.

"What you knew would happen when you came to me. I got the idiots safe away."

"Where to?"

"Passed them off to some associates. Warned them that if I ever had to rescue them again, I wouldn't."

"Did they tell you . . . ?" Her voice dropped even lower. "The warehouse where Seamus was shot, where he and Donal had been working—de Valera had been there. And had been gotten away by a crew headed by Michael Collins. I'm afraid I may have gotten you involved in the aftermath of de Valera's escape. I didn't realize until afterward."

"If you had, would it have made a difference?"

Honesty compelled her. "No."

"I didn't think so." His voice was dry. "Don't worry, I figured it out pretty fast. Hopefully with Dev off to America the Brits will give up on trying to arrest him, or anyone who helped with his escape."

"I don't think they will." Rynn hesitated. She'd overheard her father-in-law talking to a group of men in his study, and passing on information she'd obtained in such a way still made her uncomfortable. But this was Maguire, who she trusted not to misuse the knowledge, and whose safety might be at stake along with that of who knew how many other people. "Crime Special Branch is recruiting local agents to infiltrate the Dail and the IRB as we speak. They're looking to gain access to the identities of everyone involved in the network that helped de Valera escape, and are then planning to arrest them all in a single swoop."

"*Are* they?" He gave her a thoughtful look. "I'm sure there are safeguards in place. Or will be. Nothing for you to concern yourself about."

He was telling her to stay out of it, she knew. Her lips pursed.

"What did you do about . . . ?" Rynn hesitated. Even outside in the dark, with no one nearby to overhear she was *almost* certain, she was uncomfortable saying Bingle's name, or referring to him as something like *the corpse*. "Disposing of everything else?"

He knew what she was talking about. "Took care of it."

"Everything?"

"Yes."

"Did you run into any trouble?"

"Quite a bit, actually." His tone turned grim. "And just so you know, the search is still on for the government's missing man. But there's nothing to tie you to it, and as long as you're careful you don't need to worry. That particular matter is handled, and in such a way that it shouldn't come up again. If you have any sense of self-preservation at all, you'll stay out of such things in future and keep away from idiots and set yourself to enjoying your life *here*, in safety, as the wife of a good man."

Thomas liked him, too.

"I can't just forget what's happening at home," she said quietly. "I'm Irish, after all. Just like them. Just like you."

"You can do no one any good if you get yourself thrown in jail or killed. For now, the best choice for all of us is to take a step back and let cooler heads prevail. War is a terrible price to pay for peace. I'm hoping we can find our way to moving forward without it."

A number of people emerged, laughing and talking, onto the terrace. Rynn realized that the music had stopped, which meant the orchestra must be taking a break.

"We should go in," she said, conscious of the curious glances being sent her and Maguire's way.

"Yes," he agreed, and followed her back inside.

Thomas was looking for her. He was with his brother, and Alice, and Maud and Lord North, and they all spotted her almost as soon as she stepped back inside the ballroom. He was up on his sticks and as she walked toward him, his hands tightened on the grips, and he lost his smile. His eyes slid from her to Maguire, who was behind her. There was something in them—a flicker, a glint, a look she'd never seen in them before. Then she and Maguire reached the group, and greetings were exchanged, along with the normal pleasantries. Thomas was very much his affable self, and Rynn decided she must have misread the look she'd thought she'd seen in his eyes.

That is, until later, when they were back in their apartment at Hartford House, after she'd bathed and changed into her nightdress and braided her hair and, finally, dismissed Parry for what was left of the night, and Thomas came into her bedroom.

He, too, was dressed for bed. He was in his chair, and she was just turning off the light on the dressing table when he entered, which left only the light beside her bed to bathe the room in a dim, pale glow. As she was on her way to bed she hadn't bothered with her robe, and her lawn nightdress left her arms and most of her shoulders bare.

"Is something wrong?" she asked as he closed the adjoining door behind him, which he never did, so she was already alerted that this wee-hours-of-the-morning visit was something out of the ordinary before he spoke.

"I want to talk to you." There was a note in his voice that she'd never heard before.

"What is it?" Alarm, consternation, uncertainty—actually, the thought of Bingle was what jumped to the forefront of her mind—combined to make her pulse leap.

"Sit down. Please."

She sank down on the chair at her dressing table as he rolled toward her. Watching his approach, it struck her that he'd changed significantly in appearance during the time they'd been together. Besides his mustache, which had grown in full and lush, and his hair, also full and surprisingly wavy now that it was no longer cut in a military style, he'd put on weight and muscle and his coloring was healthy, with the ruddiness that came with time spent outdoors having driven out the pallor that had once so concerned her. In fact, he very much resembled the strapping youth he'd been before the war, the one she'd seen in the family portrait he'd kept beside his bed at Ballyshannon Court. Only now, that youth was a man.

"You're scaring me," she said.

"I hope not." He reached for her hand. His was warm and strong, and she curled her fingers around it. "I never want you to be afraid of me or anything else. I'm going to ask you something, and I want you to tell me the truth, and whatever that truth is I promise you that I can accept it, and nothing will happen that you don't want to happen. But I need to know."

"What on earth, Thomas?"

"Are you—involved—with Maguire?"

"What?"

He held up a hand. "Before you answer, I think you should know that I know that what you said about rescuing the dog that night you were so late getting home isn't true." His mouth twisted, a little wry, a little tender. "You really think I can't tell when you're lying? It was written all over your face. And . . ." A shadow of what looked like pain crossed his eyes. His hand tightened on hers. "I saw you leaving Maguire's hotel with him that night. I'd stopped by on the way to White's to have Meadows drop off a guest voucher for him at the front desk, and as I waited in the car for Meadows to return, I saw you and Maguire come out of the hotel, walk down the stairs to the street and then he put you in a taxi. I was . . . surprised, to say the least. You seemed very . . . taken with one another. And then tonight you went out with him onto the terrace. And when you came back in . . . well, it was easy to tell that something had passed between you that you didn't want the rest of us to know about."

"And you thought that he and I—"

"Wait," he interrupted, speaking rapidly as if afraid to let her finish. "I know I said that I would let you out of the marriage if you wanted out. And I will, if that's truly what you want. But—"

"Stop, no, you can't think that I'm having a romantic relationship with Owen Maguire! I'm not. I would never do that. I'm your *wife*. I would never play you false, I give you my word. You have my loyalty. You have my loyalty one hundred percent."

He simply looked at her. Hope was there in his eyes, and doubt, and questions she knew he wanted answers to. His hand held hers tightly, and then he reached for her other hand and held that tightly, too. She knew she could almost certainly get away with saying *trust me*, and he would. He would let the matter drop on her word.

But the doubt would remain. And it would eat away at him, and their relationship, a slow poison that would destroy it over time.

Could she tell him the truth? *Should* she?

"You're right, I was lying about the dog," she said. He winced, just slightly but she saw it, and that small gesture told her how much pain he'd been in since he'd seen her with Maguire at the hotel, and how much pain the thought of her with Maguire was causing him now.

He didn't say anything, but his eyes spoke volumes. They were vulnerable in a way that squeezed her heart.

"It was Donal." She held onto his hands as he frowned. "Donal came for me in the park that afternoon. I hadn't seen him since the night we parted, Christmas night, and I had no idea he was in London. But he'd seen my photograph in the newspaper—you know, the one with the Prince of Wales—so he knew where I was. He came to find me because Seamus had been badly wounded and they needed my nursing skills. They had nowhere else to turn. I went with him, and treated Seamus, who almost certainly would have died otherwise, and then they needed to get out of London. I went to Major Maguire for help with that. That's why I was with him at his hotel. He wasn't happy, didn't want to get involved, but he did agree to help, and then he put me in a taxi for home while he went off to deal with it. I haven't heard from Donal or Seamus since then, and tonight was the first time I've seen Major Maguire. I pulled him out onto the terrace to find out what had happened. He said he'd gotten them safe away, and he wasn't ever helping in a matter of that nature again. He told me to stay away from anything to do with the O'Reillys and the rebellion. He said you were a good man, and I should settle into my life here, and be happy."

"He said that?"

"Yes." So she'd left out the part about Bingle. That was the part that gave her nightmares. That was the part that could ruin them all. For her sake, and Thomas's, she'd told him as much of the truth as she felt she could. But she owed Donal and Seamus, and particularly Maguire, who would never have been involved if she hadn't involved him, something, too: her silence on the most dangerous part of their secret.

"You went to Maguire for help? Why didn't you come to me?"

"I didn't want to get you caught up in it. With your father being who he is, and considering his views—well, the consequences of involving you seemed far too great to risk. And Major Maguire is Irish. Even if he disapproved, which he did, strongly, I knew he'd help, and keep his mouth shut about it. And he did. And he has."

Thomas's frown was clearing. "My God. What I've been through, imagining . . ."

"I'm sorry. I had no idea you were aware of any of this."

"Rynn, my dear, your face is as transparent as glass. I knew you were lying about the dog while the words were coming out of your mouth."

"You should have said something."

"I suppose I should have. I just . . . if you want the truth, I was afraid to say anything in case that pushed you into doing something I didn't want—I *don't* want—you to do."

"Such as?"

"Decide our marriage wasn't what you wanted. Ask to end it. I know you said I have your loyalty, and I believe you, and I appreciate that. But I don't just want your loyalty. I—" He broke off, looked intently at her and seemed to steel himself. "I'm better now. I'm healing. I can almost walk again, and I think that by next summer I *will* be walking. Without the sticks. And I'm better in other ways, too. I can—I want us to have a real marriage. I want to be your husband in every sense of the word. Do you understand what I'm saying? I want *you*. Forever. As my wife."

Her heart clutched. "Thomas . . ."

"Don't say anything. Don't give me your answer yet. I want you to take some time and think about it. I've told you what I want. But I want you to have what *you* want, too. So the question becomes, what *do* you want? To be my wife, or . . . I'll give you your freedom, if that's what you choose. Even if it breaks my heart to do it." That blazing look of adoration was back in his eyes, and then he raised her hands to his mouth and kissed them, one at a time.

"Thomas—"

"Shh." Dropping her hands to cup her face, he leaned forward and kissed her. It was a full-on kiss, a deep, hungry man's kiss, and it caught her by surprise. She didn't know what her face looked like when he let her go, but when she didn't immediately say anything, his expression turned guarded. The smile he gave her was small and tight.

"Think about it," he said again, and wheeled his chair around. He was almost at the door when she recovered enough to say "Thomas. Wait."

It was only as he looked back that she realized that her fingers were pressed to her lips where he'd kissed her. With his gaze narrowing on her, she dropped them to her lap.

"Go to bed, Rynn." The words were clipped, and he turned and continued out the door, closing it behind him.

Rynn sat there, staring at the closed door and pondering her future while a thousand thoughts and feelings and images chased themselves through her mind. Her past with Donal, and the sweet intensity of their young love. Her ever-deepening bond with Thomas, and what life could be with him. What won out, funnily enough, was a kaleidoscope of visions of Bundoran that resolved into a single frame of herself standing atop the cliffs high above the Strand looking out at Donegal Bay and beyond, to the wild Atlantic Way. She was pale and still, wrapped snugly in a fringed black shawl, with her hair loose and blowing in the wind and her heart aching at—what, the sheer beauty of the scene before her? For an uncanny moment she could almost smell the salt in the air and feel the nip of the wind. Far below, the roaring waves pounded the shore . . .

And then she was back, in her bedroom at Hartford House, heart still aching a little for what she'd left behind.

Home. She missed it, missed the life she'd had, missed herself as she had been before she'd married Thomas and run away, with a fierceness that was almost a physical pain inside her. And she could have it back. She had only to say the word, and Thomas would let her go. He would do what he could to make sure the cost to her was minimal, she knew. The one who would suffer would be him.

To reclaim her freedom, she would have to turn her back on him, and on that look she'd seen for her in his eyes.

The question was, as he'd said, what did she want?

Once again it was time to choose.

Chapter Twenty-Five

After a while, Rynn stood up and turned out the lamp beside her bed.

Then she crossed the room to the door that he'd closed, opened it and padded across his dark bedroom to where a sliver of moonlight peeking through the curtains illuminated the long form that was Thomas, tucked up in bed. His chair waited nearby.

He wasn't asleep. She could tell by his breathing. He lay on his back, his head propped up on pillows because having his head elevated during the night kept the worst of the coughing at bay. She could feel his eyes on her, feel his gaze tracking her until she stopped by the side of the bed.

"Rynn? Is something wrong?" His voice was heavy, as if he were tired, or weary, which in this case were two very different things.

"I thought about it." She sat down on the bed beside him. She couldn't see much of him: the gleam of his eyes where the moonlight caught them, the darker shape that was his head and shoulders against the pristine white of the pillows. "And I made a decision. I want this to be a real marriage, too."

She heard the sharp intake of his breath. Then he reached for her even as she leaned forward to kiss him.

"Are you sure?" he asked when they broke apart.

"I'm sure," she said, and slid into bed beside him.

The earth didn't move. The stars didn't shake. But there was a sweetness to their coming together, a tenderness from him toward her that made her heart melt, a silent pledging of lives being joined even as their bodies became one.

And in the end, she wasn't sorry. Wherever this path took her, she was willing to go.

In the days that followed, they were happy. *She* was happy. Not that she didn't have regrets, because she did. She regretted that the choice she'd made meant that she could never really go home again, regretted the loss of self that came with being Lady Thomas Dunne, regretted the passing of the Rynn Carmichael that she had been into the misty realm of the past.

But she didn't regret choosing to stay with Thomas as his wife. She didn't regret choosing the life she knew they could build together. She didn't regret the safety and trust she had found with him or the knowledge that he genuinely loved her and would always put her well-being first. She didn't regret relinquishing her girlish love for Donal and replacing it with this new, more mature affection that she had no doubt would only strengthen and grow over time.

As for Thomas, happiness transformed him. His eyes were brighter, his smile was sunnier and his renewed energy and determination to get better led to him making great strides physically. His doctors still considered it unlikely that he would ever walk without the aid of his sticks, but they no longer felt it was impossible.

That was all the encouragement Thomas needed to work ferociously toward that new goal.

"How do you feel about spending next spring in Paris?" Thomas asked her as Meadows drove them home after they watched Gerald Patterson defeat reigning champion Norman Brookes to win the gentlemen's singles title at Wimbledon. A keen tennis player before the war, Thomas had followed the play with an enthusiasm that Rynn, who'd never played, couldn't quite summon. But she'd enjoyed the day, and the crowd, and the pleasure that Thomas had taken in the match. This was the first Wimbledon in four years, and the packed stadium said everything that needed to be said about the public's appetite for a return to normalcy after the austerity of the war years.

"Paris sounds lovely."

"I promised to show you the world, if you remember, and I intend to do it. Paris is just the start. Where else would you like to go?"

They discussed the merits of various destinations, not that Rynn could contribute much because, except for her present stay in England, she'd lived her entire life in Ireland. In the end, she left the itinerary to Thomas, who promised her the most fabulous trip she could ever imagine, adding that it would be the first of many. She, in turn, occupied herself with getting the house they'd leased in Kensington ready for Granny and Glenna's visit. Still unable to shake the suspicion that she was being watched and/or followed whenever she left Hartford House, she looked forward to moving into the new house with Thomas as soon as it was ready. Green Park assumed ever more monstrous proportions in her imagination, and she could hardly bring herself to glance in its direction. Although nothing happened, and she saw no one suspicious and no one approached her, she couldn't rid herself of the thought that sooner or later Bingle's death would surface with catastrophic consequences.

The feeling of dread that resulted was like a small dark cloud hovering constantly on the horizon.

Maguire returned to Ireland as de Valera's work in the United States began to bear fruit, resulting in America requesting that the Dail Eireann be given a hearing at the Paris Peace Conference and expressing sympathy with the desire of the Irish people to establish a government of their choosing. This diplomatic path to Irish independence—gaining international support for an autonomous Irish republic and thus forcing Britain's hand—had a great deal of support among the less militant wing of the Republicans. Although the struggle for independence continued, while this peaceful resolution to the Irish Question remained on the table large-scale violence did not break out. Instead, isolated incidents like the assassination in County Tipperary of an RIC district inspector by Irish Volunteers in retaliation for the ill-treatment of an Irish prisoner while in government custody kept the conflict bubbling at just below boiling point.

The big news as reported in all the papers was the Versailles Peace Treaty, signed on June 28, officially ending the Great War, which had started on that exact date five years earlier, when Archduke Franz Ferdinand of Austria was assassinated at Sarajevo. Thousands of people flocked to London in anticipation of the festivities, which were to include a victory parade featuring nearly fifteen thousand British Empire servicemen, with innumerable parties and balls leading up to it. Kensington Gardens was transformed into a camp for the troops, and every hotel, inn, rooming house and temporary lodging in the city was full to bursting. People camped out in the parks, while others slept on sidewalks and in doorways. Traffic of all descriptions clogged the streets, and the King and Queen were wildly cheered wherever they went. The newspapers were full of the patriotic exploits of the Prince of Wales, who was, if possible, even more popular than his parents. One less positive aspect of the celebrations was that every type of vice—drunkenness, drug use, prostitution—exploded out of the slums and back alleys into the mainstream parts of the city, and the bobbies worked double and triple shifts without making a dent in the epidemic of crime. The mood in the city was volatile, with hundreds of unemployed former soldiers protesting the amount of money spent on commemorating a war that had killed more than eight hundred thousand British military personnel and left the economy in a shambles.

Other, more deadly if less visible visitors found their way into London as well. The first hint that a mortal threat had come in with the crowds was a notice posted in the daily newspapers seeking more nurses at the Royal London Hospital because of a sudden influx of patients. The second was a small article in *The Morning Post* detailing a family of seven in Whitechapel who had all died within twenty-four hours of each other of a mysterious lung infection, cause to be determined. The third was word that a connection of Lord North's who was stationed in the makeshift army camp in Kensington had come down with what was suspected to be the Spanish flu. The fourth was an ominous headline in *The Telegraph* warning "Hospitals Bracing for Another Wave of Influenza."

"We have to get you out of town," Rynn said to Thomas in alarm as more people sickened and it became clear that another wave of the Purple Flu, as the Spanish flu was called because of the cyanosis that turned sufferers' lips, fingertips and toes a dreaded purplish-blue shade in the end stages, was indeed beginning a sweep through overcrowded London.

"I don't think I'm at any more risk than anyone else," he protested. "My health is much improved."

"Your lungs." Having risen from the breakfast table when she'd read the article, Rynn had already set Parry and Hinkley to packing their bags before waylaying Thomas on his way to an early-morning meeting with his bankers. "They haven't fully recovered. You still cough at night. And you're easily winded. We don't dare chance it."

"I'm not an invalid. And I'm supposed to take part in the parade."

Rynn wouldn't be dissuaded, and the Duchess, when approached, agreed with her.

"You must leave London," she said to Thomas. "As warm as the weather is, you'll find it more pleasant in the country anyway." Her face brightened. "Perhaps we should go to Ashton as well. Geoffrey and Alice can come, too, and Maud if she wishes. We can make a family party of it."

"If I must go somewhere, I'd rather go to Ballyshannon Court." Thomas looked at Rynn. "You'd like that, wouldn't you? Mother, you and Papa can come as well."

"Your father will never agree to that. No, we'll go to Ashton. But you must do as you wish, as long as you get out of town."

"Instead of Granny and Glenna visiting us in London, we'll visit them," Rynn said. "That's a splendid idea. But we must go right away."

They left the following afternoon, traveling by train to Holyhead and then crossing the Irish Sea by ferry to Dublin. There they spent the night at the Shelbourne, Dublin's most luxurious hotel, where the Irish constitution had been signed by the Dail months earlier. But despite its ties to the rebels, the hotel, with its top-hatted doormen and elegant restaurants, was a conservative bastion and a prime favorite with well-heeled British visitors. Thomas felt right at home, while Rynn, who was even more keenly aware of the change in her circumstances now that she was back among her own people, did not. It was only when she took Thomas on a chauffeured tour of the city, which still bore significant damage from the Easter Rising, that she truly started to feel that she was home again. The General Post Office, where a number of rebels had made their last stand, was entirely gone, burned out, and the backs of the buildings lining the alley behind it, through which she'd run as she and a cadre of her fellow nurses had rushed to aid as many of the wounded as they could, were still black with soot. Sackville, Abbey and Henry Streets in the central part of the city were likewise still in ruins from the fires that had swept them. Closing her mind to the emotions the lingering devastation provoked, Rynn set herself to pointing out more cheerful sights, including at Thomas's request such personal landmarks as the former Dan Lowrey's Palace of Varieties, now the Empire Palace Theatre, where her mother had last performed, the Mater Hospital, where Rynn had completed her nurse's training, and the house on Dunville Avenue, where she had lived as a young child with her parents before her mother's death had precipitated their move to Bundoran. She barely remembered any of that part of her childhood, she assured Thomas when he commiserated with her over the hurt caused by her mother's death and the upheaval that followed. If that wasn't strictly true, what was true was that she saw no point in revisiting any part of her past that was painful. She chose, instead, to enjoy this day with Thomas, and to be happy.

The next morning, they traveled on to Bundoran. Higdon met them at the train station and, because Glenna and Granny with her were off on their victory tour with the schoolchildren, drove them straight to Ballyshannon Court. No longer in use as a hospital, it still had not fully transitioned back into its former life as a private home. Much of the medical equipment had been left behind, stored in the vast cellar. The furniture that had been removed to make way for the care of patients had not yet been replaced. Full of apologies because the house was short-staffed, which she blamed on having received no more than two days' notice that they were coming, Mrs. Frampton was on hand to greet them, along with Lynette and Anna, and Cyril the footman. The slight awkwardness because Rynn, formerly considered part of the staff, was now one of the family instead, was easily overcome with the wonderful adaptability of the Irish.

After settling in, Thomas was restless and wanted to go outside. He was looking tired but refused his chair and insisted on walking with his sticks.

"You don't want to do too much," Rynn cautioned him.

"Actually, I want to do everything." He smiled at her. "Aren't you the person who told me I'll never get better if I don't try?"

"Are you really going to throw my words back at me like that?"

"All I'm trying to say is, you were right."

He looked so innocent as he said it that she laughed, gave up and went outside with him without any more protest.

It was the most beautiful summer's afternoon, and as they made their way slowly through the kitchen garden and along the path that led to the cliffs Rynn felt her spirit expand like a wilted flower soaking in water after a drought. The murmur of the surf, the cloudless sky as blue as St. Patrick's robe, the salt smell of the sea, the cooling breeze blowing in off the ocean to lift the loose tendrils of hair from her temples, called to her in a way that nothing, none of the luxuries, none of the grand houses or ballrooms or personages, none of the storied sights of the admittedly magnificent city of London, had come close to doing.

"This place suits you," Thomas said as they stood looking out over the bay. They'd only gone as far as the nearest overlook, certainly not all the way to the Point because Rynn still feared overtiring him despite his assurances that he was fine, but they could see the Strand and the sea stacks and the Fairy Bridges and the rippling ocean all the way to the horizon. Boats of all descriptions scuttled across the waves. Seagulls wheeled and cried. The sun had started its downward trajectory, and ribbons of pink and orange twisted across the sky.

"It's home." Glancing at him, she discovered that he was looking at her rather than the view.

"It's beautiful. Not as beautiful as you, not even close, but in its own wild way."

She smiled at him. "We should start back," she said, and suited the action to the words. He fell into step beside her, maneuvering across the uneven ground on his sticks with commendable skill.

The fever came on him in the middle of the night. They shared a bed now—so unfashionable!—and Rynn woke up to the feel of him shivering violently beside her.

"Thomas?"

"It's all right. It's just my head hurts. And I'm so cold."

Rynn sat bolt upright and reached for the lamp beside the bed.

As soon as the light came on and she looked at him, she knew.

Besides the shivering, he was bone pale. His breathing was labored. And his lips were turning blue.

Panic struck her clear through to her heart.

He fought to live. She fought to save him. Dr. Lowry came, masked and gowned, to do what he could. Fearful of infecting his other patients—he had left a laboring woman to come to Thomas's aid and would be returning to her—he came no closer than the bedroom doorway, making the diagnosis at a glance. He left Rynn with aspirin and oxygen syringes and little else. His parting advice, to keep him comfortable, terrified her.

"Am I going to die, then?" Thomas asked hours later between painful coughs thick with the fluid filling his lungs. Fighting for his life with every bit of nursing skill she had, Rynn feared she was losing. Night was falling again, and he was worse, far worse. The purple spots that came with advancing cyanosis mottled his cheeks. His ears had started to turn blue, slowly, from the lobes up. Swaddled in blankets, he huddled in their bed, drowsy with fever and lack of oxygen, propped up in what was almost a sitting position to help him breathe.

"No." She was on her knees beside the bed, trying to keep him with her now by sheer force of will.

"I want you to know, you are everything I could ever have wanted in this world. Could ever have dreamed of. More than that."

"You can tell me all this when you're better."

He tried to smile, grimaced instead, then started to cough again.

After that, he sank back on the pillows and closed his eyes. As midnight approached, the liquid gurgle of his breathing, the tortured rise and fall of his chest as he fought to draw in air, the spreading, mottled blue of his skin, filled her with dread.

Wet compresses, camphor to open his airways, generous doses of whiskey, quinine, nothing seemed to help.

"I love you, Thomas." Despair roughened her voice. The lamplight spared her no detail of his sweat-darkened hair, brushed roughly back from his forehead, his flaring nostrils and parched lips, parted and trembling as he struggled to breathe, the bruised look of his skin.

At first, she thought he hadn't heard, that her words hadn't penetrated the stupor he was lost in. Then his hand, which had been flaccid in hers, stirred. His closed eyelids twitched, and then they lifted.

"I love you, Thomas," she said again. Clear and emphatic, so there was no mistake.

His fingers tightened on hers. He smiled, the smallest, faintest ghost of a smile, but she knew he heard and understood.

"Rynn." It was no more than a breath of sound, but his eyes were clear and looking into hers with recognition for the first time in hours, and she felt the faintest flutter of hope. Her hand tightened on his as she gathered every remaining bit of strength she had and willed it into him.

"I've been waiting so long to hear you say that," he said. With his eyes locked on hers, something profound passed between them, a meeting of hearts and souls. The fierceness of her resolve to fight on despite the overwhelming odds had her breaking eye contact to cast a desperate glance at the medicines on the table: the aspirin, the camphor, the empty syringes of the oxygen Dr. Lowry had advised injecting under his skin. Nothing, nothing, nothing: none of it had helped.

Something had to.

Thomas exhaled with a deep, shuddering sigh. She looked back at him in time to watch the light in his eyes fade, and his lids close.

Panic galvanized her. Exhausted no longer, she leaped to her feet, grabbed his shoulders.

"Thomas! Thomas, stay with me!"

Even as she leaned over him, frantic, his face went slack and his hand went limp in hers as he died.

Chapter Twenty-Six

Rynn had only the haziest of memories of the next few weeks. On the second day after Thomas's death, after his family had been told and while arrangements were still being made for the collection of his body, she, too, was taken ill. Her battle with Thomas's killer lasted eleven days. Had it not been for the devoted nursing of Granny, who rushed to her side as soon as she could get to Ballyshannon Court, Rynn suspected she might have died, too.

But she didn't. She woke up on a sunny afternoon in an elaborate canopied bed in one of the big bedrooms at the front of the house. She knew where she was—the view out the nearest window of the manicured front lawn sweeping down to the road left her in no doubt—and the sight of the small, indomitable figure of Granny bustling around the room was immediately reassuring. But her head swam and her mouth was dry and . . . and . . .

"Thomas?" was the first thing that came out of her mouth. Through the fog in her brain burst an indelible memory even as she asked the question. "Dear God, is he . . . ?" She took a breath. "He's dead, isn't he?"

"He is. He was buried four days ago at Ashtonbury Park, in the family cemetery." Granny was matter-of-fact as she came to stand beside the bed. She did not believe in coddling her granddaughters, or anyone. In her worldview, you had to be strong to survive.

"Ah." As the memories came rushing back, the pain Rynn felt was indescribable. Gritting her teeth against it, she closed her eyes and sank deeper into the pillows propping her up.

"You're going to be all right, my dotey pet. It's a great grief, I've no doubt, but you must turn your thoughts to regaining your strength."

It was a slow process. Another week passed before she could reliably move farther than the armchair near the bed, and it was two weeks after that before she felt strong enough to dress and go downstairs. Copies of the *Donegal Vindicator,* a local newspaper, had been allowed to pile up on a table in the library. Picking one up, Rynn's breath was stolen away by its lead story. Under the headline "The Dread Scourge Influenza is Back," the article spoke of the thousand who had died of the illness in County Donegal alone since the previous year, and ended with "The Angel of Death has gathered into its fold three more of the inhabitants of the place." Thomas was one of the three listed.

Heartsick, Rynn put the paper down and went back upstairs to bed.

Mrs. Frampton, bless her, had never left, working loyally through Thomas's illness and her own, while taking every precaution to avoid infection. Cyril, too, had stayed on. With the return of Anna and Lynette—Higdon having taken up a position in Dublin—the house resumed a semblance of normality. The heartache that was Thomas's death Rynn set herself to endure, because there was simply no other choice. All the tears and all the grief in the world wouldn't bring him back. But the flu had left her physically weakened, and that, coupled with a lack of appetite and an inability to sleep, took its toll on her.

"You're pale as a ghost," Glenna exclaimed one afternoon

when she came upon Rynn sitting before a crackling fire in the music room. It was late summer, and still warm, but Rynn could not shake the bone-deep chill that her illness had left her with. Having led her tin-whistling students through the various victory parades, Glenna had rushed back home to be at Rynn's side, but Granny had kept her away until she judged the risk of infection was nonexistent. Since then, Glenna visited several times a week while she prepared for another school year.

"I'm always pale," Rynn retorted, looking at her rosy-cheeked sister in her airy linen blouse and skirt. Glenna was blooming, the very picture of good health. And happiness. Never in her life had Rynn envied her sister, but she felt a twinge of it now.

"Not like this." Glenna looked her up and down. "And you're way too thin. Are you eating at all?"

"Yes, of course," Rynn said. But she knew Glenna was right. Her cheekbones and collarbone were more prominent than they'd ever been. When she was undressed, the outline of her ribs was visible, and her hipbones showed through her skin. Her fine-boned features were almost chiseled now in their sharpness, making her eyes appear huge and shadowed and her mouth too wide. Her usual clothes hung on her, and, while the widow's weeds she'd had made up fit better, the stark black of the long-sleeved, high-necked dresses only emphasized her weight loss and pallor.

"Come on, we're getting you outside. It can't be good for you to stay in like this." Glenna tugged Rynn to her feet, and then, casting a quick glance over her sister, added, "You're not going to keel over on me, are you? Should I go get a wheelchair?"

"No." Her answer was sharper than the question called for, but Glenna's suggestion had immediately conjured up Thomas for her, and the resulting stab of pain had caught her by surprise. His chair, his sticks, everything he'd brought with him was still in the bedroom they'd shared. She'd caught a glimpse of them when Anna had opened the door and windows to air the room out and had been swamped by a wave of grief so strong she'd had to sit down on the top of the stairs. Since then, the door was kept closed. Rynn didn't think she would ever be able to look at a wheelchair with equanimity again.

Glenna's contrite expression told Rynn her sister understood her reaction, but what Glenna said was a brisk "Fine. If you get tired, you can lean on me."

They went outside and, arms entwined, walked across the lawn and around through the kitchen garden and came in the door there. It was the first time she'd been out of the house since the day she and Thomas had arrived, and she took care to steer away from the path they'd taken. But the sunshine and fresh air did her good, and she was glad her sister had insisted.

After that, she made it a point to go outside on every fine day. At first her walks were short—it was all she had the strength for—and they usually ended in the kitchen garden, where she sat on the bench near the door and communed with the cabbages and cucumbers and parsnips and scallions that grew there. The cliff walk with its breathtaking views increasingly called to her, and she finally summoned the physical and spiritual strength to venture along the path she and Thomas had taken on that last day before he fell ill.

She didn't go far, and the pain the memory conjured up as she retraced their steps made her almost regret going at all. But the next day she went farther, and the day after that farther still. When she finally made it all the way to the overlook, and stopped where they had stopped, and looked out over the wide golden crescent of the Strand and the rolling whitecaps of the bay to the wild Atlantic, she had the notion that Thomas was there with her. The sense of his presence beside her was both incredibly sad and comforting at the same time. She took in the beauty of the sea and sky with the uncanny feeling that he was seeing it through her eyes and found herself aching with grief even as she was suddenly, fiercely grateful to be alive.

"I miss you," she said to Thomas aloud. As the wind carried the words away, she felt that he heard, and understood.

From then on, she walked the cliff path almost every afternoon until she reached the Point, where she would stand for a while taking in the view. The tourists crowding the beach, the bathers frolicking in the surf, the boats in the bay, the larger ships farther out to sea—all were reminders that life went on. She rarely went any farther from the house than the grounds and the cliff walk. There was no need, as everything was provided for her. On the handful of occasions when she ventured into the village, she was surprised by how many British soldiers she saw. The streets, the sidewalks, the shops and pubs—everywhere she looked was a veritable sea of khaki. Her presence in the village elicited a mix of reactions. At first, she was overwhelmed with condolences. Friends, neighbors, acquaintances, shopkeepers—nearly everyone she'd ever met, it seemed, wanted to express their sorrow for her loss. The weight of all that sympathy was crushing. Responding to the well wishes, to the commiserating looks, she sometimes felt like she couldn't breathe. An awkward encounter right in the middle of Main Street with Donal's mother, Brigid, and sister Sarah left her feeling like she'd lost their friendship. They clearly begrudged the fact that she'd married Thomas instead of Donal even as they said how sorry they were to hear of her husband's death.

Then the Irish Republican Army, as the militant arm of the rebels was newly christened after the Dail Eireann decreed that the Volunteers and the IRB and all those fighting on their side should take an oath of allegiance to the new Irish republic, ambushed a contingent of British soldiers in Fermoy, County

Cork, and the British retaliated by sending two hundred soldiers to attack the town. The fallout raised the temperature of the conflict to fever pitch.

After that, more than a few of those she encountered seemed ill at ease in her presence, as though they didn't know quite how to react to her now that she was no longer "our Rynn" but the widow of a member of the British aristocracy and thus, by default, one of the hated Ascendancy. Mrs. Cheadle, the greengrocer's wife who was working behind the counter one morning when Rynn stopped by, spelled it out for her after two girls Rynn had once gone to school with scuttled off with no more than a muttered "good day" to her.

"What it is, you see, is that no one knows for sure any longer where your allegiance lies," Mrs. Cheadle said. Another woman in the shop, Mrs. O'Toole, who Rynn knew from years of patronizing her husband's fish shop, nodded her head in vigorous agreement.

"Husband's a sodding Brit, father's a sodding Brit," Rynn heard another woman whisper as she was leaving. "She's not one I'd be trusting, is all I'll say."

Once her eyes were opened to it, Rynn saw suspicion in the faces of enough of those she encountered that she was both angry and hurt.

Taken altogether, it was too much to face, so she simply didn't. Anyway, the truth was, she had no desire to visit the village or, indeed, to be in company. As long as she stayed inside the protective bubble that was Ballyshannon Court, nothing that had happened—Thomas's death, her own illness, the increasing acts of violence that seemed to strike like lightning bolts in random bursts across the country—felt entirely real. False as it was, that illusion was a far more comfortable state than facing up to the harsh truth.

With Mrs. Frampton and the other servants living full-time

on the property, which kept Rynn from being alone, Glenna chose to stay in their cottage in the village, which was only a short walk from her school, although Rynn offered her and Granny rooms at Ballyshannon Court. Given the increased presence of British soldiers in the town and the heightened tension that went along with that, Granny spent her nights in the cottage with Glenna while visiting Rynn most days. Although a lawyer representing Thomas's estate had come down from London bearing many documents for her to sign along with the news that, having inherited all his property including a family interest in Ballyshannon Court, she was a wealthy woman and could live anywhere she chose, Rynn did not yet feel ready to leave this place that Thomas had loved, and where he had died.

She would get there, she knew, but what she needed was time.

As November rolled around, the wind blowing in from the sea grew brisk, and the paddlers in the bay and sunbathers on the Strand went home. The summer visitors in the hotels and big houses disappeared as well. What was left behind were ghosts: of Thomas, of Molly Kincaid, of Paddy, of others she'd loved and lost. She tried not to dwell on those who were gone, instead choosing to remember happier times. She was out on her daily walk, focused on memories of herself and Glenna when they were little and spent many an afternoon wading in the surf gathering up winkles in their skirts as a way of keeping less cheerful thoughts at bay, when without warning, the world seemed to fall away and she saw herself as if from a distance. Standing atop the Point high above the Strand, wrapped snuggly in the fringed black shawl she'd acquired as part of her mourning clothes since Thomas's death, her hair torn loose from its pins and blowing in the wind, she was looking out to sea. The brisk air nipped at her cheeks and the smell of salt was all around and, far below, the waves pounded the shore.

And her heart ached with loss.

As quickly as it happened, the out-of-body sensation was gone. She stood there, shivering a little as the world around her came back into focus. Realizing that she'd seen herself exactly as she was in that moment only from a distance, as if through an objective observer's eyes, was as puzzling as it was disorienting.

Then she was hit by an overwhelming sense of déjà vu.

She'd seen herself in precisely that way before, on the night in her bedroom when she'd decided to make her marriage to Thomas a real one. She'd been contemplating her future—

The black shawl, her too-pale face, the ache in her heart—had her vision that night been a portent of what was to come?

Was it possible that Granny was right, and she had the Sight after all?

Her instant reaction was denial. From what she'd seen of the Sight—and she'd observed it in Granny over a lifetime—it was far more curse than blessing. Its revelations were too vague to be of any practical use. If it became known you possessed it, you were marked as *different*. You were avoided, or scorned, or feared, or simply eyed askance. She'd learned that from a lifetime with Granny, too.

But that night in her bedroom, had she truly been shown her future?

The idea unnerved her. She whipped around in utter rejection of it and walked quickly away, only to see a man coming along the cliff path toward her.

Her steps slowed. Instinctively wary of an unknown man in this time of trouble, she stopped and raised her hand to shade her eyes against the golden rays of the setting sun as she sought to identify him. He was dressed plainly in a gray jacket and black trousers. A flat cap pulled down low over his eyes cast a shadow over his features. But his height, and his stride, and the set of his shoulders—she knew him: Maguire. She wouldn't have thought it, had not in fact thought of him in months, but recognizing him now brought a surge of gladness with it. As he reached her and stopped, she looked up to meet those incongruously light eyes and felt something that had been wound tight and hard inside her ease.

"Where have you been?" was how she greeted him. Quite crossly, too. As if she'd been expecting him for a while. As if she had the right to know.

"France," he said, as easily as if they had last spoken the day before. "America. London. I only just heard about Thomas. I'm deeply sorry. He was a good man."

She nodded. "That's what he said about you."

He smiled, but his eyes were grave. "I'd have come sooner if I'd known. I hear you were ill as well. Ill enough that your granny summoned the priest."

She wrapped the shawl more tightly around herself. The vague memory she had of Father Doherty praying over her sick bed was enough to give her cold chills. How close had she come to dying? She hadn't asked, and Granny hadn't said. All she knew, and this was because Granny had told her, was that even in that hour of extremis she'd summoned the presence of mind to ask Father Doherty to have prayers said for Thomas's soul.

"Who told you that?"

"My sister. You remember Moira? Her farm's not too far from here. Her boy Tim drove down from Dublin with me and I dropped him off with her before I came on here. She said she'd thought about calling on you once she heard you were better, but you've been keeping yourself to yourself and no one wants to disturb you in your grief."

Rynn made a face. "Am I the talk of the village, then?"

"Not only the village. Every sailor who's passed this way in the last few months is raving on about a beautiful woman dressed head to toe in black—long black hair blowing in the wind, long black dress doing the same—that stands on the Point looking out to sea around sunset on fine days. I admit, I was skeptical until I drove up and there she was, just like they said. If I hadn't known it was you, I probably would have turned tail and run. Most of them think you're a haunt, or a witch, or a harbinger of disaster to come. The Banshee of Bundoran, they're calling you."

She looked at him suspiciously. "You're making that up."

"Devil a bit, I give you my word. I first heard of it on the ferry as we crossed to Dublin, and then again as tales of it were being bandied about on the wharf when we docked. How does it feel to know that brave men quail at the sight of you, and more than one boat has changed course to avoid the bad luck you're said to bring?"

"Now I *know* you're making it up."

"I'm not." He shook his head. But he was smiling a little, and something about his smile, about having him there, a friend, strong and dependable, someone who knew all about her and Thomas and how it had all come about and now how it had ended, blew away the fog of grief so she could see clearly for the first time in what seemed like forever.

It took her a moment to realize she hadn't replied, that she was simply standing there looking at him as they faced each other on the path, with the cliff dropping away to the sparkling blue waters of the bay on one side and the tall grass that had grown up almost as high as her waist on the other. And that he was standing there silently looking at her, too.

"Are you staying with your sister, then?" she asked, to fill the silence, and started to walk.

He fell in beside her. "Her house is too crowded as it is. I'd be bunking in with my nephews, and I'm too old for that. I stay at the Great Northern Hotel when I come."

"Tell me about France. What were you doing there?"

So he told her about France, about his efforts to get the representatives from the thirty-two countries at the Paris Peace Conference to throw their support behind an independent Ireland. As one of the Big Four, Britain scuttled that effort by refusing to allow it to come to a vote, so he set sail for America to join de Valera, now president of the Irish republic, in his effort to raise funds to support the cause of Irish independence and to cultivate support among the American public, many of whom had Irish roots.

"I must admit I did a little business along the way," he said as they reached the end of the trail and turned toward the house. "America's new law prohibiting the sale of alcohol is set to take effect this coming January, and that's caused a panic among all the bar owners in the country. Boston, New York, Detroit, Chicago—once they heard we had the goods they want, and had secure distribution channels locked down, they were all eager to make deals to acquire the very best in illegal liquor."

"How very opportunistic of you," she said, and he laughed.

"Money is power," he said. "And it's far better to have it than not. Even war respects the rich, while the poor, as we have learned to our cost, are the ones who fight and die in overwhelming numbers."

"Will there be war, then? Here?" At the prospect her stomach pitted.

"I pray not. Dev is working hard to negotiate our peaceful separation from Britain. But there are hotheads among us that feel no settlement is possible and fighting our way to freedom through armed conflict is the only answer. And Churchill, who I saw while I was in London, by the way, says he has no more time to waste on a ragtag bunch of ungrateful Irishmen. He's breathing fire to unloose the full force of the British Army on us and be done with it so Britain can move on to more important matters."

"Can we win a war with Britain?" Her heart beat a little faster at the thought. The history of eight hundred years said otherwise.

"Don't fight if you can't win, eh? Seems like a sound philosophy. The honest answer is, I don't know."

That didn't make her feel any better. She did her best to put the prospect of war out of her mind.

"Did you see . . . my father-in-law or any of the family while you were in London?" There was a catch in her voice as she spoke of the Duke. He had telephoned several weeks after Thomas's death to tell her that the lawyer would be coming, adding that the Duchess was prostrate with grief. From the sound of his voice, he'd been in little better case himself. All the family had sent letters of condolence, and she'd sent letters of her own, but other than that she hadn't heard from them, or they from her.

Their mutual loss was still too raw and painful for it to be shared.

Maguire shook his head. "From all accounts, he and his wife are holed up at Ashtonbury Park." Glancing down at her, he seemed to hesitate. "I did see your sister Penelope. She's mourning a loss as well. Her mother, Lady Somerset, succumbed to the flu not long after Thomas did. It seems they attended the Victory Day parade and Lady Somerset was stricken soon afterward, as were many others."

"Oh, no. How terrible. I'm so sorry. How is Penelope holding up?"

"As well as can be expected, I'd say. She's a strong girl. Very determined."

By then they'd almost reached the house. His car, a big Vauxhall, was pulled around to the side.

"Will you come in? I can give you a meal. Mrs. Frampton is an amazing cook."

He shook his head. "I can't stay. I have to drive on to Killybegs for a meeting. There's a boat I'd like to acquire, and this is the only night the captain, her owner, will be in port. I'll be back this way tomorrow, though, around this same time and if the meal's still on offer I'll take you up on it."

"It is." She smiled at him. The thought that he'd be back the next day lifted her spirits to a surprising degree.

"I'll look forward to it, then." He stopped beside his car and turned to give her a serious look. "I hear you've only a few servants living with you."

She nodded. "What of it?"

"There's a considerable amount of unrest hereabouts lately. You'd be safer in the village."

"I'm safe enough. And if that changes, I'll move."

"If you say so." His lips compressed, but he didn't argue. "I'll see you tomorrow."

Watching as he drove away, she realized that she was sorry to see him go.

Chapter Twenty-Seven

When Maguire returned the next afternoon, Granny was there, and naturally she joined them for the meal Rynn had promised him. Rynn had mixed feelings about Granny's presence, but the largest, most sensible part of her whispered that it was a good thing. The little glow of anticipation she'd felt all day at the prospect of his visit was almost certainly an indication of how isolated she'd been since Thomas's death and had nothing personally to do with Maguire at all. She would have felt the same had any old friend turned up unexpectedly, she told herself. But still the uptick in her spirits when he was around made her feel uncomfortable, and even the tiniest bit guilty.

When he left, she stood on the front steps watching through the gathering darkness until all she could see of his car were the headlamps as they disappeared over the nearest hill. He was heading to his sister's to pick up Tim, then driving on to Dublin, where he now lived. He would, he said as he left, be back in the area in a few weeks.

The remark had been a general one, made to both her and Granny, who'd stepped outside with her to bid him goodbye, but still it was enough to bring on another of those little niggles of gladness that were as unsettling as an unexpected twinge of physical pain.

"It was kind of Major Maguire to drive all the way from Dublin to offer you his condolences," Granny said as they went back inside. By then, she'd agreed to Rynn's suggestion that she stay the night, as there was some question as to whether, now, the roads were safe after dark for a woman alone, and had telephoned to the doctor's house, where the doctor's wife had agreed to send someone to let Glenna know. Granny had come in the pony trap, and the pony had been put up in the otherwise empty stable when she'd arrived, so there was no trouble about that. "Most men would have sent a letter, if they thought to do anything."

"He had business in Killybegs." Rynn could tell from the speculative glint in Granny's eyes what she was hinting at and did her best not to sound defensive. "And his sister lives nearby."

"So he said."

"He was a friend of Thomas's."

"Yes, he said that, too."

As the glint in Granny's eyes evolved into a twinkle, Rynn lost her patience. "He's not coming a-courting, so you can just put that notion out of your head. He's not interested in me, except as a friend. Nor I in him."

If anything, Granny's twinkle grew brighter. "If you say so."

Given that that was the second time in just about twenty-four hours that someone had answered her with *if you say so* while clearly meaning the opposite, Rynn felt she could be forgiven for the near snap in her voice when she replied with "Come on, Granny, while I've got you here let's go play a hand or two of Twenty-Five." (Granny's favorite card game, which she played on many a Saturday night in the kitchens of her cronies.) "And you'd best have your wits about you, because I'm aiming to win, too."

"If you're thinking that will ever happen, you think far too much of yourself," Granny said. Rynn silently congratulated herself as, effectively distracted, Granny followed her into the card room.

It was not quite a week later when, as she was walking along the cliff path to the Point, two masked men rose up from where they had crouched concealed in the tall grass that covered the slope beside the path to point rifles at her.

Rynn's heart gave a great leap. She stopped dead, staring at them.

"You'll be coming with us," the taller of the two said. His mask consisted of his wool scarf, which he had wound around his face, covering it from neck to eyeballs. It muffled his voice, made it sound gruff and distant. The other man's face was hidden similarly. They were mid- to late twenties, she guessed, fit men dressed in rough civilian clothes, with peaked caps pulled low to hide what the scarves didn't. If it hadn't been for the way they'd concealed their faces, she might have mistaken them for hunters out after rabbits.

"Who are you?" Instinctively she probed height, build, clothing and what little she could see of their faces for any sign that she might know them.

"Never you mind. Step down here with us and walk toward those trees." With his rifle the first man indicated the line of old oaks that marked the beginning of the woodlands behind the stable. Rynn looked where he pointed, then glanced quickly back toward the house. It was, she judged, too far away for anyone inside to hear her if she screamed, but—

"We'll shoot any who comes," the first man warned. "So I'd think twice about screaming, were I you."

"We'll shoot *you* if we must," the other threatened, raising his rifle at her. "We've no time or stomach for games, and so I warn you."

"What do you want of me?" It was all she could do to keep her voice steady. Inside, she was quivering like jelly.

"I said, *come here*," the first one said. There was a tone in his voice that told her some violent act was imminent if she didn't. "I'll not be telling you again."

Heart pounding, seeing no help for it, Rynn started down the slope.

He grabbed the front of her coat and yanked her toward him as soon as she was close enough. Even as she struggled to keep her footing he clamped onto her arm. Tucking his rifle under his arm, he started walking, long, hurried strides, propelling her with him through the grass toward the trees. The second man followed behind, his rifle at the ready. The setting sun cast a warm glow over the landscape. Rynn darted desperate looks around. The shed, the stable, the fields with their stone walls—all were deserted. The only living creatures in sight were sheep. In little more than an hour it would be dark. If she hadn't come inside by then, she would be missed. Someone—Cyril, probably—would be sent to look for her, and . . .

She would be long gone, and whatever was going to happen to her would have happened.

Too late, mourned a terrifying singsong whisper in her brain. *Too late.*

Her heart thumped like it would beat its way out of her chest.

"You're Irish," she said, desperate to make a connection. There was no doubt about his nationality. "I'm Irish, too. My granny is a Shaughnessy, from the village here—"

"Shut your mouth. Walk." Hand tightening like a vise around her arm, he shoved her along at a brutal pace.

Fight free. Run. More frantic whispers in her brain. To which another, pragmatic part of her, having taken stock of the situation, replied, *No chance of that.* They'd chase her down, or shoot her, before she'd taken a dozen steps.

When at last someone came looking for her, there would be nothing to tell what had happened. Perhaps they'd think she'd fallen from the cliff to disappear under the waters of the bay. She wouldn't be the first . . .

It was cool and dark under the trees, with each step through the carpet of fallen leaves stirring up the slightly musty smell of damp earth. Silent except for the occasional bird call. No sign of another human being, although she thought the road to Ballyshannon ran along the top of the distant ridge she could just glimpse through the trees. If she was correct, it made no difference: no traffic of any kind in sight, and the road was too far away to offer any chance of help. The path, if it could be called such a thing, cut in and out. She was dragged through undergrowth and over a creek until finally, in the lee of a giant beech, they stopped in front of a tumbledown stone cairn. Rynn barely had a chance to notice the opening before she was shoved inside it.

She stumbled and nearly fell as she missed a step that wasn't there. The space was essentially a hole, dug out below ground level. Her lightning impression was that it was small and dark and sour smelling, with fallen leaves littering a hard-packed dirt floor. A slanting stone slab formed a low ceiling hung with vines.

Her arm free now, she whirled as her captors stepped in behind her.

There were two of them, they were bigger than she was and they were armed. Together they formed a solid wall. Breaking through and getting past them would be impossible.

Whatever they intended, she was trapped.

Fear tightened her throat. She should have screamed when she had the chance. She should have at least tried to run.

The first man loomed over her. Close, too close. She took a quick, panicked step back.

"Help him." He used his rifle to point to something behind her.

"What?" She was afraid to take her eyes off them.

"You're a nurse, they say. Help him." Once again the first man gestured with his rifle.

A nurse? They wanted *a nurse*? This time she dared to glance over her shoulder.

Against the far wall was a shape—a man. Sprawled flat on his back in the dirt. Motionless. Silent. Difficult to see in the gloom.

"Go on." The second man prodded her with his rifle.

Casting another wary glance at her captors, she turned and crouched at the third man's side.

He was bareheaded, barefaced, ordinary looking. Overlong dark hair. Several days' growth of dark beard. Pale, pale skin, most likely from pain or blood loss. Maybe twenty-two or -three. From the unnatural angle of his leg, it was obvious that it was broken, badly. She leaned closer. Yes, that was his femur protruding through the wool of his trousers. The white, jagged edge of the bone was grotesque. The black splotches saturating the brown weave of the cloth were blood. Conscious, he would have been screaming with pain.

A half-empty bottle of poteen rested beside his slack fingers.

"What happened to him?" she asked.

"Lorry ran him over." The information was given grudgingly.

She touched his face. It was cold and clammy. From shock—

"Barney McShea, private, Cloughaneely Company, First Donegal Brigade," the injured man muttered, and began to toss and moan. "Look out, they're coming—Jaysus, get out o' the way, oh, oh—*ah*!"

"Shut your mouth, imbecile." The second man poked him with his foot while the first man, crouching down beside Rynn, opened the bottle of poteen. Grasping the injured man's jaw even as he struggled and gasped, he poured the liquid down his throat.

The sour smell Rynn had noted earlier enveloped her: of

course, the poteen. She was surprised she hadn't recognized it at once.

"He needs to be kept warm. If you could build a small fire—"

"No fire!" The response was explosive. Uttered so close to her ear, it made Rynn jump.

"Here, he can have my coat. 'Tis not so cold out, after all." The second man took off his coat, handing it to Rynn. Taking care not to seem to notice that his scarf had slipped, exposing his face to her view, she draped the coat over the injured man, who was seemingly insensible once more.

"Do what you can for his leg." Standing up, the first man gave Rynn a fierce look. She'd clearly heard the injured man—Barney McShea was his name, she was almost sure; it had sounded like he was giving his name and other information as required of captured soldiers by the Geneva Convention in the Great War—but thought it best to pretend she hadn't understood. Beyond the name, the identifying information made her think—no, she knew—that he must be an IRA soldier. That these must be IRA soldiers. Not that she wanted to know. It wasn't safe to know.

Hadn't Cyril had been telling Mrs. Frampton over breakfast about an IRA ambush on a convoy of British Army lorries near Finner Camp before dawn that morning? Only it had gone wrong: several soldiers had been wounded, but the lorries had broken through and gotten away. Cyril had attributed the attack to a flying column, as they were calling units that had split off from standard brigades and were constantly on the move because so many of their members were now wanted and on the run.

Was this part of the aftermath of that attack? She had to assume it was.

Keep your wits about you.

"I'll need a knife and two stout, straight sticks, about as long as his leg," she said. "The best I can do is get the bone back in place and splint it."

"Will he be able to walk, then?"

"Over a short distance maybe, with assistance."

"Eh, I'll carry him on my back if need be," the second man said to the first. "As long as he don't start the screaming again, we'll do fine."

"If I could have a knife, I could get started while one of you goes to find sticks. Stout and straight, mind, and the length of his leg."

"I'll go. You watch her," the second man said, and ducked out of the cairn as the first handed his knife over.

"Are you a nurse, then? A true nurse?" The first man watched suspiciously as she carefully cut the trouser leg away, baring the limb and the gruesome injury. The broken bone protruded through the skin halfway between crotch and knee. The flesh was torn and bloody where the bone had come through. The degree of swelling and bruising around the wound told her that it was, as she had suspected, several hours old.

"Yes. How did you hear about me?" She was busy slicing the trouser leg into long strips.

"Never you mind about that. Just fix the leg."

Don't ask questions. The more you know, the more risk you pose to them.

"I can set it, but after that he needs to be seen by a doctor. Dr. Lowry in the village—"

He gave a quick, negative shake of his head. "The doctor's being watched. All the doctors are being watched. The Brits have spies everywhere. They think we're stupid, but we know. And we know who they are."

The look he gave her as he said that burned with promised vengeance.

Rynn thought it best to redirect his thoughts to the situation at hand.

"When your friend comes back, I'm going to ask one of you

to hold him and the other to pull hard on his ankle so that the bone can be put back in place. You look to me like you're the strong one, so it should probably be you who holds him." That last was a deliberate piece of flattery, designed to get on this man's good side. If they were desperate and on the run, and she assumed they were, they might be wary of leaving behind a living witness.

The thought sent a shiver down her spine.

"I'm the one for that, all right. What is it you're doing?"

She was pouring poteen over the open wound to clean it, and she told him so. By the time the second man came back with the two stout, straight sticks as requested, she was ready for them. Telling them both what she needed them to do, she waited until they got in position. The injured man, perhaps sensing what was to come, started moving and muttering again, but she had no time or inclination to listen.

"Hold him still," she said to the first man. Then, to the second, "Pull! Now! Hard and sharp!"

He pulled, the injured man screamed and fainted, the broken bone disappeared back through the skin as she manipulated it into place and the thing was done.

After that, she poured more poteen on the wound and had them hold the sticks on either side of the broken leg while she bound it up tightly.

Sinking back on her heels, pleased with how it had gone, she saw that both her captors were looking at her. And realized to her dismay that the first man's scarf now hung loosely around his neck, too, exposing his face.

"Are you finished, then?" the first man asked.

She was already breathing hard and sweating from the work she had done. But something about his expression, *their* expressions—she could feel the hair rise up on the back of her neck.

As clearly as if they'd said it aloud, she knew they were thinking about the danger she might now pose to them.

Stay calm.

"The bone is set and splinted. To avoid the risk of amputation, though, he'll need to have Dakin's Solution applied daily for six days to the wound where the bone broke through the skin."

"What? What's that?"

"An antiseptic. Luckily the house where I live served as a hospital in the Great War, and I was a nurse there. I have medical supplies inside. Since we're done here except for that, I'll go fetch the Dakin's Solution for you."

"Amputation, you say?" Both men looked at her uneasily.

She nodded. "Without the Dakin's Solution, he's almost certain to lose that leg, I'm afraid."

They looked at each other in what was clearly a silent debate while her stomach twisted itself into knots. Her life hung in the balance, she feared.

"And you have some of this solution?"

"I do."

Another exchange of looks between her captors.

In desperation she said, "I've done what you brought me here to do. I've set his leg, and if you follow my instructions, he won't lose it. But you need to let me go get that Dakin's Solution, or it will all have been for nothing."

The first man's gaze snapped back to her. He looked at her hard, then slowly nodded.

"Get up, then," he said. To the other man he added, "I'll take her. You stay here with—" He broke off, shooting her another hard look.

She tried to appear calmly confident as she rose to her feet.

Darkness had fallen by the time they reached the outer edge of the kitchen garden. Lights were on in the house. Had anyone missed her yet? Were they looking for her? Probing the shadows in the desperate hope that someone might be about, she saw no one, not Cyril, not Mrs. Frampton, no one, out searching.

"I'm going to go inside and fetch the solution for you now," she said to the man behind her, who'd been silent as a rock during the entire trek back. His scarf was once again in place. His rifle was tucked under his arm. Which gave her hope but was still no guarantee he wouldn't shoot her as she walked away. His long silence, she feared, was the product of a wary mind weighing the risk she represented.

"And you'll be bringing it back out to me, just as nice as you please." The skepticism in his voice was unmistakable. Here was another choice: lie or tell the truth.

"You needn't fear that I'll tell anybody about this, because I won't," she said. "There's a bench beside the kitchen door. I'll put the bottle on that. You need only come up and get it. You must just pour the solution over the wound once a day. For six days, remember."

He looked at her. She could see in his eyes that he was deciding. Her jaw clenched. Her pulse thundered in her ears.

"You keep your mouth shut about this, missy," he said, and she nodded.

Then she went inside the house, fobbed off Mrs. Frampton and Cyril, who'd been alarmed when, Cyril having gone out to look, she hadn't been anywhere to be found, went to the cellar and located the Dakin's Solution, mixed it, came back outside, held the bottle up where her erstwhile captor could see and set it on the bench.

She could feel his eyes on her the whole time. The tingle in her shoulders and back as she tensed against a possible bullet didn't ease until she was safely back inside.

Chapter Twenty-Eight

Word spread. Just how she didn't know, but over the next few weeks Rynn was approached several times to attend to wounded soldiers of the IRA. Although after that first, terrifying experience she stopped her regular walks to the Point unless someone—Granny or Glenna, mostly—was with her, the next fighter needing medical attention simply came to the house. When Mrs. Frampton went down to the kitchen one morning there he was, slumped on the bench in the kitchen garden, asking for "the lady" when she went out to see what he would be about.

Alerted by Mrs. Frampton, Rynn went outside warily, only to discover that the visitor was a gangly boy still in his teens. He was half sitting, half lying on his side, his head propped on his haversack. His eyes were clouded with pain as he rolled them up at her.

"I'm after finding the lady who helped Barney McShea," he said when she asked what she could do for him. "That would be you, eh?"

"It would."

"They said you'd help me."

"Who did?"

He shrugged and closed his eyes, panting. The bloody gash on his left cheek wasn't serious, was her lightning assessment. His thick coat, however, was pierced with holes and stained with blood, and further examination revealed the cause of his distress. His left arm and side had been peppered with shotgun pellets.

"Can you walk? You're going to have to help me get you inside." She didn't ask his name, or anything else. It was safer not to know.

"I can."

With her help, he managed to get to his feet. But he slumped against her, surprisingly heavy although he was quite thin. She took him inside, into one of the small back parlors that had been closed off for lack of use. There she treated him, telling Mrs. Frampton that he'd suffered a hunting injury: he'd tripped over his own shotgun and, knowing she was a nurse and near, had come to them for help.

"Out after grouse there in the woods, I've no doubt." Mrs. Frampton shook her head sympathetically as she brought the bowl of hot water Rynn had asked for. The woods technically belonged to the Crown, and to take grouse from them was technically poaching. But since the Great War, and with all that was now going on in the country, such petty crimes were largely overlooked. "Hard as times are, I can't see anyone blaming him for that."

But Rynn noticed that Mrs. Frampton never, as she normally would, asked the young man his name, or where he was from, or who his kin were or any information that might serve to identify him.

That in itself was enough to convince her that Mrs. Frampton knew the truth. And when the young man left, having had the pellets removed and his wounds cleaned and bandaged, and having rested, and been fed, Mrs. Frampton didn't say another word about him.

The very next day, another young man appeared on the kitchen bench. Like the first, he was already there when Mrs. Frampton came downstairs not long after dawn. Taking one look at him with his bloody foot propped on the bench in front of him, Mrs. Frampton went in search of Rynn. He was more open than the first visitor, and admitted, amid groans as Rynn cut off his damaged boot, to accidentally having shot off two of his own toes with his own gun in all the excitement of his first engagement. But to see the thrice-damned Brits run as they had when their patrol was taken unawares was worth it, he maintained. The injury was at least twenty-four hours old, and Rynn suspected it had been sustained in the same skirmish that had left her previous patient peppered with shotgun pellets.

The damage to his foot was done. All Rynn could do for him was clean the wounds and cauterize the stumps. He clomped off toward the woods late that same afternoon with a sawed-off broomstick for a cane, his bandaged foot shoved into a new boot Cyril had found for him.

Rynn stood with Mrs. Frampton at the kitchen window watching him go.

"And so I suppose we're now set to lose the rest of our young men to yet another war. May God curse the English," Cyril said bitterly behind them. Surprised, Rynn turned in time to see Mrs. Frampton nodding agreement.

"May they all die without a priest." Mrs. Frampton's expression was grim, and Cyril patted her arm in solidarity. Then they both looked at Rynn with dismay as if they had only just remembered who she was and that she was there.

"And may the devil take their souls," Rynn said. Glances were exchanged, the two retainers visibly relaxed and then they all went their separate ways. But that moment had clarified the bond of allegiance that linked them: they were Irish above all. To Rynn's mind, trust among the three was no longer in question.

Yet another soldier solicited her help by simply stepping out in front of the DeLion when she was driving it back from the village. With Higdon gone, only she and Cyril ever drove the car, as Mrs. Frampton, Anna and Lynnette didn't know how and had no desire to learn. Rynn left most of the errand running to Cyril, as she didn't wish to cause any more talk in the village than she had to and the sight of a female driving a car was rare enough to give rise to plenty of that. But she did go into the village to Mass often enough to keep Father Doherty at bay, and to visit Granny and Glenna, and on this particular occasion was returning from the cottage—well before dark—when a trench-coated man walked out of a hedgerow squarely into the DeLion's path, pointing a pistol at her as he held up one hand in a silent order to stop. She slammed on the brakes—she was getting quite good at stopping where she meant to—and he walked around to her window, which, at his imperative gesture, she rolled down.

"You're the nurse." His tone made it a statement rather than a question. Even before her nod confirmed it, he was beckoning to someone apparently concealed in the hedgerow. Moments later a wounded soldier and the comrade supporting him slid into the back seat, while the pistol wielder got into the passenger seat beside her.

"We've little time," the pistol wielder said. "Bandage him up, then take us to the train station in Ballyshannon. We'll pay well for your help."

His pistol, a luger she thought, lay across his lap in such a way as to serve as a reminder of the consequences if she didn't agree. She'd already ascertained, not that there'd ever been any real doubt, from his accent and demeanor and the military belts and bandoliers they wore, that the three of them were IRA. Wounded stragglers from a flying column? Though she'd heard of no attacks in the vicinity in the last day or so, she was sure the answer was *yes*.

"I neither want nor need your money," she said coldly as she got the car going again. "And there's no need to threaten me. I help where I can. And please, point your gun somewhere else."

After a long, measuring look at her unyielding profile, he stuck the gun in his belt.

The wounded man had taken a bayonet to the side that seemed to have missed any vital organ, although the gash was large and jagged and the bleeding copious. Rynn did the best she could to pack the wound and bind it up with the supplies she had in the car, because the pistol wielder refused to allow her to stop at Ballyshannon Court for anything else, and insisted that it was a matter of utmost urgency that they be in Ballyshannon in time to catch the four-fifteen to Galway.

They made it with scant minutes to spare. As she drove away from the train station, relieved to be rid of her unwelcome passengers, she spotted the big clock on the Belfast Bank building and realized that she had only about three-quarters of an hour if she was to get back home before twilight turned the roads into a veritable no-man's-land. Roadblocks, usually by the Crown forces but sometimes by the rebels, were a constant hazard; armed stragglers from either side had been known to waylay travelers at night, and getting caught up in an ambush or military action was a growing danger.

Maguire returned on the Friday afternoon before Christmas. The day was cold and gray and intermittently rainy, which exactly matched Rynn's mood. Having turned down Granny and Glenna's invitation to join them at Glenna's school's annual Christmas bazaar, she had instead forced herself to tackle the long-dreaded, heartbreaking task of sorting through and packing up Thomas's things. The Duchess had written, requesting that she be sent an assortment of personal items including Thomas's signet ring, his pocket watch and the cufflinks that had belonged to his great-grandfather. Rynn packed those up as well. She was on her knees in her bedroom, fighting back tears as she folded garments into boxes, when she happened to glance out the window as the big Vauxhall pulled up in front of the house. Recognizing it, her spirits immediately lifted. Jumping to her feet, she flew down the stairs in time to reach the entry hall just as Cyril admitted Maguire into the house.

Maguire's hair was black and glistening with rain, his head was bent slightly as he listened to Cyril, who lacked his height by a considerable amount, and his long coat hung open to reveal an elegant suit. He looked handsome and prosperous and vitally alive, and his surprise visit was the perfect antidote to the doldrums she had fallen into.

". . . believe she is upstairs," Cyril was saying as she approached at a far more decorous pace than the unladylike run that had taken her as far as the entry hall. "If you'll wait in the—"

"I'm here." With Cyril's gaze on her, Rynn just managed to suppress the wide smile that threatened to break through when Maguire looked past Cyril to find her coming toward him. Knowing Cyril and Mrs. Frampton as she now did, she knew that Cyril would immediately retreat to the kitchen to report on the visitor and her reaction to him. They would gossip endlessly over what he said, what she said, how he looked at her, how she looked at him and what it all meant, and she didn't want to add fuel to the fire by seeming too glad to see him.

Although she was. Amazingly glad.

Something that she was afraid her telltale face just might reveal.

"Lady Thomas." Maguire greeted her with the appropriate amount of formality.

"Major Maguire." She returned his greeting as formally, although her smile broke out as, Cyril having asked Maguire if he could take his coat and being told he preferred to keep it, Cyril turned away. "Come talk to me in the library. I was in there earlier, and there's a lovely fire." As she turned to lead Maguire to the library, Rynn bethought herself of something. "Would you like some tea? And sandwiches, perhaps?" she asked him over her shoulder, ready to call after Cyril and request a tray be brought.

He shook his head. "I can't stay."

"Oh." Did she sound disappointed? She feared she did. Schooling her expression, she stopped walking and turned back to face him. "In that case, what can I do for you?"

"Actually, I've come to steal you away."

"What?" She frowned at him.

"It's Tim's eighteenth birthday. Moira's having a big to-do and lots of people will be there. She'd like you to come."

"She barely knows me."

"I've been talking you up." He smiled at her. "Besides, I owe you a meal. And Moira is the best cook in County Donegal."

"Mrs. Frampton would take issue with that."

"I'm sure she would, as would many other ladies. But still, Moira's food is not to be missed." His eyes slid over her. "And you could use some fattening up."

Rynn stiffened in mock outrage. "Are you calling me skinny?"

"Never. Willowy, maybe. Sylphlike. Fine-boned. But never skinny."

"Just because I no longer rise to your vision of female pulchritude . . ."

He shook his head. "I never said that." His eyes lost their teasing glint. "But you've lost a deal of weight, you know. And I hear that you rarely leave this place."

"Who told you that?"

"How about we say, a little birdie, and leave it at that."

Remembering how he'd given the same answer to the same question when she first met him, she gave him a condemning look. "And people think gentlemen don't indulge in gossip."

"Oh, we do. I admit it freely. The thing is, I have to put in an appearance at Tim's party or I will be in my sister's black books forevermore. I also have to be back in Dublin tomorrow morning for a meeting, and I want to talk to you. If you'll come with me, you'll allow me to accomplish all those things in the small amount of time I have available, and you'll get a good meal, good company and get out of the house. And it's got to be better than whatever you've been doing that's got you looking so glum."

"First I'm skinny, now I'm glum. You're just full of compliments today, aren't you?" She narrowed her eyes at him.

"You don't need compliments from me—you need to be rousted out of this rut you're in. Isolating yourself like this isn't healthy, and you know it."

She hesitated. The thought of going into company, especially to a family party where she didn't really know anyone and was sure to be an object of curiosity, made her shrink inside. But the idea of sending him on his way and returning to those heartbreaking boxes held even less appeal.

He clearly read her indecision in her face.

"It'll be fun, I promise. And from the look of you, you could use some fun. Along with some food."

The look she gave him should by rights have choked him. He didn't smile, but his eyes twinkled and his dimples came into play.

"Rynn. Come to the party with me."

His voice cajoled. His eyes coaxed. And he'd called her Rynn. It made her feel as if they were moving into a new phase of their relationship, from slightly distant, slightly wary coconspirators, to true friends. Wavering, she glanced down at herself. Dust streaked her skirt from where she'd been kneeling on the floor, and her hair, because she hadn't been expecting visitors, was bundled into a braid that she'd twisted into a now-untidy knot at her nape. And for all she knew she had dirty streaks on her face.

"I'm not dressed for a party."

"That's an easy fix. Go change. I'll wait." The smile in his eyes expanded to include his mouth. "Did I mention that Moira will be upset with me if I turn up without you? And if I've learned one thing in the course of a badly misspent life, it's this—never upset the cook."

She laughed. And decided.

"All right. I won't be long. You can wait in the library." She showed him the way, left him with a newspaper and headed upstairs.

She washed, and dressed in another of her black dresses, although this one was a slim silk column embellished with lace inserts at the neck and wrists, and did up her hair. The merest touch of pink by way of cosmetics on her cheeks and lips took her from ghostly pale to pleasingly porcelain, she was glad to see. The onyx earbobs Thomas had given her added the finishing touch. As she put them on, she smiled a little sadly at herself in the mirror, remembering. Then, feeling a tangle of emotions far too complex to even try to sort through, she went downstairs.

"Better," Maguire said, giving her a comprehensive look when she walked into the library. Putting down the newspaper, he got to his feet.

"If you keep this up, I'm liable to get conceited," she responded tartly.

He laughed, helped her on with her coat, and, with a word to Cyril, they were out the door.

Chapter Twenty-Nine

"So what was it you wanted to talk to me about?" Rynn asked as the Vauxhall purred along the narrow, curvy lanes that led to Moira Clary's farm. Rolling hills, grassy meadows gleaming emerald from the rain, stone walls and sheep, with mighty Ben Bulbin looming over all—even under a lowering sky the countryside was so beautiful that just looking at it lightened her heart.

"While I realize your intentions are good, you've no business acting as a nurse or anything else to any stray IRA fighters who might come your way." There was a flatness to his voice that told her that, from his point of view, there was no counterargument she could make.

Taken by surprise, she gave him an indignant look. "You really do have a gossip network, don't you? Who on earth is telling you these things?"

"That's not the point, is it? The point is, we live in dangerous times, and what you're doing is dangerous. The men you saw off to Galway? They'd just shot four RIC officers near Dungloe. They have bounties on their heads, and are being hunted far and wide across the land. You don't want to be putting yourself in the middle of that."

Her lips compressed. "I couldn't help it. They stopped me on the road, at gunpoint."

"I doubt that would make any difference if you were to be

found out. You'd be taken up for interrogation, arrested, maybe even shot or hanged. I know that you're not exactly responsible for what happened there, or with the others earlier. But what I'm here to tell you is, you need to put yourself in a position where that doesn't happen again. Move into town at the very least. You're too isolated in that drafty big mansion."

"It's kind of you to worry about me."

The look he shot her was almost savage. "It's not kind. I'm not being bloody kind. I'm using the brain God gave me to foresee a bad ending and try to stop it before it occurs. We're not just dealing with the RIC and the British soldiers anymore. Churchill has lost his patience as well as his mind and is recruiting mercenaries from among the worst of the troops that fought in the war with a plan to send them here to crush the rebellion once and for all. These are some of the most brutal, vicious men to be found anywhere, and they've no love for the Irish and no respect for military traditions. Woman or not, they'll shoot you or worse and never turn a hair."

His expression had grown so grim that Rynn felt an actual flutter of fear. Before she could reply, two young men came bounding out into the road, arms flailing wildly, with the clear intent of waving them down. Taken aback, she was relieved to hear one shout "Yard's a muddy mess, park in the grass by the barn," and realized that they'd arrived at their destination.

"Relatives of yours?" she asked as the Vauxhall bumped into the barnyard as requested. A battered buggy, a couple of wagons and a pony cart were there before them. Chickens scratching in the grass—and yes, with the barn on a slight rise, there was grass, enough of it to hold all those vehicles and keep the car's wheels from sinking in—fluttered out of the way. A horse peered at them from the barn door.

"Friends of Tim's," he replied. "Or Alfie's. Or James's. Or Joseph's. It's hard to keep them straight."

"I see you managed to bring her. Welcome to the madhouse, Lady Thomas." Moira greeted each of them in turn as, taking Rynn with him, Maguire made his way through the packed house to the kitchen where his sister was holding court as she cooked. Built of clay bricks that had been whitewashed at some point, the two-story structure was crowded to bursting and smelled of peat fires and good food and the pine of the Christmas tree claiming pride of place in a corner of the front parlor. With so many guests the house was loud with chatter, and several children darted about underfoot unchecked.

"I did." He kissed his sister's cheek, then deftly dodged a bread roll thrown by one of Moira's boys—Rynn was sure the sturdy youth was one of Moira's boys; the mop of unruly red hair was the giveaway—at another, equally redhaired, slightly older boy that just missed Maguire's ear. Alfie and James, she thought. Or Joseph.

"Oh, sorry, Owen," the guilty party said, laughing as he danced away from the other boy's retaliatory flick of a dish towel in his direction.

"Be thankful you missed, maggot." Maguire gave him a mock squinty-eyed look.

"Can I drive your car?" the older boy asked. "You said you'd teach me like you taught Tim."

"In this weather? Not likely. I've no mind to die in a ditch."

"You two, quit pestering your uncle and get out of my kitchen. Go on, *shoo.* Go find Joseph and tell him to make sure we have enough chairs set out." Moira waved hands coated in white flour at them, then glanced semiapologetically at Rynn. "They forget their manners sometimes, but they're good boys."

"I'm sure they are." Rynn smiled at her.

"If only they hadn't been spoiled so by their mother." Maguire's mournful expression earned him a withering look from his sister, to which he responded with a grin.

"Our Alfie will be going off to Trinity College next year, and our James is the best hurler on his team. And our Joseph is the kindest, best boy a mother could ask for," Moira said to Rynn with the air of one refuting her brother's words.

"Moira, I think we can add the dumplings now." The young woman, no more than eighteen, who turned from the pot she'd been stirring on the range had a pretty round face with cheeks flushed from the heat, light brown hair smoothed back into a bun at her nape and an apron covering her dress.

"They're almost ready." Even as Moira plunged her hands back into the bowl she'd been mixing, she glanced at Rynn. "Lady Thomas, do you know Katie Meagher? She's Tim's friend. And over there—" with her hands full of dough, she nodded toward an older woman slicing meat on a platter "—is my mother-in-law, Deidre Clary. And in the corner—" she looked at the comfortably plump middle-aged woman dumping bread rolls into a basket "—is our neighbor Orla Boyce. Ladies, this is Lady Thomas Dunne."

Rynn smiled at everyone in general. "Rynn Carmichael that was. And please, call me Rynn."

"Rynn it is, then. And I'm Moira." Moira lifted the bowl and carried it to the range. The other women gave their first names, with Orla adding, "I remember your mother. Rosemary Shaughnessy. Quite a splash she made, with her singing and dancing. Every man-jack of them fancied her. You're the very spit of her, God rest her soul. Oh, eh, and I'm a widow myself, like you."

Before Rynn could reply, two little girls ran into the kitchen. Their bright red hair gave their identity away even before the older one said, "Mam, the table's ready."

"Good. Take the bread out, if you would. Grace, you take the butter."

They did as asked, with the older one giving Rynn a quick,

uncertain smile as she passed. The younger girl, her long braids hanging down her back, her eyes focused on the butter dish she carried, saved all her attention for her very important task.

"Is there anything I can do to help?" Rynn asked.

Now at the range pinching off pieces of dough and dropping them in the pot, Moira shook her head. "Thank you, but once this finishes everything will be ready. Owen, if you'll look in that cupboard you'll find a cake. Carry it out to the table for me, would you, and tell everyone we'll be eating in about ten minutes." She flashed a quick smile at Rynn. "Oh, wait, there is something you can do to help. Keep an eye on Owen. He can be uncommon clumsy, and we can't have him dropping the cake."

"You heard her." Maguire took the cake—a tall, multilayered confection iced in what looked like almond paste—from the cupboard and started out of the kitchen with it. "Come keep an eye on me."

Not long afterward the party, thirty-some people strong, crowded around a table meant, perhaps, for twelve. Relatives, friends, neighbors, three full-time farmhands—beyond the core group of Maguire and Moira and her family, the gathering was a mixed bag of young and old, town and country, male and female. Rynn discovered that she knew a number of people present and was kept busy talking as the food was served up.

The meal, as Maguire had promised, was excellent. But more than that, she found to her surprise that she enjoyed the company, the laughter and teasing among people who knew each other well. Tim and his group of friends, Alfie and James and Joseph, who were stairstepped in age at sixteen, fifteen and fourteen, the little girls, Grace and Maeve, and the other relatives and neighbors made for a merry gathering. Seated beside Maguire, she was impressed by the sheer quantity of food he managed to consume, and more impressed by the obvious affection in which his sister and nephews and nieces held him, which he obviously returned.

It was a side of him she hadn't seen before, and she was charmed by it.

After the meal, after the cake was consumed and the presents opened, the guests broke into various factions. To Rynn's amusement, Tim and his brothers managed to talk—goad?—Maguire into playing outside with them.

"Are you too grand, then, to kick a ball around with us?" Alfie demanded when Maguire initially refused. (Rynn could tell Alfie from James now because, at sixteen, Alfie was larger than his brother, whom he greatly resembled, and his eyes were blue to James's green. Tim had the look of them, but he was taller and lankier. Joseph, at fourteen, had a face full of freckles, which made him easy to identify.)

"It's a sea of mud out there," Maguire objected.

"He's careful of his fancy clothes, he is. That's understandable," James said to Alfie.

"The mud's in front. We'll play in back," Joseph said to Maguire.

"There's still mud," Maguire said.

"Leave him be. He's old, you know. He'll be fearful of getting hurt."

"Old! The hell I'm old! I can play you pikers into the ground."

"He would say that," Alfie said to James in a confidential tone, which everyone could nevertheless hear quite well. "He'll be wanting to save face."

"Ah." James cast a significant look at Rynn. "No doubt you're right."

Maguire's eyes narrowed at them.

"If Owen don't want to play, he don't want to play," Tim intervened. "He's an important man now. Were we to beat him, it'd be a blow to his dignity."

"All right, that's it." Maguire looked around at his sister. "Do you have an old coat of Niall's I can borrow?"

"I do," Moira said, grinning, as the boys whooped in victory. Minutes later, they were out the door, with Maguire, stripped down to his fine white shirt and well-tailored trousers beneath a shabby old coat that reached halfway to his knees with a knit cap on his head, in their midst.

"My Niall was a broad man, but a bit shorter than Owen," Moira confided as she and Rynn watched through a window in the back door as the game got underway. The winter light pouring in through the glass highlighted the pale blue eyes she shared with her brother, although they looked far more at home on her, with her bright hair and fair skin. "I lost him at Verdun, you know." She pulled something out of her neckline. A bronze medal, Rynn saw, attached to a red ribbon with the whole suspended from a fine gold chain. "The government sent me his last pay, and this. Two bob and a medal is what they figured my husband was worth."

"I'm so sorry," Rynn said.

Moira dropped the medal back inside her neckline. "I keep it out of sight, because it reminds the kids and makes them sad. But I never take it off."

"I'm sure it's been hard on all of you."

"Getting on without Niall *has* been hard, especially for the kids. If it hadn't been for Owen, I don't know what we would have done."

"He seems very close to you and your children."

"He is. With the boys, especially, he's done his best to take their dad's place. He's done what he can to guide them, and he's provided. And not just for mine, but for our brothers' families, too. There were six of us, you know. Me, then two sisters, then Owen, then two brothers. Now there's just us two, Owen and me."

"Did your sisters leave families?"

Moira shook her head. "They passed before they could. While we were at the orphanage."

"You were at an orphanage?" Rynn didn't mean to pry, but the question was out before she could stop it.

"After our mother died, our father couldn't take care of us. He liked a drink, if you want the truth of it, and wasn't worth a lick because of it. They put us in St. Joseph's. When I was old enough, I left, married Niall and got my brothers out as soon as I could. We all worked and we weren't getting rich but we were doing all right. Then the war came, and they all joined up, Niall and Owen and Robby and Liam. Owen's the only one who came back, and he's been trying to take the place of the other three ever since. And doing a fine job of it, too. Owen didn't tell you any of this?"

"He didn't." Feeling she needed to clarify her relationship with Maguire, Rynn added, "We're not . . . seeing each other, you know. Romantically. He and I are friends."

Moira's smile was wry. "Is that how it is? Well, he makes a good friend, I've no doubt."

A shout from the yard diverted their attention to the action outside. Maguire was clutching a round ball close to his chest and running like his life depended on it, which from the look of the pack of boys chasing him, it did. Another shout went up as he apparently made it safely to wherever the goal was and started whooping with half the group as he held the ball up in triumph over his head.

"Men. They never grow up, even the best of them," Moira said indulgently, and turned away from the window with a little shiver as a draft reached them through the panes. "Come into the front room where it's warm, and we'll have a nice visit with the others while the house is quiet. Believe me, it won't last long."

An hour or so later, once again wearing his own elegant overcoat and jacket, Maguire was still flicking bits of dried mud from his trousers and shoes when he put Rynn into the passenger seat of the Vauxhall and drove away. Tim had left earlier, in the Model T that, to his loudly expressed joy and Alfie's hoots of envy, Owen had given him as a combined birthday and Christmas present. Tim's task was to take Katie Meagher home and drop off his grandmother at the train station, before returning to stay through Christmas with his mother and siblings at the farm. The girls would return to Dublin after Christmas. They were students at Hillcourt, a boarding school in the city, and had ridden the train down the previous day with their grandmother, who lived in Dublin. Old Mrs. Clary considered train travel more comfortable and far safer than the roads, and given the state of the country who could blame her? Alfie, James and Joseph attended the Bundoran Boys National School, because, as they put it, they weren't the kind of slackers to leave their mam to run the farm alone.

To which Tim, who'd left the farm to work for Maguire and at whom the thrust had been aimed, took loud exception.

"You were right, I did have fun," Rynn said as the car edged around a flock of sheep being herded down the road by a man and a dog working in tandem.

"I told you you would." Maguire was smiling a little.

"My favorite part was watching you slide face-first into the mud. And then your nephews jumping on top of you."

"Liked that, did you? At least I managed to hold on to the ball. And they'll pay, the cheeky buggers. We'll see who gets the last laugh next time I'm down."

"And when will that be?"

He shot a glance her way. It was impossible to read anything in it, but its very opaqueness told her that the question interested him.

"Sometime after Christmas. I have to go to London when I leave here, and I anticipate being away for several weeks. With de Valera still fundraising in America, Mick Collins is in charge of the IRA, and he's as bloody-minded in his own way as Churchill. There's still a few on both sides trying to keep the violence from blowing up into all-out war, and I've been asked to come add my voice to theirs." He grimaced. "Not that I think it will do much good."

"Really?" She gave him a troubled look.

"One can always hope, but as I told you earlier, the situation is getting worse by the day." They were in sight of the house now. The sun was setting, the rain had stopped and a rainbow was forming in the sky, arching above the bay and the Point and curving down over Ballyshannon Court in a scene of almost otherworldly beauty.

"Look." Rynn pointed. According to everything she'd ever been taught, a rainbow was a promise, a benediction. Or, alternatively, an augury. Of good things, she thought fiercely as her heart beat a little faster at the thought. Only of good things.

"Pretty." He was clearly unimpressed. As the Vauxhall nosed up the driveway, he added, "You want to take what I said about moving into town seriously. At least for a while. Go visit your granny and sister, stay clear of the IRA, stay clear of the RIC, stay clear of any involvement in anything that might bring you to the attention of either side. By the time I get back, I'll have a pretty clear idea about where this is headed, and then you can make whatever decisions you need to make. The key is not to get yourself killed in the meantime."

"I'll be careful," she promised as he walked her to the door. "Thank you for today. I was a little down in the dumps when you came, I admit."

"A little glum, were you?"

"Don't gloat," she warned.

He laughed. And then, as they reached the front door and Cyril, who would have been on the watch for her, could be heard on the other side fumbling with the lock, he said, "Good night, Rynn."

"Good night." Waiting for the door to open, she gave him a quick smile.

"Owen," he said.

"What?"

"You probably should start calling me Owen. Since, as you told my sister, we're such good friends and all."

She looked at him indignantly. "Does everybody you know gossip?"

He laughed again, then stood there exchanging a few cordial words with Cyril as she went inside with a deliberately casual "Goodnight, Owen," thrown over her shoulder.

Chapter Thirty

Christmas came and went. Rynn spent it with Granny and Glenna at the cottage. Not that Owen's warning had alarmed her into doing so, precisely, because she'd always meant to spend Christmas with her nearest and dearest. But with Mrs. Frampton off to visit her sister for the holidays and Cyril, when pressed, expressing a wish to go see his old mother in Drogheda, and Anna and Lynette already slated to go to their families, it seemed like a good time to close up the house for a little while just in case she was, like Dr. Lowry, on somebody's watch list.

Owen returned, as he'd said he would, but only for a lightning visit. He checked on his sister, dropped in to see Rynn—"I'm glad to know somebody listens to me" was his reaction to finding her at the cottage—and took her to dinner at the Great Northern Hotel before leaving with Tim the next day. When she asked about his progress in London, he was pessimistic.

"Neither side is willing to make any concessions. Churchill seems to think Ireland should be made to bend the knee to the Crown whatever the cost, and Mick doesn't seem to realize that he's throwing a few thousand fighters at most against the whole might of the British Empire. I think he thinks we can just worry them to death."

"You're right, the man's not courting you," Granny said with a sly smile after he was gone.

"He comes to visit his sister. He feels responsible for her and her family."

"It wasn't his sister he took to dinner."

"The man has to eat."

Quelling look clashed with irritating twinkle, and there the matter was allowed to rest.

Over the next few weeks, it became obvious that much was changing in Bundoran and the surrounding area, and for Ireland as a whole, and not for the better. The IRA had attempted to assassinate the lord lieutenant of Ireland, British Field Marshal Viscount French, in Dublin, in late December, and by doing so had infuriated the British and the Unionists. The British soldiers and the RIC, previously regarded by at least half the population with fear and loathing, were felt to be almost gentlemanly in comparison with what came next. The Crown recruited mercenaries and sent them over, just as Owen had warned.

Unemployed rank-and-file ex-soldiers with no ties to or affection for Ireland or the Irish, they arrived in batches, only a few at first and then in increasing numbers. Given a mandate by the Crown to stamp out the rebellion and annihilate any who opposed them, they openly relished the assignment. They walked the streets as if they owned them—and everyone took note, and did their best to stay out of their way. As more came, they rode around in armored lorries mounted with machine guns. Festooned with hand grenades and brandishing their Enfield rifles, they boasted loudly of the horrible fate that awaited the IRA and any who aided them.

Rude and rough, barging in where they chose, taking over as they pleased, they were regarded with dread everywhere they went. Even the RIC and the regular British soldiers stayed out of their way. Their uniforms were as crude as they were. Thrown together from leftover RIC and army uniforms, they were missized and mismatched, with RIC tunics of a green so dark they looked black paired with khaki army trousers. It was this unedifying combination that gave them their nickname: the Black and Tans.

"Think they're cocks of the walk, don't they?" Noreen Kelly, who taught with Glenna, eyed the trio of Tans, as they were known, as they pushed through the doors of George's Pub, a neighborhood gathering place off Main Street, and aggressively approached the bar. She, along with Rynn and Glenna and three other young women, were crowded into a booth in the back of the dimly lit establishment. It was early evening, dark out but not late, and, like the pub, the street outside the plate glass windows was busy. They'd just attended a musical variety performance by the Bundoran Players, and had stopped by George's for a quick bite before heading home. Rynn was there at Glenna's urging, a little uncomfortable even though she knew everybody at the table and most in the pub. She was still conscious of being regarded with suspicion in some quarters, and her black dress, which she'd refused to switch out for something less gloomy as Glenna had pleaded with her to do, stood out, she feared, among the more festive dresses of the others.

"They're thugs." Glenna made a face, and then glanced quickly down at her drink as one of the Tans swept a glance over their booth.

"*Terry O'Sullivan*," the Tan who appeared to be the leader boomed, smacking a hand down on the top of the bar as he waved a piece of paper in the face of the barmaid. Startled, Rynn realized what it was as she caught a glimpse of what was on it: a wanted poster. "Point him out."

The barmaid, Siobhan O'Leery, a war widow several years older than Rynn, jumped like nearly everyone else in the pub at the crashing sound of the slap, and went pale and wide-eyed as she found herself the object of the Tan's attention. "Eh, he's not here."

"Are you sure?"

"I'm sure," Siobhan squeaked, backing away from the bar.

The Tan turned, looking over the patrons, most of whom were frozen in place with their eyes either downcast or riveted on what was happening. The other two Tans were already roaming the aisles, searching faces for their quarry.

"Terry O'Sullivan. One-thousand-pound reward to whoever turns him in. Prison for anyone who knows where he is and does not," the lead Tan bellowed, waving the wanted poster. "For anyone who harbors him, the firing squad."

"Here, now, what's all this?" George Marley, the pub's owner, came rushing out of a back room, wiping his hands on his apron as he came. Seeing the Tans, he stopped dead, regarding them with apprehension.

"You own this place?" The lead Tan moved toward George.

"I do." Dropping his apron, George stood his ground.

"Terry O'Sullivan. Where is he?" The Tan shoved the poster in front of his nose.

"I already told them he's not here," Siobhan piped up, her voice shrill with fright.

"He's not," George agreed. "No more do I know where he is."

"But he was here." Quick as that, the Tan drew his pistol and struck George across the face with it. Crying out, clapping both hands to his face, George doubled over. The Tan brought the pistol down with force on the back of his head, then when he fell to the floor kicked him brutally.

"Next time he comes in and you don't tell us, we burn the place down." The Tan delivered a final kick to his victim. With a baleful glance around the room, he headed toward the door. The others followed.

The third one shoved the butt of his rifle through the glass in the door as he left. The sound it made as it shattered sent a last, collective shock through the pub.

Then the spell was broken. Everyone reacted, jumping to their feet, exclaiming, talking, rushing toward George, rushing to aid Siobhan, who had collapsed sobbing behind the bar. Someone locked the pub's broken door. Someone else started pointing people to a back exit. No one wanted to venture out onto the street where the Tans could be seen through the window laughing as they sauntered away.

Shaken, Rynn knelt beside George, rendering what aid she could. He was unconscious but breathing. Blood poured from the cut the pistol had made in his head. More blood streamed from his nose, which was obviously broken. Staunching the blood with handkerchiefs and napkins and towels and every other absorbent thing passed to her by those gathered around, she managed to stop the blood flow from his nose and applied a makeshift bandage to his head, tying it in place with a donated tie. She stayed beside him as several men picked him up and rushed him out the back exit, where a car had been driven into the alley to take him to Dr. Lowry. Pulled back by Glenna, knowing George would be in good hands with Dr. Lowry and not wanting to have herself identified as a nurse by a Tan or anyone else who might be watching, Rynn stayed behind. Leaving a few minutes later, she walked home with Glenna and the others. But their mood had changed from lighthearted enjoyment of their outing to anger and fear. Moving quickly through the alley, the group split up at Sea Road. All were in a hurry to get home. All were on a mission to avoid the Tans.

"The bastards," Glenna said fiercely but not too loudly as she hurried along at Rynn's side, as if still afraid she might be overheard. It was full night—later than they'd meant to stay out—with only a sliver of moon to light the way now that they were past the sidewalks and the streetlamps were behind them. As they neared the cottage, the area became increasingly deserted. Across the road, the stretch of dark fields with the dark, jagged edges of the Dartry Mountains rising up in the distance, though a familiar sight, seemed suddenly eerie and unsettling.

All at once, without any warning, Rynn felt as though she was no longer on the street with Glenna, but rather that she was a long way away, observing the scene from a vantage point that wasn't her own.

Her attention riveted on an animal the size of a small calf or large dog, blacker than the night, running away at speed across the field.

Watching it, she felt an overwhelming sense of dread.

"We can't abide this. And we won't," Glenna said. Her sister's voice snapped her back to the present, and Rynn was left to stare at the field, which was deserted, and wonder what had just happened and what she'd seen.

"Do you suppose Mr. Marley will be all right?" Glenna added, clearly unaware that anything was amiss. Unsettled by the experience, Rynn chose to dismiss it and turned to her sister.

"I hope so," she said.

"Justice needs to be done," Glenna said fiercely, and Rynn agreed.

Granny was waiting when they reached the cottage. Instead of sitting in her favorite chair before the fire sewing or reading as she was wont to do, she was pacing the floor when they entered, and she practically fell on their necks with relief at the sight of them.

"Are you well? Are you safe?" she demanded in an unsteady voice when she let them go. She was as pale as flour as she peered into each of their faces in turn.

"We're safe," Rynn assured her, looking hard at her grandmother. Granny was so rarely agitated that Rynn began to feel her own bubbling of alarm.

"But how did you know about the Tans?" Glenna exclaimed.

"No one could have told you. We've barely had time to get home ourselves."

"The Tans?" Granny scoffed. "'Tis naught to do with those villains. My loves, oh my loves, I've seen the Black Pig."

"What?" Rynn's hand went to her heart. Her mouth went dry. Glenna sucked in a quick breath.

Both knew what that meant. Every Irish man, woman and child knew what it meant. The Black Pig was an apparition seen only rarely over the centuries by those given the gift of seeing such things. It was said to portend a pending disaster. For the one who saw it, or the area in which it was seen, or Ireland. Or all three.

Granny nodded. "I did. I saw it. A little bit ago I got uneasy in myself about you and I went to look down the road to see if I could see you coming. I did not, so I turned away, and there it was. The Black Pig! Running through the field across the road, snorting and tossing its head, a fearsome sight! It looked right at me, its eyes glowing yellow through the night, then ran away and went straight through the stone wall at the end of the field—straight through it, mind, as if it had no substance to it at all—and disappeared. I thought—I thought—I could only think of the two of you."

Her voice trembled on that last.

"'Twas a dog or some such," Glenna said. But now her voice was not quite steady, either.

Granny shook her head and looked at Rynn.

"Come sit down." Ignoring her pounding heart, Rynn wrapped her arm around her grandmother, urging her toward the hearth and her chair. Though the night was not cold—windy, yes, and damp, but not cold—the cottage suddenly was. Despite the fire, and the heat it gave.

"I'll get you some tea." Glenna hurried toward the kitchen.

"You know." Clutching Rynn's hand, Granny looked up

at her as Rynn settled her in her chair. The firelight danced around them. The corners of the well-loved room were dim. "You *know*, my dotey pet. Blessing or curse, count it as you may, deny it as you will, you have it, too. The Sight. 'Twas the Pig. Joseph, Mary and all the saints, have pity on Ireland. Have pity on Bundoran. Have pity on us."

It was a donkey. Everyone, friends, neighbors, all who heard and there were many, assured Granny that that was the answer. A small gray donkey had escaped its pen and was running loose through the town that very same night, seen by many. And stones were missing in the wall—see right there, Ben Dooley, who rented the land, was stacking up more to fix the gap. Ergo, the donkey had gone through the gap in the wall and been lost to the darkness. That was what she'd seen, they all agreed with great relief. Not an apparition at all, not the Black Pig at all, but a wayward donkey.

Granny remained adamant. Rynn believed her.

Because she'd seen it, too.

That apparition she'd spotted in the field, it was no dog, or calf, or donkey.

It was—had to have been—the Black Pig.

The near certainty and all that it meant—for herself and everyone and everything she loved—made her blood run cold.

But what was there to do?

Tell no one. The attention, the skepticism, the notoriety—everything that came with having the Sight—it was nothing she wanted. It was more than she could bear.

"What do you think it means?" she asked Granny days later. Having just escaped a contingent of neighbors who'd gathered on the street outside to stare and shake their heads at the field where the Black Pig had apparently been seen, they'd retreated to the cottage's kitchen for a cup of tea. Glenna had gone upstairs to change her dress—the three of them had just returned from Mass—so she and Granny had a minute alone.

"I don't know." Seated at the kitchen table, Granny sipped her tea meditatively. "That's the curse of the Sight. I never know."

Rynn didn't say anything. *Three can keep a secret if two of them are dead.* But from the knowing way Granny was looking at her, she could tell that something had happened to open Rynn's eyes.

Something that was forcing Rynn to accept that she had the Sight, too.

Then Glenna joined them, remarking on the happy news of a friend's engagement. The conversation turned general, and, because there was nothing she could do about any of it, Rynn did her best to put the Black Pig and everything it represented out of her head.

With Mrs. Frampton, Cyril and Anna (Lynette had married over the holiday and would not be returning) back at Ballyshannon Court, and she and Glenna now too old and set in their ways to share a bedroom indefinitely, Rynn moved back up to Ballyshannon Court. Any danger that might have attached to helping the IRA soldiers she had treated had certainly dissipated over the past weeks, she was sure.

She was, as would anyone of sense, starting to give some thought to her future now that the shock of Thomas's death was fading. She couldn't, and didn't want to, stay at Ballyshannon Court forever, and she didn't want to spend her life within the limited confines of Bundoran, either, much as she loved it. But she hadn't yet decided what she did want. There were Granny and Glenna to consider. And other people, and other things, including the state of the world. She was not yet ready to put aside her nursing skills, which she had worked hard to acquire. As a trained nurse, and no longer married (because the profession, like many others, frowned on employing married women) her skills would be valued by any hospital. And if the current violence was to escalate into full-scale war, they would be needed.

Here. In Ireland.

The thought of war—more war, more death and killing—sickened her.

But she was afraid war was rushing toward them like a freight train.

She was afraid that was what the appearance of the Black Pig meant.

Glenna reported that at recess the boys marched around in play drills, using sticks as rifles.

Groups of young men could be glimpsed training in the hills.

More men were wanted and on the run than weren't, it seemed, while the Crown hunted them ruthlessly.

The IRA strategy seemed to be strike without warning and disappear. Newspapers were full of accounts of their ambushes, raids on police barracks and sabotage of roads, dams and bridges. Whispers circulated about a squad of assassins recruited by Michael Collins that some had dubbed the Twelve Apostles. The British were worse. Through their attack dogs the Tans, they burned houses and even whole villages and looted and killed indiscriminately. As terrible as the Tans were, it wasn't enough for the Crown. They were being supplemented by another paramilitary force, the Auxiliaries, who were easy to spot in their distinctive tam-o'-shanter caps, that was as bad or worse. The atrocities they visited on the civilian population were brutal.

Ireland seethed like a volcano building toward an eruption.

"Evil, conscienceless savages," Cyril said with loathing after learning of another attack by the Tans. "And the Brits as bad, paying them ten shillings a day for their dirty work. After the Great War, after we fought for them. The scum."

"Not all of them." Mrs. Frampton cast a quick, sideways

glance at Rynn. "Not Lord Thomas, for one. He was a sweet, good man, to be sure."

"It's all right," Rynn reassured her, knowing that she was worried about offending. They were all in the cellar, Anna included, sorting through medical supplies with an eye toward donating them. Rynn just hadn't made up her mind to whom, or to where. "Lord Thomas *was* a sweet, good man, and he would agree with Cyril. And he would do what he could to stop it."

The thought of Thomas brought a surge of tenderness with it. The pain was still there, but for the first time, the good memories outweighed it. That was part of the process of letting him go, Rynn realized. He would have a place in her heart forever, and she would smile whenever she thought of him. But life moved on, and so must she.

The question remained, to what?

It was only a few nights later that she was roused unexpectedly from sleep. Awakened by the sudden flare of light from the lamp beside her bed, Rynn blinked in bemusement at the apparition that was Mrs. Frampton in her nightcap and robe leaning over her.

"There's a visitor for you in the kitchen. You should come at once," Mrs. Frampton said when she saw Rynn's eyes open.

"What? Who?" Sitting up, Rynn shook her head to clear it. The shadows in the room beyond the pool of lamplight made clear that it was nowhere near dawn. "What time is it?"

"Coming up on one in the morning." She handed Rynn her robe, which was laid out at the foot of the bed.

Standing, Rynn slid her arms into her robe. Tying the soft green garment around her waist, she thrust her feet into velvet slippers. Her hair, confined in the braid she wore for sleep, was trapped inside the robe, and with a quick flip of her hand she pulled it free.

"What has happened?" Her voice sharpened as she came fully awake.

"You must see for yourself." Motioning to Rynn to follow, Mrs. Frampton turned off the bedside lamp and whisked herself out of the room. It was only as Rynn stepped into the hall that she realized that the entire rest of the house, except for a slight glow emanating from the kitchen, was as dark as her bedroom now was. Mrs. Frampton carried one of the electric torches kept beside the kitchen door in case it was necessary to go outside at night. Held high, it shed just enough light so that they both could see where they were putting their feet as they went down the stairs.

It was obvious that Mrs. Frampton thought it best not to light up the house to the point where the unaccustomed burst of middle-of-the-night activity became apparent to anyone who might be passing by on the road or, say, watching from some vantage point outside.

At the realization, Rynn's heart started knocking before she even reached the bottom of the stairs.

Chapter Thirty-One

Rynn had the worst of bad feelings as she followed Mrs. Frampton into the kitchen. The overhead light was on. Rynn blinked against the brightness as she stopped just inside the door. The homey smell of the next day's bread rising on the counter lost its soothing quality as she got her first good look at Cyril.

Wearing trousers that had obviously been hastily pulled on to supplement the nightshirt he still wore, Cyril stood with his back against the far counter with a rifle—Rynn hadn't even known he possessed a rifle—gripped in both hands. He held it crosswise in front of him, not really pointed at anyone but there. He didn't look at her or Mrs. Frampton as they entered. Instead he was focused on . . .

Rynn's eyes widened as she followed his gaze.

A man in a trench coat sat slumped at the far end of the big table in the center of the room. He was bent forward so that his head, resting on one folded arm, was on the tabletop. His other arm hung loosely at his side. His overlong hair was black, thick and wavy.

"What—" Rynn began, then broke off. *She knew that hair.* "Donal?"

Donal lifted his head even as she hurried toward him. His face was pale and drawn, but he managed a weak smile.

"Sorry to pull you into this, *acushla*, but 'twas the only place I could think to bring them." His head dropped back to rest on his arm. The breathless quality of his speech told her that he was in physical distress.

"Them?" Hovering above him, she felt his forehead, checked the pulse below his ear. His skin was warm and damp. His pulse was rapid. "Are you sick? Hurt?'

A grunt was her reply, and then a pained groan as she placed a gentle hand on his shoulder. She could feel the thick padding beneath his coat: a bandage, she felt sure.

"Come look out the window." Cyril's voice was grim. Rynn realized that he was standing where he was because it afforded him a view of the night outside the window. She took the few steps needed to join him and caught her breath.

Men staggered through the kitchen garden, singly and in pairs, a steady stream of them coming toward the house from the direction of the woods. Bathed in pale moonlight, they looked like the risen spirits of the dead.

Rynn's stomach clenched. Mrs. Frampton, who'd stepped up beside her and was seeing the same thing, crossed herself.

"Don't upset yourselves. 'Tis the South Donegal Flying Column," Donal said. "We've run into a bit of difficulty, as you can see."

"My God." Rynn swung around to look at him. "What did you do?"

"Liberated a prisoner. And some weapons. The soldiers transporting them didn't take kindly to it, but we prevailed." He'd lifted his head to look at her again, and she could see the sheen of sweat on his forehead. "They'll be hunting us. Although we did our best to cover our trail."

It was said by way of a warning.

"The first of them is at the door." Mrs. Frampton turned away from the window. Worry was in her eyes, and her voice. She clasped her hands tightly in front of her waist. She knew the consequences that might attach to opening that door as well as Rynn did.

Rynn looked at her, looked at Cyril, a question in her eyes. Did they want to be involved, to put themselves in danger? The risk was great, which they all knew. She was the nurse, and the mistress of the house. The responsibility, and any blame that went with it, was hers. They could melt away, go to bed, claim to have seen nothing, know nothing and so perhaps save themselves if anything should go wrong.

Mrs. Frampton took a breath. Her mouth firming, she turned to draw the curtains over the window. Cyril squared his shoulders, looking troubled but resolute.

She had her answer.

"Let them in," she said, and Cyril did.

Eleven men all filed in, some stumbling over the threshold only to collapse on the floor, some supporting a wounded comrade, two of them carrying a third between them in a chair they'd formed by linking hands, most armed to the teeth with rifles strapped to their backs. Seamus was among them. Of course, Seamus was among them. Where Donal was, Seamus went, and vice versa. Bearded now, with wooly curls that wouldn't have been out of place on a shaggy black sheep, he greeted Rynn with a brief, would-be jaunty smile before lowering the man he'd been helping to the floor. Pulling his and the other man's rifles free, he dropped to stretch out panting on his back, both rifles laid out on the floor beside him.

Moving from one man to the other, Rynn conducted a quick triage operation to sort the wounded into tiers of severity.

"What's this?" The surprised question had Rynn and practically everyone else in the kitchen looking in horror in the direction from which it came.

Paused on the last step of the back stairs, Anna, in her

nightclothes and robe, clearly newly roused from her bed, glanced wide-eyed around the kitchen. Before Rynn or anyone could reply, Anna's eyes lit on a lanky young man sprawled out on the floor not far from Seamus. "Brian Nolan, is that you?"

As he turned his head to look at her, she flew to his side.

"That's her fella," Mrs. Frampton said to Rynn as Anna knelt beside him, scolding and questioning all at the same time.

"It would be best if we could move to an interior room. At night, any glimmer of light . . ." Donal's voice trailed off as he took a seemingly painful breath, but then he finished with "could bring them right to us."

A chill ran down Rynn's spine.

"We're moving to the cellar," she announced. "We'll set up there." She looked at Anna. "Anna. You understand that nothing of this is to be spoken of to anyone who's not in this room."

Anna looked up at her. "You've no need to worry, Lady Thomas. *Tiocfaidh ar la.*"

Our day will come. It had become the unofficial motto of the IRA.

Rynn nodded. "All right, then. Let's go."

It was no small feat to get everyone downstairs, but once it was done and the kitchen was dark again Rynn found that she could breathe a little easier.

The cellar was built of thick limestone blocks. It ran beneath the entire house, which meant it was huge. Clusters of discarded furniture and stacks of boxes and bins and other random items filled much of the space. Its most important attribute under the circumstances was that it was windowless, with only a single door to the upstairs and another to the outside to accommodate the delivery of supplies. Even with the one overhead light and multiple lanterns set about to illuminate the small section where the makeshift infirmary was taking shape, there was no possibility that even the tiniest sliver of light could escape.

Cyril was busy setting up cots. Men lay on them or sat or

lay on the floor, waiting for Rynn to get to them. The injuries ranged from a gunshot wound to the abdomen—the most severe—to Donal's wounded shoulder and broken ribs to the multiple contusions and severe malnutrition suffered by the man they'd rescued, which Mrs. Frampton was currently helping to treat by spooning thinned porridge into his mouth.

Donal refused to identify him—"It's better for you if you don't know"—but told her, as she bound up his broken ribs, that the man's condition resulted from several months' imprisonment that included multiple interrogations that were nothing short of torture and the hunger strike he'd gone on in protest. Thanks to an informant, they'd learned he was to be moved from one jail to another earlier that day and had attacked the convoy en route. The resultant bloody battle had left, at Donal's estimation, at least two British soldiers dead and three times that number badly wounded. As for their flying column, they hadn't lost a man.

"Although it's possible Rory O'Keefe there with the bullet in his stomach might yet be the first." Donal looked a question at her as he said it. Rory O'Keefe, as Rynn now knew his name was, who'd presented with a gunshot wound to the abdomen, was the most seriously wounded and had been the first man she'd treated. With the bullet removed and the wound disinfected and bandaged, he was presently lying unconscious on one of the cots.

"The bullet missed his stomach, fortunately for him. It lodged in the peritoneum, without hitting anything too vital. If infection doesn't set in, he should recover."

"Praise be to God. He has a wife, with a babe on the way." Seated on the floor with his back to the wall in preparation for what she was about to do to him, Donal sent a frowning look up at her. "We've got to get our boyo—" he nodded at the man they'd rescued "—to the people waiting for him as soon as may be. Will it harm O'Keefe to be moved?"

"I'd recommend waiting at least several days. More likely longer, depending on how he does."

Donal shook his head. "We can't wait nearly that long. In twenty-four hours, we won't be able to smuggle a mouse out of this county. They'll have soldiers on every road, every track, every sheep path."

"Several days," Rynn said firmly. Then Donal was silenced by the roll of gauze bandages she instructed him to bite down on. Grimacing, he did as he was told, and with Cyril's help she dug out the bullet that had lodged in his shoulder, then disinfected and sutured the wound and bandaged him up. Afterward, dizzy and sweating, he collapsed on the cot that had been provided for him.

Seamus had suffered wounds from both a bullet and a bayonet, neither life-threatening. As she was treating him, Rynn noticed that he was still wearing the chain with the St. Michael's medal Molly Kincaid had given him around his neck. She didn't say anything about it, because she didn't want to cause him distress, but for a moment the thought of Molly slowed her work. Sweet-natured Molly had cared nothing about politics. All she'd wanted was to live an ordinary life, with a home and a husband and children. She hadn't deserved the fate she'd found.

Seamus must have seen her looking at his necklace, because his hand came up and he fingered the small silver medallion.

"I found him, you know," he said low, for her ears alone. "The bastard that murdered Molly. He was bragging about it, was Captain Henry Smith, and word got passed along until it reached my ears. He was on the Strand that night, the officer left in charge there after we in the *Merrow* got away from them. She came down late to the cove thinking to meet me, I'm sure, and ran into them instead. They took her prisoner, and did things to her to try to make her tell them who was in the boat and where it would likely land. Then, when she managed to break away and ran for her life, he was the bastard that shot her." Seamus's mouth twisted. From pain, Rynn thought, but the pain of grief rather than the physical discomfort she was causing him by suturing the gouge that a bullet had taken out of his side. "He told me all about it over a friendly drink at a Dublin pub, not knowing who I was. Then I came up behind him in the dark as he was walking back to his barracks and slit his bloody throat for him. Justice for Molly, the dear darling, but it does not bring her back."

His voice was grim as he finished. His eyes were wet with unshed tears.

"She's at peace now, Seamus." Snipping off the end of the thread that she used to pull the edges of his wound together, Rynn patted his shoulder consolingly. That Seamus was capable of such savagery should have horrified her, she knew, just as she should have been horrified by it as she'd watched the killing of Bingle. But it was savagery in response to savagery, born of his experiences in the Great War, and in this case it sprang from a place of tremendous love, and tremendous loss. She couldn't find it in her heart to condemn him for it. "She loved you, you know."

"I know. Far more than I deserved." He closed his eyes and flung an arm across them, shutting her out. Rynn finished up in silence and left him alone.

It was nearly dawn by the time everyone was treated. Too late, Seamus, for he was the commanding officer, decreed, for them to venture out of the cellar, out of hiding, because the hunt would be on and it would be relentless and darkness made it much easier to slip past any patrols. Accordingly, the group of them laid up for the day, with the less seriously wounded sleeping and eating and doing what they could to regain their strength. The more seriously wounded—there were four who Rynn didn't expect to be ambulatory anytime soon—lay in their cots coming in and out of consciousness as she did what she could for them.

By the time night came around again, seven members of the flying column were preparing to leave. The others would stay behind, with someone sent to collect them in a few days.

"We'll do much better taking to the hills," Donal said, refusing her offer of the car as transport. "They'll have patrols on the roads, don't you know. Our advantage is we know the countryside in a way they do not. And we know where we're going, and how to get there. Our boyo will have people already there waiting for him. They'll take him on to a safe house, and from there they'll get him out of the country."

"And what of you, and Seamus, and the rest?" Rynn asked. They were standing by the cot he'd used as he packed up his rucksack. His movements were stiff and he went white-lipped if his ribs were jarred, despite how tightly they were bandaged and the morphine injection she'd given him earlier to ease the worst of it, but still he insisted on going.

"We'll be driving the devils out of Ireland for good and all, or we'll be dying in the attempt." His belated smile was summoned for her benefit, she knew, in an attempt to ease the grimness that underlay his words. Then the smile went away as his eyes swept her face. "If I haven't yet mentioned it, I was sorry to hear about your loss. But if I'm being honest, I'm not entirely sorry that you're a widow. It may be too soon, but in times like these, life is uncertain. My feelings for you are unchanged, *acushla*. I want you to know that."

She looked up into the handsome face of the boy—no, man now—she'd loved for years. So many of her fondest memories were wrapped up in him. He was her first love, her first kiss, her first dream of marriage and family and forever.

But . . .

The Great War, and all that had happened since, had upended the world. It had altered her life, and his, irrevocably. Once they might have been made for each other. But everything that was in her—that tingly certainty, which she had to admit was most likely connected to the Sight—told her that they no longer were, that he was not the man for her, that making a life with him was not the path she was meant to take.

"But you no longer feel the same." He said it with chagrin, followed by the slightest of wry smiles, and she realized that he'd read her answer in her face. Ah, he knew her.

She smiled back at him, a little sadly as she acknowledged the truth of it. "I've changed, Donal. I'm not the girl you loved any longer. But you'll always have a place in my heart. Just not—" She hesitated.

"*The* place," he finished for her.

"Just not *the* place," she agreed.

"Donal," Seamus called over his shoulder. He, along with the other men who were going, was heading toward the outside door, where Cyril waited to open it for them. Flat caps pulled low over their eyes, coats buttoned up against the cold, rifles strapped to their backs, her erstwhile patients now had the cohesive look of a military unit. Some limped, some moved a little stiffly, some might require help if the journey was overlong or too arduous, but something in their bearing, in the look on their faces, left no doubt that these were fighting men.

"Take care." She went up on tiptoe to press a quick kiss to Donal's cheek.

"*Ach.* 'Ware the ribs," was his half-smiling response as she sank back down, and then he picked up his rucksack and was gone with a wave of his hand, out the door that Cyril had opened, away with the others into the night.

The next day Rynn went into the village to pick up a few items and get the newspapers—and not coincidentally, to see what if any talk was going around about the action the South Donegal Flying Column had been engaged in that had led to their trip to her door.

To her dismay, Bundoran was in turmoil. Khaki-clad soldiers filled the streets, moving from block to block, searching shops, houses, vehicles and any unlucky civilians who caught their eye. Military lorries loaded with Tans rumbled in from the direction of Finner Camp, setting up roadblocks on the streets leading out of town. More lorries fanned out along the roads leading to Ballyshannon and Belleek and Manorhamilton and Mullaghmore. In other words, they went rattling off in all directions. The tension among the locals was palpable. Anger and aggression emanated from the Crown forces like a stench. People hurried about their business, anxious to get home.

"What's all this?" Rynn's voice was carefully low. Her gesture encompassing the activity in the streets was equally subdued as she addressed the question to Mrs. Cheadle, who was behind the counter in the greengrocer. Looking up from adding up Rynn's purchases, Mrs. Cheadle cast a quick glance around before whispering, "Haven't you heard? Francis Gerard escaped."

Francis Gerard: Rynn registered the name with a sense of shock. Now that she knew, she recognized the man who'd been carried into her cellar from his frequent pictures in the newspapers, although he'd lost much weight since those photographs were taken. A key figure in the IRA, he'd been imprisoned since August. His hunger strike protesting his treatment had lately attracted international attention. No wonder his rescue was eliciting such a violent response!

Overhearing the conversation, other customers crowded around to add their own hushed bits of news.

"He was rescued. It was our lads that did it."

"Sure they've stirred up a hornet's nest this time."

"Near starved to death, he was. And beaten."

"Bloody heroes, I say."

"But who'll pay the price? Us, that's who."

"Hide your guns. They've arrested Pat Mulcahy and Sean

Lynch. Searched their houses looking for Gerard but found guns instead."

"'Tis a right shame, it is. A body's not safe in his own house."

"There'll be no good end to this, you'll see."

The headlines in the newspapers were equally alarming: "Convoy Transporting Notorious Prisoner Ambushed"; "Soldiers Killed in IRA Ambush"; "Francis Gerard Escapes."

The Irish Times took up a full third of their front page with a single, boldfaced word: "Manhunt!"

Reading that, Rynn's stomach sank clear to her toes.

She was still rattled when she arrived back at Ballyshannon Court. Sharing the news and newspapers with Mrs. Frampton and Cyril over supper—Anna was taking hers in the cellar, Brian Nolan having been one of the men who'd stayed behind—Rynn concluded her summary of what she'd learned with "We need to be very careful to maintain our daily routine just as it's always been."

Mrs. Frampton's lips trembled. "I'm not regretting what we've done here," she said. "I'm not regretting it, come what may."

Cyril took a more optimistic view of the situation: "If the buggers are sending lorries all over the countryside, and hunting like badgers after worms through the town, it means they've no idea where Francis Gerard or any of the rest of them are. We'll brush through this, see if we don't."

But it wasn't until the following afternoon that Rynn's nerves truly started to settle. The sun was out. The weather was mild. Spring was not far off, and the prospect couldn't help but lift her spirits. She was looking out the kitchen window ruing the overgrown state of the kitchen garden while mixing a pitcher of barley water to soothe Rory O'Keefe's stomach pains when all her newfound peace was shattered by a thunderous pounding on the front door.

Chapter Thirty-Two

Drawn by the sound and what it might mean, Rynn, Cyril, Mrs. Frampton and Anna, each hurrying from a different part of the house, converged on the front door. Coming together in the entry hall, they stopped to look at each other with fear in their faces. Another insistent pounding from whoever was outside made the oak panel shiver and at least three out of the four of them jump.

"I'll answer it," Rynn whispered, ignoring her racing heart. Whoever it was, whatever they wanted, it was her problem to handle. And if it was about the men in the cellar, as she feared, there was no point in all of them bearing the consequences. "The rest of you go into the kitchen. If this should be—if anything should go wrong—go out the back door and hide."

Making shooing motions with her hands—the others didn't leave; instead, they came together in a single unit to wait anxiously—she walked to the door and pulled it open.

The tall man in the long black coat and slouch hat with his hand raised to pound again was such a surprise that she took a step back.

"Owen." Their eyes locked. The intensity in his made her own widen. There was a grimness about him that sent her pulse leaping with alarm.

Tim was with him.

"Have you seen Alfie?" Tim burst out before anyone else could say anything.

"Alfie? No." Surprised, Rynn looked back at Owen.

"He's missing." Owen's voice was harsh. "Three days now. Moira sent for me. She's beside herself. Tim and I drove from Dublin this morning, and I brought some men with me to aid in the search. They're out looking now."

"He went to school and never came home." Tim's voice cracked. Dressed like Owen in a long coat over a suit, he was clearly distressed. With his bright hair standing on end and his eyes red rimmed, he looked younger even than his age.

"Come in." Rynn opened the door wider. The men stepped inside.

"Alfie, three of his classmates and their teacher, gone since Tuesday," Owen said. "As far as anyone knows, vanished into the mist."

"Oh, no." It was an inadequate response, she knew, but something in the way Owen was looking at her made her uneasy.

"Mr. Mulligan is the math teacher. And the hurling coach. He's a good man," Tim said. "And Robbie Conley, Jack Haughey and Ian Lenihan have been friends with Alfie and the rest of us all their lives. They wouldn't just up and leave, none of them."

"Could I have a word with you?" Owen's voice was polite but strained. His hand curled around her arm even as he asked the question. Without waiting for her reply, he glanced back at Tim. "I'll be no more than a few minutes."

"Yes, of course. Mrs. Frampton . . ." Rynn looked toward the housekeeper. Owen was already walking her away.

"I'll wager you could use something to eat, and a spot of tea while you wait," Mrs. Frampton said to Tim as she sprang into action. "Cyril . . ."

"I'll show you to the library, where you can be comfortable." Cyril, too, was on the move.

"I'll come help you." Anna hurried after Mrs. Frampton.

"Yes, that's good. Eat a bite. You've had nothing since breakfast," Owen said over his shoulder to his nephew. "I won't be long."

As Tim went with Cyril, and Owen continued to pull her away, Rynn said to Owen, "Where are we going?"

"Anywhere we can talk in private." His voice grated.

"In here, then." She took him to the music room.

Closing the door behind them as soon as they entered, he turned to her. His hand was still wrapped around her arm. Tall as he was, close as he was, he seemed to loom over her. His eyes were keen on her face.

"Tell me the truth now," he said. "Have you heard anything of Alfie?"

"No, of course not. And of course I would tell you."

"It strikes me as odd that those boys should disappear so soon after Francis Gerard was rescued by the IRA, and in the same general area. I'm told that it was a bloody fight, with casualties on both sides. My thought is that Alfie and the others might have got caught up in it somehow. And they might have needed something in the way of medical care."

Seeing where he was going with that, Rynn shook her head. "They haven't come to me. And I don't think they had anything to do with Francis Gerard's rescue. In fact, I'm sure they didn't."

His voice took on a steely note. "And how would you be sure of that?"

She sighed inwardly. But under the circumstances, much as she might wish it otherwise, she couldn't be anything less than forthright about what she knew.

"Because the men who carried out the rescue *did* come to me for treatment, and brought Francis Gerard with them. Eleven of them came on the night of the ambush, and seven of them, Francis Gerard among them, left the next night." Watching his expression darken, Rynn's voice went crisp as she told him the rest, which she knew he wasn't going to like. "The rescue was carried out by the South Donegal Flying Column. Seamus O'Reilly is the commanding officer, and he and Donal and the ones fit enough to walk took Francis Gerard into the hills to a safe house somewhere, with the goal of eventually spiriting him out of the country. Four of them stayed behind and are still here."

Owen swore. "I told O'Reilly when I hauled him and his cousin out of London that if he pulled you into his troubles one more time, I'd kill him myself, and I'm thinking I will when I have the time. As for you, do you *want* to end up in front of a firing squad? Too many people know what you're doing here for it to be in any way safe. But that's something you and I can be discussing later. For now, I want to talk to those four men."

It wasn't a request, and she had no intention of denying him, anyway. She took him to the cellar.

When they emerged, he was convinced that the South Donegal men had never so much as set eyes on Alfie and the others.

"If they'd got caught up in that ambush, at least then we'd know where to start to search." Owen looked grimmer than she'd ever seen him. "How do four kids and their teacher simply disappear? If that boy's dead, Moira's heart will break."

Mrs. Frampton came out of the library as they reached it.

"Would you bring Major Maguire some food, please?" Rynn asked her.

"I've no time to waste eating. It'll be dark soon, and I've things to do. But thank you for the offer." Owen spoke to Rynn while nodding at Mrs. Frampton as he walked past her into the library.

"Bring him something. A couple of sandwiches, some tea.

Some food he can take with him," Rynn said to Mrs. Frampton, who hurried off.

"Did you learn anything?" Tim asked, putting down his fork as Owen entered. He had quite a spread in front of him, set out on a small card table. From what Rynn could see, it looked like a leg of lamb and some vegetables and bread, with a bit of cake for dessert, all of which, except for the cake, showed evidence of having been heartily sampled.

"Nothing of worth. Finish your meal. If you faint from hunger, you'll only slow things down," Owen said.

He walked over to the window and stood looking out as Tim did as he was told. Rynn left him to his thoughts, waiting by the fire until, moments later, Mrs. Frampton appeared with a tray holding wrapped sandwiches, a cup of tea and a bottle of Guinness.

"Cyril thought he might be wanting something a mite stronger than tea," Mrs. Frampton said to Rynn in a confidential tone as she handed the tray over, nodding at the bottle.

"Thank you," Rynn said. As Mrs. Frampton left, Owen turned away from the window.

"I'm ready." Tim stood up, and Owen nodded and started to walk toward the door.

"Wait now. If Tim hasn't eaten since breakfast, neither have you." Rynn was there in front of Owen with the tray.

"I'm not hungry. I'll get something at the hotel later," Owen said.

"If you faint from hunger, you'll only slow things down," Rynn said.

Owen looked at her, grimaced at having his own words thrown back at him and reached for the tea, draining it in a few quick gulps. "I'll eat the sandwiches on the way, and save this for later," he said, pocketing the bottle. "Thank you for the food."

"You're welcome."

Sandwiches in hand, he headed for the front door with Tim right behind him. Rynn, trailing, called after them as they strode down the walk toward Owen's car, "Let me know when you find him."

She deliberately said "when," not "if," because she was afraid if they did not, or if the unthinkable happened, Moira's would not be the only heart that broke.

Owen lifted a hand in acknowledgment, and then they slid into the car and were gone.

Night came, and there'd been no word. Riddled with anxiety, wondering where Owen was and what was happening with the search, Rynn was in the cellar making a last check on her patients before retiring to bed when Cyril came down the cellar stairs. Hearing his footsteps, Rynn, who was helping a slowly recovering Rory O'Keefe take his first, tentative steps, looked his way. Cyril immediately stopped where he was—about halfway down the dimly lit stairs—and, giving her a significant look, said, "Lady Thomas, you're needed in the kitchen."

She went on immediate alert. That could mean anything, really, she told herself. But the most likely meaning—they had a visitor—quickened her pulse. Owen, back with word at last?

"Anna, will you take over for me here, please?" she asked.

Tasked with helping each patient back into his cot after the nightly walk around the interior of the cellar that Rynn had decreed was necessary for healing, Anna was sitting on a chair she'd pulled up beside Brian Nolan's cot chatting away to him. She immediately jumped up and hurried to Rynn's side.

"Don't worry, I won't let you fall," Anna assured O'Keefe as she tucked herself under his arm. Anna was small while O'Keefe was tall and large boned, so Rynn watched for a moment as they got underway. But they were managing, so Rynn left them to it and followed Cyril upstairs.

What she saw as she walked into the kitchen was the last thing she expected.

The tall, lanky boy whose shotgun wounds she'd treated stood near the back door. His light jacket was buttoned up to his neck, his cap was in his hand, his arm was in a sling that looked like it had been fashioned from somebody's shirt and a rifle was slung over his uninjured shoulder. He was, in general, dirty and disheveled and exhausted looking.

Mrs. Frampton and Cyril crouched at his feet.

As she came around the table, Rynn saw why.

Another boy, sturdily built with bright red hair, lay stretched out on his back on the floor.

Alfie Clary.

"Oh, thank God!" Dizzy with relief, Rynn dropped to her knees beside him. Owen, Moira, Tim—all of them would be overjoyed. She did a quick visual examination even as her fingers went to the pulse below his ear. It was rapid, but not terrifyingly so. His skin was hot to the touch: fever. He was clearly unconscious. A bloody gash above his left temple that extended into his hair accounted for the dried blood that smeared his face and caked his hair, she thought. As she unbuttoned his coat, the shoulder area of which was dark with blood, she looked up at the other boy. He was sitting now, in one of the kitchen chairs that had been pulled out for him by Cyril, while Mrs. Frampton handed him a glass of milk, which he drank thirstily. His rifle lay at his feet.

"Is there food?" he asked.

Mrs. Frampton nodded and turned to the icebox.

"What happened?" Rynn asked him. Alfie was missing his shirt, Rynn found as she got his coat open. Caked with blood, the shirt had been clumsily wrapped around his left shoulder and upper chest to act as a crude bandage. Its knotted sleeves held it in place. "Where have you been? Where are the others?"

"We were up near Carraig's Rock practicing our drills like we do when a lorry full of Tans came by and spotted us. They jumped out and started shooting. Alfie and I ran one way. Mr. Mulligan, Ian and Robbie ran the other. They caught those three and took them away." Finishing the milk, he wiped his mouth on his sleeve and looked worriedly at Alfie. "Alfie fell into a gulley when he got shot, and I went down after him and we hid there while they looked for us. He's not going to die, is he?"

"No." Rynn was—almost—certain. Alfie had taken a bullet to the left thigh, too, she discovered. The wound was bound by a ripped-up, blood-caked pair of drawers. As Alfie was still wearing his, they had to be someone else's. She spared a quick glance for the other boy, who clearly was in far better shape than Alfie.

"You must be Jack," she said, and he nodded. "How badly are you hurt this time?"

The slightly caustic note to her voice as she said that last was because, clearly, for him to have gotten shot in two separate incidents he had to have been doing more than "practicing his drills." The illegal rifle was more incriminating evidence.

He looked abashed. "Took a bullet to the arm, is all. It hurts like—it hurts, but it's not so bad. Not like him. I had to carry him on my back every time we moved. He's a heavy one, too."

"I'd say that makes you a hero, then," Cyril said.

"Nah. He's my friend. I couldn't leave him."

Mrs. Frampton set a plate of cold meat in front of him. Picking up a piece, he bit into it hungrily.

Any more questions could wait for later. Rynn looked at Cyril. "We need to get them down to the cellar so I can treat them properly. And we should telephone Major Maguire at the Great Northern Hotel—"

"I knew that was his car I saw," Jack interrupted excitedly. "That's a ripping machine! It's why I decided to try to bring us in out of hiding tonight. If Alfie's uncle's here, he'll fix everything so we're all right."

Jack's faith in Owen was touching. The funny thing was, Rynn shared it.

"I don't know about telephoning Major Maguire," Cyril said uneasily. "I don't think we want the operator hearing what we have to say."

Of the few telephones in Bundoran, Ballyshannon Court and the Great Northern Hotel each had one. Unfortunately, Cyril was right: the operator could listen in.

"We'll leave it for now. Let's get them to the cellar."

It was an effort—carrying Alfie down the stairs was no easy task—but they managed it. Rynn had Mrs. Frampton help her get his coat off before Alfie was deposited on a cot and piled with blankets to help warm him up. Meanwhile, Cyril was dispatched to pull the medicines and supplies needed to treat both boys from the shelves. Anna was so excited to see Alfie and Jack safe that she was practically jumping up and down. Rynn sent her upstairs for hot water while she administered a painkiller and set up an IV to get fluids into Alfie. The other patients perked up, talking among themselves as they watched the goings-on with interest.

While she waited for Anna to return, Rynn checked Jack's wound. As he'd said, he'd taken a bullet to the arm, the outer fleshy part of his upper arm just below his shoulder. The bullet had passed through, and the wound itself was not serious, unless infection should set in. The shoulder and arm were swollen and sore and would need to be disinfected, which she did before bandaging him up again. When Anna returned with the hot water, Rynn set her to gently sponging the dried blood from Alfie's wounds

"We need to let Major Maguire know Alfie's been found and he's here," Rynn said to Cyril. "Do you think you could drive over to the Great Northern Hotel and tell him in person, or, if he isn't there, leave a message for him, saying nothing about Alfie in case the message should fall into the wrong hands, but just asking him to come see me? The three of us can manage here."

Cyril nodded. "The major will be that glad to get the news."

"Likely there'll be roadblocks everywhere." Mrs. Frampton had worry in her eyes as she looked at Cyril. "They're still hunting Francis Gerard, don't you know."

"I'll be careful. Besides, a man can go into town if he wants to, can't he? It'll just be me in the car, nothing to cause concern at all."

With that, he left, and Mrs. Frampton went upstairs to find fresh clothes for the new arrivals as Rynn disinfected Alfie's wounds. Mrs. Frampton returned with nightshirts for both and started helping Jack into one while Rynn set about suturing Alfie's head wound. As she worked, Rynn considered the difficulty involved in removing the bullets from his shoulder and thigh. The thigh would be—

The sound of heavy footsteps running across the kitchen floor and then the cellar door being flung open interrupted her thoughts and had her looking up sharply in that direction. Moving faster than she would have ever thought he could, Cyril came galumphing down the stairs.

"The Tans are coming! Two lorries full of 'em, rolling up the drive!" he gasped. "They'll be on us in a trice."

Chapter Thirty-Three

Chaos was the immediate reaction to Cyril's desperate warning.

"Mary protect us!" Mrs. Frampton cried, then immediately clapped a hand to her mouth as though to stifle any further utterance. The men who could scrambled to their feet, pulling on clothes and cursing the fact that their rifles had been carried away by their flying column brethren when they left. Only Jack's rifle and the one Cyril kept for protection remained, and they were quickly snatched up.

"How many?" demanded Kevin Toomey, who was one of those Seamus had left behind. His multiple wounds had included a bullet through the left knee. Kept precariously upright by the brace that stopped his wounded leg from collapsing and his one sound leg, he had Jack's rifle.

"I didn't get a count, but the lorries were full—eight in each, I'd say," Cyril said.

Sixteen against two: impossible odds. No one said it, but from the moment of appalled silence that followed everyone recognized it.

"Close the cellar door." Rynn stayed carefully calm even as her heart lurched into a mad gallop. Cyril ran back up the stairs to obey. Fleeing upstairs would be a possibly fatal mistake—they could be seen through any of a dozen windows. She put the last suture in Alfie's head wound, snipped the thread and stood up.

"What are we going to do?" Anna moaned, bursting into

frightened tears, while Brian Nolan, who'd grabbed the other rifle, tried to comfort her. Even Rory O'Keefe struggled into a sitting position on his cot. Only Alfie remained insensible to the disaster that was at hand.

"Did they see you? Do they know you saw them?" Rynn asked Cyril as he came back down. Frantically, she tried to work out the best thing to do.

"They didn't see me. I didn't make it as far as the car." Cyril cast a wild glance around the cellar. "They're coming for this lot, I'm as certain as can be. Someone will have told them they're here."

A muffled thudding froze everyone in place for the split second it took them to figure out what it was: the Tans pounding on the front door.

"The lights are on. The car's here. They'll know someone's inside. They'll wait for the door to be answered." Rynn hoped and prayed that was the case, because it gave them a little precious time. Panic spread like wildfire through the cellar as the hopelessness of their position hit. It infected her, too, although she tried not to let it show.

"When no one answers, they'll surround the house and break the door down," Rory O'Keefe said. "There'll be no keeping them out."

"They have us like rats in a trap," Brian Nolan groaned. With the rifle in one hand, he had an arm around Anna, who wept against his chest.

The pounding on the door was so loud and insistent now that it resounded through the cellar. Distant shouts—the words were indistinguishable, perhaps a demand to be let in?—raised gooseflesh all over Rynn's body.

"They'll have to come down those stairs. We can hold them off." Brave words from Toomey. He was a banty rooster of a man with a pugnacious-looking jaw, already turning the rifle he held toward the stairs.

Until the bullets ran out. Until a Tan decided to drop a grenade into the cellar. Until . . .

"No." Rynn removed the IV needle from Alfie's arm as their only possible escape route became crystal clear. "Everybody grab a blanket and help the ones who can't walk. We're going now, out the door in the west back wall while we have a chance. Jack, can you carry Alfie a little farther?"

He could, hoisting a blanket-wrapped Alfie over his good shoulder with her help, while Mrs. Frampton rushed to unlock the outside cellar door. Rynn quickly extinguished the lights behind them as the others straggled in that direction. The booms from upstairs were heart-stopping now. The rush of cold air when the cellar door was opened was as terrifying as it was galvanizing. Once they were outside, all it would take was one Tan posted as lookout where he could see them, or rounding the corner of the west wing, or . . .

"Follow me. As quietly as you can, and as fast as you can." Rynn was first through the door, first up the shallow flight of stairs, first to push through the mass of tall rhododendrons that partially blocked the belowground entrance. A fearful glance around told her that, for the moment, the way was clear. She beckoned the others on.

The night was dark, but not dark enough. A three-quarter moon and a sky blazing with stars made attempting to escape past the kitchen garden and across the open field to the woods too dangerous. The only saving grace was that it was windy. Swaying trees and shrubs and tall grasses and the house itself cast dancing shadows everywhere. If they were lucky, to any casual glance they would be just that many more shadows. With Cyril supporting O'Keefe, Mrs. Frampton acting as a crutch for Toomey and Anna helping keep Alfie steady on Jack's shoulder as Brian Nolan brought up the rear with Cyril's rifle, Rynn chose the only other possible route: toward the cliffs.

"*Hurry*," she urged them. Speed, however, was beyond them. Gerry Healy, the last of those of the flying column who had been left to her care, hobbled beside her with the aid of Thomas's sticks. When she'd first provided him with them, the sight of him using them had brought a whole host of memories rushing back. Now, seeing them in use made her think that perhaps Thomas was with them in spirit, and she took some small comfort from that.

"That's it! Knock it down!"

A splintering crash plus that shout from the front of the house sent Rynn's heart leaping into her throat and electrified them all. Ensuing shouts left her in no doubt: the front door had been breached. Moments later, windows lighting up in rooms that had been dark confirmed it. Tans were in the house.

They had just made it to the Point when a group of Tans ran around the outside of the west wing, darting right past the sunken exit they had used. The Tans came from the back, running toward the front, which made Rynn think they'd been outside all along, keeping watch on the kitchen door.

Thank God they hadn't tried to exit that way!

"They didn't come out the back. They must still be in the house," one of the Tans shouted to someone ahead of him, someone Rynn couldn't see.

"Here. We're going down to the Strand. The way is steep. Watch your step." Voice hushed, Rynn pointed out the mouth of the path. With the cliff edge dropping away in front of them and no place left to go, the group had huddled together, ducking a little as the Tans ran past in hopes that the strip of tall grass between them and the house would provide something in the way of concealment. Now they looked down at the Strand from their present dizzying height with varying degrees of horror.

"Eh, we'll never do it," Mrs. Frampton breathed.

But with the moon riding high over Ben Bulbin now,

illuminating cliff and beach and sea in a shimmering glow, there was no choice. Situated as they were, there was no place to hide.

They went down. In short order Rynn changed from cursing the moon to blessing it. As the moonlight hit the twisty, treacherous sheep path, the exposed small stones embedded in the hard-packed earth gleamed like a thousand tiny stars, showing the way.

Without that, Rynn thought, they wouldn't have made it. Breathless, panting, the wounded members of their party dropped to the beach as soon as they reached it to sit, or lie in the case of Alfie and some others, in the dark shadow of the cliff they'd just descended. In front of them, beyond the edge of the shadow, the wide expanse of golden sand was being swallowed by the hungry surf in its relentless march up the shore. The moon itself was reflected in the dark, rolling waters of the bay. Farther out, the wild Atlantic, endlessly black until it melted into the sky, roared.

". . . hiding in the house."

". . . cellar . . ."

". . . them alive."

"Over there! . . . shed!"

Ripped apart by the gusting wind, shouts from what sounded like a search of the grounds going on above their heads blew past them in fragments. Terrified that at any moment a Tan might stumble across the entrance to the path or might think to come to the cliff edge and look down, Rynn ventured out as far as she dared—to the edge of the shadow—and looked up. She couldn't see much because of the angle, but she could see electric lanterns darting to and fro. One bobbed along the cliff edge in a systematic sort of way. Watching, Rynn realized that her worst fear was in danger of being realized: if whoever held that lantern kept on his present course, he might well discover the path down.

Heart thumping, Rynn sped back to the group.

"What's to do?" Cyril asked, low voiced, as she reached them. Already standing, he darted nervous glances up toward the top of the cliff and all around. Brian Nolan stood as well, rifle in hand. Anna clung to him like a limpet. Mrs. Frampton, clearly spent but game, rolled onto her side as the first step in the process of getting laboriously to her feet.

"We have to move." Rynn spoke to Cyril, to all of them, the urgency in her voice galvanizing them once more. "If they find the path . . ." Stiff from the descent, impeded by sand, but moving with purpose, they were already struggling to their feet. "There's a cave. This way."

She led them to Dead Man's Hole.

Once inside the narrow fissure, the darkness was absolute within a few steps. The vastness of the cavern could only be felt, not seen. The world outside seemed far away. Even the sound of the sea was muffled. What could be heard instead was a steady drip, drip, drip as if some crevice up near the ceiling had not dried out from when the last high tide had come rushing in. The smell of damp was strong.

It was a reminder that they could only hide in the cave for so long. The reason that, as children, she and Donal and the others had named the entrance Dead Man's Hole was because if you stayed too long inside it, you were a dead man.

Venturing too far from the entrance with such a group in such unforgiving darkness posed a different risk, one they didn't need to take.

"We're safe here," she said to the group she could no longer see, and forbore to add *for now.* "We need to stay together. Everybody can rest now." Various rustling sounds told her that people were sinking to the sand. "Jack, where are you?"

Jack answered. Rynn moved to stand over him. Not that she could see him, but it was clear from the position of his voice that he'd sat down.

"Are you all right? Is Alfie all right?"

"I'm all right. So's he, far as I can tell."

"I hate to get you up again, but will you come with me to the entrance? I want to talk to you, and I'd like to be able to see you while I do it."

"I can do that, sure."

Rynn called to Mrs. Frampton to come and sit with Alfie until she got back, waited until the other woman found her and sank down, then walked with Jack toward the patch of purplish light that marked Dead Man's Hole. She stopped just inside it, and he stopped beside her. He was wearing his coat, she saw, buttoned up over the nightshirt Mrs. Frampton had given him, along with his trousers and shoes. He held his arm stiffly, but that wouldn't be obvious to a casual observer and other than that there was no outer indication that he was wounded or of the ordeal he'd been through. That, plus his youthful energy and knowledge of Alfie and his family, made him the best available candidate for the vital task she had in mind.

"I need you to do something," she said to him, "but if you don't feel strong enough, or if you don't think you can, I need you to tell me so. Will you do that?"

"I will. What is it?"

"I need you to run down the Strand, all the way down the Strand, to the Great Northern Hotel." To get there, he would have to traverse a series of connected beaches with a total distance of perhaps eight kilometers. "Major Maguire is staying there. Find him and bring him back here. Tell him he needs to come in a boat, a skiff or a currach, something small that won't attract attention. Two boats, perhaps. Tell him that on the return journey he'll be carrying ten passengers. Can you do that, do you think?"

"I can do that." He looked older than his—what, seventeen?—

years as he nodded solemnly. Rynn was reminded that many of the young men who'd gone off to fight the Huns had been no older than him.

"Jack—" She stopped him when he seemed prepared to set off immediately. "We only have a few hours. When the tide comes in, the cave floods. The beach as well. Tell Major Maguire that, too."

His expression changed as he absorbed the full impact of what she was telling him.

"What do I do if he's not there?"

That was the part she didn't like to think about, the part that terrified her. She thought, hoped, prayed he would be there—but there was no way to be sure.

"Do your best to find him," she said.

"Don't worry, Lady Thomas. I won't fail," he said. His voice was full of resolve.

"Be careful," she warned. "You don't want to be seen."

He nodded and set off. She stood watching as he jogged away, following the curve of the beach, until darkness swallowed him up.

Then she returned to the others to wait.

Chapter Thirty-Four

At first Rynn thought the faint orange glow lighting up Dead Man's Hole heralded sunrise. Her heart lurched. The tide—where was the tide?

Then she realized that water *wasn't* rolling in. That the sand she was sitting on was dry. That she'd apparently dozed off with her back against the curved stone wall, and Alfie, beside her, was either still unconscious or heavily asleep, judging by his breathing. That everyone was asleep.

That it was cold. That the blanket she shared with Mrs. Frampton was mostly wrapped around Mrs. Frampton now.

"Mam?" It was Alfie, drowsily calling for his mother. His voice was weak. Seeking human contact, his hand found her leg.

Relief that he was no longer unconscious was tempered by the knowledge that the painkiller she had administered would soon be wearing off and she had nothing to give him in its place. All the medicine and medical supplies had been left behind in the house.

"It's Lady Thomas. Rynn." Keeping her voice low so as not to wake the others, she shifted positions, kneeling beside him. His pulse was elevated, but his fever had gone, she found with a quick check. She pulled the two blankets he was cocooned in more closely around him. "You were shot, but you're going to be all right."

"The Tans. I remember." This evidence that he was coherent was reassuring. There was a pause as, she thought, he looked around. Even with the orange glow—what *was* that?—the cave was pitch-dark. "Where are we? Where's Jack?"

"We're in a cave, hiding from the Tans. Jack went to fetch your uncle."

"Owen's coming?" She could feel his body, which had tensed as he began to take stock of their surroundings, physically relax. "Good."

After a moment the steady rhythm of his breathing convinced her that he was once again asleep.

The orange glow was brighter. She'd never been inside Dead Man's Hole at dawn. But she didn't think the sunrise could cause *that*.

Scrambling to her feet, she hurried to the fissure and looked out, carefully, while remaining inside.

The orange glow lit up the beach, which she was glad to see was still some way from being covered by the incoming tide. Beyond the beach, beyond the first frothy layers of booming surf, all of which, like the air itself, were tinted orange, the night remained black. Despite drifts of orange haze partially obscuring her view of it, the moon was visible overhead, having moved several degrees west since they'd taken refuge in the cave but still having a way to go before it reached the horizon. Some hours had clearly passed, but dawn was not at hand.

The orange glow owed nothing to sunrise.

A brisk wind blew in from the sea. It smelled, as it always did, of fish and salt. But there was an acrid note to it, a jarring difference–

Smoke. What she smelled was smoke.

The orange glow came from a fire. A big one. Big enough to light up the sky. And the cliff. And the beach.

It burned somewhere overhead. Which could only mean on the flat land at the top of the cliffs.

The barn? The shed? Neither would burn so bright.

Horror seized her as she came to a terrible realization: Ballyshannon Court itself must be on fire.

Oh, no. Her stomach pitted.

Her first instinct—to run out onto the beach and fly up the path—she quashed. At this point, if the house was on fire, there was nothing she could do. What she had to concentrate on was saving herself and those in her charge.

The Tans—where were they?

Fear made her heart beat faster as she looked up and down the beach. It was impossible to see anything beyond the orange glow. That left large swaths of sand and surf that were utterly, completely dark.

Listening hard, she could hear nothing over the roar of the waves. No crackling of flames. No shouts.

The thought that the Tans might even now be hunting for them along the beach sent shivers down her spine.

Jack. Had he made it to the hotel? Had he found Owen?

She cast a long, searching look out at the bay. What was out there was, simply, the dark. If a boat was coming their way, she couldn't see it.

If Jack hadn't made it through, if Owen didn't come, what was the alternative plan? With the tide coming in, the cliffs at their back, and most of them not able to move fast, if at all, she was afraid of getting trapped on the beach. Should they try going back up the path? Given the array of injuries, the climb itself would be almost impossibly arduous. And there was no way to know if the Tans were still up there, watching the house burn.

Waiting for them to appear.

The Tans could be anywhere.

With no warning at all, several men walked out of the night into the orange light, dark silhouettes striding with purpose toward Dead Man's Hole, toward *her.* She could clearly see the rifles they carried. Rynn's heart almost stopped. It was all she could do not to cry out. Instead, she clamped her lips together and shrank back, quickly, praying they hadn't seen.

Then something about the man in the lead, about his height and the breadth of his shoulders and the way he moved, registered.

She took a chance, stepped up to the entrance, looked again.

By then he was only a few strides away.

"Owen," she said. And exhaled on the most overwhelming wave of relief.

Six men, three currachs. The boats were beached just beyond the orange glow. The cave was evacuated in a matter of minutes. Scooping Alfie up in his arms like a baby—"You've worried your mam" was how Owen greeted him, to which Alfie sheepishly replied, "Sorry"—Owen carried him to the first boat, deposited him unceremoniously inside, dropped his coat around Rynn's shoulders as she climbed in next to Alfie, supervised the loading of the other boats and then took one set of oars. A man he addressed as Whelan, who clearly worked for him, pushed them out, jumped in and took the other set. Jack was the remaining passenger in their boat, while the rest were loaded into the other two.

As Owen rowed, Rynn got a glimpse of a pistol in a holster on his right hip. That, coupled with the rifle that now lay across his lap, brought home to her as nothing else had how much danger they were in.

It was clear from Owen's lack of conversation, the uncompromising set of his mouth and the very way he rowed, that he wasn't happy with at least one of his passengers. She had a feeling it was more like two. Or maybe all three of them, because after all, Jack, before acting the hero and saving Alfie, had been involved in whatever Alfie had been doing, too.

Once out of the crashing surf, the bay was relatively smooth. With no one saying anything, the only sounds were the rush of the waves and the slap of the oars hitting the water. She sat in the bottom of the boat facing Owen, with her back against the middle seat and Alfie, in his blankets, curled up in front of her with his head on her lap. From that position, Rynn could see just the tips of the shooting flames at the heart of the orange glow. Then they crested a wave, and she could spot the roof. It was fully engulfed, with fire dancing along the ridgelines and consuming dormers and chimneys. Flames leaped out of the small windows on the third floor where her room had been when she'd lived there as a nurse. Cascades of orange sparks shot skyward, then rained down like confetti. Plumes of black smoke obscured the stars.

The knot in her stomach grew so big it felt like a lead cannonball.

"By morning there'll be nothing left. It'll be burned to the ground." It was the first thing Owen had said to her, uttered in a clipped tone that, to her, reeked of suppressed anger. He'd been watching her look back at the house, she'd seen as she glanced his way. It was too dark to read his expression, but she didn't have to.

She knew him.

"Why would they do that? We were already gone. They must have known that. And it was so beautiful." She had nothing but good memories of the time she'd spent there. And Thomas—Thomas had loved it. Watching the house burn felt almost like mourning him all over again.

"It was a reprisal. And a way to warn anyone else who might be thinking about going against them."

Then they were far enough out that she could see not the whole of the house, but most of it.

Huddled in Owen's coat with an arm flung across Alfie's chest to keep him as steady as possible as the currach sliced through the waves, Rynn watched with a lump in her throat as Ballyshannon Court burned.

By the time they reached the beach in front of the Great Northern Hotel, all she could see of the fire was the distant orange glow against the sky. Because it was nearing 4:00 a.m.—Owen checked his watch—the area was deserted. The hotel itself was dark except for a pair of lighted windows that marked the lobby.

Moonlight illuminated the beach, the dock with its many boats, the great lawn that sloped down from the hotel. Rynn glanced around nervously as she stepped out of the currach. She didn't think the Tans could possibly know where they'd gone, but the night had already brought enough shocks that even the shadows seemed threatening.

"They're being taken to a safe house for what's left of the night," Owen said of Mrs. Frampton and Cyril and Jack and the others in answer to Rynn's question as they were loaded into two of the three waiting cars. As he spoke, he was putting Alfie, who was awake now and starting to grit his teeth against the pain, into the rear of the Vauxhall, where he curled up on the back seat. Sliding out of Owen's coat, Rynn folded it and tucked it under Alfie's head to act as a pillow, then slid into the front seat to give him room. Owen got behind the wheel and glanced at her.

"You'll get cold," he said.

"I won't." Rynn shook her head. "What now?"

"Tomorrow will be soon enough to start sorting this mess out. I'm taking Alfie home so that his mother can get a look at him before she expires of worry, and then we'll see. As for you, you're with me until we figure out what to do with you. You can take it for granted that the Tans know Ballyshannon Court was being used by the IRA."

Rynn's chest tightened as the full implications of what the burning of Ballyshannon Court meant hit her. Not only was the house gone, but everything in it was gone as well. The beautiful furnishings and fixtures. All the medicine and medical supplies. Her clothes. Everything of Thomas's that had been left behind. Thinking about it made her feel sick, so she tried her best to put it out of her mind.

By then they were on the road. The Vauxhall was running without lights. The knowledge that Owen was choosing to drive by moonlight rather than risk being seen and stopped by the Tans or the army or whichever of the Crown forces might be abroad in the middle of the night frightened her all over again.

"I need to get a message to Granny and Glenna that I'm safe. If they know about the fire—"

"I'll see to it that they get word. Tomorrow. If the Tans know who you are—and they're outsiders so they may not, or if they do, they may not know that Lady Thomas Dunne was once Rynn Carmichael of the village here—it's possible that they might be having your granny's house watched, in case you show up."

Rynn's insides twisted.

"Did Mam go spare when I didn't come home?" Alfie asked in a small voice. Rynn turned in the seat to look at him. He was lying down still, but his eyes were open. As dark as it was, it was difficult to make any judgment about his state, but the fact that he was cognizant enough to worry about his mother's reaction to his absence was reassuring.

"She did." Owen's reply had a steely note to it. "You notice that she sent for me. And before you give explaining yourself to her a go, suppose you tell me what the hell you were thinking."

"I didn't mean for any of this to happen. We were running drills—"

"Don't lie to me. Your friend Jack told me exactly what you were doing. The group of you were moving boxes of ammunition to a hiding spot for an IRA unit to pick up later, and this wasn't the first time you've done it, either. Something I'll be having a word with your teacher about, if he doesn't end up in front of a firing squad before I get the chance, which, if I were a betting man, I'd say he will."

"They'll shoot him?" Alfie sounded horrified.

"They'll shoot him. And your friends. And you, if they catch you." Owen's voice turned savage. "Do you know how lucky you are to be alive? To do this, after I've told you and *told* you. This isn't a game. This is a war, although I know you're too young and stupid to understand what that means. But I'll tell you, and keep telling you, because I've been there. It means if you're in it, at any time between one breath and the next you can cease to exist. One wrong decision, one unlucky step, one bad minute and, bam, you're rotting in a hole, and your people are crying for you, and none of it matters anymore because you're dead."

"Owen—" Rynn began, meaning to add *maybe this isn't the time* as Alfie shuddered and closed his eyes and shrank into his blankets.

"And you. You've no room to say a word." He turned that savage gaze on her. "You're even luckier to be alive than he is. You've been putting yourself in harm's way since the night we met. How many times have I saved your arse? This is the third time, isn't it? How many times have I told you that if you didn't keep your nose out of the bloody business you'd wind up dead? More times than I can count. And did you listen? Did either of you listen? What is it going to take to make you understand that I know what I'm talking about, and I mean what I say?"

The farmhouse was at hand, Rynn saw. Its whitewashed brick

walls shone faintly in the moonlight. Downstairs, the windows were alight—clearly Moira had been too distraught over Alfie to sleep—and there was someone standing in the shadows at the side of the yard.

A man. The darkness made it impossible to tell any more about him than that. Her pulse leaped.

"Owen." She pointed silently.

Owen made a disgusted sound under his breath and pulled into the yard.

The man came running toward them even before Owen braked. One of the farmhands, Rynn saw when the moonlight hit him.

"Major! Oh, Major, I couldn't stop it, couldn't nobody stop it!" He was blubbering as he came, and gesturing behind him. Owen, who must have understood quicker, applied the parking brake and leaped out to run past him even as Rynn saw that there were dark mounds on the grass. Several of them, in the shadows where the man had been. Owen reached them and stopped, then moved from one to another—

"They up and shot her! Mrs. Clary! Them bloody Tans!" the farmhand wailed.

Rynn was out of the car and running before he finished speaking as she realized that the dark mounds were bodies and one of them, the one Owen was sinking to his knees beside, must be Moira Clary.

Chapter Thirty-Five

The horror of it was unspeakable. Moira, her youngest boy, Joseph, and two farmhands lay sprawled in the rough grass. They were dead. A single glance told Rynn that, but she bent and checked each one. No pulse, no respiration, the bloodied bodies only faintly warm. Shot to death. Murdered.

The darkness mercifully veiled the worst details of their wounds.

There was nothing she could do for them. Owen knelt beside Moira's body, his head bent, his hands splayed on his thighs.

Rynn went to him, put a hand on his shoulder. She could feel how hard he was breathing—great shuddering gasps.

"Owen," she said.

His head came up. He didn't say a word. Instead, his arms went around her and he pulled her close and pressed his face into her waist. He was still breathing with those deep, harsh inhales.

She wrapped her arms around his shoulders and held him, silently offering what comfort she could. She could feel the weight of his head pressing against her, the strength of his arms in the tightness of his grip. The depth of his pain.

His shoulders shook. Bending over him, cradling him as she would a bereft child, she held him close, while her heart broke for him.

The farmhand reached them. He was agitated, weeping, his words emerging in bursts. "It was a carload of them. Four, altogether. They came roaring up and kicked down the door without so much as a knock. Then they came back out with Mr. James in handcuffs, and Mrs. Clary flying after them, screaming that he was just a boy and to let him go. Then Mr. Joseph come running out with a rifle to try to stop them and they turned their guns on him and Mrs. Clary cried out, 'No, stop, he's only fourteen!' It didn't make no difference. They shot Mr. Joseph, just like that. Mrs. Clary started screaming and went for them and they shot her, too, and Murphy and Doyle, who was just standing there because there wasn't nothing they could do, shot all of them one after the other, so quick you couldn't even take in what was happening until it was done. Mr. James was screaming and they hit him, and then they drove off and took Mr. James with them. I was in the barn, Major, feeding the horse, and I heard the noise and came out and I couldn't get to them to do anything. By the time I got over here it was done."

Holding Owen protectively close, wishing with every cell in her body that she could turn back time, or in some way shield him from this evil that no one could stop because it was already done, she felt him shudder. He tensed, the muscles bunching in his shoulders. The cadence of his breathing changed, steadied. Then he let her go and stood up, his arms hanging loosely at his sides, his posture that of a boxer who'd gone ten rounds but was still poised to fight.

"The Tans took James, you say?" His voice was flat. His focus was on the farmhand.

"They did. And that's not all. Mr. Tim came right after, him and some of his friends. Out looking for Mr. Alfie, they'd been, and when he saw what had been done, Mr. Tim snatched up the rifle that was laying right there by Mr. Joseph. He was crying and cursing and yelling to his friends that he was going to go rescue Mr. James and kill the bastards—begging your pardon, missus—that did this and then he jumped back in his car, his friends with him, and they all went off after Mr. James and the Tans."

"What?" Owen shot out the question like a bullet.

"That's what Mr. Tim did. He was crazed with grief. There was no stopping him."

"Damned stupid—" Owen took a breath. "How long ago? And which way did they go?"

"No more than ten minutes, I'd say. And Mr. Tim and the Tans, they all went off that way." He pointed.

"All right." To all outward appearances, Owen had himself under control again. "Qualls, I want you to carry Mrs. Clary and Mr. Joseph and the others into the house, then take the horse and ride to the village and fetch Father Doherty back here to them. Tell him to do what needs to be done and that I'll be in touch."

He was already running toward the car as he finished. Rynn ran after him.

"I'll do that, Major. I'll take care of them," Qualls called.

"What are you doing?" Rynn gasped out as she caught up with Owen.

"I'm going after them. I'd leave you here, but I think you're safer with me."

"Of course I'm going with you."

Just ahead, Alfie had the car door open and, having levered himself into a sitting position, was leaning out of it. Unable to use his wounded leg, he was nevertheless trying to sling himself out.

"Mam? Is that Mam? Has something happened to Mam?"

"Get back in the car," Owen barked at him, sprinting around to the boot, which he opened. To Rynn, who'd followed him, he added, "You, too."

He pulled his rifle from the boot, slammed down the lid. Rynn ran to Alfie, who was still trying to get out of the car. Bundling him back inside, she closed the door on him. She just managed to get into the front seat as Owen slid his rifle onto the floor and jumped behind the wheel. Slamming the car, which was still running, into gear, he shot back out onto the road.

"Did something happen to Mam?" Alfie was so frightened his voice squeaked.

Rynn's throat tightened. How do you tell a child he'd lost his mother?

"She's dead." Owen's voice was grim. "As is Joseph. Shot by the Tans, the both of them. They've taken James and we're going to get him. "

The savage bluntness of it took Rynn's breath.

"It's my fault. It's my fault, isn't it? I got them killed! Mam! Mam!" Alfie's wail pierced Rynn's heart.

"It's not your fault. If fault there is, it belongs to me. I never should have left a passel of idiot boys out here where they could find trouble when I knew there was trouble for them to find."

The very flatness of Owen's tone lacerated her heart even more.

"It's neither of your faults." Rynn glared at Owen, then slewed around to glare at Alfie. "Neither of yours, do you hear me? It's solely the fault of the Tans who shot them, so don't be putting that blame on yourselves."

There was no reply to that. Alfie subsided back against the seat with only the occasional muffled sob to be heard from him. Granite-faced, Owen too was silent, concentrating on the road as he drove like a man possessed. Hands on either side of her, Rynn held on to the edge of the seat for dear life as the car rattled and bounced. Even lit as it was by moonlight, the narrow, rutted road with its high, grassy banks on either side and hairpin turns that limited visibility to the section immediately ahead offered little in the way of forgiveness. If a car came from the opposite direction, or there was some obstruction in the road like, say, a broken-down wagon or a wayward flock of sheep, there would be little time to react. A collision under those conditions was almost a given.

"Where are they? We should have caught them by now." It was the first thing Owen had said in a quarter-hour. His hands gripped the wheel like he meant to break it. He whipped around the latest sharp curve and cursed under his breath as another dark, empty section of road unspooled before them. The windows had started to fog up, so Owen rolled his window partway down to clear them. Smelling of peat fires and wet sheep and grass, the cold air blowing in served a dual purpose since it also kept Rynn wide-awake.

They were up in the hills now, with rolling fields and the occasional farmhouse and sheep, always sheep. The moon, a pale ghost of itself, was nearing the western horizon, indicating that dawn wasn't far away. The road had seen a few branches trailing off from it, but Owen had driven straight on with the surety of a man who had a destination in mind.

"Could they have turned off somewhere?" Rynn asked. She'd been silent, too, until now. The atmosphere in the car was so heavy, so fraught with pain and tension, that any attempt at conversation would have felt profane.

"It's possible, but I think I have a fair idea of where they're going. If they've taken James, it's most likely to interrogate him. They have a secret prison up near Lough Gill where they do such things. We're close now, though, and we've not caught so much as a glimpse of either the Tans' car or Tim's."

"Tim's out here?" Alfie spoke up from the back seat. His voice was thick and raw.

"He's gone after James, too. What we're trying to do is get there first," Owen said.

"Does he know about . . . Mam?"

The tiniest wobble before he named his mother broke Rynn's heart all over again.

"He does," Owen said.

"And—and James?"

"He does," Owen said again. Paradoxically, his uncompromising tone revealed to her how much he was hurting.

Rynn's eyes stung. She wanted to weep for the pair of them, for all of them. But now was not the time. Now was the time to be strong.

The road branched again just ahead, with the main part continuing on the path they were on and another, even narrower, lane climbing up a steep hill. Rynn was surprised when Owen turned up the hill.

"I want to get a look at the lay of the land," he said in response to what must have been her questioning expression. The lane was rough and rutted, with a tumbledown stone fence on one side and a steep slope on the other. "If we're high enough, we might be able to see them on the road."

Without slowing down at all as far as Rynn could tell, the Vauxhall bumped and jolted through the darkness until it was speeding along a plateau that afforded views in every direction. The lane itself was a disappointment. It didn't rejoin the road it had left but curled back around on itself at the end of the plateau to connect with another rural path.

"There's a car," Alfie cried.

Rynn saw it, too. A big car, a saloon of some type, its headlamps cutting through the night as it raced along on the road below. It was well ahead of them, and Owen accelerated as though to catch up. Then she sucked in air as she saw, some distance behind it, a smaller car, running without lights. Knowing what she knew, it was clear it was Tim giving chase.

"Owen," she said.

"I see it." His voice was grim.

The big car below rounded one of those hairpin bends with

which the road was rife, putting it out of view of the smaller one following.

Then, to Rynn's astonishment, it did an immediate about-face, turning back the way it had come in a sliding U-turn and *stopping in the middle of the road* as the Tans inside leaped out. Shouldering rifles, they dropped into a crouch beside the car.

Ambush. As they came around the bend, Tim and his friends would be sitting ducks.

"Fuck," Owen yelped, and slammed on the brakes.

Thrown forward without warning, Rynn barely managed to catch herself before she hit the windshield. Even as she was slung back into her seat, she saw that Owen, standing on the brake, had snatched his pistol from its holster and was aiming it out the window, his eyes narrowed, his face a study in concentration. Before she had time to do more than blink at him in surprise he fired, the sound a single sharp *crack* that was loud as an explosion in the close confines of the car.

To her horror Tim's car seemed to jump up in the air before careering off the road and overturning in a field.

"What are you doing? That's *Tim* you're shooting at," Alfie screamed, surging forward in the back seat. "Whose side are you on, anyway?"

"The side of the bloody angels." The ferocity with which he said it made Rynn's blood run cold. Having wrenched the parking brake, Owen jumped out, snatched up his rifle and started firing in an entirely different direction.

Four sharp cracks: that was all it took. Rynn watched in shock as the Tans were mowed down.

"Stay put, the two of you," Owen ordered over his shoulder, and ran down the slope toward the Tans. Moments later, he reached the big saloon. The sound of two more shots being fired made Rynn wince. Apparently, two Tans had been still alive.

"There's Tim." Alfie sounded relieved. Looking toward Tim's car, Rynn saw that two, no, three boys had emerged from it and were standing up. From that distance they were small dark figures cloaked in night, but Rynn was just able to tell that one of them held a rifle.

Tim, she was almost sure.

Then she looked back toward Owen. He was moving around behind the saloon. A smaller, stockier figure now leaned against its side.

James.

She slid over into the driver's seat and shut the door. Then she eased off the parking brake, put the car in gear and drove down the grassy hill.

Chapter Thirty-Six

Only an hour or so remained before dawn broke, and out of the direst necessity they made good use of that time. The key to not becoming the target of every member of the Crown forces in the country, Owen told them with no small degree of bite, was covering up any trace of what had really happened to the Tans on that dark road in the middle of the night. Tim and his friends were a little bruised, a little shaken and more than a little upset with Owen for shooting out the Model T's tire. But once the situation was bluntly spelled out for them they were no longer upset but profoundly grateful, as Owen told them they damned well should be. By that time James had been freed of the handcuffs when the key was found in a dead Tan's pocket and had joined Alfie, who had managed to haul himself upright by hanging on to the Vauxhall's door and was standing outside the car. Tim walked over to be reunited with his brothers, and the three of them embraced, sharing a moment so emotional that Rynn, for one, had to look away.

But they had only that moment, and then there were things that had to be done. They changed the tire on the Model T and got it back on the road and loaded all the Tans' bodies into the saloon car. With Rynn behind the wheel of the Vauxhall, the three cars drove together to Lough Gill, where Owen and the older boys pushed the saloon car with the Tans' bodies inside into the lough. It sank without a trace.

With Owen once again driving the Vauxhall and James and Alfie sitting so close together in the back their shoulders touched, and Tim driving his two friends in the Model T, they journeyed on through the night. They were still on the road when dawn broke. They encountered an increasing amount of traffic the closer they got to Dublin, which was their destination, but no one bothered them, and eventually they arrived at Owen's house in Belgravia Street.

It was an elegant brick town house in a fashionable neighborhood. Pulling into the alley that ran behind the row of houses, the cars stopped outside it just long enough for Owen to escort Rynn inside and yell to his housekeeper that they had a visitor. Mrs. Yardley was her name, and she hurried downstairs in time for Owen to tell her to give his guest a room and meals and whatever else she wanted.

Having already instructed Rynn to stay inside the house no matter what, Owen left as unceremoniously as he'd arrived. A moment later, both cars pulled away.

Mrs. Yardley did everything she could to see to Rynn's needs, and in short order Rynn was provided with a bath and food. With no clothes to her name except the ones on her back—after her bath, she wrapped herself in a borrowed robe—and nothing in the way of other necessities such as tooth powder and a toothbrush, Rynn's next order of business would have been to take a taxi to first her bank, and then a department store had it not been for Owen's warning and her own fear that the Tans might be hunting her. The murders of Moira, Joseph and the others terrified as well as haunted her, and the burning of Ballyshannon Court had her picturing a wanted poster with her face on it.

The prospect gave her the shivers.

Was this, then, the catastrophe the Black Pig had warned against?

Or was there more to come?

She didn't know. There was no way to know. Which meant there was no way to prepare, or to stop anything that might be heading their way.

That was the true curse of the Sight.

Exhausted, she lay down on the bed in the lovely bedroom that had been provided for her use and tried to think through the ramifications of all that had happened and decide what was best to do going forward. Using her own common sense, with no hint of precognition to it.

And somewhere in the middle of all that thinking, she fell asleep.

When she woke, it was to find two dresses laid out across the end of the bed, and several wrapped parcels on the dressing table. Both dresses were slim and black, with fashionable dropped waists and short hems that reached only a little below her knees. One was of silk, one was of crepe and they bore labels from Arnott's, the biggest department store in Dublin. The wrapped parcels contained undergarments, stockings, night things and a selection of toiletries and cosmetics. In addition, her shoes waited on the floor in front of the dressing table. They'd been cleaned.

It was late afternoon by that time, so Rynn put on one of her new dresses and went downstairs.

Mrs. Yardley must have heard her, because she came bustling into the entry hall just as Rynn reached the bottom of the steps.

"I'm that pleased to see that dress fitting so well. I took your old dress with me, but still, you never can be sure," Mrs. Yardley said.

"Did you buy those things for me? Thank you." Rynn smiled at her.

"Major Maguire telephoned and asked me to. He told me you'd lost your things in a fire."

"I did." Rynn didn't elaborate, and after a bit more conversation Mrs. Yardley showed her to the parlor and brought her tea.

"Did Major Maguire by any chance say when he would be back?" Rynn couldn't help but ask as the housekeeper turned to leave.

"He did not. I'm sorry, miss. Sometimes he's gone for weeks at a time, but with you here . . ." Her voice trailed off. The obvious implication was that Owen was expected to return at some point in the not-so-distant future because of her presence.

"I see. Thank you," Rynn said, and the housekeeper took herself off.

There was nothing to do but wait.

Confined to the house, Rynn passed a restless few hours waiting for Owen to turn up or at least send word. Finally, when it got dark and then grew late, and he still hadn't come, she went upstairs to bed. But every time she closed her eyes, images of Moira and Joseph lying dead in the grass intruded, so finally she turned on the bedside lamp and sat up in bed to continue reading the book she'd borrowed from Owen's study. It was the true story of Sir Ernest Shackleton's harrowing trek across the Antarctic continent. Very interesting, she was sure, but she found it difficult to concentrate when she was so heartsick and worried and on edge. Truth be told, its primary attraction for her was the hope that it would put her to sleep, but that didn't seem to be happening, either.

When somewhere downstairs a clock struck one in the morning, she gave up, put the book down and padded over to the window to look out. Late as it was, there wasn't much to see. It was a quiet residential street in a prosperous neighborhood with a single streetlamp on the corner that illuminated a row of neatly kept gardens bordered by wrought-iron fences, stone steps leading up to finely carved front doors and mullioned windows marching across each house's three floors. She was just reflecting on how far Owen had come from his beginnings in Killybegs when a muffled crash from downstairs startled her.

Though she listened intently, she heard nothing more. But the sound had seemed to come from somewhere in the vicinity of Owen's study, and the thought that he might have returned prompted her to get dressed again, hastily, in the black dress she'd been wearing earlier, and go downstairs.

A single lamp was on in the entry hall—and a light was on in the study.

The study door was ajar.

Owen was in the room.

Minus his coat, wearing a white shirt and dark trousers, he stood in front of the fireplace where only the glowing embers remained of the cheery fire that had burned there earlier. His back was to the door, his hand holding a glass of what looked like whiskey rested on the mantel, and his head was bent as if he were contemplating the smoldering logs that remained.

Suddenly shy of invading his privacy, Rynn knocked on the open door.

He glanced around, saw her. His face told her nothing.

"Come in," he said. "And close the door."

She did. Without altering his posture, he watched over his shoulder as she approached. To her shock, she saw that his desk, which took pride of place in the middle of the room, had been flipped on its side, its contents scattered across the carpet.

That, then, had been the cause of the crash she'd heard.

She had no doubt whatsoever that he was the one who'd flipped it.

Eyeing him carefully, she stopped beside him.

"I would have come earlier, but I've been busy," he said. "You'll be glad to know that a message has been sent to your granny and sister to let them know you've survived."

"Thank you," she said.

"Alfie's been seen by a doctor. The bullets are out, his wounds are treated and I've shipped him, Tim, James and their friends, including Jack, off on one of my ships that left tonight for Boston. My nephews have orders to stay there. Tim can work for my operation in Boston, and I'll be enrolling Alfie and James in boarding school there. The rest are welcome to stay or come back as they please—they'll have jobs at my warehouse there if they stay—but I told them it's in their best interests to keep well out of what's coming. They can return home when it's done. But that's up to them."

Rynn finally managed to put her finger on what, exactly, was alarming her about Owen. He seemed perfectly calm, collected and in control, but there was a distance to him, a kind of dispassionate detachment to his voice, that seemed wrong under the circumstances.

"Sending them to America is a good idea," she said.

"I thought so. Tim especially is hell-bent on revenge, and his brothers are on board. As I told them, living is the best revenge. Dying means the other side won."

The barest hint of savagery colored that last sentence.

He continued, "I also made arrangements for Moira and Joseph. With Father Doherty. They'll have a joint funeral, on Friday."

Once again with that emotionless voice.

"Owen . . ."

"What?" Straightening, he threw back the contents of his glass in a single gulp, set the glass on the mantel and turned to face her. "What words of comfort do you have for me, my beautiful Rynn?"

The savagery was back, now laced with mockery.

But it wasn't his words, or his tone, that wrung her heart. It was his eyes. Red rimmed and bloodshot, they were the eyes of a man who had endured a soul-deep wound and was still suffering. Set in a face that could have been carved from stone for all the expression it revealed, his eyes, like the overturned desk, told the truth of it.

"None," she said, and took the two steps necessary to reach him. With a hand on his chest to steady herself, she went up on tiptoe to kiss him.

The sound he made as her lips touched his was animallike in its ferocity, and then his arms came around her and he was kissing *her*, fiercely, desperately, like she was his only hope of salvation in a ravaged world.

After that, what happened, happened. He made love to her there, on the carpet in front of the dying fire, as fiercely and desperately as he'd kissed her. His need awakened her own as he took his own heart-stopping brand of solace from her body and she responded with a passion that she never would have suspected herself capable of. This was a different kind of loving than she had experienced before, darker and deeper and wilder, culminating with a shattering intensity that changed her view of love, and men, and herself, forever.

Afterward, after they'd regained their breath and, for Rynn, her sense of perspective, she went upstairs and fell into bed with him and they made love all over again.

"So." Owen propped himself up on an elbow to look down at her. Supremely conscious that she was naked beneath the sheet that she'd pulled over herself when he'd first stirred in a laughably late effort to preserve her modesty, and that her hair lay in wild tangles against the pillow and that the cold daylight pouring in through the open curtains was certain to be less than flattering, she narrowed her eyes at him.

"So?" she repeated.

"So are you going to ask me?"

"Ask you what?"

"What every woman in the world asks a man after a night like the one we just spent."

"And what would that be?"

"Do you love me?" He assumed a mocking falsetto.

For a moment she simply looked at him. He was far better at hiding his emotions than she was. His stoic facade was nearly perfect.

But she knew him. The pain he was keeping inside was soul deep.

"Actually, that wasn't the question I was going to ask you," she said. "Although I do have a question."

"Oh? In that case, please, ask away."

"What's for breakfast? I'm starving."

He stared at her for a second, then broke into a wide smile. And she was so glad to see him smile that she could feel the warmth of it penetrating clear through to her heart. Then he rolled on top of her and kissed her breathless and—well, what came after was a revelation. Finally, he propped himself up on his elbows in an apparent effort to keep the bulk of his weight off her. Looming above her, he met her eyes and said, "You don't have to ask me, you know. I do. Quite madly. I have done, I think, since the most beautiful girl I'd ever seen in my life tried to blackmail me on the deck of my own ship."

She narrowed her eyes at him. "It wasn't blackmail. Paying was only fair, since you were keeping the guns. And I'll wager you made a nice profit on them, too."

He smiled, and once again she felt the impact. "As I believe someone once said to me, only a fool doesn't take advantage of opportunities."

She smiled back at him. Then she stopped smiling, looked at him very seriously and said, "Just so we're clear, I love you, too."

"Ah," he said by way of acknowledgment. Then he kissed her again.

And kept her in bed until noon.

Chapter Thirty-Seven

It was Friday.

Spring had come at last. The sky was the same shade of blue as Owen's eyes and Donegal Bay and the wild Atlantic beyond it had turned sapphire, with gently rolling waves topped with drifts of white lace for as far as the eye could see. Even the seabirds seemed to embrace the mild weather. Instead of screaming and diving as they usually did, they soared gracefully above the water. The surf itself had nothing more to say than gentle murmurings.

Moira and Joseph had just been laid to rest in the little cemetery on the hillside above the Church of Our Lady Star of the Sea. From the look of it, every soul in Bundoran, as well as most who lived in the surrounding villages and the nearby countryside, had turned out. The crowd of mourners was enormous. Anger and outrage mixed with the grief that hung heavy in the air.

Rynn was not part of that crowd. She stood with Owen on an even higher hillside some distance away, where they could see without being seen. He was being careful with her, because, as he told her, although no word of her being wanted or searched for had reached his ears, that didn't mean she wasn't being hunted. It might only mean the hunters were being quiet about it.

The blackened ruin that was all that was left of Ballyshannon

Court was just visible from where they stood. She grieved its destruction, but the far greater loss of Moira and Joseph put it in perspective. Buildings could be rebuilt. Lives were lost forever.

Owen had stood with his head bowed and a face like stone throughout the service. The only time he'd shown emotion was when the two coffins were lowered one after the other into side-by-side graves. With her hand curled around his arm she'd felt him tense. If his eyes had glistened briefly, she'd been tactful enough to look away.

"Mick's in the right of it," Owen said as the service concluded. "There's no negotiating with Churchill and his bloody band of warmongers. I've let Mick know I'll be throwing in with him. The only thing we can do with this murdering lot is treat them like the snakes they are and drive them the hell out of Ireland."

Rynn looked at him with worry in her eyes. Michael Collins's tactics embraced guerilla warfare, ambushes, assassinations, bombings, with no more than a few thousand warriors to throw themselves up against the might of the entire British Empire. The odds against success were enormous. The cost of failure was . . . unimaginable.

"You'll be going back to Dublin to work with Mick?" The fear that he would be putting his life at risk there made her throat tighten.

"I will."

A series of explosions in the distance jolted her out of her thoughts. Plumes of smoke rose above the hills to the north. The crowd at the funeral, almost to a person, turned to gape in that direction. On the roads surrounding the cemetery, a rush of activity drew her gaze: the Crown forces, the soldiers and RIC officers and Tans and Auxies, all of them that were on hand to observe and harass and arrest, were leaping into their armored cars and machine-gun-fitted lorries and big saloons and tying themselves up in knots of traffic as they did their best to race toward what was obviously an attack.

"Finner Camp." There was a wealth of satisfaction in Owen's voice. "That'll be the IRA, freeing those boys and their idiot teacher and anyone else they're keeping in their damned prison, and blowing the damned camp up while they're at it." A grim smile just touched his mouth. "While the murdering bastards were all lined up here menacing us at Moira's and Joseph's funerals, seemed like the perfect time to hit them."

"That was brilliant." Admiration for the ingenuity of it lightened her spirits a bit.

"It was. And that's the kind of thinking that's going to win this for us." He looked down at her, and his tone changed. "Well, Lady Thomas, what's it to be? I can see you safe away to America, where you'll be well out of this mess, or back to England, if you prefer." His face had turned expressionless, as she'd learned it tended to do when he spoke of things close to his heart.

Their eyes met. She could read nothing in his.

But she knew him.

He was attempting to send her away just like he'd done with his nephews, to protect them from what was coming, to keep them safe.

She would be smart to let him. But . . .

Once again it was time to choose.

A carefree existence in England or America or anywhere, basically, where Ireland wasn't fighting for her life.

Or war, and the fear and pain and suffering that went along with it.

She chose.

Owen.

Ireland.

And the side of the angels.

"I'm not going anywhere. I'm a nurse. I'll be needed here," she said.

"Is that so?" His eyes narrowed at her. Those light blue eyes that always made her think of the Irish Sea were shadowed with grief and pain. But what she could see for her at their backs made her heart race.

"It is. And you can't talk me out of it, or send me away." Her gaze was as unyielding as his.

"There is an alternative, I suppose," he said slowly. "If you're dead set on charging into danger, you could always go home with me."

She smiled at him.

"I could," she said.

And she did.

Because she knew, *knew*, with no help needed from the Sight at all, that this was the country, the cause and the man that were meant for her.

★ ★ ★ ★ ★

Acknowledgments

The story didn't end there, of course. Not for the rebellion and not for Rynn and Owen. This was, rather, the end of the beginning. The Irish War of Independence raged on until a ceasefire was declared in July 1921, after much loss of life on both sides, and the Anglo-Irish Treaty ending the conflict was officially signed on December 6, 1921. The guerilla tactics of ambushes, raids and assassinations conceived by Michael Collins succeeded where eight hundred years of various Irish uprisings had not: in victory for the rebels. With the creation of the Irish Free State, a self-governing dominion, centuries of British rule in most of Ireland came to an end. Only Northern Ireland, divided from the rest of the country by terms of the treaty, continued under British control.

But a true peace remained out of reach. Almost immediately, pro-treaty and anti-treaty factions turned on each other, Irish against Irish. Six months after the treaty was signed, open conflict broke out once again. The Irish Civil War raged for another eleven months.

On August 22, 1922, Michael Collins was shot to death in an ambush by IRA anti-treaty forces. Eamon de Valera lived on to serve his country for many more years, dying of pneumonia in 1975.

I've tried to be true to the characters and viewpoints of the real people who inhabit this story, including Michael Collins and Eamon de Valera, Winston Churchill, Andrew Bonar Law, Mrs. Freda Dudley Ward and HRH The Prince of Wales, later Edward VIII. I've equally tried to be true to the events leading up to the Irish War of Independence and the escalation of the conflict.

Months of research and thousands of pages of reading material into actual people and events were tempered with a liberal dose of creative license over the year-long process of actually writing the book. Any mistakes—and there are sure to be some, despite my best efforts—are my own.

I loved writing *The Moonlight Runner.* I hope you love it, too.

It takes a village to produce a book, and this one is no exception. I want to thank my wonderful editor, Annie Chagnot, whose diligence, insight and wise counsel were invaluable. I also want to thank Margaret Marbury, Erika Imranyi, Greg Stephenson and the entire team at Park Row Books. I couldn't ask for a better home for *The Moonlight Runner*!

My brilliant agent, Robert Gottlieb, deserves way more in the way of gratitude than a mere "thank you" can convey, but thank you, Robert, for your guidance and unfailing support. Thank you also to everyone at Trident Media Group. What would I do without you?

And finally, thank you to *you*, for reading this book. I appreciate you so much! My readers are the best!